GW00865417

MURDER ON THE STRIKE OF FIVE

M P Peacock

Cover image:
Birch Trees - 365 25-2-2011
by Suzanne Schroeter, 2011
https://www.flickr.com/photos/shezamm/
ⓘ ⓢ CC BY-SA 2.0
https://creativecommons.org/licenses/by-sa/2.0/

Murder on the Strike of Five

ISBN-13: 978-1537126753
ISBN-10: 153712675X

By M P Peacock

http://www.mppeacock.co.uk

The moral right of the author has been asserted.
All rights reserved.
Copyright 2016

DEDICATION

To our parents, Lawrence and Felicity Youlten

CONTENTS

CHAPTER ONE

At nine o'clock in the evening on the twenty-third of February 1917, Inspector Vladimir Lesnoy, of the Moscow division of the Special Corps of Gendarmes, left his desk at headquarters carrying a small suitcase and hurried outside to hail a passing cab.

The journey to Yaroslavsky railway terminal was not long, but Lesnoy sensed menace as well as the threat of snowfall in the air, and was anxious to avoid being caught up in anything which might delay him. The cab driver would only allow his horse to go at a cautious pace as the streets had been plunged into darkness since five o'clock in the afternoon due to the rationing of fuel which had led to the imposition of the 'gas hours' on the city.

A newspaper vendor on the street corner brandished a late edition and called out 'Revolution in Petrograd! Read all about it!' Lesnoy shook his head in exasperation.

'What is the world coming to?' the cabbie called to him over his shoulder. 'My wife had to queue for bread for five hours today - five hours!'

'Mmm… disgraceful,' Lesnoy replied. It was surely only a matter of time, he thought, before the revolution reached Moscow. Already there were strikes and riots and a general atmosphere of unrest. Then, just this evening, as he was about to leave, a report had come in of a disorderly rabble,

1

led by a small cabal of well-known troublemakers, marching angrily towards Count Shuysky's palace.

He had made a swift exit before he could be called upon to attend the scene. There were other officers who could deal with the revolutionaries - Lesnoy had bigger game to hunt. A significant piece of intelligence had come in from a town called Verkhneudinsk, over 5,000 kilometres east of Moscow, near Lake Baikal. The report detailed a murder in which the victim's body had been hacked into pieces and placed inside a hessian farm sack. At last, ten years after Lesnoy had first heard of the 'Potato Sack Killer', as the popular press liked to dub him, he had the opportunity to apprehend the psychopath.

At last, the distinctive outline of Yaroslavsky station's fairytale roof loomed up before them in the dark.

'Whoa there!' The cabbie pulled up his horse and Lesnoy hopped down, paid, and patted the horse on the nose, relieved to have escaped from the police station. The horse snorted loudly, emitting clouds of steam into the freezing air and Lesnoy looked up at the imposing station building, the white stone carvings and decorative mosaics gleaming in the moonlight. Then he took stock of the scene around him.

Where the city streets had been deserted, the station was thronging with a crowd of several hundred. For a moment, Lesnoy was taken aback, but, given the latest bulletin from Petrograd, this exodus was not in the least surprising. Predictably, the station entrance had become log-jammed with bodies, pushing and shoving in their attempts to enter the concourse, but coming up against the static and ever-growing queue at the ticket office.

'*Politsiya! Politsiya!*' Lesnoy, brandishing his official identity card and using his small case as an improvised body shield, battered his way through the sea of serge overcoats and fur hats from which an malodorous steam of human sweat and breath evaporated.

He thanked God that his official papers - hastily signed

off just an hour before, as soon as the message from Verkhneudinsk had come through - let him bypass the ticket queue. However, he needed to call in at the station telegraph office where a smaller line snaked its way round the edge of the room.

Once again, Lesnoy flashed his card to jump to the head of the queue. The customer at the desk in front of Lesnoy glanced behind him as the clerk counted the number of letters in his message and Lesnoy instinctively captured a mental snapshot - mid-forties, close-cropped auburn hair, tweed coat. The clerk spoke in a low voice, but Lesnoy tuned in. '"Meet train stop Spassk Primorskiy stop twelve days stop Zayats stop." Is that correct sir?'

'Yes, thank you, that's correct. How much will that be?'

A cell in Lesnoy's brain lit up. The message itself could be harmless enough, but he had been trained to observe everything and sift through every piece of information to identify the unusual and the suspicious. The man's accent was distinctive and his grammar almost too correct to be a Russian native. And the name - Zayats - that name had come into his consciousness just a few days previously in a highly confidential note which had been circulated among the higher ranks of the Moscow police.

An English agent, Dominic Hare, was thought to have arrived in Moscow, motive unknown, but to be identified and observed as top priority. The agent's name had immediately conjured up an image from Lesnoy's favourite childhood stories. His father, an eminent Moscow medical man, had passed them on to the young Volodya from his own boyhood - the fables of Aesop. And the character 'Zayats' had unexpectedly lost in a race against the tortoise. Zayats was the Hare.

The clerk at the far end of the desk became available and Lesnoy made his way along to send his own telegram. 'To Ilya Brilyov Verkhneudinsk Gendarmerie stop arrive train six days stop Inspector Vladimir Lesnoy stop.'

That task completed, Lesnoy could relax a little. He

glanced up at the telegraph office clock before leaving - ten past ten, just over one hour to go. Returning into the hustle and bustle of the main concourse, he bent to pick up a small paper pamphlet which had been unceremoniously discarded:

Fourth Thursday Meeting
of Progressives and Intellectuals
International Working Women's Day,
6.00pm,
Moscow West Workers' Meeting Hall.
Speakers:
Viktor Skobelev, Valeriya Amosova, Alexander Zhuravlev

Lesnoy snorted, derisively. Three grainy photographs, a hatchet-faced woman flanked by two men, completed the page.

Ha! Skobelev and Zhuravlev, Lesnoy mused. Well-known names - and faces - at headquarters. Odds on it's this lot behind the Shuysky Palace disturbance. Well, it could get violent if Skobelev is involved - he's got form. Zhuravlev is a different type altogether, fancies himself an intellectual - the pen is mightier and all that nonsense.

Lesnoy folded the leaflet and stuffed it into his coat pocket. Beyond the ticket queue, the crowd thinned out a little. As he passed the door into the first class waiting room, he glanced in but decided to continue through and out onto the platform. His superior at the Special Corps of Gendarmes, Kirill Belyakov, knowing he was travelling on this particular Trans-Siberian train, had asked him for a favour. A valuable, top-secret shipment of gold was being transported to Vladivostok and there were some concerns about its security. With all the trouble starting, they couldn't spare anyone to act as an official escort, but could Lesnoy please keep an eye on things.

Out on the platform, Andrey Tokar, a sleek, well-fed

middle-aged man with unnaturally black pomaded hair under an astrakhan hat, was overseeing the loading of about five dozen small wooden crates into a special secure carriage of the train. Tokar was a senior employee of the State Bank of the Russian Empire.

'What have you got in here, guv, solid gold?' joked a cheerful, red-faced railway employee, one of a team doing the loading. Tokar ignored the question and glanced nervously at the man who had just appeared beside him. Lesnoy's interest in the gold was peripheral, but he was amused to recognise Tokar.

'Good evening Mr Tokar, I'm glad to see at least some of the gold has made it from the bank to the station.'

'Sorry? Do we know each other?'

The policeman produced his identity card and introduced himself as Inspector Vladimir Lesnoy of the Special Corps of Gendarmes.

'You know my boss; we helped you with that "awkwardness" at the bank last year...'

Tokar blushed deep borscht red and stuttered, 'That is all history. I had the word of the Chief of Police that no further action would be taken against me.'

'Yes, yes of course. Please calm yourself, Mr Tokar,' said Lesnoy, 'I thought the crates would be bigger and more of them. Is this the complete load?'

'The crates can't be any bigger - they'd be too heavy to lift.'

Lesnoy nodded. 'So what's the total value here?'

Tokar glanced around to check nobody else was within earshot. 'Should be enough to buy fifteen tanks and twenty-five thousand rifles. It's safer to move it out in these small quantities. I've lost count of the amount of gold I've had to transport on this godforsaken route - three times in this past year at least. Back and forth to Kazan, back and forth to Vladivostok.'

Lesnoy nodded again, but his thoughts had wandered. Keeping an eye on this consignment of imperial gold bars on its way out of Moscow and out of the greedy clutches of the upstart revolutionaries wasn't a problem. However, once they got to Verkhneudinsk he had his own matter to attend to, while the gold continued on to Vladivostok and beyond.

If Tokar had been expecting sympathy from the Inspector, he wasn't getting any. He noted Lesnoy's cold, expressionless eyes and the slight sneer permanently attached to his thin red lips and shuddered. Not the ideal travelling companion, he thought, but there again, this was not a social trip. He should probably feel reassured by his escort's ruthless demeanour. If Lesnoy was being paid to protect him, then protect him he surely would, even if he had to kill in the process.

Inside the first class waiting room, Ekaterina, wife of Captain Pavel Ozertsov, despite being swaddled in her finest fur coat, huddled close to her husband, trying to gain some extra warmth. The journey from Oryol, several days earlier, had been tedious and uncomfortable and she was not looking forward to another long train journey, possibly several weeks of discomfort and tedium.

Her husband put a protective arm around her and she smiled up at him. Although they had been married for almost three years, Pavel's long spell as a prisoner-of-war in Germany had made him almost a stranger. He had returned from the war to her damaged, his left-hand ring finger obliterated by a German bullet wound, the wedding ring itself lost in some muddy battlefield. She wondered whether years from now some young farm worker might dig it up and marvel at his luck in literally striking gold, presenting it proudly to his peasant-girl fiancée.

Ekaterina's own wedding ring, safely ensconced inside her fur-lined mittens, had survived, but she blushed with shame and the smile disappeared from her beautiful face when she thought of her own, invisible scars. Pavel, his privileged upbringing battered by deprivation, disease and hard labour, quite understandably thought he had experienced the worst of what war can bring. Ekaterina was not so sure. Bitter and ashamed, she had kept her unhappy experiences a secret from her husband and she wanted them to remain that way. No good would come from sharing her own pain.

Pavel had returned from Germany, released in a prisoner-of-war exchange and invalided out of the army. His family, of noble blood, but liberal-minded and resigned to the new social order that was inevitably coming to Russia, had sold off or given away most of their estates and moved abroad, some to Western Europe only to find themselves caught in the horrors of the war there, others to the United States, land of the free and limitless opportunity. Pavel had been keen to join the exodus to America and Ekaterina had been only too relieved to leave behind the dark memories associated with their home, with Oryol and with Russia in general.

She glanced around nervously at the other travellers. A young girl, dark-haired and pale-skinned, but flushed, had just arrived in the waiting room. Ekaterina appraised her clothes and fine features and identified her as someone of her own class. The girl looked familiar, someone she might have seen in a box at the Moscow Opera, perhaps, or at one of the balls she had attended in the city. The girl's companion, of a similar age and type, but blonde, seemed to be in charge, checking documents and sorting out their luggage. Both girls looked anxious and frightened.

Ekaterina could tell that Pavel was also appraising the crowd, wondering who else would be travelling *spalny vagon* - first class - like themselves. The two young girls looked likely candidates. A tough-looking auburn-haired man in his forties was harder to place - possibly a foreigner.

The dark-haired girl, Countess Tatiana Shuyskaya, was casting her gaze anxiously about while her maid, Sofia, organised their tickets and luggage. The crowd out on the concourse looked malnourished and ill-dressed. She herself had, at her father's request, dressed in her least ostentatious clothes. Having run, dragged by Sofia, from the palace, she was looking more dishevelled than she would normally dream of appearing in public, but the situation was a desperate one and her life was in danger. She surreptitiously eyed the well-dressed couple - the attractive woman in expensive furs, the haunted-looking man in a cavalry officer's greatcoat - and assumed that they too were escaping from the troubles.

Back out on the platform, Tokar was trying, without success, to engage the Inspector in small talk. Lesnoy's replies were gruff, his manner curt. He had the cold, expressionless eyes of a hawk and, like a hawk, he missed nothing. Ignoring Tokar's dreary, complaining voice, he watched, from the darkness of the platform, through a grimy window, the travellers in the first class waiting room which was lit by the waxy yellow glow of oil lamps.

The man calling himself Zayats was standing alone in the far corner, his back to the wall, clearly assessing his fellow travellers in a similar manner. Lesnoy's attention was next drawn to an attractive blonde whom he had noticed earlier, when she had been struggling through the station entrance with an equally pretty dark-haired girl in tow. The two of them looked quite well-to-do, but somewhat flushed and flustered. It was curious that they were travelling alone; most likely their parents were aristocrats, anxious for their daughters' safety now that the revolution was building up steam. Two young girls, all alone. Perhaps they would need some 'protection' - a service which Lesnoy specialised in. Fleetingly, a smirk replaced his habitual sneer and he gave a soft snort, causing Tokar to glance at him in surprise.

Suddenly, though, Lesnoy felt his heart thud and the brief smirk was quickly wiped from his lips. His gaze had wandered from the blonde to a couple, certainly a cut above the rest of the crowd by virtue of their superior dress, who were standing near the window next to the platform. They had their backs to Lesnoy, but at that moment they turned to each other and smiled, anxiously but lovingly and the man placed a protective arm around the woman. As the interior oil lamp lit her profile, Lesnoy immediately recognised her and a shock ran through him. 'Kiki…' he murmured softly.

He looked more intently at the man. No, he hadn't seen him before, not in the flesh at any rate, but of course he recognised him. He remembered that first time at the house in Oryol, in Ekaterina's bedroom, when she had made such a pretence of reluctance. She had reached for the silver-framed photograph of her handsome husband, resplendent in his cavalry uniform, and turned it face down on her dressing table before drawing the curtains.

CHAPTER TWO

January 1894
Saints Cyril and Methodius Parochial School
Letter to Mr and Mrs Stukov
Dear Mr and Mrs Stukov,
Further to your complaint, I have spoken to the child in question about his very unpleasant bullying of your daughter. He has been punished appropriately and I have every confidence that these incidents will not happen again. We will, of course, monitor the child closely to ensure the well-being and safety of your daughter.
Yours sincerely,
Mr Oleg Bogdanov, Headteacher

February 1894
Eight years ago, Irina Maslova thought as she pulled a fine-toothed tortoiseshell comb through the Countess's long dark hair. Was it really possible that this was the eighth time she had dressed the Countess for the big winter ball? Irina smiled wistfully to herself as she remembered the day she had been promoted; it had been a big surprise and the cause of some tittle-tattle among the other chambermaids.

Count Nikolai Lvovich Shuysky had told Mr Pluckrose, the chief of his household staff, to promote Irina. The Count had just returned from his honeymoon with his new wife, Anastasia, Countess Shuyskaya. He had proudly opened the door of the black and yellow landau, drawn by a pair of pure-bred Arab horses from the Shuysky stable, and guided his slim young bride out of the carriage and into the entrance hall of the Shuysky Palace. Mr Pluckrose had arranged all the palace staff in a line to welcome their master and to meet their new mistress.

Irina recalled standing at the end of the long line of servants waiting to greet the young couple upon their return from their six-week-long trip to visit the Countess's Italian cousins at their palazzo on Lake Como in Lombardy and then on to Budapest where the Count's uncle owned a magnificent villa right on the west bank of the Danube. It was one of those bright Moscow days in August. The sun, already high in the sky, had cast brilliant sunbeams through the skylight high above Irina's head down into the cool, dimly lit hall. The murmured introductions that echoed off the marble floors reminded Irina of her visit to St Basil's cathedral to pray for her brothers and sisters far, far away on their farm near Lvov.

She remembered the butterflies flapping with enough energy to break out of her stomach and then the first cold stab of jealousy at the sight of her former lover, the Count, holding hands with his pretty young wife. For one heartbreaking moment Irina had wanted him to gaze at *her* with that big satisfied grin and those boyish puppydog eyes. She had wanted him to adore *her* and not this new girl. She had wanted the excitement and romance of a new life, untroubled with fear and doubt. It was clear that the Count and Countess were very much in love, but not in the forbidden, urgent, hidden way that Irina and Nikolai had loved. Nikolai and Anastasia were different: open, romantic lovers, lit by the sun.

Irina recalled the song that one of the Scottish kitchen girls had taught her: 'She was poor but she was honest,' the song had started, and ended, 'It's the same the whole world over. It's the poor what gets the blame. It's the rich what gets the pleasure. Ain't it all a bloomin' shame?'

Finally, the newly-weds had reached the end of the line where Irina had been positioned. Irina found it impossible to look at her new mistress in the face. She looked instead at the Count who gave her a courteous smile and an almost imperceptible wink as he introduced her to his wife.

'Countess Shuyskaya, may I introduce you to Miss Irina. Miss Irina was my mother's favourite chambermaid and will become your personal lady's maid. I assure you, my love, that you will not find a more loyal and devoted servant than Miss Irina. She will do anything you ask of her.' Irina had blushed at the memory of their nights together and her slow, secret, barefoot walk back to her room before dawn. Irina's jealousy had been tinged with relief; Anastasia's arrival meant that Irina's impossible affair with the Count had finally come to an end.

All the downstairs staff had agreed: the Count Nikolai and Countess Anastasia made a very handsome couple. Irina was pleased to see that the Count appeared so happy and, even when the other servants made ribald comments about the messy matrimonial bed and the trail of hastily removed garments and undergarments in the private apartments, she still felt satisfied, somehow, that the man she had once loved so dearly had found a beautiful woman of the right social standing.

More than once during their affair, Nikolai had kissed Irina's naked body and discussed his desire, his historic duty to procreate, to sire a large family of little Shuysky Counts and Countesses, 'At least three boys and three girls,' he had told her between kisses on her naked belly. So when, six months after their return from Hungary, the Count announced that the Countess was expecting a child, Irina felt another moment of great loss, but she managed to smile and when Konstantin was born she joined the other servants to drink a toast to the health, wealth and good fortune of the young couple and their new baby.

Looking at the huge smile on the Count's face and his obvious pride at becoming a father had helped Irina feel genuinely happy for him. Irina had imagined her love for Nikolai as a dance around a bright candle. Every hour, every day, every week that passed since their two summers of passion, she imagined dancing further and further away from the candle that they had once shared.

A second baby son, Georgiy, arrived in 1889. Eighteen months later, Countess Anastasia suffered a miscarriage and after that, Irina sensed a shift in the relationship between the Count and his wife. Anastasia seemed exhausted - from childbearing, the demands of her two delightful but exuberant boys, her charity work and the hectic social whirl in which the couple engaged.

So in late 1892, when Irina had been summoned to visit the Count in his private drawing room one evening when the Countess and the boys were away visiting her parents, it seemed quite natural that she and Nikolai fell upon each other wordlessly, as if nothing had changed.

Irina nudged herself out of her guilty daydream. The Countess was sitting at her dressing table surrounded by a selection of jewels, while Irina stood behind her, brushing Anastasia's long dark hair before twisting it into curls, piling it up into an elaborate style and decorating it with hairpins each topped with one of the famous Shuysky diamonds.

'You look tired tonight, madame.'

Anastasia sighed. 'Yes, I wish I didn't have to go to the Vronskys' ball. Countess Vronskaya always looks so elegant and I - well look at me - I'm so fat, I look like a watermelon on sticks! Never again!'

'Once you've had the baby you'll soon be slim again,' Irina said, soothingly.

Anastasia instinctively rested her hand on the large bump beneath her grey silk dress and smiled.

'I'm praying for a beautiful baby daughter, Irina. I love my boys, but they're so boisterous and messy. I so want to have a girl, a little doll whom I can dress in pretty clothes.'

Irina finished pinning the Countess's hair and gently lifted up the heaviest, most sparkling piece of jewellery on the dressing table, a two-part gold necklace set with large diamonds and rubies in a modern style bought from Boucheron's new shop in Paris. Irina placed the lower part of the necklace carefully around Anastasia's naked shoulders and began to do up the complex set of clasps that held the upper part close against the Countess's neck like a choker made of golden chains. Suddenly, Anastasia flinched forward and clutched her stomach.

'Oh! Oh my God!'

'What is it, madame?'

'The pain! Quickly - loosen my gown.'

Irina's nimble fingers swiftly undid the row of silk-covered buttons running down the back of Anastasia's dress and worked the tightly knotted laces that pulled the Countess's corset tight. Anastasia gave a deep gasp of relief and agony combined.

'I must…' she said, rising from her chair. Irina helped her over towards the edge of the bed, but Anastasia suddenly doubled up and clutched her middle again.

'No! Oh, no, I think…'

A small pool of liquid darkened the pale pink pile of the carpet, turning it a shade of deep rose.

'Madame! I must fetch the doctor. I will go to tell the Count that the baby is coming.'

'It's too soon; I have another month yet. Oh!' The Countess knelt on the floor by the bed, her head on the embroidered silk coverlet, her features contorted in agony. 'Yes, hurry, Irina, I do need the doctor…'

Irina rushed from the room and down the sweeping marble staircase, arriving in the Count's first-floor study out of breath and almost unable to speak. 'Sir, sir…'

Count Shuysky turned languidly from his desk, smiled and raised a wry eyebrow. 'Calm down, Irina. What is taking the Countess so long, is she still sulking about having to go to the ball?'

'Sir, the baby is coming.'

The Count stood abruptly and tugged on the bell-cord to summon Pluckrose.

'Are you sure? I thought she had several weeks left?' Irina simply shook her head. Pluckrose arrived instantly and was immediately despatched to fetch the family physician. The Count enfolded Irina in his arms and kissed the top of her blonde head.

'Thank you, Irina. Now please go and look after the Countess until Doctor Lesnoy arrives.'

Three hours later, the Count, returning to his study, heard a high-pitched cry from upstairs and his heart clenched. A short while afterwards, the doctor poked his head round the door and smiled.

'Congratulations, Count. You have a beautiful baby daughter. A little small, but healthy, and your wife is fine. Irina is tidying her up and then you may go and see her. I'll be back in the morning to check on them both.'

The Count entered his wife's bedroom and found her sitting up in bed with a tiny bundle in her arms, a cocoon of fine white wool with a little dark-haired head peeping out. Irina was picking up the grey silk dress which had been abandoned on the floor and then placing the diamond and ruby necklace back in its velvet-lined case.

Anastasia smiled at her husband. 'Look what we have, Nikolai - a lovely daughter.'

Count Shuysky kissed his wife on the forehead and moved the woollen shawl a little to see the baby's face. She looked pink and healthy, her rosebud lips sucking at the air.

'What shall we call her?' Anastasia asked.

'You can choose, my dear. I know how much you wanted a daughter.'

'Then I'd like to name her after my mother. 'Tatiana' - what do you think?'

'Countess Tatiana Nikolaevna Shuyskaya? Yes, I

approve,' and he kissed her again and stood to leave. Both women followed him with their eyes as he disappeared through the bedroom door.

'I think he's pleased to have a daughter, don't you agree, Irina? I wonder if he'll buy me another necklace to mark the occasion? I think I'd like diamonds and emeralds this time. Countess Vronskaya has a beautiful emerald necklace…' but Irina wasn't listening. As the baby let out a small kitten-like mew, wanting her first milk, something stirred inside Irina and her heart pummelled against her ribcage in fear. Of course she had known, deep down, but this was real now. A living, moving creature, growing inside her. How much time did she have left? She tried to calculate. Four months? Maybe only three? She must think what to do. How much longer could she keep her secret? I must tell the Count, she decided. After all, it is his child, she thought defiantly, his secret too. Irina's heart sank. I must tell the Count - but not now.

The following morning the Count was again in his Study, when a tentative knock on the door announced Doctor Lesnoy, looking grave. 'The Countess has a fever, a serious one, I'm afraid. I will stay with her and do what I can, but…' and he shook his head sadly. The Count rose immediately. 'I must come with you,' and the two men left the room together.

By early evening, the mood in the Shuysky household was sombre. The little boys, six-year-old Konstantin and four-year-old Georgiy, had tearfully kissed their mother goodbye and she had stroked their silky heads and murmured to them that they must be good boys for their father and look after Tatiana, their little sister. Miss Greycourt, the English governess had taken the boys to the nursery and the priest had been summoned to administer the last sacrament to Anastasia before she slipped out of consciousness for the final time.

Finally, The Count was left alone with his wife. He lay beside her on top of the bedcovers, holding her hand, now cold and white, and lifting it to his lips. 'I'm sorry, Anastasia. I truly loved you and I tried to be a good husband, though... though I know I didn't always succeed...' Tears came to his eyes and he sobbed himself into a deep sleep beside her still body.

Three-and-a-half months after the birth of Tatiana Shuyskaya, in the family's dacha at Novinki, forty-four kilometres south of Moscow, another baby's cry was heard. The look on Doctor Lesnoy's face was grim as he drew the sheet up over the mother's face, put away his stethoscope and clicked shut the brass clasp on his black leather bag. Another new life; another tragic death.

Mrs Chekhova, the gardener's wife, was holding the screaming infant, desperately trying to calm it.

'You will have to find a wet nurse for the child,' the doctor said. 'There must be some woman in the village who wants some extra money. I'm sure the Count will pay her well. He wants this baby to be properly cared for.' Mrs Chekhova raised her eyebrows curiously, but the doctor avoided her gaze and turned to leave. At the door he hesitated and turned.

'She is to be called Sofia,' he said, 'Sofia... er... Ivanovna Maslova.'

In the hallway, his young son was waiting for him. 'Come on, Volodya, I've finished here. It will be very late before we get home. Your mother will be wondering where we've got to.' The boy noticed how tired and drawn his father looked, but just put his small hand in his father's larger one and the pair clambered into the carriage and rode away in silence.

June 1894
Saints Cyril and Methodius Parochial School
Letter from Headteacher to the parish priest
It is with regret that I have to inform you that we have had to expel an eight-year-old boy from the school due to his extreme and disturbing behaviour. The most recent misdemeanour, in which he pulled the wings off a butterfly, caused great distress to his classmates who witnessed it. However, this was just the latest in a long string of incidents of bullying and cruelty.

His mother died when he was a baby and his father shows little interest in the boy or concern for his violent tendencies. We have tried to nurture his compassionate side, but to no avail, and the decision to expel him has been a last resort.

He is a highly intelligent child and we understand his father has managed to secure him a place at another school in the town.

Yours faithfully,
Mr Oleg Bogdanov, Headteacher

CHAPTER THREE

January 1900
Letter from Anatoly Shylapnikov, farmer, to his cousin.
Dear Fyodor,

It is with a heavy heart that I write to you to ask for your assistance and to give you a warning. In my last letter of woe I told you that the oats never germinated and that the May frost had burned and stunted the potatoes just as their shoots appeared. The late summer rain and terrible humidity brought the blight onto the rye crop. We have only harvested one tenth of what we collected last year.

To cut a long sad story short, I decided I must sell Grusha, the bay mare you admired last time you were visiting. I had to sell her because without feed, she would have starved anyway. Two days before I was due to take her to the livestock auction in Voronezh, I came in the early morning to check her only to find that she was not in her stall.

My first thought was that she had been stolen, but then I saw a trail of blood drops on the stable floor. I followed it out into the yard but then it disappeared. One week later my neighbour, fishing in the big carp pond in the village, hooked a hessian sack with my horse's head in it - my Grusha, no doubt of that, even though the worms were chewing her eyes and nose. She had been decapitated with an axe by the look of it and her head put into a potato sack and dumped into the pond.

We searched the woods behind the long meadow and found the rest of her. An awful sight and smell that haunts me still. Who would do such a thing? To steal a beautiful animal is perhaps understandable, if despicable. But to slaughter her so brutally just for the sake of what? Fun? Spite against me? That is surely inhuman.

I went to the gendarmerie in Voronezh to report the crime. The rural crime inspector said I was not alone in my misfortune and three other horses, all mares, had been killed in the last few weeks. So make sure you lock up your horses securely. Who knows where this monster will strike next?

The poverty in which my family and I now find ourselves is now a great concern; my children are certain to go hungry. For their sakes, I am begging you to assist us. Please forgive me. I pray your harvest and luck are better than mine. Any help you can offer would be a blessing.

Your humble and broken cousin, Anatoly.

June 1900

'Ninety-seven, ninety-eight, ninety-nine, one hundred! Ready or not, here I come!' Vladimir removed his hands from in front of his eyes, turned around and quickly scanned the dacha garden. At thirteen he was starting to feel rather too old for such childish games, but he had to admit it was fun to be free from school and away from Moscow at the Shuyskys' dacha for a few weeks.

Vladimir's father, Dr Lesnoy, had told Vladimir that Count Shuysky was worried because his own son had never really mixed with 'normal boys'. So at the age of nine, Vladimir had been volunteered by his father to befriend Count Konstantin. Now the Count and his younger brother Georgiy were nowhere to be seen. However, a flash of pink gingham from behind a rosebush and the flutter of a yellow striped dress from behind the lilac tree, combined with some barely suppressed girlish giggles, instantly gave away the whereabouts of the two little girls: Konstantin's six-year-old sister, Countess Tatiana, and her best friend, the gardener's daughter, Sofia.

I'll pretend I can't see them, Vladimir thought to

himself, looking around the other end of the lawn where the cherry trees were. Standing beneath one of the trees, he heard a crack and a twig fell onto his head. He looked up and saw Georgiy.

'Georgiy! I see you in the cherry tree.'

'Damn you, Volodya! Why didn't you get those stupid girls first - everyone can see where they are.' Georgiy swung down from the tree and dropped lithely into the long grass.

'Yes, well they're just babies - and girls, too. We have to make allowances. Come on, let's find Konstantin. I think he's behind the shed - you go round that way and I'll go this way.'

As Vladimir rounded the corner of the shed he saw his Konstantin's bare foot disappear between two large wooden water butts resting against the shed wall.

'Georgiy!' he shouted 'block Konstantin! He is hiding between the barrels!'

Georgiy and Vladimir closed in on their quarry. Konstantin appeared from his hiding place, looking sweaty and red-faced from the heat.

'Okay, you got me Volodya. How did you know where to look?'

Vladimir smiled. 'That's easy. I followed your trail.'

'What trail?'

'The trail you left last time we played.'

'But there is no snow, not much dust, where is the trail? Tell me how you know.'

Vladimir laughed. 'I followed the trail of your habits. You hid here last time we played. I bet you would hide here again next time we play.'

'But, that was ages ago, must be three or four years now. How can you remember that kind of thing? It's not fair.'

'I don't know. I just can. Come on - let's find the girls!'

The three boys raced across the lawn towards the flowerbeds. Behind the rosebush and lilac tree, the girls were standing with their fists over their eyes, giggling uncontrollably.

'I can't see them anywhere, can you, Georgiy?' said Vladimir.

'No! They've completely disappeared. Do you think the wolf has got them?'

'Or a bear!' And with a deep growl, Vladimir grabbed Tatiana from behind, making her stop giggling and start shrieking. Sofia squealed too, grabbed her friend's hand and pulled her away from Vladimir's grip. 'Run, run, Tati!' she shouted and off she sprinted, pulling Tatiana in her wake. 'Come on, slowcoach!'

On the terrace, a jug of fresh cherry juice and a plate of seed buns were waiting for them. Konstantin poured them each a glass and they sat down, all laughing and a bit grubby. Mrs Chekhova appeared through the French doors with a large iced cake on a floral china plate. It had six miniature candles, their small flames almost invisible in the evening light.

Tatiana gasped. 'Oh! I forgot. It's Sofi's birthday!' She jumped up and hugged her friend then embraced Mrs Chekhova who placed the cake carefully on the veranda table. 'I do so wish you were my mama, Mrs Chekhova! If you were my mama then Sofia could be my little sister.'

The gardener's wife blushed. 'Now, Miss Tatiana. Your father wouldn't be pleased to hear you say that. Miss Greycourt looks after you very well, I'm sure.'

'But she's not my mama, she's just a boring old governess from England. She doesn't make yummy cakes for me.'

At that moment, the Count himself appeared on the terrace with an armful of packages and said, 'Oh what a fine cake! Who is the birthday girl?'

'Papa!' Tatiana hugged her father's legs. 'What have you brought? Presents? For me? Oh thank you fine sir. Most pleased if I do.'

'They're presents for Sofi, you little *dura*,' said Georgiy.

'Georgiy! Don't speak to your sister like that.'

'Sorry Papa,' he muttered ungraciously.

The Count laid down the parcels on the table and started singing with a melodious baritone voice in lightly-accented English. 'Happy birthday to you, happy birthday to you, happy birthday dear Sofia, happy birthday to you.'

Sofia ran embarrassed to Mrs Chekhova and clutched her skirt, hiding her face from the Count. 'Mama, what did that man say?'

'I don't know, dear. I think it was in English'.

'It's the "Happy Birthday" song in English,' Tatiana told her friend, "Like '*S dnem rozhdeniya*".'

Sofia looked at Tatiana with a confused expression on her face. 'But what is English?'

The boys all laughed and pointed at her. 'Ha! Sofi doesn't know what English is,' shouted Konstantin, gleefully.

'Two little *dury*, Tati and Sofi,' mocked Georgiy.

The Count gave his sons a look of displeasure, picked up the largest present and offered it to Sofia. '*S dnem rozhdeniya*, Sofia,' he said, gently. Sofia looked anxiously at Mrs Chekhova then, unable to resist the gift, carefully pulled the red ribbon bow and slowly unwrapped the white tissue paper, revealing a pale green silk dress.

'It's beautiful,' she gasped, curtseying to the Count. 'Thank you, sir.'

Tatiana was frowning petulantly.

'What about me?' she pouted. Her brothers nudged each other and pulled faces, rolling their eyes and made grabbing actions with their hands.

The Count ignored his daughter and presented another, smaller package to Sofia. Inside was a book of poetry. 'Thank you, sir' she said, more hesitantly, 'But I'm afraid I cannot read.'

The Count and Mrs Chekhova exchanged glances.

'Well, Sofia…' the gardener's wife began and paused, lost for words. Another glance was exchanged and the

Count took over.

'Soon you *will* be able to read, Sofia. When the holidays are over and the boys go back to school, you are to return to Moscow with Tatiana and begin lessons with Miss Greycourt. That will be fun, won't it?' Despite his best efforts, the Count didn't manage to sound entirely convincing and though Sofia managed another 'Thank you, sir,' in a more subdued tone, the Count noticed that the little girl was clutching more tightly still at Mrs Chekhova's skirt.

CHAPTER FOUR

August 1907
Newspaper report from the Kazanskii gazeta
Police in Spassk are investigating the brutal killing of a man,
believed to be a homeless vagrant. No identification has been possible,
due to the mutilation of the body. A boatman on the Volga found the
body floating in the river, chopped into pieces and tied into a hessian
sack. The sack is of the type used to transport and store potatoes, but
police have been unable to identify its provenance.

September 1907
Tatiana and Sofia stood at the front door of the Shuysky
Palace in Moscow watching the footman load the last of
Miss Greycourt's trunks onto the back of the carriage.
Miss Greycourt dabbed at her red-rimmed eyes with her
lace-edged handkerchief and turned to the girls with a
sorrowful look.

'Adieu, mes petites! Adieu ma petite Tatiana; adieu ma
petite Sofia,' she said in a resolutely English accent,
embracing them each delicately in turn. The girls
submitted to her hugs with a wry glance between them.

'You have both been excellent pupils, my dears. Your
English is better than some of the girls I taught in London
and I am so very proud of your beautiful piano-playing -
nobody would guess you were only thirteen years old if

25

they heard you. Do practise your duets during the holidays - you know how the Count loves to hear you play together. Now, Tatiana, you must make the most of your new school in Paris to perfect your French. Sofia, you have achieved so much for a girl of your class; now you must learn all you can from Mrs Belikova. She is getting on in years and the Count will soon rely on you as his housekeeper.'

With that, Miss Greycourt gave one last watery smile, descended the stone steps from the palace and was helped into the carriage. The girls stood and waved as the horses trotted down the drive to the main gate, then turned into the road. As soon as it was out of sight, they both breathed a sigh of relief and turned to each other with huge smiles on their faces.

Within seconds, however, Tatiana's smile had faded and been replaced by an anxious frown. 'I wish I didn't have to go to that stupid school in Paris. I don't care if I can't speak perfect French and I don't ever want to go to a ball, so what's the point of learning to dance?'

Sofia said nothing but shrugged resignedly. 'Come on, you know the Count wants you to be packed and ready to leave tomorrow morning. Let's go and choose which dresses you should take.'

In Tatiana's room they were almost finished when the Count knocked on the door and came in. Tatiana flung herself into his arms. 'Papa! I don't want to go. Please let me stay here with Sofia so we can both take care of you.'

Her father said nothing but held her at arm's length and pulled out a small package from his pocket. 'I bought this to give to your mother when you were born…' He tailed off, shaking his head sadly. 'Now it's for you to take to Paris.'

Tatiana's smile returned and she ripped off the tissue paper, letting it fall on the floor. Inside the little blue leather box was a pair of emerald earrings decorated with tiny diamonds.

'Papa! You're an angel - I love them,' and she unclipped her pearl earrings, carelessly dropping them on the bed, and rushed to the dressing table mirror to put on her new acquisitions. Sofia bent to pick up the discarded tissue and earrings.

'Why don't you let Sofia have the pearls,' suggested the Count. Tatiana turned and waved an impatient hand. 'Oh, yes, of course; whatever she wants. These are much better.'

After dinner that evening the Count sat alone on the large button-backed sofa in the drawing room, sadly gazing into the flames of the fire which blazed in the hearth. Of course it was right and proper that Tatiana should go off to the *Institut de l'Assomption* in Paris. It is where her mother had gone to be 'finished' and where Tatiana herself would be polished to perfection, as bright and sparkling as one of the Shuysky diamonds. He would miss her, though. So much. He sighed and gazed up at the ceiling, blinking back his tears.

His reverie was broken by the sound of girlish laughter and the drawing room door burst open. Tatiana and Sofia romped in like a pair of boisterous puppies. Tatiana was holding some sheet music up as high as her arm would stretch and Sofia was jumping around her, trying to snatch it away.

'Come on, Tati, you said I could choose which part to play. It's my turn, you know it is.'

'No, I want to play primo and you can do secondo. It's my last chance after all. I'll be gone tomorrow and then you'll have to play both parts yourself. Do you think you'll be able to grow an extra pair of hands?'

Tatiana rushed over to her father and flung herself on his lap, her arms around his neck. 'Tell her, Papa; tell Sofia I must play primo.'

The Count said nothing but twisted his neck to look at Sofia who rolled her eyes and stomped her foot, but immediately grinned.

'Oh, yes, of course you can, Tati. I'm only teasing.

27

Come on Your Highness, Miss Prima Ballerina Tatiana, your Papa is waiting for his Mozart.'

The girls sat down on the velvet-covered music stool at the keyboard of the mahogany Steinway grand piano and within seconds the echoes of their high-pitched squabbling voices had dissolved away to be replaced by the lively opening of Mozart's Sonata in D.

As the final bright major chords sounded, the Count clapped and cheered. 'Brava! Brava! Oh goodness, my dearest Tatiana, whatever am I going to do without you. The palace simply won't be the same.'

The girls came quietly over to sit one on either side of him. Tatiana took her father's hands in hers and there was a long silence, filled only with the occasional explosive crackle of the wood on the fire and the tinkling chime of the ornate French clock on the mantelpiece striking the quarter hour.

'Dear Papa,' Tatiana raised his hands up to her lips and kissed his fingers tenderly. 'I'm only going to school for a few months and Sofia will be here to look after you. Mrs Belikova is going to teach her to cook and sew and look after the house, so she'll be ever so useful.'

The Count smiled and turned to Sofia.

'You must ask Mrs Belikova to allow you to have your evenings free so you can dine with me just as you always have…'

'Well maybe once a week or so,' Tatiana interrupted, 'But it may not be convenient every evening.'

'Not convenient?! To whom? I don't want to sit all by myself in the dining room, pecking at my food in solitary splendour and staring silently down the length of an empty table. No! Sofia must beg to be excused her evening duties. I will instruct Mrs Belikova myself and there's an end to it.'

Tatiana frowned slightly and Sofia said nothing. Another log popped and the clock chimed the half hour. A discreet tap on the door heralded the arrival of Mr Roberts, who had replaced Mr Pluckrose as head of household the previous year.

'Good evening, sir. Will you and the young ladies be taking hot chocolate in the drawing room tonight or in your bedrooms?'

'We'll have it in here, please, Roberts,' said the Count, wistfully. 'Our last hot chocolate together for many moons.'

Tatiana brightened and patted his cheeks playfully. 'Oh, come on Papa, don't be melancholic on my last evening. I'd like extra chocolate, please Roberts, and extra cream and some Turkish Delight. And Sofia would like the same, wouldn't you, Sofia?'

'Yes, that would be lovely, thank you.'

'Come on, let's play the Adagio while we're waiting for our chocolate,' Tatiana commanded, 'And I'll let you play primo this time, Sofia,' she added, graciously.

Delicious though the hot chocolate was, it was not enough to lift the Count's pensive mood as he drained his porcelain cup. He set the cup and saucer back on the tray with the silver chocolate pot and turned to Tatiana.

'Will you play that piece I love - the Chopin?'

'The E-flat Nocturne? Of course, Papa. It's my favourite, too.'

She returned to the piano and began to play. The Count and Sofia listened, rapt, and the crackling of the logs grew ever quieter as the fire died gradually down to its embers. The Nocturne ended and Tatiana stood.

'Sofia will play to you when you want music, won't you Sofia?' Tatiana tried to sound cheerful.

'Of course - and we can read poetry together,' Sofia picked up on Tatiana's cue and also tried to inject an upbeat note into her voice.

Suddenly the Count smiled. 'I know! I can teach you chess, Sofia. I've been missing a chess partner ever since the boys left.'

Tatiana and Sofia exchanged glances, amused and horrified in equal measure.

'No, papa!' Tatiana exclaimed, laughing. 'We hate chess!' and, laughing, she flung her arms around her father and hugged him as tightly as she could, until the laughter turned to quiet sobs and she thought her heart would crush under the weight of her sorrow.

CHAPTER FIVE

March 1912

Newspaper report, Pravda

The search for missing ballerina, Ludmila Rusina, ended last night when the body of the 19-year-old, who had been missing since her performance in the first night of Ravel's Daphnis and Chloë, was identified. Identification was made difficult by the fact that Miss Rusina had been brutally hacked into pieces, but as she was still in costume there can be little doubt that it is indeed her. A spokesman for the Mariinsky Theatre in Saint Petersburg where Miss Rusina was a member of the corps de ballet, said 'Ludmila Rusina was a talented dancer with much promise and all her colleagues at the Theatre are in deep shock at this news. Her family has been informed.' Police found the body inside a jute sack when they searched the shores of the Neva river just outside the city, after a tip-off from a member of the public.

June 1912

'Sofia! Sofia!' Count Shuysky appeared at the top of the stairs down to the entrance hall of his palace, brandishing a letter.

Sofia, who had been discussing the week's flower arrangements for the palace with the head gardener, came to meet him and bobbed a brief curtsey. 'Good morning, sir. How may I help you?'

31

The Count smiled. 'Sofia, how many times do I have to tell you - there's no need to curtsey. Look at this!' He waved the letter at her. 'It's from Tatiana. School in Paris has finished and she'll be home tomorrow afternoon. Is her room in good order? I want everything to be perfect for her. What should we ask Cook to make for her first dinner?'

The next twenty-four hours were a whirlwind of preparations. Tatiana's bed was made up with fresh linen and the silk curtains and rugs were taken out to the palace gardens to have the dust beaten out of them. Sofia went out to the garden herself to oversee one of the gardeners cutting a dozen red roses - Tatiana's favourite - Sofia wanted a large bunch of perfect blooms to display in a crystal vase on her friend's dressing table.

As the hallway clock struck four, the sound of carriage wheels could be heard crunching on the gravel drive. Sofia hurriedly removed the housekeeping apron and headscarf that she wore when involved with housework and quickly checked her blonde hair in the gilt-framed mirror at the bottom of the grand marble staircase. The Count, who had also heard the arrival of the coach from his study, met Sofia in the hall and the pair of them walked briskly to the front door where the butler was waiting.

'Come on, Roberts, open up - my little girl is home!'

Sofia scarcely recognised the elegant apparition who alighted from the carriage and walked daintily up the stone steps. She had only seen her friend once since she left for Paris. Sofia was just a few months younger than Tatiana but during her four years in Paris, Tatiana had evolved into a sophisticated and fashionable young woman.

She was dressed in a beautifully cut long dark blue travel suit made from very fine cashmere that accentuated her slim silhouette. On the side of her matching hat was a fan of five white feathers each tipped with a flash of incandescent electric blue. Later in the servants' dining room the staff would discuss why the Countess's luggage had monogrammed 'LV' rather than 'TS'.

The Count, suddenly feeling very antiquated, took a step towards Tatiana, bowed, took her hand and kissed it with mock formality. Then, laughing with pleasure at her return, he twirled her around as if in a dance. He wanted to admire her, to remember this image of his Tatiana as a fashionable, modern European woman forever. Then he put his arms around her and embraced his daughter warmly.

As he stood back, Sofia took a step forwards and opened her arms as if to initiate an embrace with Tatiana, only to drop them to her side when she heard Mr Roberts clear his throat in a clear warning that protocol was about to be breached. Sofia converted her hug into a curtsey and a bow and Tatiana's face lit up as she recognised her old friend. 'Sofia, oh Sofia, how lovely to see you after all this time. You look well. It is so wonderful to be home. Nothing ever changes in Russia, does it? It is so comforting to have strong roots.'

Upstairs in the bedroom, Sofia pointed out the new needlepoint cushions on which she had embroidered cherry blossoms and a small bird.

Tatiana laughed. 'Oh, how charmingly old-fashioned! You are sweet, Sofia. And thank you for the roses, you did choose the roses, didn't you? Of course in Paris roses are quite out of fashion, the emphasis is on natural forms and grasses are all the rage this season.' She bent over the bouquet to inhale the heady scent. 'Well, never mind, you did your best and these are fine for now.'

Perhaps she noticed Sofia's crestfallen face, because she immediately shook her head, held out her hand and smiled - a proper, broad grin, just like the old Tatiana whom Sofia remembered. 'Oh, listen to me - sounding like such a horrid Parisienne Mademoiselle. I'm really so pleased to be back and it's going to be such fun now that you're head of housekeeping and can make sure that everything is just the way I want it. Poor old Papa can be such a stick-in-the-mud sometimes. I want parties and music and...'

'I think he worries about everything that's happening here. Not just the palace, but in Moscow and Russia. It's not the same as it was when you left, Tatiana. There is so much unrest and the Count thinks it's better for you, I mean the aristocracy, to keep a low profile. That's why he kept you in Paris all those years. He thought it would be safer.'

Tatiana yawned. 'Oh, well, I know all that, but we can enjoy ourselves just a little, can't we? Come on, Sofia, let's go and ask Papa who has been invited to dinner. I hope you will join us tonight, as a special treat?'

'Well, yes, I usually...' Sofia tailed off, suddenly feeling uncertain about what life was going to be like now Tatiana was home. Was she her friend or her servant? What should she call her? 'Tati' sounded too informal, 'Countess' too formal. Should she say 'Miss Tati' or 'Miss Tatiana', or maybe 'Mademoiselle' was more acceptable? Were the cosy suppers - just she and the Count enjoying a simple meal - going to be replaced by formal dinners every evening? The best porcelain and silver, fancy menus, and Sofia herself stuck in the kitchen overseeing a team of disgruntled servants whose minds were more on revolution than on roast beef?

As Tatiana tripped happily down the stairs in front of Sofia, as carefree as the little girl playing in the dacha garden twelve years earlier, Sofia followed with a heavy heart.

CHAPTER SIX

July 1914
Newspaper report from Oryol Gazeta
Residents in the village of Redkino are living in fear since last Sunday when they awoke to the news that the barbaric 'Potato Sack Killer' has struck at the heart of their community. The well-respected Bobrov family who farmed a smallholding on the edge of the village were murdered last Saturday night. Mr Vasily Bobrov, 36 and his wife Olga, 28, were found dead in their beds by a relative who had come to help on the farm. The body parts of their three young children, all under five, were found in hessian sacks in the duck pond.

The relative in question was too upset to be interviewed, while the Oryol Chief-of-Police, Leonid Golovanov, was quoted as saying 'This is the most horrific crime which I have had the misfortune to investigate in all my years in the district. With very little evidence we are keeping an open mind in the investigation, but it does appear to bear all the hallmarks of the so-called 'Potato Sack Killer'. We believe this evildoer to be the perpetrator of a string of serial killings dating back at least seven years and in a number of different localities in the west of Russia.'

Anyone with any information which could lead to the arrest and conviction of the murderer should contact the Chief-of-Police directly.

At half past ten in the morning on the first of August 1914, Captain Pavel Ozertsov said farewell to his wife

Ekaterina. She stood at the open doorway of their elegant home in the countryside near Oryol, a city 360 kilometres south west of Moscow, and watched as he mounted his horse, Belaya Iskra, and trotted off to rejoin his regiment, the Fourteenth Cavalry Division of the Tsar's Imperial Army.

As he reached the road, he turned for one last wave. He noticed Ekaterina brush away a strand of her beautiful auburn hair which the summer breeze had blown across her face. His heart lurched with the realisation of her vulnerability. She was his new bride, far from her family; he should be there to take care of her. But he was a soldier, an officer, and now that Russia had entered hostilities against the Austro-Hungarian empire, his duty was to his country.

It would be two years and one month before Pavel and Ekaterina were reunited. Two years of anxiety and loneliness for Ekaterina and two years of frustration and imprisonment for Pavel.

At ten thirty-five in the morning on the first of August 1914, almost two thousand kilometres away in Saxony, Bruno Berthold, an eighteen-year-old private in Kaiser Wilhelm's Army, kissed his mother goodbye and walked down the dusty road that led from Borsdorf, the village of his birth, towards his regimental barracks in Leipzig. Bruno's regiment would soon be mobilised and deployed to defend East Prussia from Russian aggression.

Three weeks later, on the twenty-third of August 1914, Bruno watched the twenty-two horses of Pavel's squadron canter across a field towards the dry ditch where he and his platoon had been positioned. With a mixture of fear and excitement he grabbed his Mauser rifle and loaded the first bullet that he would use that summer. He waited for the order to open fire. When, after what seemed to be a very long wait, the *Zugführer's* order came, he forgot all his training and shut his eyes just as he pulled the trigger. Truth be told, Bruno was just relieved that his rifle was pointed in the general direction of the enemy horses.

Bruno's first bullet flew high over the Russian cavalry, making a curious zipping noise. His second shot fell short, kicking up a puff of brown dust from the field of beetroots. The third round hit Captain Pavel Ozertsov's hand, shattering his left ring finger. In an instant the lead bullet turned the inside of the officer's glove into a bloody mess of blood, splintered bone and cartilage. The bullet passed out of the glove, followed by a shower of blood droplets, with just enough energy to bruise Pavel's left hip.

Shocked, but not in any real pain, the cavalry officer watched impassively as the split finger of his glove flapped in time with the galloping motion of his horse. He watched, emotionless as the gold ring which Ekaterina had slid onto his finger at the Cathedral of Archangel Michael in Oryol that spring, slipped out of the broken glove with a slop of blood, bounced off his knee and into the beetroots, never again to be seen.

Another round, fired by Bruno's friend, Private Hans Groener, hit Belaya Iskra right in the heart. The horse dropped like a stone; Pavel was trapped by his leg under the dead animal and later that evening was taken prisoner by the German infantry. He eventually ended up in a prison camp in Fürstenburg, north of Berlin, from where he spent two years writing long, melancholic love letters to his wife.

For Ekaterina, the late summer of 1914 was almost idyllic. Her brother-in-law, Maxim Ozertsov, his wife, Maria, and their four young children were living nearby. They had a large circle of friends and Ekaterina was included in the tennis parties, riverside picnics and alfresco luncheons which filled the month of August.

Of course she wished that Pavel could have shared in this social whirl, but she wasn't going to let his absence spoil her fun. She was popular with the young men who were all determined to enjoy themselves to the full before they finally felt obliged to enlist. Her pale, delicate prettiness and thick auburn hair, which always seemed to have a tendril or two escaping provocatively at the side, made men feel protective towards her. But they all behaved in a most gentlemanly way - her very recent marriage to a much-admired cavalry officer ensured that they kept a respectful distance at all times and Ekaterina herself knew just how to far to go with a flirtation to remain on the respectable side of coquettishness.

The second week of September, however, brought a sudden cooling in the air, heavy rain, and the upsetting news from Ekaterina's in-laws that they were packing up and leaving Russia for America. The parties and picnics ceased and one mid-September evening Ekaterina found herself sitting in their drawing room after supper, in the midst of tearful goodbyes.

Maria embraced her sister-in-law tenderly.

'Oh, my dear Katya. I wish we didn't have to leave you, but Maxim is so worried about what is happening in Russia. When Pavel returns you must try to persuade him to join us.'

That autumn, with Maxim and Maria gone, Ekaterina retreated into solitude. She kept the letters from Pavel in a drawer in her dressing table, having read the first two and decided against reading any more of them. They were too sentimental, wallowing in the romantic self-pity that Russian men are prone to in times of trouble.

The battering of the autumn wind and rain gradually denuded the trees of their leaves and the roses of their petals. Ekaterina felt depressed and lethargic and spent whole days sitting on the cushioned window seat in her bedroom, gazing out at the garden.

One grey morning in early October her gloomy reverie was broken by the arrival of a policeman. Inspector Vladimir Lesnoy brought a letter from Colonel Mirskii, of the Fourteenth Cavalry Division which briefly noted Pavel's detention in Germany and the continued payment of his salary, though at at a much reduced rate. Lesnoy noticed both Ekaterina's fragile beauty and her apparent lack of emotion as she read the official notice. He gave her his official visiting card and decided then and there that he would pay 'particular attention' to her well-being.

This campaign of attention started a week later when Lesnoy returned one lunchtime. 'Madame Ozertsova, I was just passing by and thought I ought to pay you a visit, just to check that you are not suffering too much in these difficult times.' Ekaterina, though not physically attracted by the policeman's saturnine looks, was lonely and bored. In addition, she recognised that he had the power to make her life difficult if he chose to do so.

She invited Lesnoy to join her for lunch: borscht, followed by a smoked pork, onion and potato pie. He asked if she had any vodka to wash it down and, somewhat reluctantly, she produced a bottle, untouched since Pavel's departure. After a painfully quiet meal, at which Lesnoy, well-oiled by the excellent vodka, tried in vain to flirt with Ekaterina, he laid his cards on the table.

'Madame Ozertsova,' he said, carefully keeping his manner formal. 'I understand that your relatives have gone to America and you are now all alone in the area. You should realise that in these violent times your servants are as likely to be a danger to your well-being as a guarantee of your safety. Did you, by chance, hear about what happened to the Bobrov family just a couple of months ago? Mr Bobrov hacked to death, Mrs Bobrova raped and murdered. Their three children all put into potato sacks and drowned in the duck pond like baby kittens. And the perpetrator is still at large.'

Ekaterina stiffened; she instinctively knew what was coming next. Beautiful women, even beautiful married women, knew how these offers of protection worked. The local gendarmes in Oryol were well-known for their 'protective services'.

Ekaterina avoided eye-contact with the policeman.

'Yes, I have heard that story. My servants were most upset by it. Their version was that none of the farm workers was involved and that it was actually the latest in a series of violent murders stretching back years - the Potato Sack Killings.'

'Madame Ozertsova, dearest Ekaterina - may I call you Ekaterina? We are friends, are we not? You need protection. A beautiful young widow like you is vulnerable, very vulnerable to the social crimes of the criminal peasant class.'

Ekaterina considered correcting Lesnoy, reminding him that her husband was a prisoner-of-war, lightly wounded by the Germans, not dead and buried by any means, but she said nothing and continued to sit, rigidly upright.

'I insist on it. Without my protection you are in grave danger.'

Ekaterina turned her sea green eyes towards Lesnoy and looked at him directly for the first time. 'I understand,' she said in a monotone. 'But I am not a rich woman. How should I pay for the special protection which you so graciously offer?'

Vladimir Lesnoy stood up, walked around the table and stopped behind Ekaterina. He rested his hands on her shoulders, slowly slid them together and rubbed the downy hair at the back of her neck. She froze. Fear, anger, sorrow, but also the tiniest frisson of excitement: all these emotions filled her. She knew what she had to do and pretended to smile and patted his hand in a fake show of affection. He grabbed her jaw, twisted her head around and kissed her hard on the mouth. Ekaterina could taste the blood where his teeth pinched her lips. She felt nothing but hatred for this man and contempt for herself.

Lesnoy's weekly visits continued, always on a Tuesday afternoon when Ekaterina's maid Galina, the only remaining live-in servant, had her half-day off. Months went by. Ekaterina felt as though she were sleepwalking through life, floating high above and looking down on this strange, distorted version of her existence in which she had somehow become inveigled.

Late one Tuesday afternoon, when Lesnoy had been there for several hours and Ekaterina had left the bedroom to wash and change, Lesnoy idly opened the dressing table drawer and pulled out one of Pavel's letters.

'My darling Ekaterina,' he read, 'My beautiful, green-eyed Kitty; my adorable little Kiki-Cat, how my soul yearns for the soft touch of my Kiki's pretty hands…'

Lesnoy smirked and glanced at the next letter.

'My own precious Kiki kittykins, how I long to be with you again, body and soul as one…'

He snorted in derision and hastily replaced the letters and shut the drawer as he heard Ekaterina's approaching footsteps. The bedroom door creaked as she opened it and Lesnoy turned to smile at her.

'I yearn for your soft touch, pretty Kiki!' he mocked.

'Don't you dare…' she spluttered furiously and her Gorgon-like stare might have turned a more sensitive man to stone. Lesnoy was immune to her rage. 'Ooh, pretty Kiki kittykins, I love it when you're angry!' Ekaterina turned on her heel and flounced off, leaving Lesnoy smiling to himself in her bed.

The passing weeks and months became a year. A second year crept by in cruel slow motion. Ekaterina felt like an empty shell, used and abused but unable to break free, almost complicit in her own humiliation. Then, in August 1916, almost two years after she had first watched the policeman walk up the drive, he arrived one Tuesday afternoon and stood in the hallway, regarding her coolly and announcing that he would not be staying.

'I've been promoted to the Tsar's Special Corps of Gendarmes. I leave for Moscow tomorrow morning.'

They looked at each other in silence as the hall clock loudly ticked each passing second. Eventually Lesnoy shrugged. 'I think we both know it was soon going to be

41

over anyway.' Ekaterina said nothing.

'I hope your husband returns soon. Before your looks fade too much. You're always so pale and listless nowadays.'

Ekaterina imagined slapping his insolent face, but instead clenched her fists so hard that her nails dug into her flesh. She welcomed the sharp pain. Lesnoy opened the front door and walked out. As he shut it behind him Ekaterina heard his mocking voice one last time.

'Goodbye, Kiki; au revoir.'

Ekaterina heard the latch click shut and sank to the floor in a heap, overwhelmed by a huge flood of rage, relief and self-recrimination. She wept and wept. Then she composed herself and went upstairs to run a hot bath in which she scrubbed herself clean.

In a fresh dress, her hair tied back from her face in a severe bun, she sat at her dressing table and opened the drawer. With a delicately-carved ivory-handled letter knife, unused for almost two years, she opened the remainder of Pavel's letters and read each one several times over.

Ekaterina picked up the framed photograph of her husband which had been placed face-down on the dressing table surface since Lesnoy's first visit, and set it upright. Then she pulled out a fresh white piece of writing paper, her pen and inkpot, and began to write.

'My dearest Pavel, I hope with all my heart that you are safe and well and pray with all my soul that you will return to me soon…'

A month passed. And then one crisp, gold-burnished September morning as Ekaterina sat at her window while Galina brushed her hair, another tall, dark-haired man walked up the drive towards the house. This one dressed not in a policeman's uniform, but in the uniform of a cavalry officer. He walked with a slight limp and was almost unrecognisable in his gauntness.

Ekaterina's heartbeat halted, then pounded violently.

'Pavel?' she murmured. Then 'Pavel!' and she rushed

from the room with her long auburn hair still loose, down the stairs and out onto the front steps where she flung herself into her astonished husband's arms.

CHAPTER SEVEN

January 1917, London

Columba livia domestica, Major Dominic Hare thought; city doves, feral pigeons, flying rats. Different names for the same thing. He smiled ruefully to himself as he remembered how many different names he had adopted over the last fifteen years. He looked at his watch. His meeting with his boss, Captain Sir George Mansfield Smith-Cumming, Head of Military Intelligence, Section 6 of His Majesty's Secret Intelligence Service, and Commander Augustus Willington Shelton Agar, the Royal Navy's Russian expert, wasn't for another twenty minutes. Not enough time to walk over to the East India Club for a drink and he didn't really want to sit on a cold, damp bench looking at the ducks dabbling around in St James's Park lake either. He gripped the silver eagle's head that formed the handle of his walking cane and decided to amble slowly around the outer path of the park. It would give him time to think.

At that moment three huge pelicans flew low across the lake.

That really isn't a good omen, Dominic thought. He remembered that the huge white birds were of Russian origin. Descendants of the Great White Pelicans that the Russian ambassador had given to Charles II, over 250 years previously. 'Please God, don't send me to Russia, not at this time of year.' he muttered to himself; however, he knew that if Commander Agar were involved it wasn't likely to be good news.

Agar was Executive Officer on the cruiser HMS Iphigenia, the warship used by the Secret Intelligence Service for Russian operations, and Dominic knew that Russia was in turmoil. However, without any opportunities for birdwatching, winter in Russia wasn't on Dominic's list of preferred destinations.

Did they have pigeons in Russia? he wondered. Even the most hardy city pigeon wouldn't be able to survive a Russian winter. He would much prefer to go back to Africa or the Middle East for his next assignment. He wondered if he might have been a swallow in a previous life.

No, he thought, not a swallow; I'm nothing but a bloody *cuculus canorus*, a common or garden cuckoo. Untrustworthy, manipulative, dowdy. A Janus. Unloved and unlovable. Cruel and ruthless. Hated by everyone. The first thing cuckoo fledglings did was to push the eggs of their adopted families out of the nest. He had killed in the past, though he had never actually murdered anyone, at least not in cold blood, not with his bare hands; but he could if he had to. If he was ordered to.

Thirty minutes later he was waiting outside Room C on the second floor of Admiralty Arch. He stood looking out of the window at the traffic slowly rumbling around Trafalgar Square. The damp evening smog caught in the dreary haze of the gas lamps. The telephone on the receptionist's desk buzzed once, quite loudly. Dominic resisted the urge to turn around and look at her.

'Yes sir,' she said into the phone and placed the handset back into its cradle. 'Excuse me, Major Hare, Sir George and Commander Agar will see you now.' In one smooth action Dominic turned on his heel, crossed the corridor and opened the door.

His heart sank as he saw the two men inspecting a large map of Russia printed on canvas spread over the chart table.

'Hello Major, do come in. Have you met Commander Agar?'

Dominic saluted the naval officer. 'No need for formality here, Hare. Now Commander, this is the chap I was telling you about.' Agar stepped forward and offered Dominic a firm handshake. Smith-Cumming continued, 'Major Hare has just returned from an assignment in Persia. According to our friends at the war cabinet, without Persian oil the war would be over in six weeks. Major Hare's mother was a Russian princess or some such and he studied Russian at Oxford, so he is quite fluent in the noble lingo of Gogol and Pushkin.'

Dominic leaned over the table to look at the map. 'Are you sending me to Russia, sir?'

'Yes, we have a special job for you. Our man in Petrograd tells us that the whole country is heading for revolution. The Russian Army is thoroughly demoralised and on the verge of mutiny. Most of the soldiers and sailors are starving and are starting to desert the front lines. If the eastern front collapses, the Germans can focus all their strength on the western front, which isn't good for us. We are presently inclined to back someone called General Kerensky. But you don't need to worry about that. What you need to know is that the Russian Imperial Bank in Petrograd has been shifting its gold bullion reserves eastwards, away from the unrest. From Petrograd it goes by armoured train to Moscow and from Moscow it either goes to Kazan, here,' Smith-Cumming jabbed at the map with his finger, 'Or all the way across the country on the Trans-Siberian railway to Vladivostok.' The head of MI6 traced the thin black line that marked the railway eastwards across Russia, past the southern shore of Lake Baikal, along the Russian border with China and finally down to the city of Vladivostok on the Sea of Japan.

Dominic looked at the map. 'Five thousand miles of steppes and forest.'

'Five-and-a-half thousand miles, actually,' Smith-Cumming replied. 'We are doing a deal with this General Kerensky chap. He needs guns, ammunition, vehicles and aircraft, even tinned beef and biscuits and we are going to sell him exactly what he needs. Our dear King and his cousin aren't the best of friends, but blood is thicker than water and all that.' The head of MI6 paused for breath. 'Any questions, Major?'

'Not really, I understand what the background is,' replied Dominic.

'Well, the "commercial arrangements" have not been going as smoothly as we had hoped. To tell the truth, we have been badly cheated in an earlier exchange of arms for bullion - it seems that an insider is trying to divert our gold. What His Majesty's Secret Service wants you to do, Major, is to observe the transfer of quite a considerable amount of gold from Moscow to Vladivostok, where Agar's man on HMS Suffolk will take charge of it. This time we want our payment, in full, fair and square.'

CHAPTER EIGHT

January 1917

Sofia stopped at the tall music room door and listened intently to the waltz being played on the grand piano. She tapped lightly on the door and after waiting a moment she pulled the door open and entered.

Sitting at the piano was Tatiana, wearing a fashionable dark grey silk gown with sheer three-quarter length sleeves. She looked intently at the sheet music propped in front of her while she plonked out a slightly ponderous waltz. After a few bars she let out a frustrated groan and banged her hands hard onto the keys, producing a random, angry, discordant cacophony of sound.

'Aghhhh'

'That sounds very modern,' Sofia said. 'Is it by Bartók? Or maybe Debussy?'

Tatiana laughed and launched into an improvised jazz piano piece, her slim fingers racing and hopping all over the keyboard. Sofia couldn't help but smile at Tatiana's musical skill and she clapped when Tatiana had finished.

'Who composed that? Is it dance music? How do you dance to it?'

'Oh my dear Sofia, you really must get up to date,' Tatiana said, starting to play again. 'Nobody "writes" jazz; I improvised it. Don't you know there is a revolution in music going on?' She switched to a lively, syncopated rendition of La Marseillaise.

'Have you decided what music you will be dancing to at your Birthday Ball?' Sofia asked.

'I'm working on the dance programme now. Of course, Papa will insist on some of this…' and she launched into a limping, clumsy rendition of Strauss's Blue Danube.

The girls laughed.

'We need to talk about this,' Sofia said, offering Tatiana a piece of white card.

'What is it?'

'The proposed menu for your birthday banquet'

'Oh, delicious, let me see.'

Tatiana took the card, placed it on the piano's music stand and started to read out loud.

'Starters: Canapés of Beluga caviar from the Caspian Sea on Melba toast; Chicken and wild mushroom vol-au-vents; Smoked salmon, sour cream and dill blinis. Followed by French onion soup. What happened to the *ukha* soup with gold flakes?'

Sofia squirmed uncomfortably. 'I spoke to Cook and we didn't think it was a good idea.'

'Whyever not? It was served at Princess Anastasia's Winter Ball.'

'Yes, mademoiselle, we are aware of that. Cook has the recipe, from the Romanovs' own chef, Monsieur Cubet.'

'So why isn't it on the menu? I specifically requested it.'

'Well, mademoiselle, are you sure that it's a good idea?'

'What do you mean?'

Sofia paused and then said 'We, that is Cook and I, don't think that serving gold flakes in a soup is a good idea.'

'Is it fantastically expensive? Papa says money is no object for my ball.'

'That's not the problem, mademoiselle. Cook looked into it and the gold leaf is so thin and delicate that it only costs a few kopeks per person'

'So why isn't it on the menu?'

'Well,' stuttered Sofia, starting to blush, 'Don't you think that it might seem a bit extravagant and insensitive to put real gold into a soup? It isn't so much the cost, but the message it sends. What with the war and the troubles in Petrograd, not to mention how cold and hungry everyone is at the moment.'

'Oh Sofia, please don't bring politics into everything. This is my Birthday Ball. For just one evening, I want to forget the outside world. All my friends and family want to celebrate like we did in the good old days.'

The two young women stared at each other in silence, neither one willing to give ground.

Finally Tatiana said, 'I insist that the gold *ukha* is put on the menu.'

'Mademoiselle, I don't...'

'Let them eat gold, Sofia; I don't want to argue about it - let them eat gold!'

'Very well, mademoiselle,' Sofia was seething inside, but attempting to maintain a polite exterior. 'If everything else is in order, I'll tell Cook that you and the Count have approved the menu but that the Tsar's *ukha* with gold flakes should be served instead of the onion soup.'

Tatiana scanned the rest of the menu and passed it back to Sofia. 'Yes, that looks fine. Tell Cook, "Well done".' Then she turned back to focus on the piano music.

Sofia gave a half-hearted curtsey and carried the card out of the music room and down to the kitchen. She placed it on her desk and started writing a list of things to do.

A cheerful rat-a-tat-tat on the door of Sofia's office next to the kitchen, and a cheeky greeting of '*Dobroye utro ocharovatelnyy tovarich*,' interrupted Sofia as she sat at her desk a few days later, checking the to-do list.

Without looking up she smiled. 'Good morning Mister Skobelev,' she said, putting emphasis on the word 'Mister'.

'Did you really just say "Good morning charming comrade"?'

'I did,' said the handsome young man at her door. 'We live in revolutionary times, Comrade Sofia; the world is changing and you are certainly charming.'

Sofia couldn't help but smile. Viktor continued, 'I hear that Vladimir Ilyich, our dear leader himself, might be returning to Russia soon.'

'Lenin?' Sofia exclaimed in surprise, 'Who told you that?'

'Ah, that is for me to know and for you to find out, Comrade Sofia. But I have my sources.'

'Viktor, are you still mixing with the revolutionaries? You know that if the workers and peasants take control we won't be ordering any overpriced groceries from you.'

'Not "if", my beautiful and intelligent Comrade, but "when",' laughed Viktor.

'Listen, "Comrade Viktor," I still have a lot of work to do and, while it is always a pleasure to hear the latest revolutionary news from you, I really must be getting on.'

'I have your special ingredient here,' Viktor said, holding out a small square envelope. 'The gold.'

'Oh, thank God for that. The menus have been printed now.' She pulled a gold-edged card from a brown paper package and handed it to Viktor.

'Clear *ukha* with gold leaf. Sounds like the kind of thing they ate during the last days of the Roman Empire. I wonder if it is an omen? Decadence and excess among the ruling classes enhance the pre-conditions of violent revolution.'

'Well, I told the family not to do it.'

As Sofia turned to place the envelope containing the gold leaf onto a shelf, Viktor slipped the menu card into his jacket pocket, unnoticed.

'You should come with me to next month's Fourth Thursday Meeting.'

'Fourth Thursday? What an odd name!'

'It's held on the fourth Thursday of every month. Here…' Viktor handed Sofia a small paper pamphlet which read:

> *Fourth Thursday Meeting*
> *of Progressives and Intellectuals*
> *International Working Women's Day,*
> *6.00pm,*
> *Moscow West Workers' Meeting Hall.*
> *Speakers:*
> *Viktor Skobelev, Valeriya Amosova, Alexander Zhuravlev*

Underneath these details were three grainy photographs. One was just about recognisable as the man standing in front of her.

'Is that you, Viktor? You're going to make a speech? I'm impressed. Who are the other two?'

'Valeriya Amosova is chairperson of the Moscow Working Women's collective and Alexander Zhuravlev is a poet.'

'A poet? How romantic!' Sofia looked closely at the dark, attractive, if somewhat blurred young face gazing out of the page at her.

'Ha! He doesn't waste his ink on *burzhui* love poems, Comrade Sofia. He writes his verse to whip up passion in the hearts of the workers, to inspire them, to give them strength in their souls to fight for a new Russia of soviets.' Viktor looked slyly at Sofia. 'You think he's good-looking, eh?'

'Well, he's all right. It's hard to tell.' She blushed and put the pamphlet hastily down on the table. 'Right, I must get on now.'

'But you'll come to the meeting?'

Sofia hesitated. She was intrigued. Viktor's revolutionary friends seemed to represent the future, while life in the palace seemed firmly frozen in the past.

'Maybe. If I'm not too busy and only if you promise

that I'll get the best price possible for a half kilo of Beluga caviar. And it must be from the Caspian Sea. None of your cheap carp roe from a muddy duck pond in your granny's village.'

'I'll give you a good price for the caviar, but that gold is going to cost you.'

'Name your price, Viktor,' she shrugged. 'It's not going to cost *me* one kopek. What the Countess wants, the Countess gets - she has absolutely no idea of the value of anything. We could charge the Shuyskys ten times the price and they would be none the wiser.'

Viktor grinned delightedly and tapped the side of his nose.

'I like your *naglost*, comrade. I shall recommend you to Valeriya as someone who would be useful on her committee.'

Sofia rolled her eyes in exasperation, collected her papers and stood up briskly.

'Enough of your nonsense, Viktor, I must get on or there will be no ball.'

Viktor gave her a mock salute and shut the door behind him.

Sofia breathed a sigh of relief and looked around her, frowning distractedly.

'Now,' she thought. 'Where did I put that menu card?'

CHAPTER NINE

January 1917

Later, Sofia would look back at the sound of that tinkling bell as the moment when the regular axis around which her life had gently rotated for the last twenty-three years was about to be tilted.

The silver-plated, brass bell that announced this shift in Sofia's life one Friday afternoon, was one of eighteen silver bells, all attached to a long, black-painted board by flat coiled metal clock springs. The bell board was hung on the long wall of the servants' hall in full view of anyone sitting at the long wooden refectory table.

The springs on the board were connected to thin metal cords made of twisted copper wire that ran along hidden conduits and tubes through the walls and under the floorboards of the palace. Occasionally the wires would run over brass guide wheels and cleverly engineered spring-loaded levers that enabled the cord to go around corners and change direction.

In the public rooms, such as the Dining Room, the Living Rooms and the Ball Room, the wires were attached to thick ropes made from three twisted strands of silken, golden-coloured cord, handmade in Bologna, with a large golden tassel at the end. In the private rooms such as the bedrooms, a thinner red rope was used with a more modest tassel. When the Count wanted to attract the attention of his butler, Mr Roberts, from his study, he would tug a silken rope made of two dark grey strands and one bright canary yellow strand made to match the exact colours of the Shuysky family coat of arms.

When one of these ropes was pulled, the wires and wheels and levers and springs running under the floors and walls all shifted a few centimetres towards the 'upstairs' end of the system and the 'downstairs' spring contracted just enough to bounce and shake the appropriate bell on the board in the servants' hall. The bell continued to bounce for a few seconds after it had rung, allowing the servants to see which room was demanding their attention.

When the bell system had been installed, almost all the domestic staff employed by the Palace had been English or Scottish. Only the carriage drivers and gatekeepers were native speakers of Russian and they tended to be rough-and-ready Cossacks recruited from the Count's vast estates on the Eastern Steppes of Russia. Wide, flat, open prairies where horsemanship, loyalty to tribe and family honour defined the lives of young men. So, above each bell, written in white painted letters, was the name of the room in English. Sofia had noticed that nobody had ever painted over the English names and replaced them with Russian; tradition and inertia were powerful forces in Russia.

Only two of the eighteen bells had been used regularly since the Shuysky boys had left Moscow to fight the Germans two years previously. The Count had also been travelling for much of the time: back and forth to Petrograd for meetings of the State Council in Marie Palace; abroad to act on affairs of state on behalf of the Tsar. When he was in Moscow he was often at the House of the Unions on Bolshaya Dmitrovka Street in the Tverskoy District - the so-called 'clubhouse' of the Assembly of the Nobility.

The most frequently used bell was the one marked 'Bedroom Five'. It usually rang between half past nine and ten o'clock in the morning, most often on a Friday, Saturday or Sunday. The bright metallic ringing usually indicated that Countess Tatiana wished to take breakfast in her bedroom, rather than descending the main staircase to the buffet presented in the breakfast room. Sofia knew that the Countess went dancing on Thursday, Friday and Saturday nights.

The other bell which the Countess rang on a regular basis was the one marked 'Music Room'. This would ring at about half past four in the afternoon when Tatiana and her guests wanted tea and cakes to sustain their energy for dance practice. Since her brothers, Konstantin and Georgiy, had gone to fight, the Music Room had taken over from the Billiard Room as the social hub of the Palace.

When the bell marked 'Study' rang on that January afternoon, Mr Roberts, the Head Butler and last remaining English servant, commented on the unusual event in heavily accented Russian. He reluctantly stood up, put on his long black jacket and gave one quick tug on each of the cuffs to remove any imaginary creases at the elbows. 'I'll be back shortly, no doubt,' he said gruffly.

Just a few minutes later the butler returned and told Sofia that it was her whom the Count wished to see. Sofia walked up the main staircase, knocked once on the Study door and paused, waiting for the Count to call 'Enter!' She rotated the engraved glass door knob and pushed the door open. And so began the unexpected new chapter in Sofia's life.

'Ah, Miss Maslova, Sofia, welcome, welcome. Please sit.' the Count said, pointing at an armchair set in front of his desk. Sofia sat and gently smiled at his awkward formality.

'Good afternoon, sir. How may I assist you?'

'The world is turning upside-down, Sofia. We are cursed to live in an age of change. I have certain anxieties about the future and need you to help me to make the necessary arrangements to keep my Tatiana safe.'

Sofia felt bemused. She had no idea what was going through the Count's mind, but tried to look suitably efficient and in control.

'Of course, Sir, I am at your disposal.'

The Count nodded, an intense look on his face.

'I know that I can trust you to be discreet. No hint of this conversation can be communicated to anyone, not even Countess Tatiana and certainly not to any of your colleagues downstairs.'

'Of course, Sir,' Sofia said, slightly perplexed at the intrigue. 'As you know, your wish is my command. How exactly can I be of service?'

The Count took a small key from an inside pocket of his velvet jacket and unlocked the lower right-hand drawer in his magnificent walnut wood bureau. Sofia couldn't see exactly what he did next, but he seemed to reach into the back of the drawer and press something. She heard an unobtrusive click, then he pulled out a second, slightly larger key.

The Count stood up and went over to the far left-hand section of the vast built-in bookcase which lined one entire wall of the Study. He removed the thickest book from the middle shelf - Tolstoy's *'Voyna i Mir'*, Sofia observed - and reached into the gap with the key. She heard the key turning in a hidden lock, then he drew something out and returned to sit at his desk.

The Count placed a large, dark blue velvet bag with a drawstring on his desk. Sofia thought she could hear the distant tinkling of rain falling on the lake at the dacha. The sound seemed to be coming from within the bag. The Count pulled the drawstring open and reached into the bag, pulling out a fistful of small stones which he gently scattered onto the green leather top of his desk. Light from his desk lamp bounced and glittered from them, lighting up the room.

'Diamonds!' Sofia gasped. Her mind was in a whirl, a myriad conflicting thoughts shooting through her brain like the Perseid meteor shower. What help did the Count require? What could he be expecting her to do for him?

Count Shuysky seemed to read her mind. He gazed at her steadily. 'These are for the two of you: an escape plan, an insurance policy.'

'The two of us?'

'Yes, my dear Sofia, you and the Countess Tatiana.'

'But why?' Sofia stammered. 'What escape plan do you mean? I don't understand…' She shook her head in agitation, unable to continue speaking.

The Count tried to smile, but it was a sad smile and Sofia could see tears glistening in his tired old eyes.

'Dear Sofia, life here as we know it is over. The *dvoryanstvo* - the aristocracy - is like a herd of woolly mammoths, lost and wandering around the Siberian marsh. As the snow melts in spring we will find ourselves sinking into a stinking bog. We have failed to evolve. The Shuysky family, like all the others, has no place in modern society. Look at what is happening around us - not only here, in Moscow and Petrograd, not only in Russia, but all over Europe - Germany, Austria, France, even England. We are relics of a dying world, destined at best for imprisonment in a *katorga* or at worst for the guillotine. What is it that the revolutionaries say? "First up against the wall when the revolution begins!" Our only hope is to help our youngsters escape.'

Sofia could hardly breathe. Her chest was tight, but she had to speak.

'But escape where? How? I can't imagine…' She shook her head again in disbelief and clutched at the edge of the desk, as if to steady herself against being physically thrown topsy-turvy.

The Count spoke calmly and reassuringly. 'I believe America is the future. I want you and the Countess to take these diamonds to California. My lawyer has a cousin there who will meet you and help with any necessary paperwork on arrival. You will travel from Moscow to Vladivostok on the Trans-Siberian railway. From there you can buy passage on a steamer to San Francisco. All I need you to do is to prepare a minimum of clothes and other essentials which you and Tatiana will need for the journey and to organise the travel arrangements - paperwork, visa, tickets and so on. For the time being I don't want to worry Tatiana with this plan - we will tell her nearer the time, when everything has been organised.'

'When will this take place? What about Tatiana's birthday celebrations? Are they to be cancelled?'

'No. I want you to make all the arrangements straightaway, but without drawing attention to it. Word from Petrograd is that it's just a matter of time before Moscow will become a place of danger for the aristocracy, but until then we carry on as normal. As long as you're ready to move as soon as it becomes necessary, all should be well.'

'But what about the diamonds? Won't it be dangerous to travel with them?'

'That is another task I need you to carry out, Sofia. I would like you to think up some way of carrying the diamonds which is secure and secret. I know you're an intelligent and resourceful girl and I'm sure you'll be able to invent a clever scheme.'

'But Sir, won't you come with us? Tatiana won't want to leave here without you,' she hesitated a moment, 'And neither do I.'

The Count bowed his head sadly and Sofia's heart went out to him. She noticed the silver threads which now ran through his once thick, dark hair and the wrinkles which lined his handsome face.

'I am too old for such change, Sofia. For better or for worse, my life is here and I must see it through, put my affairs in order, and survive as best I can when the new regime comes. Tatiana is tougher than she looks and I know you will look after her. You have been a true friend to her, more than that even, more like a sister.' He looked up at Sofia and gazed intently into her eyes. Sofia felt strongly that he was trying to convey some meaning to her.

'And your sons? Konstantin and Georgiy? What will they do?'

'They will have to survive as best they can. Who knows what their future holds, so far away, in the thick of that terrible war. I pray every day for their safe return and that, when all this horror is over, they will be able to join their sister - and you - in America.'

To Sofia's dismay, the Count suddenly covered his face with his hands and his shoulders began to shake. She pushed back her chair and stood, hesitantly, by his desk. Then she walked around and paused behind the Count's chair before tentatively patting her hand on his shoulder.

The Count immediately placed one hand over hers.

'Don't worry, sir,' she whispered. 'Of course I will do everything you have asked. Leave it all to me.'

The Count breathed in - a deep, shuddering breath. 'Thank you, Sofia. My Tatiana is very precious to me and I am entrusting her to you. Your reward will be half of the diamonds. When you arrive in California you will be able to live like a Countess yourself.'

As Sofia left the room the Count opened another drawer in his desk and took out a piece of thick, creamy paper embossed with his personal letterhead - Count Nikolai Lvovich Shuysky and the Shuysky coat of arms. He dipped his pen into the black ink cupped by the silver and enamel Fabergé inkwell on the desktop and tapped the nib carefully on the rim to rid it of excess liquid. He thought of all the official letters he had written in his various roles on the State Council or on issues concerning the Assembly of the Nobility. None had been as difficult to compose as the two letters he had to write now.

He thought of his beautiful, clever daughter Tatiana. How would she react when she learned the truth about him? He was too cowardly to tell her face to face. How could he bear to see the shock and disgust on her face? He thought of Sofia, so loving and loyal, such a lively and intelligent companion during those lonely years when Tatiana had been away. Did she somehow sense the blood bond between them? Again, he was too ashamed to reveal the truth about her parentage directly to her. However, he could not send his daughters off, so far away, to begin their new lives on the basis of a half-truth - a *lie* if he was being brutally honest with himself. No, he must set down the truth in writing and keep the letters ready to give them when the time came for them to leave.

The ink had dried on the pen nib, so he dipped it into the inkwell again and began to write the first letter.

'My beloved Sofia…'

Sofia went straight to her room instead of returning downstairs. A maelstrom of thoughts was churning inside her head and she needed to make sense of them. Only a few days ago she had been conniving in Viktor's scheme to fleece the Shuyskys out of a minuscule fraction of their enormous and utterly undeserved wealth. She had been thinking about leaving her position of servitude to throw in her lot with the radicals. Now, she was plotting with Count Shuysky to protect his spoilt daughter and smuggle his stash of diamonds out of the country. She was seriously considering what it would be like to live the life of a rich American.

Bozhe moi! My God! Those diamonds! she thought. One could quite conceivably feed, clothe and house the whole of Moscow's poor with the contents of that velvet bag. What should she do? She thought of Viktor and his deeply held socialist beliefs, his rabble-rousing rhetoric and the fiery passion in his soul. She thought of Tatiana fussing over which dress to wear, teasing Sofia with French phrases which she didn't understand, prancing around the Music Room with her wealthy friends for hours to learn the latest dance steps.

Then she thought of the Count, a widower for so long, his brave sons away for years fighting for their motherland, his beloved daughter in danger of death - or worse - at the hands of the ever more angry mob. She thought of the happy summers at the dacha when she had been too young to understand the concept of class divide. She thought of the years in the palace schoolroom with Miss Greycourt, giggling with Tatiana over the pointlessness of chanting a list of the Kings and Queens of England.

Of course she believed in equality, in justice, in fair distribution of wealth. But, she realised, she also believed in something else, something which - to her at least - was even more important. She believed in love, loyalty and, strangely perhaps because she didn't have one, she believed in family. The Shuysky family.

CHAPTER TEN

January 1917

Letter from Grigory Zyuzin, Moscow Chief-of-Police, to Ilya Brilyov, Verkhneudinsk Chief-of-Police.

Esteemed Brigadier Brilyov,

We have recently had a breakthrough in our ten year long investigation of the serial killer popularly known as 'the Potato Sack Killer'. We have reason to believe that he is now living and working in the Verkhneudinsk area and I am sure you will join us in wishing to apprehend him before he carries out yet another heinous crime, this time in your jurisdiction. To this end, I would be grateful if you could be so good as to afford all possible assistance to the senior detective, Inspector Vladimir Lesnoy, who has been leading investigations into this case. He will be arriving in Verkhneudinsk by train in the next few weeks, further details of his travel arrangements to follow. We would request that he is met at Verkhneudinsk by one of your officers of equal rank and accommodated with a desk and lodgings, ideally close to the Office of Gendarmes.

Yours faithfully,
Brigadier Grigory Zyuzin
Chief-of-Police
Moscow

Sofia knocked on the study door.

'Enter,' the Count called in a loud voice.

Looking serious, Sofia entered and placed two garments on his desk. The Count picked one up and inspected her handicraft. It was a tailored, sleeveless bodice made of soft, white brushed cotton. Across the front and back, narrow white ribbons tufted out from the fabric giving the garment the appearance of a newly planted field of white grass. The Count turned it over and inspected the twelve sturdy cotton strips at the back which could be used to tie it shut. He put the first bodice back onto his desk.

'And this one?' he asked, using two hands to lift up the second bodice. He pulled a grim face, 'It is rather heavy. What is it like to wear?'

'I have put it on myself and found it quite wearable, at least for short periods of time. It certainly isn't the most flattering garment I have ever made, and I wouldn't want to go dancing in it, but under a coat or a jacket it will be almost invisible. I used gravel from the drive to take the place of the diamonds. I'm not sure but I think that the diamonds might be slightly heavier. There are twenty pockets on each bodice, each one can hold about fifty cubic centimetres of stones. I think you estimated that each bodice should hold about one litre.'

The Count pulled a silk ribbon that held one of the pockets shut and lifted the flap to look at the small brown stones.

'Ingenious, how clever of you to think of using gravel.'

'I washed it and then dried it carefully, before I filled up the pockets. It's all perfectly clean.'

The Count reached over and tugged at the bellcord. 'I think it is time we talked to Countess Tatiana.'

Moments later a single tap at the door announced the arrival of Roberts.

'Look at this, Roberts, the bodice that Miss Sofia has made for the diamonds.' The Count handed the heavy bodice to Roberts who felt the weight of it in his hands. 'Filled with gravel from the drive,' he added.

'It is quite heavy, Your Lordship. Will Countess Tatiana be able to carry such a weight?'

'That's what we want to find out. Could you please find her and tell her that we request her presence here in my study.'

'Of course, Sir,' Roberts turned and went to find the Countess. Sofia wondered how such a large man managed to glide so smoothly and silently, as if he were on wheels.

'So, Sofia, I'm impressed, it looks very good,' the Count said. 'Can you fill the second bodice with diamonds so we can test it on the Countess: we need to confirm that the design is really practical.' He reached into his desk, brought out the dark blue velvet bag and spilled a great pile of diamonds onto his desk.

'I've borrowed this from the kitchen to help load the pockets,' Sofia said showing the Count a small kitchen scoop made of wood. 'Cook uses it to measure out tea leaves when he is blending.' Sofia picked up the first bodice and opened a pocket with her index finger. She dipped the scoop into the pile of diamonds and carefully poured them into a pocket. A second scoop of glittering stones filled the pocket up. She tied the flap tight shut with the tiny ribbon and opened the next pocket.

'I think that once the design has been tested and filled with diamonds I will sew the pockets shut,' Sofia said.

'Yes, that's probably a good idea,' said the Count. 'It's important that diamonds don't escape by accident.'

Once all the pockets were filled, the Count turned to look out of the window while Sofia put the remaining diamonds back into the velvet bag. He gazed out at the snowy garden.

'Things are not going well, you know. The war is hell, the strikes are getting out of control and the communists are winning more and more support. We have no one to blame but ourselves. I tried, Sofia; I tried my best to be a good patrician and employer. It is not easy.'

'Oh, Sir, you are the kindest and most caring master we

65

could wish for. All the servants downstairs say the same.'

'What do they say about the war and the unrest in Petrograd?'

'We all agree that the war is a terrible mistake, that the British system is probably the best we can hope for. The Royal family must stop dictating to us and the Tsar should let the Duma take the lead.'

'The Duma?' the Count snorted a derisory laugh. 'That bunch of self-serving dimwits? That's what you get when you give the illiterate masses and the criminal classes a vote. I despair of the whole situation, Sofia, I despair.'

There was a pause.

'Is everything else organised?' he said.

'I think so. I've packed money, enough to buy our train tickets at Yaroslavsky station and dollars for when we reach America, letters of introduction and passports for Miss Tatiana and myself. I've packed one of the Countess's trunks with winter travel clothes and boots. All we need now is to try on the bodices and prepare a set of clothes for the day that we leave. I'm not sure what to do about the voyage to San Francisco. There is very little information on boats departing and the availability of passenger berths.'

'Good, good. Well, as long as you have some American dollars in cash you can buy your way onto a steamer. I don't think that will be a problem. What happens when you arrive in California?'

'I have received a letter from Mr Danchet, your lawyer's cousin, who practises law in San Francisco. He tells me that if we travel first class on a passenger ship we will be able to pass immigration tests on the liner. If we have to travel second class or steerage we will disembark at a place called Angel Island in San Francisco Bay and there we register our desire to enter into the United States. It will be for one or two days at most, while they perform health and educational checks. It seems that we will be free to go quite quickly. Mr Danchet says that all our property will be confiscated but he assures me that in America everything will be returned to us. Most importantly I have a visa letter signed by Mr Maddin Summers, the American Consul General in Moscow, which should ease our passage.'

'Well done, Sofia - once again I am extremely impressed by your organisational skills. I am sure that Mr Danchet will be able to assist you and Tatiana if necessary. Once you arrive in California you should find a hotel and then start looking for a house to purchase. I hope that you will continue to assist the Countess even when you have left Russia.'

A knock on the door announced the arrival of Tatiana. This, thought Sofia, was going to be an interesting conversation.

CHAPTER ELEVEN

Thursday 23rd February 1917

At five o'clock in the afternoon the Palace was a hive of activity as everyone in the household buzzed hither and thither preparing for Tatiana's ball that evening. When Sofia, briefly visiting the kitchen to check with Cook about the timings for the banquet, saw Viktor waiting, her heart sank.

'Good evening my heavenly Comrade Sofia,' Viktor said, offering Sofia a posy of rather sad looking wild flowers, 'May I say how lovely you're looking this evening.'

'Heavenly?' Sofia laughed, 'That doesn't sound very socialistic. I thought you communists were planning to ban heaven and the afterlife for workers like me. Didn't Marx say that heaven is the "opium of the people" or something like that? Anyway, what are you doing here? I thought you had already delivered everything for tonight.'

'Sofia! Have you forgotten? Today is International Day of the Woman Worker. I am proud to salute you with a suitably respectful greeting and, as is traditional in these circumstances, a bunch of flowers.'

'Well, thank you, Comrade Viktor, for the flowers, but I can't possibly come to your meeting. I've got far too much to do here.'

'We had a deal. I got you the Beluga caviar - with great

difficulty I might add - and you agreed to come to the meeting. You don't have to stay long. It's only fifteen minutes there on the tram, you can have a beer to toast the working women and be home again by half past six. Cook has everything under control, haven't you Cook?'

Sofia saw a wink pass between the two men.

'Go on, Miss Sofia,' Cook encouraged her, 'You deserve an hour off before it gets really busy. Everything's ahead of schedule in the kitchen.'

'Well, I don't know...'

'You can meet a few of my friends - Alexander Zhuravlev, that young poet I told you about - he's going to be there,' Viktor urged.

Sofia brightened a little. 'Oh, well, yes I would like to meet him. I don't know...' she pushed her hair back from her forehead in a gesture of agonised indecision, 'I'll have to go and ask the Countess. Wait here a moment.'

Tatiana was putting the finishing touches to the flower arrangements in the entrance hall. She was glowing with happiness and rushed, smiling, towards Sofia, taking her hands and whirling her around on the marble floor.

'Oh, Sofia! I'm so excited about tonight. It's going to be my best Birthday Ball ever. All thanks to you - you've organised every detail so brilliantly. Everything's ready and absolutely perfect. All we have to do now is get dressed and enjoy ourselves.'

'We?'

'Yes, of course! I know you're needed to help serve at the banquet later on, but you are going to join in with the dancing, aren't you. Oh, please say you are - you know two of those young gentlemen who've been here for dancing practice keep asking me if they might book you for a dance or two!'

Sofia looked at Tatiana in surprise. 'Really? Oh, well, yes - of course I'd love to. It's just that I wondered if I might be spared, just for an hour, to go to a meeting. I'll be back well before the ball starts.'

'A meeting?' Tatiana frowned uncomprehendingly.

'Yes, it's a… well I think there might be a poetry reading and some… some light refreshments.'

Tatiana smiled fondly at her. 'Of course you must go, then. Have fun, but please don't be late back. I shall book you in for the first dance with Mr Zyuzin and the second with Mr Lopatin. And don't worry about dressing me, I'll ask one of the other girls to help.'

Sofia and Viktor just missed a tram and didn't arrive at the packed meeting hall until almost six o'clock. What must have been a crowd of three hundred or so were milling around looking for somewhere to sit. Sofia was impressed that so many people knew Viktor, but he didn't actually introduce her to anyone and there was no sign of the poet. Several comrades said something to him about 'Looking forward to the revolutionary oratory' and 'Petrograd today, Moscow tomorrow.' Viktor just worked his way through the throng with a brief word here and a curt nod there, with Sofia trailing along behind him, becoming more and more uncomfortably aware of the passing time.

The large hall clock struck half past six and Sofia tapped Viktor on the shoulder.

'Viktor, I must get back now. Thank you so much for inviting me, it's wonderful to see how much support you have for the cause. Don't worry, I can find my own…' But in response, Viktor glared at her, grasped her wrist and led her through the crowd, up a short set of wooden steps and onto the stage, where there were seven seats and a small table covered in a bright red cloth with the words 'Long Live the Equality of the Woman' painted in yellow letters.

Viktor pointed at a chair. 'Sit here.'

Sofia felt extremely uncomfortable. 'No, no Viktor, I can't sit up here. I am… I must go.'

Viktor pulled her towards him, twisting her arm and

not letting her move. He put his face so close to hers that she could see the wrinkles around his eyes, the whiskers on his chin and smell the stale tobacco on his breath. She froze in horror.

'Listen to me, my dear *burzhui*-bitch, Sofia,' he hissed through gritted teeth, 'You are nothing but a class traitor and pathetic moll of the oppressive tyrant, Count Shuysky. Please be so kind as to sit your pretty little arse on that chair. Don't move, don't say anything, don't twitch one muscle without first asking my permission. If you disobey me, I promise that you'll be beaten and abused by the heroic red guards and then, once they have finished taking their base pleasure, thrown naked from the Bolshoy Kamenny Bridge onto the icy Moskva where the Gendarmes will find your broken and bruised body tomorrow morning. Do you understand me, Comrade Strumpet?'

Sofia felt the blood drain from her head. She felt faint with terror. Limp as a ragdoll, she let herself be pushed backwards by Viktor onto the chair. Why had she come to this awful place? What did Viktor want from her? How could she possibly escape? Irrationally, she was concerned that Mr Zyuzin and Mr Lopatin would be angry that she had failed to dance with them. She felt faint and dizzy.

'Good, good comrade. That is good,' Viktor said in a sinisterly soothing tone, letting go of her arm. 'You stay nice and quiet.'

Sofia sat, terrified.

'Order, order!' Viktor shouted, raising his arms in an effort to quieten the audience. The crowd was not paying attention to him so he raised his fist and smashed it hard onto the table.

The audience fell silent. All eyes were upon him.

'Order! Comrades, silence your chatter! Would the members of the Fourth Thursday Organising Committee please come up to join me on the stage.'

The chatter of the crowd restarted as four men and a

woman climbed the wooden stairs at the side of the stage and sat down on the wooden chairs. None of them so much as glanced at Sofia, but nervously she looked askance at each one in turn. At the far end sat a middle-aged skinny intellectual type with wire-rimmed glasses and a neatly trimmed beard; next to him a chubby red-faced factory worker with huge, dirty fingers and a black bushy beard. Then there was an older man with white hair and a white beard and a threadbare blue pinstriped suit that had clearly seen better days. Alongside him, behind the table, was the stony faced woman in her forties, Valeriya, hair scraped back into a bun, flanked by a baby-faced young student with a fluffy beard that was struggling to make an impact. Sofia wondered if beards were somehow obligatory for committee members. Viktor took the sixth seat next to Sofia. Sofia realised that none of the committee had looked her in the eyes. Her feeling of unease deepened.

Valeriya stood up and walked to the front of the stage. The chatter dwindled as she glared chillingly at those members of the audience who were still talking. Finally, silence was achieved.

'Comrades of the revolution. Welcome to this Fourth Thursday Meeting. Happy International Day of the Working Woman,' she said, cheerlessly. A great shout went up from the large crowd. 'Comrades, comrades, please, silence. We have something special to show you. Something special to share with you. Viktor, please come forward.'

Viktor stood up. Sofia felt sick. What was he going to do? Why had she agreed to come to this meeting?

Viktor cleared his throat.

'Comrades, working women, workers. We, the Moscow Central Fourth Thursday Committee invite you to celebrate this special day of women workers with bread and beer.' The crowd clapped and stamped their feet with approval.

'Sadly, there is no cheese, no meat, no fat. But what is mine is yours!' Another huge cheer shook the hall. Viktor raised his hands to quieten the audience. 'I know some of you are wondering who this woman is.' He turned to look at Sofia and pointed at her with a piece of white card. Her heart lurched violently as she recognised it immediately. The missing menu.

'This evening, at our party to celebrate our solidarity with oppressed working women around the world, we will eat a humble meal of black bread and watery beer, no butter, no cheese, not even stale cheese.' The crowd laughed, loving Viktor's introduction.

'At the same time as we honour our women comrades, there is another party. A party which Sofia Maslova here,' he jabbed the menu card accusingly in Sofia's direction, 'Has been organising for her employers. A party that we workers and peasants haven't been invited to. A party to celebrate the birthday of one woman. Countess Tatiana Shuyskaya.' Sofia shuddered on seeing the shower of spittle issue from Viktor's lips as he spat the name out in disgust.

'Is Countess Tatiana a worker?'

'No!' roared the crowd.

'Is Countess Tatiana, with her diamonds and rubies, satin and silk, a spoiled brat?'

'Yes!' bellowed the crowd.

Once again Viktor held his hands up to quieten their shouts and catcalls.

'What's this? What's this?' Viktor asked the crowd, waving the white card. 'I've got a little list, I've got a little list.'

Sofia suddenly realised what was going to happen. She needed to escape. To warn the Count and Tatiana and their guests. Viktor was rabble-rousing. She had no doubts about what his aim was.

'This little list is the menu which Countess Tatiana and her guests are guzzling this evening: Caviar, French

Pastries, and…' here he paused for effect, switching to a mocking, refined, effeminate accent, 'Golden soup.'

A voice from the crowd shouted, 'What the hell is that?'

'Let me tell you, comrade. Clear *ukha* fish soup with 'flakes of real gold'. Flakes of gold! It is here in black and white. Gold. The Countess and the Count and their *burzhui* cronies are eating soup made of gold, while we, if we are lucky, will have a mouthful of lukewarm water flavoured with mouldy potato skins.'

The crowd stood up and shouted angrily, waving clenched fists in anger at this evidence of the excesses of the evil, greedy *dvoryanstvo*. Sofia decided that this was her chance; she stood up and ran down the steps off the stage only to be confronted by the screaming mob. She could see the exit door at the back of the hall, but the crowd was so dense that she knew she could not possibly reach it.

Viktor shouted 'Stop her!' but the noise was so tumultuous that his words were lost.

She felt someone grasp her elbow and tried to shrug them off, 'No, no! Let go of me!'

'I can help you,' a calm voice whispered in her ear. 'This way, come with me; there is another exit, behind the stage.' Sofia surrendered herself to her guardian angel, a tall, thin, dark-haired young man wearing a grubby, dark blue Imperial Navy coat and a dark blue cap. As the mob jumped up and down, shouting and gesticulating in a furious class war dance, he pulled her round the side of the stage and bundled her unceremoniously out of a small door at the back of the hall into the freezing night.

'Go back and warn the Shuyskys. Their lives are in danger. Go!'

Sofia met the young man's dark eyes fleetingly, and she recognised him as Alexander Zhuravlev, the poet on the leaflet. Then adrenalin surged through her and she ran as fast as she could back towards the palace, barely registering the sound of two gunshots which came from inside the hall as she rounded the corner onto the main road.

The crowd in the hall was chanting 'Storm the palace! Storm the palace!' over and over again. Viktor called for silence. Such was their fury that they did not listen.

A gunshot rang out. Alexander Zhuravlev was on the stage, pointing a smoking pistol up in the air. He fired a second time. The crowd fell silent.

'Comrades!' Alexander said in a deep, well-educated voice. 'Comrades, stop! Violence is not the way. Yes, the Shuysky Palace, their diamonds, and even their gold-flaked soup must become property of the Moscow Soviet. But violence now will destroy our ethics. Confiscation of property - yes, restorative justice - yes, popular revolution - yes. But a revolution without justice is no revolution; it is mob rule. We already have a mob ruling us. A mob of kings and queens and counts and countesses. Let's overthrow the aristocratic mob, but without blood, without destruction. A bloody revolution is not going to change anything. We must not act in the same way as they do.'

The audience shouted and whistled and booed their dissent. Alexander slipped his pistol back into his inside coat pocket. Viktor stood next to the new speaker shaking his head in mock sorrow.

'Listen, comrades, listen. Comrade Zhuravlev, esteemed poet of the workers, has delivered some impressive rhetoric,' he said in a soothing voice, his hands gently rising and falling, palms down, in a gesture of appeasement while he scanned the crowd. 'Let's go to the palace. We will tell them that we are a little bit sad and a little bit disappointed that our invitation to Countess Tatiana's Birthday Ball has been lost in the post... *Then* we will burn the palace down!'

The crowd erupted into a hysterical mixture of anger, sanctimonious outrage, and bloodthirsty glee. Viktor smiled a fake smile, waved at an invisible 'friend' in the audience and then turned and nodded at the three security guards who had slowly manoeuvred themselves into position behind Alexander, who was looking exasperated.

Alexander's annoyance was replaced by a hot stinging pain in his head, a flash of bright green light and then the sound of his boots scraping across the stage and down some stairs. He later recalled the voice of one of Viktor's thuggish 'Red Guards' saying, 'Sweet dreams, comrade poet' as they dumped him like a sack of potatoes into the void under the stage.

CHAPTER TWELVE

Sofia was not able to run as fast as she wanted. Her long dress and best shoes made it impossible to move much faster than a brisk walk with occasional scuttling sprints which she managed by grabbing her skirt and lifting it up so that her feet did not get tangled.

She knew the way back to the palace. She scurried through the dark streets behind the Dorogomilovo Cathedral towards Borodinsky Bridge. Just as she arrived at the bridge she heard the clang-clang of an electric tram bell. She lifted her skirt up to her knees and ran as fast as she could towards the tram stop where a Number 31 tram had paused to let off passengers.

Sofia waited impatiently for the passengers to step down from the rear car, before pulling herself on board, still shocked at what had happened. She sat on one of the wooden benches and, in a daze, bought a ticket from the conductor, who looked at her face and said, 'Is everything all right, Miss?'

She nodded and turned to look out of the back of the carriage, worried that she was being followed. The tram carried Sofia over the bridge and then along Arbat Street before turning onto Vozdvizhenka Street where she stepped off. Her tears, panic and guilt combined to make her feel sick and dizzy at the same time. She stopped briefly to orientate herself at the corner of Nizhny Kislovsky Lane. Passers-by looked at her tear-stained face and whispered; she heard one man say, 'She looks like a hunted animal.'

Back at the meeting hall, the mob had finished shouting abuse at Alexander Zhuravlev and was happily singing the Internationale with the passionate ferocity only found in large groups of very angry, drunken people. Viktor was still on the stage looking at a roughly sketched map of the roads around the palace. He was leading a tactical discussion with the burly looking men who had dragged Alexander from the stage.

'Ilya, You go to the front gates and start shaking them backwards and forwards. While you do that, I'll go to the merchants' delivery gate on the side lane and try to get in. It isn't a strong door; if I have to, I'll unlock it with my Nagant.' He tapped his hip where a Nagant M1895 service revolver sat snugly in a brown leather holster.

The song finished with a final rousing shout of 'Tomorrow the Internationale will be the Human Race'. Viktor rolled up the sketched map and the three men nodded complicitly. They briefly shook hands, wished one another luck, and turned to face the audience.

As the song ended, more cheers followed. Viktor raised his right arm, his clenched fist gripping the red cloth which he had pulled from the table. His face was emotionless. 'Comrades. The time has come,' he started. He waited for silence. 'Comrades.' He paused once again as the crowd shushed an old man who had started to cough. The mob wanted to know what Viktor was going to say.

'Comrades, it is time. It is time to march, not to sing. A moment to shout with rage, not whisper poems. A moment of bravery, not fear. We need to send the Shuyskys a message, a warning. This message is not just for Count Shuysky and his family. Our action will send a message to all the *dvoryanstvo* and their cronies. Tonight, when we burn the Shuysky Palace, when we destroy all the *burzhui* art and icons and tapestries and statues and fine china and when we reclaim the family silver and sequestrate the Shuysky gold and diamonds, then our message will be heard loud and clear: Count, you have sucked enough of our blood, you and your family of vampires. I say away with all these damned parasites! Burn them all; they are nothing but scum. Burn their rotten palace to the ground. Comrades, attacking the Shuysky Palace is not the start of the revolution, that will come soon enough. And it is certainly not going to be the end of the revolution: there are many palaces that will need to burn before we are done. This action is merely one small step on the long march to freedom. Smashing windows, kicking down doors, confiscating stolen property. That is what we do, that is what we do best. We, the Moscow Workers' Soviet, we say enough is enough. We start now. Reds march, Reds attack!'

A great roar filled the hall and Viktor, still holding the red flag clenched in his right fist, raised his arm straight up, above his head. He marched down the steps from the stage and pushed his way through the crowd who clapped him on the back and encouraged him. As he passed the rows of chairs the chanting mob joined behind him. Viktor finally stepped into the dark street. His followers filled the full width of the street behind him and once again started singing the Internationale.

Viktor led from the front, enjoying the power he felt over the scared, timid pedestrians whom they passed.

As soon as Sofia arrived at the palace, she banged on the gate and shouted for Lavr, the Cossack gatekeeper.

'Lavr, Lavr, they are coming. The Bolsheviks are coming, Lavr. Lavr, let me in, they are coming!' She sobbed and clung to the heavy, cast iron gates. After what seemed an age, the tall, languid, moustachioed gatekeeper came out from the gatehouse still buttoning his long grey and yellow uniform coat. He drew back the bolts and opened the gate just enough for Sofia to slip in.

'Lavr, get ready. Get the guard, get everyone. We must defend the palace.'

Lavr looked at Sofia and said nothing.

'Lavr, they are coming. We have ten, maybe twenty minutes before they get here.'

Lavr looked at her and said, 'The Count is in the ballroom. I'll delay them as much as I can, but these gates are old and not secure.'

Sofia took his hands. 'God bless you Lavr, we all depend on you now.' She turned and ran down the gravel driveway and up the stone steps to the front door of the Palace.

She banged on the door, which was opened immediately by the palace *shveytsar* and his assistant doorman who went to roll out a red carpet for her. 'Quickly, quickly Anton, tell the staff that the Bolsheviks are coming. Find Mr Roberts, tell him to warn the servants, we must clear the palace.'

Sofia ran into the mirrored ballroom and scanned the brightly lit party for the Count. Women in beautiful gowns, men in their evening suits and dashing uniforms, swirled around the dance floor. She couldn't see her master anywhere. She ran around the edge of the room as fast as she could and stepped up onto the dais where the dance orchestra was playing. She interrupted the conductor, who looked at her crossly before recognising her desperation. The waltz came to a ragged stop. The dancers groaned in disappointment at the dance being cut short and turned to look at Sofia.

'Ladies and gentlemen, your highnesses, please excuse this interruption. I have some very bad news. A group, a mob, a very angry mob of Bolsheviks, is coming to attack the palace. Please all make your way out of the ballroom through the garden doors and leave the palace by the tradesman's entrance. Please hurry, there's no time to lose.'

The gilded youth of Moscow looked at Sofia with open-mouthed astonishment. They all seemed paralysed. The waltz music echoed in Sofia's head, one-two-three, one-two-three, and at the end of the second bar the whole room erupted into a mass of pushing and shoving, shouting and screaming as the party guests rushed, like a flock of frightened sheep, towards the doors. Within moments the ballroom was cleared, leaving the Count and Tatiana alone in the middle of the room.

The orchestra, still seated on their platform, struck up the melancholic folk song, 'As I Walk Alone Along The Road'. Sofia stepped down from the dais and walked across the polished oak parquet floor to join a tearful Tatiana and the Count, who was trying to comfort his daughter. He smiled a rueful smile at Sofia.

'The time has come. Sofia, Tatiana, you must now follow the escape plan. Go immediately to my study and change into your travel clothes. Collect your personal bags. I'll arrange for Roberts to fetch you and the emergency trunk. We will all meet in ten minutes at the small garden gate by the rose garden as we planned. Hurry! We have no time to lose.'

The two young women looked at each other and at the Count. 'Go now!' he urged and clapped his hands together. Sofia followed Tatiana out of the ballroom and upstairs to the first floor landing and quickly along the corridor to the Count's study. There Sofia unbuttoned Tatiana's ball gown and undid her stays. As soon as Tatiana was naked, except for her French bloomers, Sofia started to undress herself.

Soon they were wriggling into the cotton bodices that were almost stiff with precious stones. Travel dresses, socks, sturdy leather boots, fur hats, coats and mittens completed the outfits. A rapid knock sounded at the door and Tatiana said 'Enter'. The Count stood at the door with Mr Roberts who appeared, as he always did, reliably unflustered even in the face of impending chaos and violence.

81

'Papa,' Tatiana whispered, taking his hands, 'Papa, I don't want to leave you.' The Count drew her into his arms.

'My precious girl, I am an old man, I come from a different era. I was born here in the palace and I will die here. I am quite useless now. You go my beautiful, darling daughter, go into the world and do great things. Be generous, be gracious and be grateful for everything. You must escape from here, do everything you can to survive, make your way to California and rebuild your life. Love life, my darling, love life.' Tatiana sobbed, her shoulders shaking with the enormous sorrow of her loss.

The Count kissed Tatiana's head and looked solemnly at Sofia. 'Sofia, please accompany the Countess to the station, as we arranged.'

'Goodbye, sir. And thank you.'

'For nothing, my dear, for nothing. God bless you both'

Sofia took Tatiana by the hand and the girls followed Roberts down the stairs and into the garden for the last time.

Alexander came to, disorientated and confused by his blurred vision of the old costumes and props that were stored under the stage. He was not sure what was up and what was down before he rolled over and his brain began to understand what he was looking at and where he was. He checked his coat pockets, and was glad that his heavy pistol was still in his inside pocket and his precious notebook of poems was still safely wedged in the large outside pocket. 'Sofia' he whispered to himself, 'Oh my God, Sofia.' He pushed himself up and staggered up the steps and out of the hall.

Lavr looked anxiously through the palace gates and tried to identify from which direction the chanting was coming. In the moonlight to his right, he saw the dark silhouette of a man walking purposefully around the corner from Arbat Street into Vozdvizhenka. Lavr looked more closely at the figure; the man was too far away to discern any detail, yet Lavr noticed that he was walking down the middle of the street between the tramlines. As Lavr focused on this strange behaviour, the first line of demonstrators appeared just a few steps behind their leader. Lavr looked at the mob for a moment, and gave the gate's iron bolts one final check to ensure they were firmly seated in the stone recesses in the pavement. As he glanced back through the gates a large black car turned into the main road. It stopped and then juddered as the engine stalled.

Lavr could see the cap of the uniformed chauffeur in the front seat and four party guests in the rear. Lavr whispered an unholy prayer to Saint Olga of Kiev as the chauffeur tried and failed to restart the flooded engine.

Viktor marched briskly towards the limousine. Without pause, he drew his revolver and shot the chauffeur directly in the face. The bullet splintered a hole in the brittle glass of the windscreen, glanced off the driver's cheekbone and shattered the paper-thin bone at the back of his eye socket. The lead bullet swooped once around the inside of the chauffeur's skull, killing him instantly. In the back of the car the four young party goers were screaming at each other. A tall, slim young woman wearing a long ball gown under a fox fur jacket opened the door furthest away from the crowd and made her escape, running towards the palace gate. Lavr drew back the bolts and pulled the gate slightly open to let her and her companions back into the palace grounds.

The woman slipped through the gap followed by two young men. One was dressed in black tie with black leather shoes so highly polished that Lavr noticed the moonlight reflected in them, the other in the black and grey uniform of an Artillery officer. They squeezed through the gate and turned to look for the final passenger.

83

The fourth passenger, Viktor's second victim that night, was shot in the shoulder as she ran towards the palace and never made it to the gates. Viktor went onto one knee beside her as if to offer her first aid and ripped the gold necklace from around her neck then twisted two diamond and gold rings from her fingers.

As he did this, the crowd overtook him and surged against the gates, gripping the iron bars with their bare hands and starting to pull and push them backwards and forwards. 'We are the people!' the crowd chanted, 'We are the people!'

CHAPTER THIRTEEN

Slowly at first the rhythmic force gathered pace as the hinges of the ornate iron gate started to loosen and pull out of the stone walls, like a rotten tooth being wrenched one way and then another by a dentist. The crowd felt the gates weaken and then the hinges give way on one side. The gate suddenly swung around and struck Lavr, who was trying in vain to push back against the crowd, on the side of his head. He collapsed unconscious as the first of the mob ran through the gap whooping and shouting their delight.

A young woman, Elena Chelskaya, ran up the short flight of stone steps expecting to find the front door locked, but it swung open at her first push and she found herself in the entrance hall. She was armed with nothing but a red flag tied to a stick of wood. As she entered she stopped and gazed at the splendour of the decorations. Marble, intricate plaster work with golden highlights, a huge painting of a battle decorated one wall. A bronze statue of an Arab horse looked almost alive as it reared up, nostrils flared, teeth bared, terrified by the lion jumping onto its back, the lion's claws and incisors about to clamp onto the horse's neck and shoulder, bringing it down to its bloody death. Elena felt as though she were that lion's claw, one small part of a ferocious, hungry beast.

85

As more revolutionaries entered the hall they all stopped, partly in awe of the beautiful interior, and partly because they did not really know what to do next. Their angry voices turned into timid whispers as if they were children at a church service. From the top of the stairs came the deep voice of the Count. 'Welcome to the Shuysky Palace. Please do not destroy anything. These objects bear precious witness to history. Take what you must but please do not destroy anything.'

Elena ignored the old man, dipped her red flag into the fireplace and set light to the red banner she was carrying. Once it was well and truly alight she moved away from the fire, held her burning staff like a javelin, pulled her arm back, stepped forwards two strides then accelerated into a short run and launched her burning missile directly at the Count. It flew up over his head and hit the tapestry that hung behind him on the first floor landing. Within moments it was alight. Soon the whole ground floor was ablaze as revolutionaries set fire to curtains, the ornate wooden chairs and tables.

Elena ran up the stairs with a handful of others and started to vandalise the palace, tipping over china urns, slashing and ripping paintings, and setting fire to anything that looked flammable. Their objective was clear from their chants 'Throw them off the balcony, throw them off the balcony.'

The Count had retreated to his Study and stood looking at the door, waiting for it to burst open; he had decided not to struggle. All he saw were the wispy plumes of smoke starting to slide under the door and into his darkened office. He coughed and walked around his desk to sit in his favourite chair. It was then that he noticed the fat envelope addressed in his own fine Cyrillic handwriting to Countess Tatiana Shuyskaya and Miss Sofia Maslova. His heart sank as he picked up the letter, laden with secrets and shameful truths that needed to be aired. This letter was to have launched a new era for the Shuysky dynasty. A wholehearted future, looking ahead, not dragged back by mistakes of history and the sucking, cloying mud of the past. A fresh start. A new chapter of honesty, vitality and, he hoped, humility.

The ground floor of the palace was soon well ablaze. Cries of 'Wine!' and 'Brandy!' came from the kitchens and basement attracting Elena and the remaining vandals from the upper floors. Viktor was going up the stairs as they ran down. Viktor was on a mission, he went systematically from room to room looking for something specific, his focus was not distracted by the fire downstairs. Eventually he stopped in the Games Room. He pushed a billiard ball across the green baize cloth of the billiard table. As the ivory ball silently travelled the length of the table he heard the hacking cough of an old man over the distant crack and hiss of burning.

He walked to the door at the far end of the room and turned the handle. Just as he went to push the door open he was interrupted by the authoritative voice of Roberts.

'Pardon me, sir, Do you have an appointment with Count Shuysky?'

Viktor turned away from the door, pulled his revolver from his belt and pointed it at the family butler. 'No, not a formal invitation, but I think this will do,' he said and shot the butler in the throat.

The bang of the shot reverberated through the palace. Roberts raised his hand to the wound in his neck and looked at the blood on his fingers. As he fell to the ground, his lungs rapidly filled with blood. A second shot from Viktor's revolver ripped open the old Englishman's aorta.

Viktor smiled at the pool of blood that leaked out from the butler's body and turned towards the door again, gingerly pushing it open with the tip of his boot.

'I have been expecting you,' said the Count from his chair behind the desk. Viktor strode into the room and glanced over his shoulder to make sure nobody was hiding behind the door. He marched over to the desk stood looking at the Count.

'Shuysky?'

'Yes. What is your name?' the Count replied.

'It doesn't much matter, but I am Skobelev. Viktor Skobelev, Head of the Workers' Vanguard of the Moscow Soviet.'

The Count looked with contempt at the intruder and the revolver that was being levelled at him.

Viktor walked around the desk and stood behind the Count's chair. He pushed his fingers into the gap between the Count's neck and his shirt collar and twisted the collar roughly. The Count choked and tried to grab Viktor's wrist. Viktor punched the Count on the side of his face with his revolver. 'Where are the diamonds?' he shouted, 'Tell me where they are or I'll…'

'You'll what?' said the Count coughing out the words.

'I'll, I'll…' Viktor punched the Count again.

'Listen Skobelev, you have done enough. Go now. Leave me to burn to death in my home. There is nothing for you here.'

'Where are the diamonds, you leech?'

'Long gone,' the Count half laughed and half coughed, 'Long gone.'

Alexander arrived at the palace gates. He sprinted up the drive into the smoky entrance hall. Nobody was around. He didn't know where to start looking for Sofia so he went to the bottom of the stairs. The explosive report of a revolver from upstairs startled him. He drew his own pistol and ran upwards. The sound of a second shot came from the room across the landing. Alexander paused at the door and listened. Nothing. He entered and found the room empty. Cautiously, he edged around the billiards table to discover the butler's body face down in a pool of thick red blood.

As he looked down at Roberts, voices came from

inside the Study and Alexander gently pushed the door open.

'Let's play a little game,' Viktor said. He stepped around the Count to face him. 'You know how to play "The Gun of God" game don't you?' He rotated the cylinder of his revolver and counted. 'I have three unfired bullets, and look, there are seven chambers in total. How do you like the odds? Better than fifty-fifty - it's your lucky day, old man.' He spun the cylinder, grabbed the top of the Count's head and forced it back against the chair. 'Say "ahhh", just like at the doctor's.' Viktor shoved the gun hard into the Count's mouth. The Count cried out and gagged on the barrel of the gun. 'Where are your diamonds?' Viktor asked in a gentle voice. The Count shook his head and made ugly vomiting sounds as tears streamed down his cheeks. Viktor pulled the trigger and the revolver just clicked. He spun the cylinder again without taking the gun from the Count's mouth. 'Question two: Where are your fucking diamonds?' Again the Count shook his head. Viktor's finger tightened on the trigger but it was Alexander's revolver that fired first. His shot hit Viktor's arm and knocked him sideways. As Viktor slipped over he fired his revolver into the Count's chest. Alexander ran across the Study, jumped onto the desk and fired three shots into the wounded Bolshevik.

The Count was still conscious although bloody bubbles were forming at the side of his mouth and more blood was trickling out of his large, aristocratic nose. 'Please… give this to my daughter. Please… help… give this… to my… Tatiana.' His hand was tapping the envelope, pushing it across the desk towards Alexander. Alexander took the envelope and looked at it. The name 'Sofia Maslova' leaped out at him.

'Where are they?' Alexander asked.

'Yaroslavsky Station… to Vladivostok. There is money… take it. In the drawer… take it. Give her the envelope. Promise me you will do this.'

By the time Alexander had pulled the roll of banknotes from the drawer of the bureau the Count was dead. Alexander leaned over and gently closed the Count's eyes, murmuring one of his own poems:

And so the cursed Soviet is born,
An ugly infant,
Baptised in fire and blood, screaming
'Death to the past' and
'Bourgeois scum must die',
While sucking on the breast of horror
Without pity.

A volley of shots from the garden and the sound of a ceiling collapsing brought him back to reality. He'd better get cracking.

CHAPTER FOURTEEN

By ten to eleven the great crowd of people at Yaroslavsky Station had been herded onto the second class *kupé* and third-class *platskartny* carriages. A uniformed railway official opened the door to the waiting room and announced, 'Ladies and Gentlemen. Final call for the eleven fifteen train to Vladivostok. Calling at Samara, Chelyabinsk, Omsk, Krasnoyarsk, Irkutsk, Baikal, Verkhneudinsk, Chita, Kharbin and all intermediate stations before terminating at Vladivostok. The first-class carriage is now ready for boarding.'

Tatiana and Sofia stood up and Sofia waved her gloved hand at a porter to signal that they needed assistance with their baggage. The old man loaded Tatiana's beautiful Louis Vuitton trunk and her matching leather case on to the trolley. He went to take Sofia's carpet bag but she remembered the orders given to her by the Count and insisted on carrying the precious cargo herself.

Having adjusted the load, the porter asked them to follow him to the train. Sofia looked at Tatiana and tried to imagine what she was thinking. Sofia had a bad feeling about the fate of the Palace. She imagined it being vandalised and the beautiful paintings and sculptures being destroyed. She wondered if the mob would smash the grand piano in the music room. What would they do in the kitchens? How would the other servants be treated? And the horses, the Count's famous stable of purebred Arab horses. Surely they wouldn't harm such beautiful animals? She felt close to tears.

Tatiana, meanwhile, was in a daze. She couldn't truly comprehend what was happening to her: her life, her past experiences and future plans seemed to have turned to smoke in a matter of minutes. The flight from the palace, the angry mob, it all seemed like a bad dream. Her objective was to get to San Francisco. She must focus on nothing else. 'Escape, survive, rebuild; escape, survive, rebuild,' she kept repeating her father's advice silently in her head. 'Escape, survive, rebuild.' Step-by-step: escape, from the palace to the station; onto the train; off the train and onto the steamer.

It seemed simple enough, but she felt anxious. She imagined people were looking at her, wishing her dead. She followed the porter to the train and climbed on board. The uniformed steward welcomed her, asked for her name and requested that she follow him to their compartment.

He slid back the door and gestured her to enter with a small bow. The compartment was almost exactly the same as the one she had taken each year to Paris. Not exactly luxurious, a small metal sink and two single beds took up most of the available space. It looked quite comfortable but she wasn't sure how two such different young women would get on in such a claustrophobic environment. She would have to draw upon her experience of attending boarding school to survive the long railway journey. Then they had to face the eighteen day voyage by steamer across the Pacific Ocean.

Poor papa, she thought. How will I cope without your wisdom and kindness? I pray to God that you are well. Just at that moment Sofia arrived with the luggage. Soon everything was stowed away and they lay on their beds looking at the ceiling.

'What time do we actually leave?' asked Tatiana.

'A quarter past eleven,' Sofia replied. The locomotive's steam whistle sounded. 'That must be five minutes to departure.'

Alexander Zhuravlev ran through the castle-like main entrance of Yaroslavsky Station, across the concourse and out onto the platform marked 'Vladivostok'. Further up the platform the locomotive was hissing great billowing clouds of steam that created a thick mustardy coloured fog in the cold air. Alexander ran past the first heavily armoured wagon, clad in sheets of riveted steel plate and bristling with a cannon and several machine guns. Ahead he could see the figure of the train guard silhouetted in the yellow mist. Alexander ran further along the frosty platform, past the second carriage which had iron-bars bolted over the windows towards the guard who was standing by an open door. The guard looked up and down the platform one last time, spotted Alexander running towards him and shouted 'All aboard!', lifting his silver whistle to his lips.

Alexander shouted, 'No, wait! Wait, please!' As he reached the guard, out of breath, he gasped, 'Is this the train to Vladivostok?'

The guard scowled. 'Yes it is. Do you have a ticket, sir? If not, you can't travel.' Alexander ignored the railway man and climbed onto the train.

'Wait, sir, if you don't have a ticket…' the guard repeated, warningly. Alexander fumbled in the pocket of his battered greatcoat and after a short struggle pulled out the thick roll of banknotes.

'Here, look! I have money. I have to be on this train. Please… I can pay.' He waved the notes at the guard, who looked disapprovingly unimpressed. The young man in front of him looked thoroughly scruffy and disreputable, but also quite desperate. The guard shook his head in resignation, lifted his arm towards the distant locomotive and blew his whistle hard, the locomotive whistled loudly in reply and as it rolled forward the guard stepped onto the train and shut the door behind him. He waved his hand impatiently at Alexander, shooing him out of the way.

'All right, all right. I'll be coming through the train later - you can buy your ticket then. But you can't stay here in the armoured section. You'll have to get off at the next station and move into the second-class carriage.'

'I have to travel first class. Please.'

The guard looked incredulous, but a closer look at the wad of notes which the young man was still waving around convinced him that he did, indeed, have more than enough to pay for a ticket in *spalny vagon.*

'Let me check.' The guard pulled a piece of paper from his jacket pocket, unfolded it and held it up to a smokey oil lamp so he could read it. Alexander looked around the dimly lit carriage that was gently rocking from side to side as the train left Yaroslavsky Station. Behind him and running three quarters of the length of the wagon were iron bars that went from floor to ceiling, creating a large cage within the carriage. In the cage was a neatly arranged stack of fifty or sixty small wooden crates, each about the size of a shoe box, with loops of rough hemp rope as handles and the double headed imperial eagle branded on the end. The far end of the cage was hidden behind a heavy red velvet curtain.

'What's in there? A Siberian tiger?' he asked.

The guard ignored his question. 'There is one first class bed left; you will have to share a compartment with Mister Zayats. Go through this door, down to the other end of the restaurant carriage and into carriage number five. You are in compartment number three. Go on, quickly now, you can't stay in the security wagon, I've told you.'

'Thank you, thank you.' Alexander stuffed the banknotes back into his pocket and opened the door that led into the next carriage just as the train began to pick up speed. He didn't notice that, as he had pulled the bank notes out of his pocket, both his notebook and the envelope entrusted to him by Count Shuysky had fallen onto the floor.

Alexander walked through the restaurant car which was decorated with more red velvet curtains, brass oil lamps and sets of ornately upholstered chairs arranged four to a table on one side of the carriage and two to a table on the other. At the end of the restaurant car was a small kitchen galley with two attendants who greeted him politely before going back to storing packages of food and bottles of wine. Alexander opened the next connecting door and felt the icy blast of night air and the noisy rattle and clank of the train as he hurriedly stepped over the metal foot plates that formed the floor of the passageway from one carriage into the next.

He pushed open the next door and found himself in the warmth of the brightly lit sleeping carriage. A small diagram inside a simple frame attached to the wooden wall in front of him showed the arrangement of the four first class sleeping compartments, each with its own tiny bathroom.

He made his way along the corridor past the first door which was half open. As he passed he glimpsed a woman sitting on the bed with her hand to her throat before another figure, male, reached out and closed the door with a snap.

The next door was shut but he could hear female voices coming from inside. The following door was marked with an ornate brass number '3'. He tapped, turned the handle and entered. There was nobody inside. Alexander noticed a leather trunk on the floor by one of the single beds and an attaché case on the same bed, but the other one was empty. Still in his greatcoat he collapsed, exhausted, on the narrow berth.

Inspector Lesnoy, unpacking his belongings in the berth at the far end of the armoured wagon, had overheard the exchange between Alexander and the guard. He emerged from his cabin just in time to see a tall, thin figure in a greatcoat disappearing through the door at the other end into the first class accommodation. Lesnoy walked past the cage where Tokar was also unpacking and glanced in, but the banker either didn't notice him or pretended not to.

As Lesnoy reached the corner of the cage he noticed, on the floor, an envelope and a notebook with a well-worn leather cover. He picked them both up. 'Tatiana Shuyskaya, Sofia Maslova,' he read on the envelope. He flicked through the notebook. It was about one quarter full of writing.

Blood red sun sets on the bitter Moscow evening,
Ragged flames burn in the hearts of the young men…

Lesnoy laughed to himself. Poetry! He looked at the inside cover of the book. Alexander Zhuravlev. Oh yes, that trouble-maker. What's he doing here I wonder? After a moment's deliberation he dropped the book back on the floor.

He looked again at the envelope. Shuysky, eh? Well, well. I think I need to have a little look at this. He turned round and returned to his compartment to put the letter somewhere safe.

CHAPTER FIFTEEN

The next day was flat and grey. The train huffed and puffed along, heading East towards the sunrise. The open, muddy fields and occasional ramshackle village gave way to woods. Only the silver birch trees were easy to identify. One leafless tree in a forest of leafless trees is difficult to distinguish from any other leafless tree in the same forest. When the forest stretches, not for miles but hundreds of miles then the trees all meld into one.

With every hissing beat of the locomotive, with every rotation of the great steel wheels, the traumatic events of the previous day and the past weeks and months and years, slowly receded across the misty horizon.

Dominic Hare was an early riser. 'Up with the lark,' was one of those annoying expressions that had stuck in his mind from his Sussex childhood. He remembered a summer's day, lying in a grassy field staring up at the blue sky, trying to spot the tiny lark, hovering so high up above him, which was singing such a clear and beautiful song. The Englishman was washed, shaved, fully dressed and drinking black tea with jam in the dining carriage before Alexander had even started to blink himself awake.

Dominic found himself staring, semi-hypnotised, at the passing forest. It put him into a trance. The flickering of the trees and the rhythmic rattle and squeaking of the train

97

took him back to previous railway journeys across India and Africa. As he gazed out of the window he started to make a mental list of things he needed to do. One, establish that the train was running on time. Two, estimate the amount and weight of the gold in the armoured wagon. Three, calculate the transport requirements and manpower needed to shift it. Four, estimate the number of armed guards on the train and their weaponry. Five, assess his fellow first-class travellers to identify risks. Six, befriend Tokar: that needed some consideration. Seven, look at the railway map to work out the best place from which to send his next telegram.

When Alexander finally awoke it was late morning. He was exhausted and it took a few moments for him to work out exactly where he was and why. A series of horrible visions flashed through his mind in reverse sequence: running through the streets from the burning palace to Yaroslavsky Station; the Count dying in his arms, blood foaming out of his mouth; Viktor's death; the mob, running to the palace; Sofia's terrified face as he shooed her out of the stage door at the back of the hall.

Suddenly he sat up. Sofia! He reached for his greatcoat and searched frantically through the pockets. The letter. Where was the letter? And his notebook? Had he dropped them in the street or been pickpocketed? He thought back to the station, panicking and jumping on the train. At the palace he had pushed the money and the letter into the same pocket, so when he had pulled the roll of banknotes out he must have pulled the letter and notebook out too. Damn. At least it was on the train. He'd have to find it quickly: who knows what trouble might ensue if the letter got into the wrong hands.

Alexander quickly dressed and left his compartment. He wondered whether the door from the dining car through to the armoured wagon would be locked. He looked out of the window. The train was called an express, but it was trundling along at a snail's pace. He could probably jump off the train, run alongside and jump back on through the external door of the armoured car if necessary. Assuming that door wasn't also locked, which it probably was. Ah well, he might have to throw himself on the mercy of the steward.

There were three passengers having breakfast in the dining car. An exhausted-looking couple sat at one table, the man reading a book, the woman looking dreamily out of the window. A single man occupied another table. 'Morning, room-mate!' the man greeted Alexander as he passed.

'Oh! Good morning!' Alexander didn't stop but continued along to the other end of the carriage. His heart lifted as he turned the handle and found it opened. Thank God! He crossed into the armoured car and looked around, hoping that the irascible guard wasn't suddenly going to appear. Then he looked down at the floor and again gave thanks as he saw his notebook.

His relief was short-lived, however, as there was no sign of the letter. Panicking, he flicked through the pages of poetry, hoping the letter had slipped inside, but no. He paced up and down the corridor, knowing that it wasn't likely to be anywhere else. Damn! Surely it must be on the train, in this carriage. Had someone else picked it up? Well, all he could hope was that it would eventually find its way to the Countess and Sofia. But he felt wretchedly guilty that he was somehow letting down the Count by not delivering it safely into the girls' hands. What should he do? Was it better to tell them that there had been a letter and have to admit that he'd lost it? Or to keep quiet about it? He would have to think carefully.

Back in the dining carriage, Ekaterina looked at Pavel. They had both ordered tea along with ham and eggs for Pavel and a sweet bread roll filled with cream cheese for Ekaterina. She looked at Pavel and smiled, a warm glow of

affection washing over her. He was reading a book,'
Vyuchite angliyskiy samostoyatelno' - 'Teach Yourself English'.

She wondered what California would be like. A land of
peasants, gold diggers and uneducated cowboys by all
accounts. Would Pavel ride a horse and carry a revolver?
She smiled as she realised that riding horses and firing
guns was exactly what Pavel had done as a cavalry officer.

'Darling Pavel,' she said, 'When you have taught
yourself English, could I borrow your book?'

He smiled at her. 'I'll teach you English, my beautiful
wife. We can learn together.' She smiled back, glanced at
his poor scarred hand holding the book, then she shut her
eyes and let the train rock her to sleep.

Pavel gazed protectively at his sleepy wife. He was
focused on learning English from his Berlitz phrase book.
Chapter 7: Used to (to be, to have, to want)... he read. *Exercise
One: I used to be a doctor/teacher/student.* I used to be a
student. Easy enough. His mind wandered. I used to be a
soldier.

He forced his attention back to the book. *Exercise Two:
I used to have a boat/house/dog.* I used to have a horse, he
thought, remembering his beloved Belaya Iskra. I used to
be a patriot... I used to be a cavalry officer. But no longer.
He glanced at the ugly stump of his ring finger and
remembered being in the German prison camp.

As a cavalry officer on a fine stallion, Pavel had
commanded respect. Once in the camp, the old rules, the
old certainties had quickly broken down. He remembered
how one morning a young soldier had swung a punch at
him for 'talking like a posh *durak*'. Another soldier,
Corporal Igor Cuprinov, a great fat man with bad breath,
piggy eyes and crude features that gave him the appearance
of an overgrown potato, had spat at the back of Pavel's
head while they waited in lines for the weekly roll call.
Pavel could not remember why Cuprinov had spat at him.
Perhaps merely because he was an officer.

The thin soup made of pig bones and gristle with black

bread was the same for officers and enlisted men. They all drank from metal cups, no matter what class, rank or education. He remembered once looking at a perfectly round, glistening puddle of melted fat floating on the surface of his lukewarm soup. A year ago he would have spat it out; now he had looked at it, thinking that with this globule of pig fat he could survive another twenty-four, maybe thirty-six hours. Survival in the camp depended not on social position but on energy; energy enabled violence; violence enabled power; power ensured survival.

Fighting became second nature to him. He avoided punching with his injured left hand. But somehow his aching fist added a ferocious, angry edge to the violence, which earned him a degree of respect within the camp. That he had been captured so soon after the start of the war meant that he had been one of the original group who slept in open fields, chopped trees and dug foundations for the camp that would eventually hold him and several thousand of his comrades.

He had been at an advantage because he could read and write and knew something about the law: knowing how rules and regulations applied to their living quarters, clothing, food and medicine. His daydream took him back to the typhus epidemic. The delirium and panic of the infected. The groaning and moaning of those with the headache which made them feel that their brains were going to burst. The rash and spots. The urgent pleas to the German camp administration for soap and razors and hot water to try and control the spread of the lice and fleas that were as murderous as the machine gun and barbed wire out on no-man's-land.

How he had survived he did not know. He had killed two men in the camp. The spitter, Corporal Cuprinov, was dispatched with a single crushing punch to the throat after the Corporal had tripped him up in an act of direct, provocative insubordination. The other soldier he killed had pulled a sharpened spoon on Pavel in an attempted robbery. Pavel had easily twisted the spoon out of his attacker's hand and sliced open the man's jugular vein, leaving him to bleed to death on the sandy ground.

His efforts to learn German had impressed the guards and they had appointed him a kind of unofficial translator and negotiator. They had given him a book called 'Learn German in Ninety Days'. He had completed the course in just forty. I used to be a cissy, he thought. Now I am a monster, a remorseless machine, capable of killing. As the breakfast plates were cleared he looked at his sleeping wife. I choose to use this power to be a protector. To protect Ekaterina. To protect our future together.

Sofia lay in bed looking blankly at the ceiling of their compartment. It seemed that after their escape she and Tatiana had run out of things to say to each other. She could not bring herself to discuss the minutiae of daily life: 'Breakfast, Miss Tatiana?' 'Which dress will you wear, mademoiselle?' Their circumstances made such observations sound overwhelmingly trivial. Nor was it going to be possible to discuss the big issues: life and death, war and peace. She felt dislocated. Not just physically and geographically but emotionally. She realised that she was not here as a result of any act of her own free will. She was here because the Count had decreed that she should be here. That she should leave Moscow. That she should start a new life in California. Maybe his plan was a good one. Maybe the Count had good reason for this scheme, but more than anything she craved autonomy. She wanted her way of seeing, her way of dreaming and her ambitions to guide her future, not the diktat of some old man, no matter how much power he wielded.

Tatiana felt equally lost. But her feeling of loss was more like that of a rudderless, anchorless yacht drifting across a huge ocean with torn sails, no crew, no compass. All her certainties and shelters, her guiding stars were gone. She could feel her sense of entitlement slowly ebbing away as each wave rocked her. She tried to imagine what the next phase of life held for her. Would California really be sophisticated enough? Cowboys and earthquakes: she did not know much more about California than that. She loved Mother Russia in spite of all her complexity and cold. She loved the dancing, the music, the history and passion. Could a young country like America really compete with all that her homeland could provide?

She sat up and pulled the curtain back from the window. 'Oh look, Sofia! Trees, and more trees. Oh, there's another tree.' Sofia couldn't help but laugh at Tatiana's silly wit.

'I am trying to sleep, Miss Tatiana,' she said, 'But please, let me know if you see any trees.'

'There are millions and millions of trees here. They are all beautiful.'

Sofia sat up and the two girls both fell into a kind of daze, just staring silently out of the window. The endless snow and black trees flowed hypnotically past. It was bleak. Tatiana wondered about her father. The attack on the Palace just twelve or so hours before seemed like a disjointed, muddled dream. She was relieved to be on the train, but what would her dear Papa be doing? Had he managed to escape? And her brothers, what would become of them? The only good thing that the revolutionaries might do would be to stop the war against Germany. Then Konstantin and Georgiy could come home. But if the palace had been destroyed then where would they go? She leaned back and felt the sharp edge of one of the diamonds hidden in her bodice poke the skin of her shoulder. She shifted uncomfortably.

Sofia was thinking about the previous night, too. For some reason she was most worried about Lavr the gatekeeper. He would have almost certainly been killed. She shut her eyes and imagined that awful Viktor aiming his pistol at the solemn, dignified Cossack and shooting. She imagined blood staining the snow and the rush of dirty boots into the palace.

Andrey Tokar was feeling low. It was the third time in the past year that he had made this journey. He knew what to expect. Endless days of trundling; innumerable stops in provincial towns; meal after meal of grey meat, boiled potatoes, cabbage, beetroot soup. Nothing delicious, nothing tasty. Less than twelve hours since leaving Moscow and he recognised the symptoms of depression. A reluctance to get out of bed. Obsessive over-thinking of past mistakes, manic anxiety over the future.

He had a pile of books with him. During the first journey he had ploughed through half of the first volume of 'Capital' by Karl Marx. The other two parts remained unread. Bored and confused by Marx, he had turned to the collected poems of the romantic poet Mikhail Lermontov for mental stimulation. On the second trip he had read a number of shorter books and plays. On this occasion he had brought Tolstoy's War and Peace with the ambitious intention of reading it cover to cover.

Of course none of these so-called Marxist communists had ever actually read the complete works of their economic guru. Tokar doubted if many of the socialists had even read the Communist Manifesto pamphlet. No wonder Lenin and his gang were so popular - their followers didn't have to read Marx, just chant the slogans and regurgitate the carefully distilled, simplified ideas about nationalisation, central planning and soviet democracy. 'A spectre is stalking Europe - the spectre of communism'. Perhaps he ought to try 'Capital' again, try to understand. The unrest in Petrograd and now in Moscow was just the beginning. What would become of him? he wondered. Even a soviet government would need money managers and economists. Maybe his future would be better if the revolutionaries actually took control. Who knew what the future held? All he did know was that for the next few weeks he would be caged, like an animal being transported to the Moscow circus.

Inspector Lesnoy slept. His snores were starting to irritate Tokar who could hear them through the thin wall between his curtained-off bed in the cage and the adjacent sleeping compartment. Then the snores stopped abruptly as Lesnoy awoke and Tokar breathed a sigh of relief, opening the Tolstoy at the first chapter. As he began to read, '*Well, Prince, so Genoa and Lucca are now just family estates of the Buonapartes…*' he was oblivious to the fact that on the other side of the partition, Lesnoy was smiling to himself as he began to imagine all the entertainment he could create to mitigate the boredom of this long journey.

CHAPTER SIXTEEN

Pavel closed the curtains to shut out the dark February night on the other side of the train window. Ekaterina, dressed in an off-the-shoulder, finely-pleated red silk Fortuny gown, sprayed a generous puff of *L'Heure Bleue* into the air in front of her and stepped through the mist of tiny droplets which deposited themselves on her neck, face and shoulders.

'Is that what you are wearing?' Pavel asked.

'Yes, why, don't you find it suitable?'

'No, no, you look gorgeous,' he said, putting his hands on her waist and pulling her backwards towards him.

'Maybe it is too fancy? Am I showing too much skin for a train journey?' Pavel nuzzled his face into the left side of her neck and kissed her gently. He paused and took a deep breath in through his nose.

'You smell divine, Katya.'

Ekaterina smiled and brought her left arm up to hold his head against her skin. 'Pavel, tell me. Should I wear something more modest? I want to make a good impression on our fellow passengers. First impressions are so important: my mother told me that people decide what they think of you in less than five seconds. Those Moscow girls will be wearing something fashionable. I don't want to be forced into the role of the dowdy country cousin.'

106

Pavel laughed into her neck and kissed it again. 'My love, you could wear a muddy potato sack and still look like an angel. You are far more beautiful than those silly young girls. None of the men on this train will be able to take their eyes off you.'

At that moment the dinner gong sounded.

'Dinner will be served shortly, ladies and gentlemen. Dinner in five minutes,' the steward said, banging on the gong as he walked down the corridor.

Pavel took his wife's hand to lead her to dinner.

'No, not yet, it is better to be fashionably late.'

Five long minutes later Ekaterina nodded at Pavel.

'Would you kindly escort me to dinner, Captain?'

Pavel took her hand, kissed it, opened their compartment door and led Ekaterina into the dining carriage.

As they entered, Dominic, who was sitting at the first table facing the narrow door from the wagon lit, smiled politely and murmured '*Dobriy vecher,*' to the couple.

Alexander, sharing the table with Dominic, turned and raised himself from his chair slightly with a courteous inclination of his head.

'*Zdravstvuyte.*'

Pavel and Ekaterina politely nodded in return. 'Good evening... hello...' The other passengers looked around to see who had just entered.

Pavel steered his wife down the aisle towards the next table which had four empty seats. He gestured her to the window seat facing forward and he sat opposite her. Pavel gazed with unrestrained happiness at his wife, a huge smile spread slowly across his thin angular face, still slightly gaunt from the months of starvation in the camp. Ekaterina looked at his reflection in the window.

'Pavel!' she said, blushing, 'Stop looking so pleased with yourself. You look like the cat who got the cream.'

'My love, my wife, my best friend and lover, I feel *exactly* like that lucky cat,' he said, *sotto voce.* 'You make me so happy and now we are on our way to a new future, I want the world to know it.'

Ekaterina turned away from the reflection and looked at Pavel directly. She reached out and gently stroked his left hand, being careful to avoid the sensitive, shiny scar that covered the stump of his missing finger.

'My friend,' she whispered, 'My lover, my handsome champion, I am honoured to be your wife.'

As they gazed into one another's eyes a dark shadow fell over their table.

'Good evening Captain, Madame. May I introduce myself? I am Inspector Vladimir Petrovich Lesnoy, of the Special Corps of Gendarmes. I was wondering if I might join your table?'

Pavel looked up at the man standing by their table. He was tall and well built with a nose that seemed to descend from the top of his head in one smooth line. Pavel thought the new arrival looked rather like a bird, a falcon maybe or a raven, with his dark oiled hair, tanned skin and deep set eyes, framed by thick black eyebrows. He had the look of a hunter.

Pavel stood up and shook Lesnoy's hand. 'Of course, Inspector, please sit with us. You are most welcome. I am Captain Pavel Fyodorovich Ozertsov and this is my wife, Ekaterina Yurievna.'

Ekaterina looked at the stranger and felt the blood drain from her face. Her eyes performed a strange, uncontrolled flickering dance from left to right and back again. She felt sick, terrified. What was *he*, of all people, doing here?

Lesnoy, smiling with a sly, conspiratorial smirk clicked his heels together and bowed stiffly to Ekaterina. 'Madame Ozertsova, it is an honour to meet you.'

Ekaterina's face had turned to stone. She could not breathe, let alone talk. Her heart began a spasmodic fluttering.

Pavel looked at his wife and tried to understand her

lack of etiquette. Just as he started to tell her to acknowledge Lesnoy, Ekaterina spoke up.

'Inspector, please do join us, please sit.'

Sofia glanced surreptitiously down the aisle at the policeman, trying to get a glimpse of him without letting him notice that she was looking. Lesnoy. Why was that a familiar name? But no, she didn't recognise his face. She had seen him enter the restaurant car from the far end and assumed that he was part of the railway security team. But if that were the case, why would he be mixing with the passengers? She watched him raise his hand and beckon over the steward. The steward nodded respectfully and disappeared towards the kitchen returning shortly with a bottle of what looked like vodka.

Tatiana sat opposite Sofia, waiting for her food. She had ordered a piece of grilled chicken with boiled potatoes and cabbage. She wondered what her father was going to eat that evening, and her brothers. Were they out in the cold, fighting the German invaders, or marching back to Moscow now to fight the Bolsheviks? The whole world was a horrible mess. She felt a sudden desire to stand up and jump off the train. She would walk back to Moscow if she had to. She would go and find her father. Together they would find Georgiy and Konstantin. Then she would take them all to Paris. But she knew that it was an impossible dream. She sat in a glum silence, waiting for her meal.

Tatiana and Sofia ate in silence. They had nothing to say to each other. No friends in common, no shared experiences, no bond beyond the summers they had spent together at the Shuysky family dacha so long ago it might as well have been another life. The dining car was no place to start a conversation about their escape and their anxieties, so they sat in silence, eating the bland, beige food.

Once they had finished eating Sofia looked down the

aisle once again. An older, well-dressed gentleman had stood up from his table and was walking down the carriage towards her. He nodded a polite 'hello' and pushed open the door that led into the mysterious 'security wagon'. Sofia flinched at the gust of cold air and the noise of the train but couldn't resist trying to get a glimpse of what lay behind the door. All she could see was the canvas and metal wall that made up the connecting passage between the two cars.

'It is full of the Tsar's gold, apparently,' said a deep, well-modulated voice. Sofia looked up at a tall, skinny, somewhat scruffy young man who had been dining with the older man.

'Really?' She smiled broadly. 'How exciting!'

He extended his hand to shake Sofia's. 'Perhaps you don't remember me, Miss. We met briefly last night in rather unpleasant circumstances. My name is Alexander Borisovich Zhuravlev. I'm so pleased to see that you managed to get safely away from Moscow.'

Sofia looked at him in astonishment. 'Yes! How extraordinary, Mr Zhuravlev. I am Sofia Ivanovna Maslova and this is my friend Coun...' she came to an abrupt halt, suddenly in a panic about revealing Tatiana's aristocratic identity to this Bolshevik poet. 'I mean, Miss Tatiana... Tatiana Sh... um... Tatiana Nikolaevna Shuvalova.'

Alexander smiled at Sofia's poor attempt at hiding the name of her companion, but didn't reveal that he could guess perfectly well who Tatiana was. 'I am very pleased to meet you both.'

'Please - sit down with us and tell us more about the gold.' said Sofia.

Alexander sat next to her. 'I don't know much. My dining companion, Mr Zayats, tells me it is being sent from the Royal Mint to Vladivostok, I imagine it will be used to buy weapons and material for the Tsar's army to kill and maim his own people. It is a shame on Russia that he should do such a wicked thing.'

Sofia changed the topic of conversation. 'Are you travelling for business, Mr Zhuravlev? A Navy posting on a ship at Vladivostok, perhaps,' she said, looking at his threadbare Navy greatcoat. It struck her as a little odd that a man with such vehemently expressed political views should be travelling first class.

Alexander hesitated. 'I used to work for the office of Naval Intelligence in Petrograd, but no - my journey is not work-related. I'm trying to earn a living as a writer, mostly pamphlets and posters for different groups. My real passion is poetry, but it's a struggle to get paid for writing verse.'

'A poet! did you hear that Tatiana? Mr Zhuravlev is a poet.' Tatiana nodded sullenly and looked out of the window, imagining the pitch black forest which was surely there, though invisible.

'Might we hear one of your poems?' Sofia asked, gazing into Alexander's dark brown eyes.

'It is mostly boring stuff.'

'No love poems?'

'Just one or two, but I cannot remember them.' He blushed.

'I learned this one by heart a long time ago,' Sofia said:

Black night.
White snow.
The wind, the wind!
It will not let you go. The wind, the wind!
Through God's whole world it blows.
The wind is weaving
The white snow.
Brother ice peeps from below
Stumbling and tumbling
Folk slip and fall.
God pity all!

'It is by Alexander Blok. I cannot remember the rest.'

111

'It is very atmospheric, and most appropriate, Miss Maslova.' Alexander turned to Tatiana. 'Miss er... Miss Shuvalova, do you know any poems?'

Tatiana did not turn from the window but started to speak quietly as she continued to stare into nothingness:

The world's great age begins anew,
The golden years return,
The earth doth like a snake renew
Her winter weeds outworn;
Heaven smiles, and faiths and empires gleam
Like wrecks of a dissolving dream.

She paused and a tear trickled down her cheek.

'Shelley,' Alexander said. 'He is a great inspiration to my own work.' He paused. 'May I say, Miss Shuvalova, that you recited that verse most beautifully'.

He turned to Sofia. 'I will leave you both in peace, good night.'

CHAPTER SEVENTEEN

The next morning, Tatiana flopped down on the narrow bed in the compartment she shared with Sofia and let out a groan.

'How much longer, Sofia? It's only day two and I don't think I can bear any more. How could Papa do this to us? I'd prefer to be put up against a wall and shot than die of boredom on this wretched train. And this bodice thing - it's awfully uncomfortable. Some of the diamonds are digging into my skin. I'm going to take mine off when we go to for dinner this evening. It makes my bust look lumpy, like a ploughed field and it's so tight I can't eat properly. Not that the food is worth eating - it's disgusting. I wish we were at home so you and Cook could make me something delicious.'

Sofia sighed.

'All right, let's change - we'll have to pack the bodices into the bottom of the trunk and lock it. We're well away from Moscow now, so the diamonds should be safe, but we must put them on again after Novonikolayevsk - that's bandit country.'

Tatiana sat up and turned her back so that Sofia could undo the long column of tiny mother-of-pearl buttons down the back of her dress, and then the little ribbon ties on the bodice. She wriggled out of the offending garment

113

and, breathing a sigh of relief, lay back onto the bed.

There was a pause, then Sofia cleared her throat. 'Er, Tatiana, please could you…'

Tatiana turned towards her. 'What?'

'Well, please could you undo my buttons?'

'Oh! Can't you manage them yourself?' She let out a theatrical sigh. 'Oh, very well then, I'll have a go.' Laboriously she fumbled her way down the buttons, taking three times as long as Sofia had and frequently tutting and complaining about how difficult it was.

At last, both girls were in their petticoats, feeling much more comfortable, Tatiana seemed almost happy for the first time. They smiled at each other and Tatiana hugged her companion.

Sofia looked searchingly into Tatiana's dark eyes. 'I cannot go on like this. *We* cannot go on like this. What am I? Your friend or your servant? I hate it. I hate the ambiguity.'

'I'm sorry, Sofia, I'm not used to all this. Can we be friends again? I mean real friends, best friends like when we were little girls at the dacha? Do you remember those games of hide-and-seek with Kostya and Georgiy? You know, sometimes I think that going to that school in Paris, having to learn how to be a lady, was the worst thing that ever happened to me. I was much happier before.'

'Do you mean that?' Sofia asked dubiously.

'Yes - I do. From now on I'm not going to be your mistress and you're definitely not my servant. We're just going to be friends like we used to be. We'll help each other and…'

Sofia, who had grown quite wary of her former friend over the last few years, returned Tatiana's embrace warmly, then held her at arm's length and smiled again.

'I'm so happy you said that. We're going to need each other's friendship more than ever. If we're going to survive this awful journey we have to be able to trust one another. We are away from Moscow, but there's such a long journey ahead. Come on, I'll get our other dresses out of the closet and we can help each other with the buttons again.'

Tatiana groaned. 'I wish we could just go to dinner in our petticoats. Who cares what anyone thinks? There is nobody here to impress. I really don't care if we shock all these stupid people on the train.'

Sofia raised an eyebrow. 'Are you sure? How about Alexander? Maybe you'd like to impress him? I imagine he is in his compartment, right now, struggling to write a poem about you.'

Tatiana blushed and tried to suppress a smile. 'I'm sure he'd be even more inspired by the sight of me in my petticoat. Anyway,' she said, changing the subject deliberately, 'What about that striking-looking detective? He might take great pleasure in arresting you if you appeared at dinner improperly dressed? I think you might actually rather enjoy being locked up by him. I saw you looking at him in a certain way, Sofia Ivanovna! Am I right?' Tatiana laughed.

Sofia rolled her eyes.

'Yes, I was looking at him, but not because I like him. I just thought there was something a bit familiar about him and I was trying to work out whether I had met him before. His name - Lesnoy - wasn't that the name of your father's old doctor?'

Tatiana frowned. 'Yes, I think you're right. Do you think they're related? I find Inspector Lesnoy rather scary. Have you noticed how he seems to be listening to everyone's conversations? What do you think he's really doing on the train?'

Sofia gave this some thought. 'I'm not sure. Let's invite him to join us at our table this evening and we can try to find out more about him. What do you think?'

Tatiana clapped her hands together and laughed, 'What fun! We can investigate the investigator!'

'All right, but be careful Tatiana, we shouldn't trust

him. Don't tell him anything he doesn't need to know. And no mention of California or diamonds.'

'Don't worry, I'm not as silly as you think, Sofia. I promise to be discreet.'

Alexander and Dominic had both woken with splitting headaches after a bout of heavy drinking the previous evening. It was mid-morning before the two men eventually dragged themselves out of their narrow beds and sat symmetrically in their striped flannel pyjamas, unshaven and hair awry, squinting against the thin, weak shaft of sunlight which pierced the narrow crack at the edge of the curtains.

Alexander indicated his blue and white striped attire.

'Thanks for lending me these, Dmitry, they are very comfortable.'

'My pleasure, dear boy. Couldn't let you go to bed in your day clothes for a second night running. God you look rough, though - expect I do too. Certainly feel it anyway. Reckon we need the hair of the dog, er... *opohmelka*?' He pulled out his attaché case and placed it on top of the bedcovers.

Dominic opened the case, which did not appear to be locked, and took out a bottle of vodka which he handed to Alexander. 'Here, try this.' As Alexander pulled the cork out, Dominic shut the case.

Alexander took a swig from the neck of the bottle and almost choked on the bitter, foul taste.

'Oh, God!' he spluttered, shaking his head and grimacing while handing the bottle back to Dominic.

'That bad, eh?' Dominic laughed, before gulping it down himself. 'Bloody hell! It *is* that bad!' He rammed the cork hard back in the neck of the bottle and placed it on the small shelf by his bed. He stood up creakily and ruffled his short auburn hair, making it stand on end.

'Tell you what, I'll go and get us some tea from the samovar. And why don't you give me your clothes - I'll ask

116

the steward to get them laundered. I've got some spares you can borrow.'

Alone in the compartment, Alexander felt his eyes drawn towards the attaché case. He was enjoying the company of his travelling companion, but there was something odd about him. He couldn't quite put his finger on it, but definitely something odd. They had played cards the previous afternoon; Alexander had suggested *Preferans*, the two-player version called *Gusarik*. Dmitry was not familiar with it, though he had picked it up quickly and then taught Alexander a simple game called gin rummy in return.

Alexander glanced at the bottle of vodka. Perhaps he would be doing Dmitry a favour if he returned it to the case, he told himself. He checked the cork was firmly back in the bottle and clicked the clasps on the case, making the lid spring open. Inside was a pistol, three passports and a small bottle of clear liquid, unlabelled apart from a small skull and crossbones and, underneath, the word 'poison'. Poison? *Yad*? Alexander felt a guilty rush of adrenaline and his heart fluttered. He quickly closed the case and left the vodka where it was on the shelf before hurriedly withdrawing to the tiny bathroom.

CHAPTER EIGHTEEN

That evening, now dressed more comfortably, Tatiana and Sofia entered the dining car to find Inspector Lesnoy already seated, a tumbler of vodka in his hand. Sofia approached him and bobbed a slight curtsey. 'Inspector Lesnoy, would you care to join us for dinner? We would be most happy if you would.'

Lesnoy's thin, red lips formed a slight, self-satisfied smile. 'Not as delighted as I would be, I'm sure, Miss... Miss, er, Maslova is it not? And you must be...' Lesnoy winked at Tatiana, '"Miss" Shuyskaya?' Tatiana and Sofia exchanged nervous glances. *Cher*! thought Sofia, they could hardly deny Tatiana's true family name. At least he had been discreet enough to avoid using her title.

'Yes, I am Sofia Ivanovna Maslova and this is my friend, Miss Tatiana Nikolaevna Shuyskaya.'

Your "friend"? Indeed! I had thought... well, never mind. What could be more delightful than to have dinner with you both; we can all become "friends" can't we?' Sofia could hear the quotation marks he deliberately put around the word and wondered what he meant by it. Although part of her was attracted to his powerful, saturnine face, she was also repelled by his manner. He was, she felt, an expert trouble maker.

Tatiana looked at Lesnoy as he sat at their table. She

remained silent. Now that Sofia had mentioned that there was something familiar about Lesnoy, she was beginning to see it too, though she couldn't exactly place him.

'So, my dear "friends", I hate to drink alone; what can I get you? I recommend most highly this excellent vodka. Or would you prefer something more, shall we say, ladylike?'

'I would like a glass of warm water, please,' murmured Tatiana, uneasily 'With lemon but no sugar.'.

Sofia flashed the policeman a brilliant smile. 'May I have a glass of champagne, please, Inspector?'

He raised a dark eyebrow and clicked his fingers towards the barman. 'A bottle of champagne and a glass of warm water!' he commanded, without turning to look at the boy.

Captain and Mrs Ozertsov entered the dining car and the Captain clicked his heels together and gave a small, formal bow to the two girls. 'Good evening, ladies... good evening Inspector Lesnoy.' Sofia noticed a slight change in tone as he acknowledged the policeman, but Lesnoy appeared oblivious.

'Captain, my dear lady, how delightful to see you!'

Pavel and Ekaterina smiled at Sofia and Tatiana. 'We have not been introduced yet,' said Pavel, 'This is my wife, Mrs Ekaterina Yurievna Ozertsova and I am Captain Pavel Fyodorovich Ozertsov.' Sofia introduced herself and Tatiana.

'Are you joining us for dinner, Inspector?' asked Pavel.

'I am sorry Captain, but I have been honoured by an invitation to join these two lovely new friends and how could I refuse?'

'Indeed, Inspector, we would not expect you to pass up such an attractive invitation. Another time, perhaps.'

As they turned to seat themselves at the next table, Sofia noticed Ekaterina frown and give her husband a nudge and a brief, annoyed, shake of her head.

Finally the last two first-class passengers entered the

restaurant car. Mr Hare and Alexander appeared together. Sofia noticed how Tatiana's face suddenly lit up at the appearance of the young poet. She realised how keen Tatiana was to have him sitting with them, but she did not wish to appear rude to Mr Zayats. Luckily, Zayats also seemed to read the situation.

'Alexander, will you excuse me if I sit with the Captain and his wife? I had promised to give them some advice about travel in America.'

Sofia smiled at Alexander. 'In that case, Mr Zhuravlev, do please sit with us - we would love to hear some of your poetry tonight, wouldn't we Tatiana?'

Tatiana smiled, nodded and shyly looked out of the window. Alexander sat down beside her.

'Poetry! Please, please no, I beg of you!' groaned Lesnoy. 'My most hated memories of school are those turgid afternoons we spent learning vast chunks of Zukovsky and Pushkin. Even worse, Homer's Aeneid - in its original Latin. Aargh! Saints preserve us!'

'Er, actually it was Virgil who wrote the Aeneid... at least I think that is correct,' Alexander said, hesitantly.

Tatiana smiled at him. 'Yes, Homer wrote the Iliad and the Odyssey - in Greek. You should know that Inspector.'

'Huh - well, it was a long time ago,' Lesnoy turned to Sofia. 'Your friend has clearly had an expensive education - in Paris, no doubt. How about you, Miss Maslova, are you also well-versed in the classics?'

'No, not really. Tatiana and I studied together with our governess until we were thirteen, then Tatiana went to Paris and I stayed in Moscow.'

'A governess! Just like something from an English novel. Was her name Jane Eyre, by any chance?' Lesnoy chuckled at his own joke.

'No - Miss Greycourt,' Tatiana said, before Sofia had a chance to kick her under the table.

'Miss Greycourt? Now that rings a bell,' Lesnoy looked closely at each girl in turn and Sofia suddenly felt uncomfortable. 'I'm sure I once heard of a Miss Greycourt when I spent a summer at the dacha of a friend I once had - Konstantin Shuysky. Of course - I thought your name sounded familiar. My father was Doctor Pyotr Mikhailovich Lesnoy - your family doctor. I was invited to your dacha south of Moscow one summer, July or August 1900 I think, to play in that glorious garden. Like an English garden, no? Don't tell me you two are the little sisters of dear old Kostya - what an amazing coincidence!' And he slapped the table in genuine happiness and downed the remainder of his vodka in one swig.

Sofia looked anxiously at Tatiana. They exchanged puzzled faces, what should they say?

Tatiana spoke first. 'Yes, I am Konstantin and Georgiy's sister; Sofia is a friend - a dear friend - of the family.'

'I do remember you now, Mr Lesnoy,'

'Please Sofia, call me Vladimir. We are old friends, after all!' he interrupted.

Sofia continued. 'So you were there the summer I celebrated my sixth birthday. But I am not a Shuysky myself. My real mother, Irina Ivanovna Maslova, died when I was born. I was brought up by Tugan Chekhov, the head gardener at the Shuysky's dacha, and his wife Galina.'

Lesnoy leaned back in his seat and smiled happily. 'Ah! Those were the days! You should have seen it, Mr Zhuravlev, such a beautiful garden, filled with flowers and fruit trees - an idyllic setting for a very privileged childhood. Now that would have been something to inspire one of your poems, wouldn't it?'

Alexander murmured something non-committal and looked awkwardly at Tatiana, though he tactfully avoided commenting on her unexpected change of name.

'I'm not sure Mr Zhuravlev is inspired by those very conventional subjects, Vladimir,' explained Tatiana. 'Revolutionary fervour is more his thing...' but she was cut short by a hard stare from Sofia, who had also gave her a second kick under the table. Alexander was taking an extra long drink of water to cover the fact that he was blushing furiously.

At the adjacent table, Ekaterina was trying not to eavesdrop too obviously on Lesnoy and the young women, while her husband and Mr Zayats talked about different travel routes across America.

'Shuysky - of course,' she thought, 'We went to a ball at their palace once, many years ago.' She went off into a reverie, remembering the dress she had worn and the handsome young men she had danced with, coming to with a start when she realised her husband was saying her name.

'Ekaterina, Katya, are you still with us my dear? Mr Zayats was asking you a question.'

'So sorry, Mr Zayats, I was day-dreaming.'

'I was just explaining to Mr Zayats our reasons for being on the train - about wanting to leave all the turmoil and start a new life in America,' said Pavel. 'He has some contacts in Washington, at the Russian and British embassies. Perhaps they could be useful to us.'

Ekaterina smiled and tried to look interested. 'Yes, indeed, Mr Zayats. What was it you wanted to ask me?'

'Oh, I was just asking your husband what profession he intends to pursue once you are settled in your new home. He is interested in training in the law. I was wondering whether you had any ambitions to a career yourself?'

Ekaterina laughed nervously. 'Me? Work? Oh, goodness, I'd never thought of that. Is it normal for ladies of my class to work in America, Mr Zayats?'

'The world has changed a lot since the beginning of the war, Mrs Ozertsova. Certainly in England, many of the ladies, of all classes, have taken on roles which have been left vacant since so many of the men are away fighting. A lot of them work in factories or on farms, but in my experience ladies of the upper classes, like yourself, often volunteer as nurses.'

'It is surely not quite the same situation in America, though?' asked Pavel.

'No, but the women are even more emancipated there - working in offices and so on.'

'Well, perhaps I shall have to give it some thought. What do you think, Pavel? Would you enjoy having a working wife?'

The Captain gave her a fond, indulgent smile. 'If you would find it amusing to work, then by all means. I hope, though, that there will soon be a houseful of "Petits Ozertsovs" to keep you busy. Three boys and three girls would be perfect, don't you think?'

Ekaterina blushed and reached for her husband's hand. 'That does sound perfect - and the best job in the world for any woman. How about you, Mr Zayats, do you have a wife and children?'

'Sadly not. My way of life isn't compatible with being a family man. I've never been in one place long enough to settle down.'

Ekaterina sipped at her wine. 'How very intriguing - it sounds a most exciting and glamorous life you lead. You seem to know a lot about England. Have you spent much time there?'

'Yes, I was born there to a Russian mother and English father. But nowadays I travel all over the world.'

At the other table, a plentiful intake of vodka and champagne had ensured a convivial atmosphere. Having got past the initial awkwardness of discovering their childhood link, Tatiana and Sofia felt more relaxed in the Inspector's company.

Tatiana pressed her nose to the window and cupped her hands around her eyes. She shivered. 'How bleak it is outside. I can't see any signs of life anywhere. Does anyone live out here?'

'Not many humans, I would imagine,' said Lesnoy, 'But bears and wolves aplenty.'

Sofia suddenly turned to Lesnoy, smiling, 'Do you remember, Vladimir, one time at the dacha, when you pretended to be a bear to frighten us? You grabbed Tatiana and made her scream.'

'Like this?' Lesnoy moved his hands towards Sofia suddenly as if to grab her neck, but stopped short seeing the startled look on her face. 'Sorry, Miss Maslova, I didn't mean to scare you.'

Alexander laughed. 'I don't think Miss Maslova is so easily scared, Inspector. Do you agree, Miss Shuyskaya?'

'Oh, yes, Sofia could wrestle a bear any day. I completely rely on her to protect me, don't I, Sofia?'

Sofia just smiled and Alexander said 'Well if you're ever too busy, Miss Maslova, please let me know and I'd be happy to act as the Countess's protector.'

Tatiana looked sharply at Alexander. Countess? So he knew after all. She hoped he wouldn't hate her for it.

Lesnoy wagged his finger at Alexander. 'Aha! You young men, eh? I knew there was romance in your soul, not just revolution. Come now, why don't you turn your hand to love poetry - I'm sure these ladies would appreciate it.' He gulped down the last of his coffee. 'However, if you will excuse me, I must just trot along to visit my friend Mr Tokar.'

The Inspector stood up, bowed to the ladies and strode off in the direction of the bullion carriage. Tatiana, Sofia and Alexander looked at each other.

'So, what do you think, friend or foe?' whispered Sofia.

'Friend, surely,' said Tatiana. 'He's in the Special Corps of Gendarmes, on the side of the Tsar, so he would protect us from the revolutionaries. And his father was Dr Lesnoy - my Papa thought very highly of him both as a doctor and as a friend. He seems quite *sympathique*, although a little heavy-handed with the vodka.'

Alexander looked at his coffee cup but didn't speak.

'Come on, Alexander, what do you think of the Inspector,' Sofia demanded.

'Well, I'm not sure… I don't want to speak ill of your family friends…'

'Oh, don't worry about that. Vladimir wasn't ever a real friend - just a rather awkward, clumsy little boy as far as I remember, not much like his father at all. So go on - what do you really think?'

'He makes me nervous.' Alexander seemed unwilling to elaborate, but Sofia pushed him for more.

'Why? Because he's loud and overbearing and rather too keen on his drink? I know you're a poet, but surely you're not so very sensitive?'

Tatiana frowned at her. 'Don't be rude, Sofia. Let Alexander speak.'

'It's not just his manner,' Alexander explained, 'I have good reason to be wary of him. I…' he looked nervously at each girl in turn, 'I am worried he may be on the train to arrest me. He's probably just waiting until we reach a station where there's some godforsaken Siberian *katorga* camp where he can lock me up.'

Sofia laughed. 'Why would he want to arrest you? For crimes against literature? I'm sure your poetry isn't that bad!'

Tatiana smiled at Sofia's impertinence, but turned to the window again so as not to let Alexander see.

'No, I hope not,' Alexander himself couldn't help smiling at her blunt approach. 'You and Tatiana will have to be the judge of that. But my subject matter is controversial. I write from the heart, I write what I believe in - freedom, equality, comradeship - and my philosophy is to fight with my pen, not with a sword or a bomb. But the establishment, men like Lesnoy, see me as a threat. They think I choose my words deliberately to stir up dissatisfaction and incite rebellion.'

'And is that true, Mr Zhuravlev?' Sofia looked at him boldly and directly in the eye and Tatiana turned towards

125

him to gauge his reaction. Alexander returned their gazes frankly, with a look of earnest sincerity.

'Yes, I wish to inspire my fellow men to create a better society. Ideally not with violence nor with bloodshed, but sometimes...' he tailed off and looked away.

'Sometimes?' said Tatiana, encouragingly.

'Sometimes, I fear, there is no other option.'

Inspector Vladimir Lesnoy had left the dinner table in high spirits. His week on the Trans-Siberian railway might turn out better than he could possibly have imagined. Plenty of vodka, the food was passable, and the other passengers were, well, how could he put it - full of possibilities.

The Shuysky girls - that was a turn-up, and both clearly unaware of their dirty little secret. He would have to hold onto the letters while he worked out how to use the information to his best advantage.

The soppy poet - well, he could have a bit of sport with him too. Lesnoy had bigger fish to fry than that little sprat, but he would enjoy watching him wriggle and squirm.

Then there was Ekaterina. Ah, Katya! Or 'My Kiki' as he had enjoyed teasing when he found out her husband's playful nickname for her. She had been one of his favourite 'war widows', maybe even *the* favourite. Though after almost two years he had grown tired of her and hankered after something younger and less world-weary. She was still beautiful, yes, but she had lost her bloom. That tired and anxious expression in her eyes - hardly surprising given what she had been through, but not what a man really wanted to be looking at in bed. Her husband? Captain Ozertsov was a bit of a dark horse. Lesnoy considered his options with this pair. Blackmail potentially? Or just the good old-fashioned fun of creating a rift and watching the relationship crack.

Anyway, time enough for all of that to take its course. Right now he wanted to remind Tokar of his presence.

The banker was sitting in solitary splendour at his little table inside the cage. There was something incongruous about the prison-like surroundings, the cold metal bars and bare wood contrasting with the plump, slick-haired little official eating his dinner off the fine china and cutlery of the Tsar's Imperial Railway's first class service.

'Good evening, Mr Tokar,' Lesnoy managed to exude his characteristic menacing bonhomie, 'I trust you enjoyed your meal. What a shame you have to dine all alone in this miserable cage.'

Tokar wiped his lips with the linen napkin, careful to avoid staining the crest of the Russian Empire and looked warily at Lesnoy as if to say, 'Well I had been enjoying my meal until you came along,' though he actually said nothing.

'The cargo all looks very secure. How many crates were there at the beginning of the journey? I expect they're all still there - more or less, anyway.'

Tokar banged his wine glass down in exasperation at his visitor's barely-disguised insinuations.

'What exactly do you want from me?' he spluttered irritably. 'I told you at the station, that matter you referred to, it has all been dealt with. The slate has been wiped clean. I gave your superiors certain valuable information and in return...'

'Calm yourself, dear sir,' Lesnoy interrupted. 'You flatter yourself if you think I'm here on your account. Frankly, you're not worth bothering with. I just popped by this evening to pay a friendly visit and check that you are comfortable. Can I get the steward to bring you some more wine? Or are you ready for coffee? Your wish is my command.'

Tokar relaxed a fraction but still looked wary.

'So what is your business on the train, Inspector? May I know or is it confidential?'

'Well, I can share it with you, my good fellow. After all, we are both working for Tsar Bloody Nicholas. I am here to puruse a notorious murder case, solving a series of ugly killings, closing in on a very unpleasant, no - let's not beat about the bush - an evil criminal, a psychopath who has been at large for possibly at least ten years of cruel and unusual murders.'

'Indeed?' Tokar looked impressed and interested, 'And are you certain of solving the case?'

'Nothing is sure. I am getting close now. If I succeed it will be the pinnacle of my career. My name will be made: Inspector Vladimir Lesnoy of the Special Corps of Gendarmes will go down in history as the dogged and unrelenting police genius who solved the Potato Sack Murders.'

Tokar was, in spite of himself, impressed. 'My goodness, what a horrible business. A colleague of mine had a cousin whose gardener was one of the early victims. I would say you are absolutely right. If you have solved these abominable crimes, you will indeed make history.' The little man heaved himself off his uncomfortable-looking chair and came to the front of the cage. He stuck his plump, clammy hand through the bars.

'Let me shake your hand, Inspector. I would like to be able to tell my grandchildren that I once had the honour of meeting the man who solved the case of the Potato Sack Killer.'

CHAPTER NINETEEN

Ekaterina opened her green eyes and pulled back the side of the curtain. Weak sunshine filtered into their sleeping compartment, illuminating Pavel's left hand which lay protectively over her waist. She rolled onto her back and snuggled under the eiderdown to warm up her shoulder. Unable to sleep, she lay staring at the ceiling as the train clattered further and further East.

Her stomach tightened as she recalled the situation that she found herself in. What on earth was Vladimir Lesnoy doing on the train? Of all people, Vladimir, from the fire into the flame! She was aware that Pavel had noticed her odd reaction to the Inspector on the first evening, but felt reasonably sure that she had quickly composed herself and covered up her shock at seeing him. She had pleaded tiredness soon after, leaving the dining car early to avoid a whole evening of his company. But there was no avoiding the disturbing truth that, sooner or later, she would have to talk to him. I hate him, my God I hate him, she thought. Her lips moved silently as she focused her distaste on the man and forced herself to confront the shame she felt for the ease with which she had betrayed her husband. The sun flickered through the endless birch trees and for a brief moment the tempo of the train's wheels changed as they passed over a set of points.

Pavel shifted restlessly.

Ekaterina slid her right arm from under the quilt and placed her pale hand over his wounded, scarred hand. She gently ran her fingers over the back of his hand avoiding touching the tight shiny scar that sheathed the ugly stump of his ring finger.

He muttered something that sounded like a warning and then groaned as if reliving the charge across the German beetroot field. Ekaterina rolled onto her side and looked at him. Still drawn and hungry looking. His eyes sunken and surrounded by dark rings.

She had only done what she had had to do in order to survive. A woman had limited options without a man to protect her. Pavel had disappeared to fight and her world had turned upside-down: Russians fighting Germans, communists striking against factory owners, anarchists murdering religious nationalists, tenant farmers struggling against their own sons and daughters. It was a catastrophe; her beautiful, serene, future - all wrecked. All her certainties dashed.

She looked more closely at Pavel's face. Not as handsome now as he was when they had married. But for better or worse he had come back from the prison camp with a plan.

'Pack one trunk and one suitcase.' he had ordered, 'We are leaving tonight.' No discussion, no debate; she had enjoyed his authority. The war had made him into a man, the real man she had dreamed of as a girl, not the prancing, pampered cavalry officer who had wooed her, but a rougher, tougher man. Less the dandy, obsessed with army protocol, dance steps and the gold braid of his uniform. More a man not afraid of a fight. She had noticed his harder, crueller approach as a lover. So very different from the timid, romantic she had waved off to war.

Ekaterina lay back, closed her eyes and tried to organise her thoughts. What do I know for sure? She started to list the facts, placing her thumb on her index finger.

One: Pavel knows nothing. She had managed to hide her relationship with Lesnoy, though it was hard not to blush beneath his rude gaze at the dinner table.

She touched her thumb on her middle finger. Two: I am a survivor. We live in difficult times. I did what I had to do. I'll do the same again, or worse, if I have to.

She moved the tip of her thumb onto the tip of her ring finger. Three: I do love Pavel. I made a mistake with Lesnoy. Lesnoy must be silenced before Pavel discovers something. Anything.

She brought her thumb and little finger together. Four: I must act sooner rather than later. Every day that passed made his betrayal more likely.

That left the question: how could she silence the policeman? She restarted her count, her thumb placed on her index finger once again.

One: I can use my feminine charms, smile at and flirt with him. Appeal to his better nature. She dismissed this as unlikely. She knew that the relationship with Lesnoy had ended because he had chosen to end it. She had been relieved, but the truth was that he had grown bored with her, she had lost her allure for him. In any case, after nearly two years as his mistress she had gained insight into his true nature. He would get more of a thrill from causing trouble between her and Pavel than from any mild flirtation.

Two: Blackmail? His relationship with her had been immoral on her part, unethical on his. If his superiors in the Gendarmerie found out about his unprofessional behaviour he would surely lose his job, his status, his reputation. Wouldn't he? Ekaterina felt doubtful. Then angry and bitter. These men were all the same. The whole of the Oryol police force was probably indulging in sordid little affairs, their 'special protection' racket. They would all cover for each other, nod and wink and slap each other on the back. What chance would she have, just her word against his?

131

Three: I could kill him. Could I kill him? She tried hard to imagine the reality of such a course of action. Pavel used to tease her about her squeamishness. She had flinched and shuddered even when he had swatted a mosquito buzzing irritably at the bedroom window one night just before he had left for the war. She gritted her teeth and forced herself to imagine murder. Plunging a knife into Lesnoy's heart. Would she have the strength? Imagine the blood! Borrowing Pavel's gun and shooting him in the head. Her hand would shake. Imagine the brains splattered. No! It was impossible. Lesnoy was a snake, but she was incapable of killing a fly, let alone a snake.

Four: Bribery. She had valuable jewellery with her. She could easily spare one of her necklaces. Not the emerald one which Pavel had given her on their wedding day; nor the diamonds which had been passed down from her grandmother and mother. But the ruby and diamond one with the matching bracelet, inherited from an unmarried great-aunt. It was worth plenty, but had no sentimental value for her. She breathed a sigh of relief at the thought of handing it over to Lesnoy, buying his silence. She knew it was the sort of language he understood. The language of money, the language of greed.

CHAPTER TWENTY

Pavel stood behind his wife, fastening the clasp on her diamond necklace and admiring her lovely face in the portable dressing-table mirror she had brought from home as one of her 'essentials'. He smiled when he remembered her attempts to pack for the journey. One trunk! One suitcase! She had shaken her head incredulously then spent the next hour pulling everything out of her extensive wardrobe and flinging innumerable dresses on the bed, trying to decide what to take.

'Should I take the chartreuse green silk or the rose chiffon?' Pavel hadn't replied, preoccupied as he was with sorting out important paperwork, documents they would need for the journey, money, a letter to the estate manager. 'Pavel! Are you listening? It's important - which dresses should I take?'

'You look beautiful in anything, Kiki, you know I adore you whatever you wear - in fact you look especially irresistible when you're not wearing anything!' He had let the paperwork slide to the floor to get up and embrace her, but she had pushed him away in fond exasperation.'

'Pavel - not now!' She had smiled in spite of herself. 'You told me yourself we have to hurry. And don't call me "Kiki" again - I keep telling you I don't like that ridiculous nickname any more.'

Now, in the train compartment, he kissed the top of her head. 'You're right - the green dress is perfect - it brings out the colour of your eyes. Just like a cat, a kitty-cat, a Kiki-cat…'

Ekaterina slapped him on the wrist. 'I have warned you enough times,' she scolded, 'And as punishment, I'm not going to sit with you at dinner?'

'What? Who are you going to sit with? I hope I'm not going to lose you to the charming English spy or the sensitive young poet.' He hesitated, 'Or the rugged Inspector?'

Ekaterina got up from her seat and busied herself with smoothing out her silk skirt. 'Don't be ridiculous,' she snapped, 'He's awful. They're all awful. No - the Countess and her friend asked me to join them for a ladies' night.' She paused and looked at Pavel. 'You don't mind, do you?'

Pavel smiled at her and pushed back a tendril of hair which had fallen over her eyes. 'Of course not - that sounds an enchanting idea. The men can talk war and you girls can talk wardrobes.'

Ekaterina rolled her eyes. 'We three 'girls' as you call us have more brains than all you men put together. If women ruled Russia, we'd have sorted everything out for the best without all this awful bloodshed.'

Tatiana and Sofia were already seated when the Ozertsovs entered the dining car and Tatiana excitedly patted the seat beside her for Ekaterina to join them. Pavel looked down the aisle. Mr Zayats and Mr Zhuravlev were deep in conversation at the table at the far end of the carriage. Pavel hesitated a split second before deciding to ask if he could join them, but at that moment, Inspector Lesnoy entered the carriage behind him.

'Ah! Captain! Have you been jilted by your wife? How unfortunate! You are most welcome to join me this evening - we can hit the vodka hard without any disapproving looks from the ladies.' He slapped Pavel on the back, then clicked his fingers for the steward. 'A bottle

134

of vodka and the menu, quickly now.'

At the other end of the carriage, Dominic surreptitiously glanced behind him and murmured to his companion, 'I think we've had a lucky escape, Mr Zhuravlev.'

'I'm not sure what…?'

'I just meant that I'm somewhat relieved to have managed to escape the close attention of the Inspector again. I heard him giving you a bit of a grilling yesterday evening.'

Alexander gave a wry smile. 'I was worried it was going to go that way, but luckily he doesn't appear to see me as a serious threat to national security - just a rather pathetic poet.'

'He doesn't subscribe to the belief that the pen is mightier than the sword, then?'

'No - more of a brute force type, I'd say. In any case he was far more interested in trying to flirt with Miss Maslova. The young ladies realised that he was the son of their family doctor and a friend of the Countess's brothers. They knew him as a child.'

'Interesting. Well let's hope the ladies keep him nicely distracted for the rest of the journey. Then we'll be safe.'

'He's cornered the Captain tonight. I must say Ozertsov isn't looking exactly delighted with his dining companion.'

'No, I can imagine, but at least he's got nothing to hide from the Inspector.'

'Unlike us, you mean?' Alexander asked. 'I suppose he does make me a little uneasy, but as I said, I don't think he's actually on the train for the purposes of apprehending a pacifist poet.'

'Even a pacifist with a pistol and a reputation for rabble-rousing?'

Dominic gazed steadily at Alexander, who didn't reply immediately.

'You've been looking through my belongings, then.'

Dominic smiled. 'Of course. It's my job. And it means we're quits, doesn't it?'

Another pause, then Alexander laughed ruefully. 'All right, we're quits. I didn't mean to be rude. I was going to replace your vodka, but then I saw what was in your attaché case. I'm in a somewhat confusing position at the moment. A peaceful revolutionary - with a pistol, I grant you, but I would only ever use it in self-defence - and at the same time a wanted man. There are some in the Gendarmerie who consider those like me who wage the revolution with words rather than bullets, even more dangerous than the violent types. And now, on this train, I'm not actually here in my role as revolutionary or poet.' He shook his head in a gesture of bewilderment.

'So why are you here, Mr Zhuravlev?'

'I'm here as a kind of undercover chaperone.'

Dominic raised his eyebrows quizzically. 'Chaperone?'

'At the request of Count Shuysky - to keep an eye on the Countess and Miss Maslova. Only, they don't realise, so please don't let them know.'

'Of course, if that's how you prefer it. Does it matter, though? Why should you want to keep your role as guardian angel a secret from them.' Dominic smiled at his young companion. 'Don't you think the Countess would appreciate your protection? She would probably see you in a new light?'

Alexander blushed and shrugged. 'Perhaps, but it's not simple. She doesn't know her father's fate. Sending me to keep an eye on his daughter was his dying wish. If you'd told me a week ago that my next assignment would be acting as nursemaid to the pampered offspring of a Moscow aristocrat, well, I wouldn't have believed it.'

Ekaterina's diamond necklace glittered in the flickering candlelight and Tatiana sighed. 'You do look lovely, Mrs Ozertsova. I fear Sofia and I have let ourselves go. It's so hard to keep up appearances on a train.'

'We're supposed to look a little down-at-heel, don't forget,' Sofia reminded her friend. 'Your Papa was worried we might present an easy target for the revolutionaries.'

Tatiana shrugged in exasperation. 'Well we're safe now, aren't we? Couldn't we wear a little jewellery tomorrow night? To cheer ourselves up? There aren't any revolutionaries here to tear it from our necks.'

'What about Mr Zhuravlev?' asked Ekaterina, 'I hear he's one of the leading lights in the movement?'

'He wouldn't do us any harm. He's an idealist, a champion of the oppressed and I admire him for it, but he's a gentleman,' said Tatiana.

'And Tatiana thinks she can twist him around her little finger. She thinks she can make him believe that she's just a poor little rich girl - as deserving a case as any little poor girl from the Moscow slums, dressed in rags and begging for food.'

'That's unfair, Sofia, I admire his high-minded principles. It's not my fault that I was born into a wealthy family. I don't even know what I'm doing here. What do I care about saving the Shuysky jewels - I'd have preferred to stay with Papa, whatever the consequences.' Her eyes welled up with tears.

Sofia put a reassuring arm around her and tried to change the subject. 'Tell us about yourself, Mrs Ozertsova. Are you also escaping revolution?'

'Please, call me Katya.' She sighed and fiddled with her necklace. 'Yes, I suppose you could say we are. We'd only been married a few months when my husband was sent to war. He's seen the way the world is going, the changes that are coming. In fact he has sympathy for the revolutionary cause, but he doesn't like their methods and he knows they will have little sympathy for us. We've both been through a lot in the last three years and we want to start a new life, far away from all this.' She gestured out of the window. The landscape outside was invisible in the pitch blackness, but they all knew how bleak it was in its emptiness and that the cities, for all their glitter and glamour, were equally bleak.

'Your husband…' Sofia said, hesitantly, 'He must be a very brave man. I've noticed…' she tailed off, unsure of Ekaterina's reaction.

Ekaterina smiled, resignedly. 'His hand, you mean. Yes, he was badly injured in the fighting and taken prisoner in Germany for two years. It has changed him - and not just physically.'

There was a hush. Tatiana mused on how quickly her light-hearted admiration of Katya's necklace had turned to darker, less frivolous subjects.

Sofia broke the silence first. 'It must have been hard, being left behind. Were you in Moscow?'

'Pavel thought I would be safer out of the city, so I stayed at our dacha in Oryol, near his brother's family, although they soon decided to get out altogether and go to America.' She smiled. 'That's where we're going now: to the other side of the world; to a new life.'

'*Na zdorovie!*' Lesnoy raised the first of many glasses to his table companion and swigged back the vodka with a satisfied smack of his lips.

Pavel chinked his glass carefully against the Inspector's and sipped tentatively. He wanted to keep his wits about him this evening. Lesnoy was not his ideal dinner companion, but since he was stuck with him, he might as well take advantage of the situation and try to find out… find out what? He wasn't exactly sure; he just had a feeling that there was more to discover.

'So, Inspector, you must thank your lucky stars that you were so busy protecting Mother Russia from home-grown criminals that you managed to avoid a fate like mine.'

'Indeed, Captain. It hasn't been exactly a picnic here while you've been away, I can assure you, but on balance I believe you did have the worse deal. I'm not surprised you want to get your lovely wife out of here now you've done your bit.'

'Do you have a "lovely wife", Inspector? Waiting anxiously for your return?'

'Ha! Unfortunately not. Never met the right woman. Or rather I've met an awful lot of the right women, but either it wasn't the right time or I didn't seem to be the right man for them. You know what, though, sometimes I think that maybe I've been lucky. More variety, if you know what I mean.' He winked lasciviously at Pavel who forced himself to smile politely.

'Each to his own. Personally, I'm very happy to have found the right woman for me. Strangely enough, I felt it more on my return from war than I did as a newly-wed. When there's so much brutal misery in the world, a happy home life seems more valuable than all the Tsar's riches.'

'Bread and peace! Long live the revolution! Is that what you're saying, Captain? I'm surprised, I confess - had you down as a royalist through and through.'

Ozertsov realised that he was the subject of a subtle interrogation. Unsure how best to react, he shrugged. 'Life's not that black and white, though, is it? Royalist? Revolutionary? Basically, we are all as bad as each other. What I do know is this: if there's going to be violence, I don't want to be part of it - not on either side. I've had my fill.'

Lesnoy nodded. 'I can understand that. A wise decision.' He jerked his head in the direction of Tatiana. 'I understand the young ladies are of a similar mind. At least the Countess's father decided to have them shipped out of Moscow, to somewhere safer.'

'Countess?' said Pavel looking at the three young women engaged in an animated discussion, 'Of course, Tatiana Shuyskaya. I think we have friends of friends, or cousins of friends, in common. She must be worth her weight in gold.'

'Weight in diamonds more like.' Lesnoy grunted.

'And the other two? I got the impression that the young chap - a poet isn't he? - was a bit of a revolutionary himself. Isn't it bit strange his travelling *spalny wagon* with the rest of us toffs?'

'I think he's as surprised as I am,' replied the Inspector. 'Quite a change for us lower class types to mix in such esteemed circles.' Lesnoy's habitual sneer appeared. 'I imagine the possibility of getting closer to the lovely Countess Tatiana and her wealth is probably enough to turn any man from red to white.'

'What about Mr Zayats? Any idea what his game is?'

'He's obviously English, a government agent I suspect. Probably thinks we backward Russians haven't got a clue, but we've got him on our "list of visitors" at police headquarters.'

Pavel looked surprised. 'You're very frank, Inspector. I thought all that kind of intelligence would be strictly confidential.' He wondered whether it was the vodka loosening Lesnoy's tongue, or just that he didn't care about keeping secrets.

'Pah! These English spies think they're frightfully important, with their ridiculous "perfect" Russian, diligently learned at Oxford, and their special technical kits, all neatly packed into a Savile Row briefcase. Truth is, Zayats, as he calls himself, is just a glorified bodyguard.'

'Guarding whose body?'

'Well not exactly a body. I imagine he's here to ensure that the gold consignment gets to the end of the line and then onto a ship bound for the United Kingdom. King George is very kindly helping his dear cousin to hold onto power by selling him tanks. The alternative is too awful for His Majesty to contemplate. If the workers revolt successfully here, it might give the English working classes ideas above their station.'

'So effectively, this Englishman is fighting on the same side as you? So why all the subterfuge? Why is he pretending to be Russian when he's not?'

Lesnoy made a balancing gesture with his hands. 'Who knows? The English like their little games - makes them feel important. On the other hand, there may be more to him than meets the eye.'

'Such as?'

'I was watching him at the station. He sent a telegram.'

'That's not unusual is it? He'd just be letting his bosses know when when to expect him at Vladivostok, to lay on extra security.'

Lesnoy leaned forward and tapped the side of his nose. 'Almost exactly right, Captain, apart from one important detail.'

Pavel looked questioningly at Lesnoy.

'"Meet train Spassk Primorskiy."'

'Spassk Primorskiy? Where the hell is that?'

'I checked the timetable, It is some one-dog-town, or a village, a day and a half from Vladivostok'

'What do you mean?'

'That was the telegram he dictated: "Meet train Spassk Primorskiy". Odd don't you think? Surely the idea is to get the gold all the way to Vladivostok so it can be shipped out.'

'Yes, I see what you're saying, but maybe he's asking for reinforcements at Spassk Primorskiy. Are you going to investigate further?'

'Reinforcements...' Lesnoy chuckled, 'Yes, I suppose that is one option. Bandits or gangsters might be another.'

'Gangsters? You must investigate, stop him, warn the authorities.'

'Well, that's not what I'm officially here for, as you know. My real job is too important to allow myself to be distracted. On the other hand...'

Pavel waited, but Lesnoy didn't elaborate. 'On the other hand...?' he encouraged him.

'On the other hand, I'm not averse to watching him, having a bit of sport with him - making him a squirm a bit. Dig a bit deeper. What do you think, Captain?'

'Not my idea of entertainment, I'm afraid. Life's complicated and miserable enough without making it worse. I wouldn't want anyone doing it to me and I wouldn't do it to anyone else. However, if you think that our security on the train is at risk, you have a duty to act, don't you?'

'Indeed, Captain, your sentiments are very proper, very correct. I salute you, sir!'

Pavel had an odd feeling that the Inspector was mocking him. A strange man, undoubtedly. He thought back to the first day on the train when he and Ekaterina had both sat with him. He'd had the same uneasy feeling about Lesnoy as he had now. A strange man, a dangerous man. Something unscrupulous about him, feral even. Like a hawk zooming in on its prey and enjoying its quarry's fear as much, if not more than, the taste of its blood. Pavel had been aware of Ekaterina's tension sitting next to him. She hadn't liked him either - she was a good judge of character - and had barely spoken during the meal, before leaving early on the pretext of exhaustion.

He looked across at her now, relaxed and laughing with the two younger women. He smiled. How lovely they looked - all of them Russian beauties - dark-haired Tatiana, blonde Sofia and his graceful, auburn-haired, green-eyed wife. She must have sensed his gaze because she returned it, smiling warmly at him and raising her fingertips to her lips to blow him a subtle kiss. You're a lucky man, Pavel, he thought to himself, a very lucky man.

CHAPTER TWENTY-ONE

Over a mid-morning cup of coffee, alone in the dining car, Dominic Hare, alias Dmitry Zayats, thought back over the last three days. Outside, the snow-covered landscape swept past in a blur, mile after mile of emptiness, with barely any sign of habitation. He had heard that the name 'Siberia' came from the Tatar for 'sleeping land'.

'Dead' would be closer to the truth, he thought, bitterly. At the age of forty-two, he had done enough of this sort of mission. He'd done enough for his country, his king, his fellow man. Time to do something for himself, to start to live the life *he* wanted to live.

Returning to England probably wasn't an option, as much as he loved the place. An idyllic childhood in Sussex, university at Oxford, working in London, holidays in the West Highlands of Scotland - all beautiful places, wonderful memories and he would feel nostalgia for them for the rest of his life. But no, it was time for a fresh start, somewhere completely different, somewhere he wasn't known. One final change of name and he would be ready to embark on a new life.

America! He thought, filling his cup with the remains of the coffee pot and downing it in one gulp before it chilled. Land of the free, land of opportunity. And with a million dollars in his pocket he could have the time of his life. A penthouse apartment in some swish part of New York? A weekend place in the Hamptons? He continued to muse. Maybe he would invest in a vineyard on the west coast?

There would be time enough for those decisions. First of all he had to make sure that everything went according to plan on this side of the ocean. It all came down to being prepared. He had his basic scheme in place, now he had to consider all the variables, the factors he had no control over. Worst case scenario, what might he have to contend with?

The weather was the first factor. His team on the ground should be equipped - a reindeer-drawn sleigh if necessary, if conditions were too bad for a truck to get near enough to the railway.

The second factor was the people. Mentally, he ticked off a list of his travelling companions, assessing whether or not they could pose a threat. First, the Countess and Miss Maslova. He knew not to underestimate women - there were a few formidable females working in British Intelligence. He'd come across them in meetings in London and once on a mission in the Far East in his youth when the lady in question had got him out of a hole. However, he felt fairly confident that this pair were too focused on their own survival to be bothered about him.

His cabin companion, Alexander? Not quite sure about him. A revolutionary, yes, so he might subscribe to the Robin Hood ethic if the opportunity arose. Alexander portrayed himself as a pacifist poet but, as Dominic had discovered, the young man had a pistol and a commission to guard the girls. If he falls in love with one of them as well, who knows what he might do if he thinks they're under attack. Should he let him in on the plan so he didn't turn trigger happy in the heat of the moment? Not ideal, he thought; the fewer people who know, the better.

Captain and Mrs Ozertsov? Like Tatiana and Sofia, they were likely to be more focused on their own plans. An interesting couple, intelligent, sophisticated. They'll do well in the New World. I might even keep in touch, look them up some time. It was a shame he had to disrupt their travel plans, but it was only temporary. The main danger was that Pavel might find his military instincts coming to the fore - a threat to the Tsar or the Tsar's resources? Gut reaction - out comes the gun. There were two viable options: either pre-warn him or hide his pistol the night before so it wasn't to hand at the crucial moment. On balance the latter seemed the better choice.

Then there was Lesnoy to consider. He had been putting off involving himself in conversation with the Inspector - wanted to assess him from a distance first, as it were, work out what he was up against. But he needed to bite the bullet and find out exactly what the man was up to. He'd overheard snippets of his conversations with the other passengers, just enough to confuse things really. Was he there simply to provide police back-up to the bank official? Or was he journeying towards a specific mission somewhere in Siberia? He had the impression that Lesnoy had a link to the Countess, too, and there was also a tangible tension between him and the Ozertsovs. Damn it! Dominic thought, why can't the wretched man act in a more straightforward manner? Why the cloak and dagger act? Then he chuckled to himself, thinking of his own labyrinthine persona.

There was one more person to take into account. Dominic checked his pocket watch and decided to pay him a visit before lunch. He walked down to the far end of the dining car, checking over his shoulder for anyone who might observe him, before opening the door to the armoured freight car.

Andrey Tokar was sitting at a table, reading a thick doorstep of a book. He looked up as Dominic entered and, somewhat to Dominic's surprise, gave a delighted smile. I suppose the poor fellow must be glad to see anyone. It must be pretty grim in here with almost no natural light, he thought.

'Good morning!' Both men spoke at exactly the same moment and both laughed.

'Let me introduce myself - Dmitry Zayats, I'm a passenger in *spalny vagon*. Just thought I'd come along and say hello. Someone mentioned there was a chap in here, all by himself - can't be much fun, eh?'

'Absolutely right, Mr Zayats.' The bank official rose and stuck his right-hand through the bars, offering as much as he could muster of a handshake. 'I'm Andrey Tokar, Bullion Transport Officer of the State Bank of the Russian Empire.'

'Ah! Very pleased to meet you, Mr Tokar.' Dominic nodded his head in the direction of the stack of small crates at the rear of the cage. 'I presume you are here to keep watch over some very valuable cargo.'

Mr Tokar looked a little uncomfortable. 'Top secret, I'm afraid, Mr Zayats. Bank security protocols and all that, you understand. Probably shouldn't even let you stay in here, but, *chert voz'mi*! I'd go mad if I couldn't have any human contact. The stewards are supposed to lock the carriage door every time they pass through, but of course they don't, thank goodness, it's far too inconvenient.'

Dominic nodded sympathetically. 'No, no, of course, I quite understand that it's all got to be hush hush. On the other hand…' he beckoned Tokar back to the bars and leaned forward to whisper to him. 'I'm actually here to keep an eye on things as well - part of your team, you might say.'

Tokar stepped back, eyebrows raised. 'Really? Well, how very odd. Nobody has informed me that there was any additional security detail on the train. No offence, Mr Zayats, but do you have any identification?'

'I'm sorry, Mr Tokar, I realise you won't have been informed about my role here. My position has been endorsed at the highest level…' he paused.

'The President of the bank?' asked Tokar, seeming

somewhat flustered. He shook his head, tutted and began muttering, 'My superiors promised not to involve him - oh dear me, there really wasn't any need. The whole matter was sorted out, they promised...'

'No. No indeed, not the bank's president, not at all,' Dominic reassured him. 'When I say the *highest* level, I mean the *very highest*.' He raised his eyebrows meaningfully. 'You understand what I'm saying?'

'Not... surely not... not the Tsar himself?' Tokar almost hissed, his stress palpable. 'Good God, man, what the...'

'Confidentially, I am here on behalf of the Tsar's cousin, King George of the British Empire. He's anxious to help defend Russia against the revolutionaries, frankly because it's in all our interests. Nobody at your bank knows about this extra layer of protection which has been put in place. When it was suggested to them they took it as some kind of insult and blocked the idea immediately. I'm merely here on an external contract, as an observer, making sure everything goes smoothly on the passage from Moscow all the way to HMS Suffolk at Vladivostok. After that the Royal Navy is responsible for delivering the umm... the 'cargo' let's call it, to the Bank of England.'

Tokar relaxed a fraction. 'So it's nothing to do with the... the business last year?'

'Business last year? No, not at all, no idea what you're even talking about, dear fellow.' Dominic deliberately tried to appear completely unconcerned, though he made a mental note to try to find out what that 'business' had been.

'To put it simply, I'm here on behalf of the Government of the United Kingdom, to keep an eye on the... the cargo, and to make sure you're happy with everything. I'm here to check you feel safe and secure, that sort of thing. Can I report back that you haven't had any problems, no security issues? Is there anything you need?'

Tokar finally breathed a sigh of relief. 'No, everything's

147

absolutely fine apart from the boredom. I was locked in here just before the train left Moscow. The key stayed in Moscow. It is for my own protection, of course, so no one can come in, point a gun and force me to open up.'

'And there'll be a bank official at the other end with a duplicate key to open up?'

'Precisely. When we arrive at Vladivostok my colleague arrives with a duplicate key and lets me out. Then we oversee the carefully vetted team who have been appointed to take the cargo onto the ship... HMS Suffolk, as you said.'

'And that's when His Majesty's Royal Navy takes over responsibility.'

'Indeed,' Tokar smiled for the first time since Dominic had initially entered his carriage. 'Thank you, Mr Zayats, you have reassured me a great deal. A man like you, clearly highly regarded by the British elite, looking after my interests and those of Russia. I'm sure the Tsar - and your King - ought to be very grateful.'

Dominic's practised eye gave a final once-over to the carriage, assessing the layout, the quantity of cargo and the size of the crates, and stored it photographically in his memory.

'I'll take my leave, then, if you don't mind, Mr Tokar. It has been a pleasure meeting you - I'll come back another time for a longer chat if you like. Anything I can bring you?'

Tokar picked up his book and let it drop onto the table with a bang. 'Well if you've got anything more exciting than this dreary tome... a detective novel? Sherlock Holmes, perhaps?'

'I may well have the very thing for you, Mr Tokar.'

'And a bottle of vodka would be very welcome - why not come and share it one evening?'

'Thank you - I shall'

CHAPTER TWENTY-TWO

That particular evening, however, Dominic Hare had other plans. He'd done his preparatory work, made the necessary observations. He was ready to take on Inspector Lesnoy.

In his cabin, he and Alexander were vying with each other for space in which to dress. Both men were making a particular effort to look their best that evening and each of them noticed.

'Dining with the young ladies this evening?' Dominic asked.

Alexander grinned sheepishly. 'Yes, they've asked if I would. They want me to take this,' and he held up his battered notebook.

'A poetry reading? Excellent,' Dominic said. 'I'd like to read some of your work myself some time.' He noticed Alexander's slightly anxious look. 'Not tonight, though, don't worry. I'm not going to cramp your style with the Countess. I'm hoping to grab a word or two with the Inspector actually.'

'Good luck with that, Mr Zayats… Dmitry. You're ready for your interrogation, then?'

'Yes, Alexander, and hoping to do a bit of grilling myself.'

Dominic made sure that he arrived early in the dining car and sat down at the furthest table, ready to greet the

Inspector when he entered from the direction of the armoured carriage. He accosted the steward as he passed. 'A bottle of the best vodka, please.'

Lesnoy came through the door just as the vodka was being delivered and Dominic greeted him enthusiastically. 'Inspector - would you care to join me this evening? We haven't had the chance to have a proper conversation.' Lesnoy paused by Dominic's table and turned his hawk-like gaze on him. Dominic continued, 'I'm very interested to hear your views on the situation in Moscow. Now, first things first, let me pour you a glass of this first class vodka.'

Lesnoy's eyes lit up and he sat down with alacrity. 'Excellent, Mr Zayats, a man after my own heart - getting your priorities right I'm pleased to see.'

'Absolutely. So, four days on the train, well away from the Moscow troubles. Is this a journey you do often, Inspector?'

'No, thankfully. My days on the beat in Moscow, or being sent out to various godforsaken villages in the surrounding area, are just about over. I've been lucky enough to achieve rapid promotion and the reward is to be comfortably installed behind a desk at Gendarmerie Headquarters most of the time.'

'Surely talent, rather than luck, Inspector. You are clearly doing important work in Moscow Division. A toast, to you and your continued success.' Dominic filled their glasses with the vodka and raised his glass in a salute to the policeman.

Lesnoy smiled and shrugged. 'Well, I've had success in some important cases, but there's still an element of luck involved - being in the right place at the right time.'

Dominic nodded. 'Yes, it's remarkable how one's career can turn on such things. Did you always have ambitions to join the police?'

'My father was a doctor - a very successful and well-respected physician who made a name for himself among the higher echelons of Moscow society. He would have liked me to follow in his footsteps and until my late teens I went along with his ambitions. I even studied for one year in the Medical Faculty at Moscow University.'

'How interesting. May I ask why you didn't pursue your medical career further. Was your father not disappointed?'

'If he had still been alive, I am sure he would have been very disappointed, but alas, he died the summer after my first year of study. It was a turning point for me in many ways.'

'I can imagine. From my own experience, the death of my parents was something of a catalyst in the reevaluation of my life. Did you simply realise that you had been trying to fulfil his ambitions rather than your own?'

'Yes, in part, but I had also experienced some unusual, somewhat disturbing situations during my first year which encouraged me to pursue a different path.'

'How interesting. May I ask what experiences those were?'

The Inspector hesitated momentarily before replying. 'Yes, certainly, Mr Zayats. There were several, minor incidents of a similar nature, but the one which made the greatest impression occurred in the spring of 1906.'

Dominic raised his eyebrows in query, encouraging Lesnoy to continue.

'Perhaps I should wait until we have finished eating. The subject matter is rather too gory for the dinner table.'

'Of course, if you prefer. I've got a pretty strong stomach, but in a confined space such as this it's probably better not to risk putting anyone else off their food!' Dominic glanced meaningfully at the next table where Sofia and Tatiana were sitting. Tell me more about your present journey. I assume you've been dragged away from your comfortable office chair for the important task of overseeing the cargo next door?' Dominic jerked his head in the direction of the armoured carriage.

Lesnoy smiled. 'Yes, that's what everyone seems to

151

assume. It's true that with my sleeping cabin right next to the cargo, I am well-placed to keep an eye on things.'

'Are you saying that's not the primary reason for your presence on the train?'

'Not the primary reason, no, although between you and me it doesn't do any harm for Mr Tokar to know that a member of the Tsar's Special Gendarmerie is close at hand.'

Dominic smiled, knowingly. 'Ah, yes. I had a little chat with Mr Tokar earlier today. He seemed a little worried about some "business" that had occurred last year. Of course I had no idea what he was talking about, but now that you mention it, I'm guessing there was some police involvement.'

Lesnoy put a finger his lips and leaned forward across the table. Dominic noticed that the vodka bottle was all but empty, though he had carefully rationed himself to one glass. Unsurprisingly, the Inspector's speech was beginning to slur.

'Can't say too much, my dear fellow, but all I will say is this - you're not wrong. One of last year's consignments of… well, the cargo as you call it, was a little lighter at the end of the journey than it had been at the beginning. Bloody fool!' Dominic jumped as Lesnoy unexpectedly brought his fist angrily slamming down on the table, making the glasses and cutlery rattle.

The conversation at the other tables halted as everyone turned to look at Lesnoy. Dominic realised he only had a limited time to get all the information he needed. He'd witnessed this alcohol-related personality change on previous evenings.

'Bloody fool, absolutely,' he murmured, soothingly. 'But just tell me, Inspector, now we've finished eating, about the incident which inspired your very successful change of career. You mentioned that there was a specific…'

'Yes, yes, ghastly incident,' Lesnoy continued with a

certain amount of glee. 'Spring 1906, I was doing my stint as a student in the pathology lab. They brought in the body of a child. Bad enough in itself, of course, but this was much worse. It - or actually she, because I remember thinking that it was particularly nasty being a little girl - she had been hacked into pieces and tied inside a potato sack. Awful, absolutely bloody awful. And I had a sort of epiphany. Decided that rather than analysing the aftermath in a rather detached, scientific manner, I'd much prefer to be out there tracking down and apprehending the monster who'd carried out such an awful crime and ensuring he was punished.'

'So you turned your back on medicine and joined the police?'

'I completed the year, though my heart wasn't in it. Then that summer my father died and, although I was sad, it also felt like an opportunity.'

'To follow your calling?'

'Exactly.'

'And, tell me, Inspector, what happened to the Potato Sack Murder case. Did you ever track down the perpetrator?'

Lesnoy sat back in his seat and placed his fingertips together.

'I thought all Russian citizens knew about this very famous unsolved mystery. But then you really are not a "son of Russia", are you Mr Hare?' Dominic's expression was impassive and he ignored Lesnoy's use of his real name, but felt as though a ranging shot had been fired at him. 'It was a frustrating case,' the detective continued, 'a case that haunted me. For a long time I felt despair that it would never be solved. I built my career on an almost visceral desire to look that bastard in the face one day and know that I could send him to the firing squad, or at least a life sentence in the Sakhalin *katorga*.'

'So his atrocities were the spur which helped you make such a success of your career?'

'Quite correct, Mr Zayats. And *now…*' he emphasised the word and paused dramatically.

'Now?' Dominic was agog, sensing even in Lesnoy's vodka-slurred voice a sense of climax and resolution.

'Now - I have him. That is why I am here, on this train. Very soon that scene I have imagined for more than ten years will be a reality.'

Tatiana picked up Alexander's notebook and read:

The drowsy garden scatters insects
Bronze from the ash of braziers blown.
Level with me and with my candle
Hang flowering worlds, their leaves full-grown…
Where the pond lies, an open secret,
Where apple bloom is surf and sigh,
And where the garden, a lake dwelling,
Holds out in front of it, the sky.

While she read, Alexander held his teacup to his lips longer than necessary to take a sip, in order to cover his embarrassment.

'That is beautiful, Mr Zhuravlev. I do love the alliteration of "*bronze from the ash of braziers blown*". Is that a recent poem?'

'Er, no, um… actually it's not one of mine.'

'Oh! Well it's very good. Who wrote it?'

'A poet called Boris Pasternak. I've met him several times at the Moscow writers' club. He read that poem to us just before Christmas and I asked if I could copy it down. I liked the imagery and, yes, the alliteration too.'

'*The drowsy garden…* it sounds so peaceful and warm. Doesn't it remind you of those summers at the dacha, Sofia? The sound of the bees humming and us running around pulling petals off the roses to make our own perfume. Do you remember how cross Mr Chekhov was when he saw what we were doing to his garden? The roses were his pride and joy.'

A contemplative look had come over Tatiana and she leaned her elbows on the table and her chin in her hands and gazed through the window into the black nothingness.

She is dreaming of her former life, thought Alexander with a pang. A life which she will never live again. He thought to himself how easily in his mind he had condemned girls like her. Girls born into wealthy families, daughters of Counts, girls with palaces in Moscow and pretty dachas in the countryside, with governesses and silk frocks and diamonds. She is being very brave, he thought, braver than I am. She has been wrenched away from all her comforts and flung into the unknown, bundled into a cramped train compartment with the minimum of possessions and set hurtling off, through the wastes of Siberia towards some unknown destination.

While he wondered, not for the first time, how he was going to speak to Tatiana about her father's death, Sofia was leafing through his poetry notebook.

'This is interesting:

The linnet in her cage is but a toy,
Her pretty feathers just a prison cloak.
The world looks through the bars, she sings her song,
But then they turn away, she sings alone.

Is that all?'

'No - it's one I've not finished.'

'What's the next verse going to be?'

She passed the notebook across the table to Alexander, who reached inside his jacket for a pen.

He began writing:

The linnet sings alone in minor key;
She fears the endless sky, turned bloody red
With the hell of hunting hawks above,
The sparrow's miserable death beneath.

The linnet's master takes a golden key
On silken thread and opens up her cage.
'Fly, little bird,' he coaxes, 'Fly!'
She flies, but is she free? He will never know.

Sofia twisted her head, trying to read as Alexander wrote. 'Wouldn't *"miserable sparrow's death"* be better than *"sparrow's miserable death"*?'

Tatiana turned her gaze back to her companions. 'Sofia! That's rather rude. It's Alexander's poem - you can't change it.'

Alexander smiled. 'Well, you might have a point. It's only a first draft. I quite often change words around, but I think here I do mean that it's the death that's miserable, not the sparrow.'

'Can I see what you've written?' Tatiana asked, shyly. Alexander pushed the notebook over to her and she read it in silence, then sat back looking thoughtful.

'I suppose the linnet is a rich girl, living in a gilded cage. She seems to have everything, but she isn't free and when she gets her freedom, she might not even survive. Is that right?'

Alexander nodded and smiled. Tatiana continued, 'And the sparrow is the poor girl. You don't say what her life is like, or whether or not she's happy, but her death is miserable. Why is it miserable, I'm not sure I understand that bit?'

Tatiana was looking directly into his face, her large brown eyes earnest and worried. He felt touched that she was taking his work so seriously and his heart gave a little lurch. He could hardly trust himself to speak without betraying the emotion he was feeling, but she was still gazing at him so seriously, wanting an answer.

'I suppose I wanted to convey… well, I wanted to show that the sparrow's death was miserable in the same way that its whole life had been miserable. That's different from the sparrow herself being miserable. Do you see?'

'Yes, I think I see now,' Tatiana replied. She smiled at Alexander. 'Is that the end of the poem or will you add more?'

Sofia broke in. 'I think the linnet should fly off to find the sparrow's grave and weep over it. Actually, I think I could write a better poem altogether, Alexander, something a lot more stirring. Here, let me borrow your book and pen.'

Without waiting for his assent, Sofia pulled the battered leather-bound notebook over, gently prised the pen from Alexander's fingers and looked at the dining-car ceiling for inspiration. Alexander didn't object and Tatiana didn't rebuke Sofia for her rudeness either. The two of them were lost in their own world.

Pavel was trying to suppress a smile. His wife noticed and smiled back. 'What's so funny?'

The Captain cocked his head towards the Tatiana's table.

'The young people and their poetry - oh, to be so romantic and naive again!'

'You *are* a romantic, Pavel, darling. Remember those beautiful letters you wrote me when you were imprisoned? They were very poetic.'

'Huh - I never knew if you'd even received them. You didn't reply at any rate.' He looked wounded.

'I kept them all, and I'm sorry I didn't write back. It wasn't because I didn't care. I was so unhappy, I didn't know what to say. I didn't want to make life worse for you.'

Tears filled Ekaterina's sea-green eyes and Pavel hated himself for stirring up her unhappiness. He leaned across the table towards her and clasped her hands in his. She looked down and had to stifle a sob as she looked at his injured fingers.

'Oh, my poor darling - what you had to endure. How can you bear to listen to my whining.'

'Ekaterina, my beautiful Katya, listen to me. We both had to endure some horrors. There's more than one kind of awfulness in war. At least my physical scars are tangible. Sometimes it's harder to come to terms with the emotional scars of loneliness and uncertainty. You were just a young bride, barely home from our honeymoon, all alone in a place you didn't really know.'

Ekaterina sniffed and shrugged. 'It's all in the past now. I don't want to dwell on it. I won't pretend I'm not anxious about this new adventure, but I'm sure it's for the best.' She tried to smile bravely, but Pavel noticed how she was deliberately avoiding looking at him. He squeezed her hands in his in an attempt to make her meet his gaze.

'Don't you think that maybe you need to dwell on it? Well, not dwell exactly, but talk about it. It was painful, talking about those two years in the prison camp and I couldn't have shared it with anyone except you, but it felt better once I had. I can't force you to talk about what happened - I wouldn't want to force you - but think about it. If you want to talk, then I want to listen. When you're ready.'

Ekaterina made herself look steadily into his eyes. Such deep, sad eyes. Full of sorrow, but at the same time full of strength and hope. She loved him so much. How could she possibly share the details of her own sordid 'prison of war' and risk losing him.

A clatter from the end of the carriage made her jump. Pavel rolled his eyes. 'That idiot again! Doesn't Lesnoy ever learn when to stop? No wonder he hasn't found a wife to share his life with. What sane woman would put up with his drunken temper?'

'Yes, it's horrible.' Ekaterina spoke through clenched teeth.

'You really can't bear him, can you, my dear? I noticed how you flinched away from him even on the first day. You're a good judge of character, to have recognised his shortcomings so soon. Thank goodness we never came

158

across him in Oryol.'

Ekaterina said nothing. Everyone had finished their tea and Tatiana and Sofia were saying goodnight to them all.

'You look tired, beautiful wife,' Pavel murmured tenderly. 'Shall we go to bed?'

'Shall we go to bed? Shall we go to bed?' a mocking, sing-song voice echoed. Lesnoy had lurched drunkenly up the aisle behind Pavel and had to rest his hand on the Captain's shoulder to steady himself.

'Go to bed? Capital idea, Captain Ozertsov, sir. If I had a gorgeous wife like that, I'd take her to bed in a flash myself.' As Lesnoy lurched on down the carriage, Pavel saw how Ekaterina's pretty mouth was twisted in disgust. What a boorish fellow, he thought in annoyance. No idea how to behave himself in public. Still, if the revolutionaries eventually overrun the country, a man like that could become the Tsar.

CHAPTER TWENTY-THREE

The train trundled on through the forest, over bridges, past snowy farms, iced-up villages. There was little sign of the coming spring. Every night the condensation froze on the inside of the window.

Inside the train Alexander lay alone on his bed, thinking about Tatiana. He had never had these feelings for anyone before. He felt awkward and tongue-tied whenever she was near him, yet he looked forward to seeing her every time he entered the dining car. How strange that he should have fallen in love with a Countess, a symbol of the very society he professed to hate, to want to destroy. If love were logical, he would have fallen in love with Sofia. Sofia was beautiful, intelligent, resourceful - and a member of the proletariat, exploited by the Count and his family. He liked Sofia - liked her a lot. But he didn't love her. He loved Tatiana. He loved her vulnerability, her romantic, poetic soul, her sweet, sad smile. He loved her, in spite of her aristocratic sense of entitlement and oversensitivity, or was it because of those qualities? He didn't know. Nothing made sense, nothing had turned out as it should have done.

But loving Tatiana was also an enormous burden. While on the one hand he felt his heart was almost bursting with love and joy, it was also weighed down by a great, dark boulder of dread. Every day that passed, his feelings for Tatiana grew. Every day that passed, the horrific story of what had happened at the Shuysky Palace weighed heavier on his heart. Naively he had hoped that the further they got from Moscow the easier it would be for him to tell her the truth of what happened during that night of fire and blood.

Alexander had thought about introducing the subject several times. At first it had seemed hard because he didn't know her; then it seemed much harder because he knew her so much better. More than five days after the train had pulled out of Yaroslavsky Station he still had not found the right moment, the right place or the right words to tell her about her father's last moments.

Alexander also felt hampered by not having the Count's letter. He could at least have mitigated the tragic news of Tatiana's father's death if he had been able to pass on a tangible memento to her. He cursed himself for his carelessness in losing it. He still believed it must have fallen out inside the train as he boarded and pulled the money out of his pocket. But how was it that his notebook had been exactly where he thought it would be, but not the letter? He wondered what the letter had said. What would the Count have wished to say to his daughter that he couldn't say to her face? And to Sofia, too? Her name had also been on the envelope, he remembered. It gave him an idea, though. If there were certain thoughts which the Count preferred to convey to his daughter in written form, then surely that was his, Alexander's, best bet as well. Was it a coward's way out? Perhaps, but the thought of having to look directly into Tatiana's beautiful brown eyes and speak those wounding words aloud was too horrible to contemplate. He might as well be stabbing her in the heart.

Yes, he was a writer, a poet, a 'wordsmith' - a term which aligned him more closely with the workers of the world, the revolutionary brothers with whom he desired to stand shoulder to shoulder. Better to play to his strengths.

In 1903 he had left school in what was then still Saint Petersburg and started work as a junior statistician in the Reports Department at the Office of Naval Affairs. He was responsible for collecting telegraph dispatches from the field commanders and using them to compile figures and maps for the Imperial Russian Fleet's daily status bulletin. Not long after he had started work, Japan declared against Russia and every morning he was the first to read the 'status reports' sent by radio telegram from the commanders of the four imperial fleets: the Black Sea Fleet, the Arctic Fleet, the Pacific Fleet and the Baltic Fleet. It fell to Alexander to collect and tally the losses.

After a few months Alexander had to start writing as well as counting. The editor had been demoted for obfuscation and sent to the Office for Naval Archives. Upon his promotion Alexander had been told, or rather ordered, by Admiral Ivan Grossinov, no less, that under no circumstances should he try to hide bad news. 'Lead with the disasters,' he was told. 'Lead with the sinkings, the deaths and mutilation caused by self-inflicted explosions, the latest sailors' mutiny, the supreme incompetence of the officer corps. Then mitigate, inform and try to explain. Never hide anything from me or the high command.'

Alexander had quickly developed a particular skill at this form of communication. His second year at the department in 1905 had seen him apply the rule of 'brutal honesty' almost every day during the war against Japan. Every morning the telegrams from the Pacific Fleet had included bad news. Every day Alexander had introduced his bulletin with the latest naval catastrophe.

Towards the end of the war in September 1905 he had written a series of tragic reports from the Battle of Tsushima. Thousands of sailors had drowned in the Sea of Japan. How was it, then, that one brief missive to one pampered rich girl about the death of one aristocratic old man could be causing him such paralysis?

His pen hovered above the paper as he considered his

opening words. 'Dear Countess Shuyskaya,' or was 'Dear Tatiana,' more appropriate, warmer and more sympathetic? Then he stalled. Where to start? His invitation to read poetry at the Fourth Thursday meeting? Helping Sofia to escape from the baying mob? His attempt to reach the palace and save lives? No, he determined. No, don't bury the bad news. Tell it how it is.

'My dearest Tatiana,' he wrote, 'Your father is dead. I am so very sorry...'

CHAPTER TWENTY-FOUR

Sofia was seated and Tatiana was standing behind her in their compartment, brushing her friend's long blonde hair. 'How do you want me to arrange it tonight? Shall I put it up?'

'Yes please.' She passed Tatiana some hair clips from the table and Tatiana tried her best to pin it up elegantly. She put her head on one side to appraise her efforts. 'Oh dear, Sofia. I never realised what a skilled hairdresser you are.'

'It's just practice, Tatiana, practice. After a few years your fingers will just do it automatically and you won't even have to think about it.'

Tatiana sighed, unpinned the blonde tresses and made another attempt. 'Hmm, a bit better. What do you think? Will that do?

Sofia smiled. 'Yes, that's fine. I'm dining with Mr Tokar tonight. Quite honestly it doesn't bother me what I look like.'

Tatiana looked shocked. 'Dining with Mr Tokar? In that nasty, cold armoured carriage? Why?'

'I feel sorry for him - Mr Zayats told me that Mr Tokar is lonely, with hardly any company all day, eating by himself every evening. Besides, I thought it would give you and Alexander the opportunity to dine *à deux* - I'm fed up

164

with playing gooseberry.'

Tatiana tapped her playfully on the head with the hairbrush. 'Excuse me, Sofia, there's no need - and I'm sure that you are able to put Sacha at his ease better than I can. When we're on our own he gets completely tongue-tied.'

'Well maybe you need to encourage him a little, give him a chance to untie his tongue. He just needs practice, Tatiana, lots of practice!'

In the dining car, everyone else was already seated. Ekaterina and Pavel were dining alone again; Dominic and Inspector Lesnoy were together at another table. Alexander was sitting alone and got up to bow to the girls as they arrived. Tatiana sat down opposite him and Sofia continued down the aisle towards the armoured car.

Mr Tokar visibly brightened as Sofia closed the carriage door behind her.

'Miss Maslova! How delightful! I wasn't sure you'd come - thought you might change your mind about dining in these dismal surroundings with a dull old man like me.'

Sofia smiled charmingly. 'Not at all, Mr Tokar! I'm sure we'll have a very pleasant evening. I have something for you from Mr Zayats.' With a flourish, she presented a copy of 'The Valley of Fear'. 'I believe this is the latest Sherlock Holmes mystery to be translated into Russian. Mr Zayats would like to have it back when you've finished, but he assures me it is such a page-turner that you'll race through it.'

Sofia sat at the little wooden card table which the steward had unfolded in the area next to the cage. She smiled at the banker, who was beaming with pleasure both at the prospect of reading the new Conan Doyle novel and the delight of an attractive young face to admire for the next hour or two.

Back in the dining car, Alexander and Tatiana were so deep in conversation they had barely touched the food in front of them.

'You didn't bring your poetry with you this evening,' Tatiana remarked after the steward had cleared away the plates. 'I was looking forward to hearing you read some more.'

'Oh, I'm thinking of giving up writing. Sofia has convinced me that she could compose a better poem than any of mine!'

Tatiana giggled and joked, 'You know, I wouldn't be surprised if she could.'

Alexander picked up his napkin and pretended to dab tears from his eyes.

'Ah, Sacha, don't cry! I'm sorry; I didn't mean it. Your poems are wonderful.'

Tatiana looked at Alexander fondly and continued, 'Sofia is a surprising person, you know. She can turn her hand to almost anything. I can't imagine how I would have survived these last days without her. She has been part of my life since we were little girls, but I took her for granted for far too long. This last week, though…' Tatiana shook her head and bit her bottom lip, 'This last week…' tears filled her eyes, 'Since that awful night… I simply couldn't have survived without her.'

Alexander suddenly realised that these tears were real. He quickly passed the bright white linen napkin to her as she broke down sobbing. Alexander felt that his own heart was about to shatter into a thousand tiny pieces. He couldn't bear to see her like this. He patted her shoulder in a timid, ineffectual way, like a cat tapping on the surface of a goldfish pond.

'Papa… oh my poor Papa…' she whispered.

Alexander's rapidly throbbing heart skipped a guilty beat. Had she discovered her father's fate? He listened carefully to Tatiana's small voice, 'Oh my poor, poor Papa, when will I see you again?'

No, he thought, she still doesn't know. He would have to be strong and give her the letter he had written describing the final moments in the life of Count Nikolai Shuysky.

Tatiana uncovered her face and took a deep breath. She put down the napkin and dried her tears with a dainty lace-trimmed handkerchief. She looked straight into Alexander's eyes and attempted a smile. He held her gaze, and felt himself spinning down into their dark, deep centres. He wanted to capture that moment in words. Later he would write, '*Like falling into caliginous liquid pools of strong coffee.*'

'I must be brave, mustn't I?' she said in a weak, tired voice. He nodded gently, thinking, yes, yes my beautiful, fragile Tatiana, you must be brave and I must be brutally honest; but I will wait one more day. He took her hands in his and raised them to his lips. He gently kissed her fingertips. She stroked his right hand, tracing a V-shape from the tip of his thumb down and up to the tip of his index finger.

'The poet's hand,' she said. 'Will you write a poem for me, Sacha?' He nodded, unable to speak for fear of betraying all the emotions which were swirling around inside his head and his heart.

'How much longer, Pavel?' Ekaterina was looking out into the dark night. She had pushed aside her plate, less than half eaten. Pavel sighed. 'Ten, eleven, twelve days? I'm not sure. It is one quarter of the way around the world, I've heard. A very long way.'

Ekaterina looked around wearily. 'Such a long way. We have done the right thing, haven't we? We've left our home, everything familiar and we're going to - to what? I don't know what to expect. What will my life be? What will our life be?'

Pavel took her hand and squeezed it reassuringly. 'Remember what is happening in Oryol, in Moscow, all over Russia. What used to be familiar is no longer recognisable; what we thought of as home may have been destroyed. What we left behind - it no longer exists, for us. No going back - remember?'

Ekaterina said nothing, but turned back towards the window. Pavel continued, 'But let's not think about what we've lost. It's nothing compared to what our new life will bring. Just imagine, my dearest: children, a home, friends, freedom. All will be well - I promise you.'

Ekaterina turned to him again, the ghost of a smile lighting her face. 'Thank you, Pavel, thank you for your optimism. You are quite right - all will be well.'

She squeezed his hand in return, fiercely and looked at him as though seeing him properly for the first time. 'The truth is, I will be happy even without any of those things. I will be happy as long as I have you.'

Lesnoy downed the latest in a long series of vodka shots and slammed the empty glass on the dining car table.

'Pass the vodka,' he slurred at Dominic who was sitting opposite him, 'There's a good fellow.' These last words were spoken in English with what Lesnoy obviously intended to be an exaggeratedly upper-class accent. Dominic looked at him coldly and did not respond.

'Come on!' Lesnoy waved his glass aggressively into Dominic's face. 'Isn't that what you say in England? "There's a good fellow"?'

Dominic shrugged and muttered, in Russian, 'Maybe that is what they say in England,' emphasising the word 'they'.

Lesnoy tapped his glass. 'Come on, do you want me to die of thirst?' Dominic stood suddenly and up-ended the empty vodka bottle above Lesnoy's head, 'Sorry "Dear Fellow", it's all gone!'

Lesnoy had flinched as Dominic did this; now he stood up, his swarthy features suffused with rage, grabbed the empty bottle and flung it to the floor where it smashed to hundreds of sharp shards that skated and spun across the dark wooden floorboards. Everyone in the carriage jumped in surprise and fear and Lesnoy looked around slowly and defiantly.

'What's the matter?' Then the look of anger metamorphosed into a sly grin and a mirthless laugh. 'I thought you might all enjoy some entertainment. No? To break the tedious monotony of our endless, endless journey.'

He clicked his fingers loudly and summoned the startled young barman, who scurried over, trembling with fright.

'Come on, come on - clear it up now and bring another bottle.'

The boy disappeared to fetch a broom and a dustpan along with another bottle of vodka which he placed in front of Lesnoy with an obsequious bow. 'I'm afraid this is the last bottle, sir,' he said in a low voice. 'There won't be any more until Verkhneudinsk when we will take on new supplies.'

'Verkhneudinsk? That's two days away at least! How am I meant to tolerate this torture without a plentiful supply of your best Zorokovich? Bah!' He opened the new bottle with a squeak and a pop of the cork against the glass neck and poured himself another generous shot.

The rest of the carriage, who had been reduced to stunned silence for a minute, began, warily at first, to talk again and the murmur of conversation gradually resumed its normal buzz.

Dominic had been appraising Lesnoy coolly during this whole unseemly outburst. Definitely not a 'good fellow' he thought. A loose cannon, certainly, and one who could cause him enormous problems. He wondered how much the Inspector knew. Dominic knew his Russian accent wasn't perfect, but his English identity wasn't a particular secret. Commander Agar had suggested he should try to blend in, given his background and competency in the language. In his official role, keeping an eye on the gold, it was really only while in Moscow that he'd needed to keep a low profile so as not to attract the interest of the revolutionaries. On the train, though, he and Lesnoy were both protecting Imperial Russian interests.

The only real danger, surely, was if Lesnoy knew Dominic's real plan. And how could he? Nobody knew that - not Commander Agar, not General Sir Mansfield Smith-Cumming, not poor old Tokar. The only possible weak link was Boris, his contact at Spassk Primorskiy. But he was far away and neither knew nor cared what Dominic's ultimate intention was, just as long as he got his ten per cent commission for helping with the ambush.

Dominic's train of thought was interrupted by the drunken policeman sitting opposite.

'Mr Zayats - here - let me fill your glass.' Lesnoy, his mood mollified by the trickle of warm vodka sliding down his throat, was now exuding an air of silky bonhomie. Dominic was not prepared to let his guard down. He didn't trust this man. Lesnoy raised his glass and Dominic responded.

Lesnoy leaned forwards, breathing fumy breath into Dominic's face. 'Did you enjoy stories when you were a little boy, Mr Zayats?' Dominic nodded, non-committally. 'Excellent! Of course you did! What stories did you enjoy? What traditional Russian folk tales did your mother tell you, while you sat on her knee by the fire in your dacha in the Russian woods? Eh?'

Dominic's mind was racing, frantically trying to conjure up something buried in his deep subconscious. Years of training, however, ensured that his surface remained composed and cool. 'I was brought up in Sussex, England, but I remember Baba Yaga... The Firebird...'

Lesnoy leaned back in his dining chair, fingertips placed together, nodding and never once taking his gaze away from Dominic's face. 'Yes, yes, very nice stories. But you know what I liked to hear the most? My father used to tell me the story of *The Cherepakha and the Zayats*, Mr Zayats.'

Dominic smiled coolly back at his inquisitor. 'Yes, that

is a good story. The Tortoise and the Hare, the Fox and the Crow, the Dove and the Ant. But they are fables by the Ancient Greek slave, Aesop, not Russian at all.'

Lesnoy wagged his finger at Dominic. 'Aha! I knew you were a clever man, Mr Zayats. A classicist it seems. Did you perhaps read Greats at Oxford?'

Dominic felt as though he were in a game of chess and pondered his next move. Actually, no, this was more like a game of poker. What was his best strategy? He decided to lay his cards on the table.

'No, I read Russian and Arabic. At Magdalen.'

It was Lesnoy's turn to play his hand. 'I am certain that both languages have been very useful in your career at the British Intelligence Service.'

'Indeed,' Dominic acknowledged, curtly.

The tension in the atmosphere was palpable. Was that all that Lesnoy knew? That he was English, working for MI6? Well, he'd soon find out.

Lesnoy continued, 'Excellent, Mr Zayats, or may I call you Mr Hare now that you have been so frank with me?'

Dominic nodded, silently and Lesnoy continued, 'But to return to that fascinating fable... Do you know what I enjoyed most about it? The hare was outwitted by the tortoise. The cocky hare reached the finishing line only to find that the old slowcoach, the tortoise you understand, had got there first and was waiting for him. Now, Mr Zayats or Hare or whatever your name is, I wonder who might be waiting for you at the end of the line, at Vladivostok? Or perhaps the hare will be tempted to cheat and finish the race early?'

Dominic kept his breathing slow and regular, his cool exterior belying his quickened heart rate. He does know something. Well what's he going to do about it? He's leaving the train at Verkhneudinsk. On the other hand, he can send a telegram from there, put someone onto the case.

'No, no, sadly I've got to go all the way. Vladivostok or

bust! I won't get my medal for Distinguished Service from King George unless I deliver the Tsar's gold bullion safely onto HMS Suffolk.'

'Indeed, Mr Hare. And there are no ships at Spassk Primorskiy, are there? No sea. No ships. No medal.'

The lightning dart of fear which shot through Dominic's body left barely a trace, but Lesnoy had a practised eye. Hell and damnation! Dominic thought. I'll have to act. Should I send a telegram myself at the next stop, change the rendez-vous? Or should I deal with Lesnoy? Those were his only options and he didn't have very long to make a decision.

CHAPTER TWENTY-FIVE

Dominic Hare climbed out of bed and searched his trouser pocket for a handkerchief to wipe the condensation from the inside of the window so he could see out. Having done so, he realised that it wasn't just the window which was misted up - a thick fog had enveloped the world outside and it was impossible to see anything at all.

We could be anywhere, he thought. He knew that the train was due to arrive at Verkhneudinsk in around twenty-four hours, but it was going so slowly, crawling along at tortoise-pace he mused ruefully, remembering the previous night's uncomfortable conversation with Lesnoy. Who knows if it would be on time? He had known the weather might throw his plans off kilter, though he'd been thinking more about the snow than the fog. Ah well, he considered, phlegmatically, not much I can do about it. Boris and the local team must be used to all this sort of thing, surely, and maybe the lack of visibility might even work to their advantage. He should send a telegram when the train next stopped, confirming arrangements.

Alexander stirred in his bed, and rolled over, away from the dim window light. Dominic looked at the young man's peaceful expression and smiled indulgently. Should I hide his pistol now, he thought, before he wakes up, or wait until he's out of the room? On balance, the latter was probably a safer bet.

Alexander had been dreaming a happy fantasy in which he and Tatiana were married, with seven rosy-cheeked children, living in a modest wooden dacha in some idyllic forest clearing, where the sun always shone and nobody had ever heard of either the Tsar or Bolsheviks. They lived their own simple, self-sufficient life, with some pigs, an apple orchard and a brook of clear water running through the garden where the children sailed miniature boats made of leaves and twigs.

As he woke, the idyllic dream faded rapidly and reality rushed to fill his consciousness, flooding it with less welcome thoughts. Today is the day, he told himself, firmly. Or at least tonight's the night. He would finish the letter and at dinner he would make an excuse and slip it under the door of Tatiana's compartment on his way to bed. It would be easier for him to talk after she had read his letter.

Pavel had woken early and spent a couple of hours looking at the map of America which Dominic had lent to him. Another vast, wide continent, but surely filled with possibilities from west to east - San Francisco, Chicago, New York - he tried the names out in his mind, hoping for some sudden illumination to tell him where his future might lie.

He was relieved that Ekaterina was sleeping soundly and apparently peacefully. He knew she was troubled by something more than the upheaval of the flight from Oryol and the discomfort of the journey. He was determined to make everything all right for her so she would be happy again. He yearned for the same happy Ekaterina whose radiant smile had so warmed his heart as she walked down the long cathedral aisle at their marriage. Three years ago, yet it seemed like yesterday; or like a lifetime. He frowned slightly, unsure which it was.

Ekaterina woke later than usual. The fog kept the cabin

dim and gloomy. She had lain awake for several hours after retiring to bed the previous night, turning her turbulent thoughts over in her mind again and again. At last they had settled into a kind of peaceful resolution. Do nothing, a soothing voice from deep within her consciousness had told her. Do nothing. It was nothing. It was a different you - it was not you. Relax. You have a new life, you have an opportunity for happiness and peace of mind with the man you love. Anything else is nothing. It does not exist. Do nothing. Do nothing. And with that mantra echoing in her mind, she had finally slipped into a deep, undisturbed sleep.

Sofia checked through their belongings as she did every morning: the bodices at the bottom of the trunk, the papers and money in the carpet bag, the jewellery boxes in the Louis Vuitton case. Everything was just as it should be. She rested the palm of her hand against the inside of the window until she could bear the cold no longer then, mischievously, laid her hand on Tatiana's brow.

'Ouch - you beast,' squealed her friend, woken abruptly from the most delicious dream in which she and Alexander were lined up for a family photograph on the sweeping marble staircase of the Shuysky Palace in Moscow. Alexander and herself at the head of a glockenspiel-like arrangement of miniature Tatianas and Alexanders, all dressed in white lace frocks or sailor suits.

'Come on, lazybones - we'll be late for breakfast.'

'I'm not hungry - you go in without me.'

'Not hungry? You really are love sick. You still need to eat, you know.'

Tatiana groaned, pulled the pillow from beneath her head and flung it at Sofia. 'Leave me alone, Sofia, I was in the middle of a lovely dream and you spoiled it.'

Sofia picked the pillow up from the floor where it had fallen by the cabin door and noticed that underneath was a folded note, addressed to her. She glanced round at

Tatiana who had pulled her blankets right up over her head in an attempt to get back to sleep and carefully opened the letter, trying hard not to rustle the paper.

'I know more about you than you know about yourself. We must speak privately. Tonight, come to my cabin, after dinner. VL'

Sofia felt a hot flush engulf her. VL, Vladimir Lesnoy? What could he mean? 'I know more about you than you know about yourself'. She felt annoyed at his presumption yet at the same time she couldn't help but feel intrigued. She couldn't possibly go alone to his cabin; but at the same time, she had to go - she had to find out what he knew about her. She folded the letter as small as she could and hid it at the bottom of the carpet bag.

CHAPTER TWENTY-SIX

As dinner time approached, Sofia could feel butterflies in her stomach. She had avoided the Inspector all day, ignoring him at breakfast and lunch and staying in her cabin the rest of the time. Tatiana seemed in a good mood. She was trying to persuade Sofia that they should wear some jewellery to dinner.

'Oh, please - I don't mean necklaces and tiaras, just a pair of earrings. I'll wear my diamond and emerald ones that dear Papa gave me and you wear your pearls. It'll make us feel so much better, dressing up just a tiny bit.'

Reluctantly, Sofia retrieved the two pairs of earrings from the case. She clipped on the pearls and looked in the mirror, turning her head from side to side. It was true, the creamy lustre of the pearls lifted her complexion and her spirits.

But her spirits sank when they entered the dining car. They were the last to arrive. Captain and Mrs Ozertsov sat at one table with Mr Zayats. Alexander and the Inspector were sitting opposite each other at another table. Tatiana would want to sit with Alexander but she really couldn't face another evening of Lesnoy's drunken boorishness. Oh well, she thought, and resigned herself to sitting next to the Inspector. She was going to have to speak to him later anyway.

177

Tatiana sat down next to Alexander with a happy smile on her wide mouth. Lesnoy looked pointedly at Sofia and patted the seat next to him. Sofia gave him a cool, half-hearted smile before sitting down. He leaned towards her, murmuring, 'You received my note, I trust, Miss Maslova?' She nodded, looking straight ahead. 'And you will allow me the pleasure of your company later? Alone?' She nodded again, relieved that Alexander and Tatiana were too engrossed in each other to have heard the exchange.

The steward approached their table with menus and looked nervously between them and the other group of diners.

'I am sorry sir, but as I said yesterday, stocks are running low. We have Omul, a white fish from Lake Baikal, two portions of duck, venison and some beef steak. But, unfortunately there is no vodka left and we have just a limited amount of wine. We will be taking on supplies tomorrow morning at Verkhneudinsk. May I take your orders, please, ladies and gentlemen?'

The food arrived and the conversation began to flow. Alexander and Tatiana both looked more entranced by one another than ever. Sofia began to feel less tense in the Inspector's company. He's not so bad when he's sober, she thought. The grilled fish which she and Tatiana had chosen for their first course was really quite fresh and tasty. The wine put a warm glow into Sofia's veins and she began to relax. As the main course was served, however, Lesnoy suddenly got to his feet.

'Excuse me, Miss Maslova, there is something I need from my cabin.'

He returned a minute later with a half bottle of vodka, looking very pleased with himself.

'This is more like it,' he said, settling back into his seat with a satisfied sigh. He gave Sofia a wink. 'I saved a bit of "little water" from dinner yesterday - I knew they were running out.'

Sofia's heart sank. She knew that even half a bottle of

vodka was enough to make him thoroughly antisocial once again.

'My friends, please drink some with me.' The three of them declined politely and the Inspector looked relieved. Sofia noticed he didn't offer any to the other table - probably because he knew Mr Zayats and Captain Ozertsov would take him up on the offer.

Alexander ordered another bottle of wine and they tucked into their main courses - duck breast in a bitter cherry sauce for Tatiana and Sofia, venison stew with dumplings for the men.

'This reindeer meat is a bit chewy,' Lesnoy complained. 'I should have had the steak like the Captain.' He inclined his head towards the other table, where the steward was placing their main courses in front of them.

'Captain, I say, that's a good looking piece of meat you've got there,' Lesnoy called out to them, staring at Ekaterina. Pavel looked round in some surprise at being so rudely interrupted.

'Yes it looks rather good, doesn't it?' He picked up his fork and steak knife and cut into it. 'Very tender, too, and just the right amount of pink in the middle.'

After they had finished their dinner, Sofia returned to the subject of poetry.

'What was the name of that poet you mentioned, the one at the writers' club?' Sofia asked Alexander.

'Boris Pasternak - he published a collection last year called *"Over the Barriers"*. I did have a copy but I couldn't bring it with me - I had to leave in rather a hurry unfortunately.'

The Inspector snorted. Sofia felt herself tense up. He'd finished his vodka and she sensed that his mood was changing.

'Ha! I wondered why your clothes didn't fit. Borrowed from Zayats, I suppose,' he scoffed. Alexander blushed and looked as though he wished the carriage floor would swallow him up. 'What was the big rush, eh? Running away

179

from something?'

Alexander ignored him. He drained his teacup and spoke softly to Tatiana.

'I have something to attend to. Ladies, will you excuse me, please?'

'Of course,' Tatiana sounded surprised and looked concerned. 'Are you feeling unwell, Sacha?' she asked him, quietly.

'No, I'm quite well thank you, Tanya. Just a little tired and I have something urgent to do - some important and difficult writing I must finish tonight. I will see you tomorrow.' He lifted her hand, kissed it and made his way towards the wagon lit.

'Where's he going?' the Inspector boomed as Alexander left the dining car. 'Was it something I said? Ha!' He half laughed and half snorted at his "joke" and once again the three diners at the other table turned to look distastefully at the drunken policeman.

'Mr Zayats! Mr Hare!' Lesnoy picked up his empty bottle and waved it in Dominic's direction. 'Mr Hare! Don't forget that bottle you promised me.'

Dominic ignored this, but Lesnoy repeated himself, louder: 'Don't forget, Hare, Zayats, whatever your name is, you promised me a bottle of vodka.'

'All in good time, Lesnoy, all in good time. I'm still finishing my meal here.'

'I say, Captain Ozertsov!' Lesnoy now seemed intent on interrupting the conversation at the other table. 'Did you enjoy your steak, Captain?' Pavel murmured his assent, but seemed disinclined to pursue the conversation. 'Stuck up cavalry tosser,' Lesnoy muttered. Sofia felt her irritation at Lesnoy's drunken behaviour swell to fill her brain with contempt and anger. How could such an *alkash*, a drunken fool, know anything important about her?

'If you drink any more of that vodka I will not be visiting you tonight,' she hissed at him, hoping that Tatiana, who was looking out of the window, would not

180

hear. Lesnoy looked at her with unfocused eyes, lifted his glass to mock her with a toast.

'Oh yes you will, my dear.' Lesnoy turned towards Ekaterina and called across the aisle, 'May I say, Madame Ozertsova, how very lovely you are looking tonight. Quite good enough to eat.'

Pavel went to stand up; he looked ready to punch Lesnoy, but Ekaterina put out her hand to stop him. 'Ignore him Pavel, darling, he is a drunken idiot.' Ekaterina glanced at her husband and saw how furious he was. 'I'm very tired Pavel, would you mind if I left the table. You mustn't rush - stay and finish your steak.'

Pavel grimaced and muttered, 'I don't think it is a good idea for me to remain in this company much longer. I won't be long, my love.' He stood to let her leave the table and she turned to the other young women. Tatiana, who was now alone on one side of the table, shivered.

'Oh, my dear Tatiana, you look cold,' Ekaterina exclaimed. 'Here, let me give you my shawl - I'm going to my cabin so I won't need it again tonight.'

'Oh - there's no need...' Tatiana began, but Ekaterina had already taken off her shawl and wrapped it around Tatiana's shoulders with a smile.

'There, now you look more comfortable.'

'So kind of you - it's a lovely shawl and what a delicious scent,' Tatiana buried her nose into the shawl. 'I shall wear it all night.'

Ekaterina smiled, 'It is *L'Heure Bleue*, by Guerlain,' and turned to leave.

'Goodnight, Countess, Miss Maslova.' She ignored Lesnoy.

The Inspector was staring at her very deliberately. As Ekaterina moved forward he stuck his knee into the aisle to brush against her dress. She pulled her long skirt in, as if trying to avoid even the slightest contact.

'Goodnight...' Lesnoy said to her. 'Goodnight, Kiki.'

His voice was low, but despite his inebriation he spoke

181

clearly. The effect of his words on Ekaterina was unmistakable. She did not look at him but in profile Sofia noticed the look of revulsion and fury on her face and the way she froze momentarily, her jaw clenched, before sweeping out of the dining car.

Sofia was equally struck by the reaction of the Captain across the aisle. As Lesnoy said 'Kiki,' Pavel, who had been raising his wine glass to his mouth, also froze, his fist clenching the stem of the glass so tightly that his knuckles turned white. As his wife left, he stared across at the Inspector, who was now trying to force Sofia to take his jacket.

'If you're cold, Countess Sofia, I'll keep you warm.' He sniggered at his crude joke, 'You blue-blooded girls have such thin skin. Here, let me lend you my jacket.'

Sofia tutted in annoyance and tried in vain to refuse the offer. 'I'm fine, Inspector, really there is no need...' but he was having none of it.

'No, no, I insist. You can return it later, when it's convenient,' and with that he removed his grey jacket and draped it around her.

'I am tired, Tatiana, shall we leave the men to themselves?' Sofia said.

Tatiana picked up the hint. 'Yes, I am also very tired. Will you excuse us, Inspector Lesnoy, it has been a long day.'

'Oh, yes, off you go, Countess Tatiana, Countess Sofia.'

Sofia opened her mouth to object, but thought better of it and the two girls left.

As soon as the men were alone, Lesnoy waved his hand at Dominic, 'What about that bottle of vodka you promised me, Mr Zayats. Haven't I been patient long enough? You have finished eating and I could drink an ocean!'

Dominic sighed and stood up. 'Very well, Inspector, but I hope you have your roubles ready - it's a very special bottle you know.'

No sooner had he gone than Lesnoy also got up, much to Pavel's relief.

'I'm going to my cabin,' Lesnoy slurred. Pavel nodded but said nothing.

'If you see the English, tell him to bring the vodka to my cabin.'

'Very well,' Pavel murmured, not looking at him.

Lesnoy staggered off unsteadily towards the armoured carriage. Pavel watched him close the door behind and then stood up himself. He stood by the table for a moment then glanced around to check that no-one was watching before swiftly exiting the dining car, leaving it empty.

Alexander had arrived back in his cabin half an hour previously. Thoughts were churning around in his head, chiefly to do with Tatiana and what he had written. He took the letter from under his pillow where he had hidden it, read it through one last time and signed it 'Alexander Zhuravlev'. He did not have a proper envelope, so he carefully folded the paper into a neat triangular package, pressed the edges flat and wrote 'Countess Tatiana Shuyskaya' on one side. Then he opened the door of his compartment, quietly stepped into the corridor and walked the few steps to the door of the next compartment. He crouched down on one knee, as if genuflecting at a holy altar, and slid the triangular package under the door. Despite his professed atheism, the young poet muttered a few words in prayer for the soul of the Count and added a plea for Tatiana to reciprocate his love. Having completed his mission he returned to sit on his bed. His heart was pounding, yet he also felt a strange sense of relief. There was no going back now. She would know the truth about her father's death. She would be upset, of course. But perhaps she would come to him, seeking comfort and consolation? Or would she be more inclined towards 'shooting the messenger'? He sincerely hoped not.

He let his thoughts drift on towards the future. What

would he do now? Having done all that the Count had asked of him, he could - should, even - do the right thing and alight at the next station and take the next train going back to Moscow, where he could rejoin the workers' and peasants' struggle for 'Land, peace and bread'. His heart was telling him otherwise - at least he should accompany Tatiana to Vladivostok, ensure she arrived safely. But then what? She was supposed to be boarding a ship to America, to start a new life in California. Did he want to go with her? No, he was needed here; yes, she was the woman he loved. He shook his head sadly, confused by his conflicting dreams. No, he didn't want to live in America; but, yes, he wanted a life with her.

Perhaps he should think about leaving Russia. Was he safe here anymore? That hateful policeman, Lesnoy, had become more and more threatening, one moment pretending to be charming and interested in his poetry, the next insinuating that he had enough information on Alexander to arrest him and send him to a *katorga* where intellectuals were worked to death in nickel mines or felling trees. Alexander's waking nightmare jolted him back to reality; suddenly he felt very insecure. His greatcoat was hanging on a hook by the door, he patted the outside of the pockets, just to reassure himself of the existence of his pistol. He frowned - he couldn't feel anything heavy or hard. He unbuttoned the internal pocket where he kept it and shoved his hand in. Nothing.

He knelt to look under Dominic's bed. The leather attaché case was there, with the bottle of vodka next to it. Alexander pressed the latches on the case and it clicked open. The passports were still there, also the small vial of liquid, but no pistol - not Dominic's nor Alexander's. He picked up the vial to have another look.

By the time Ekaterina returned to her cabin, her earlier mood of calm resignation had been replaced by one of almost manic desperation. *Ublyudok!* That bastard! she thought, flinging herself onto her bed. How dare he! Why is he trying to ruin my life? He's nothing but an evil sadist. A devil. I can't let him get away with it. She buried her face in her soft, downy pillow and let out a sob of frustrated despair mixed with furious anger. Would it be better if she ended it all? Could she bury her head into the soft pillow and simply stop breathing? Would that work? Would she just drift off into welcome, suffocated oblivion? Probably not, but it had given her an idea.

Tatiana and Sofia arrived back at their cabin door. As they passed the Ozertsovs' room a faint sound of muffled sobs emanated from it and the girls glanced at each other.

'Is Ekaterina all right?' Tatiana asked.

'No, I don't think she is. Did you notice? Lesnoy said something to upset her. I think she probably wants to be left alone. Pavel will be back soon - he'll know how to handle Lesnoy.'

Tatiana opened the door. She hesitated, and bent down to pick something up from the floor.

'What's that?'

'Nothing, I dropped my handkerchief.'

Sofia didn't enquire further, although she thought it had looked like a letter, not a handkerchief. She was too distracted to care very much, wondering how she was going to find an excuse to get away from Tatiana so she could visit Lesnoy.

Tatiana removed Ekaterina's shawl and folded it neatly on the bed. 'I'm so tired, Sofia; I must go straight to sleep. Would you help me to undress?'

Sofia undid Tatiana's buttons slowly and in silence, thinking all the time. As she undid the last one, she said, 'I ought to return Inspector Lesnoy's jacket.'

'All right, I'm going to sleep. Don't wake me up when you get in.'

'I won't be long.'

Sofia left the compartment. Tatiana hurriedly slipped

on her nightdress. Then, her hands trembling, she pulled the folded triangular paper from beneath the shawl and her heart stumbled as she recognised the handwriting on it as Alexander's. She unfolded it, smoothed it flat and scanned the page, expecting to find a poem or a declaration of true love.

A jumble of ugly, cruel words jumped at her from the page: 'father', 'dead', she read, shocked, unable fully to comprehend the meaning. She reread it: 'Your father is dead', 'murdered', 'Viktor', 'revolutionaries', 'fire', 'manservant', 'blood', 'pistol', 'dead'. No! Please, no! she thought. Her heart clenched in agony and her hands were shaking with fear and loss. She read on, 'promise', letter', 'train', 'lost', 'profoundly sorry', 'Zhuravlev'. She stuffed the heartbreaking, brutal letter under her pillow, crawled, sobbing under the bedclothes and cried herself to sleep.

Sofia hurried back to the dining car, hoping to find Lesnoy still there. If he were on his own she wouldn't have to go to his cabin. She felt her face go stony as she saw that he had gone; the restaurant car was empty of passengers. Only the steward remained, clearing debris from the tables. He ducked down and started to look for something under one of the tables.

'Excuse me,' Sofia squeezed past him and continued into the armoured car. She was relieved to find that Mr Tokar was nowhere to be seen, apparently already asleep behind his curtain. She reached her destination, hesitated for a moment, took a deep breath and knocked on the door.

'Come in, darling, come in.' Lesnoy's slurred voice called.

Dominic returned to his cabin to find Alexander asleep. His government issue case was still under his bed, but he could tell that somebody had been sticking their nose in where it was not wanted. The almost invisible layer of talc that he had gently dusted onto the latches had been partially wiped off. That someone, most likely the young poet who was sleeping, or pretending to sleep, had been more inquisitive than careful. He smiled to himself; curiosity killed the cat, maybe the poet too. He pressed the tiny button under the leather handle and released a hidden compartment at the base of the case. Dominic checked inside. Three pistols: his own, Alexander's and Pavel's, all present and correct.

He shut the secret compartment, closed the case, pushed it back beneath the bed and picked up the vodka bottle. He held it up to the light. He and Alexander had only had a single, throat-burning, swig each. Would it pass for a full bottle? He could top it up with water. Then another idea took hold. This is war, Dominic said to himself grimly, and in war, death is inevitable.

A minute later, having pushed the cork back into the bottle as tightly as possible, and twice turned it upside down to ensure it was well mixed, Dominic ensured the door to his cabin closed quietly behind him and made his way to sell Lesnoy the vodka.

The steward was just finishing off clearing up in the dining car.

Dominic nodded at him. 'Good night'.

'Good night, sir. Er, excuse me sir, but was it you who had the steak?'

'No, that was Captain Ozertsov.'

'Ah, yes, thank you sir.'

Dominic shrugged. The exchange seemed a little odd, but he was focused on his own assignment. He passed the caged crates in the armoured wagon - no sign of Mr Tokar - and raised his hand to knock on Lesnoy's door. He hesitated, hearing a voice - a woman's voice, he thought - from within.

He rapped on the door which opened slightly and Lesnoy peered out, his face flushed. Dominic held out the bottle and Lesnoy reached to grab it. Dominic pulled his arm swiftly back. 'Two roubles, please, Inspector'.

'Two roubles? You are joking! One rouble, nothing more.'

Dominic's face remained impassive. 'Two roubles is what I paid for it,' he lied, 'It is top quality, not homemade potato alky; you won't go blind.'

'Oh, yes, yes, very well,' Lesnoy muttered, shutting the door again. Dominic listened carefully but there was no further sound of the female voice. Lesnoy returned and dropped two silver coins into Dominic's hand. 'At that price it had better be good stuff,' he grumbled, shutting the door again. Dominic waited and listened.

'Diamonds… protection… arrangement…' he could hear Lesnoy say. So, there *was* someone else in there. At the sound of the cork stopper being pulled from the vodka bottle, Dominic turned and quietly walked away.

CHAPTER TWENTY-SEVEN

It was the creeping chilly stillness that finally woke Andrey Tokar from his alcohol-infused dream. Day after day, night after night, the train marked its steady progress across Russia with a relentless rumbling, click-clacking and a gentle creaky swaying. At night the train gently rocked Tokar into a deep, restful sleep. Whenever the train stopped, to replenish its supplies of water and fuel, the rhythm, and Tokar's sleep, were broken.

Tokar lay awake on his narrow mattress. Silence descended upon the train. A silence broken only by the occasional calls and distant shouts between engineers and firemen, murmured discussions between station masters and porters.

Tokar fumbled for the gold pocket watch that he kept under his pillow. He popped open the cover by pushing down on the winding crown and squinted closely at the white watch face, barely illuminated by the dim yellowish light that glowed from behind the sooty glass chimney of the oil lamp.

Confused for a moment, he thought that one of the hands must have fallen off, before his befuddled, still slightly drunken brain realised that the hands were almost exactly lined up and it was just past midnight. Tokar kept his watch on Moscow time. He tried to remember which

189

time zone the train would now be in. Yesterday had marked a week since Yaroslavsky Station. So now it must be Thursday morning, six or seven days out of Moscow, and another six or seven days to go before Vladivostok. Yesterday he had glimpsed the vast expanse of Lake Baikal; was Baikal in the Irkutsk or the Yakutsk time zone? Irkutsk, he thought, Moscow plus five, that would make it just a minute or two past five o'clock in the morning local time.

Tokar sighed and sat up. What a strange dream he had just had! He paused; now he was awake he wanted to know where he was. He swung his legs out from under the blankets into the cold. He wrapped his warm blankets around his pale, doughy shoulders and shuffled across the cold wooden floor to the window. He pinched the corner of his blanket between his thumb and fingers and used it to rub a circular spyhole in the frosty condensation that had collected on the inside of the glass.

He peered out, moving his head slightly from side to side to avoid his view being blocked by the iron bars that were securely bolted to the outside of the wagon.

The distant hiss and occasional mechanical clank of the locomotive echoed across the deserted, moonlit station. Tokar could not see the name of station, nor was there anything of the town that might have given him a clue as to its location. The only thing he could see clearly was the silhouette of an ornate onion-shaped dome sitting on top of a church tower. The crunch of boots on the snow-covered platform announced the arrival of the new driver and fireman. A few minutes passed in silence as Tokar looked at the confused pattern of snowy footprints that decorated the platform.

The locomotive's steam regulator released a jet of high pressure steam and the familiar chuffing of the engine resumed. The armoured carriage jerked backwards as the locomotive was reversed from the water tower and re-attached to the front of the train. The impact rattled down from one carriage to the next, like a line of dominoes falling in a destructive wave. Tokar held up his watch to the moonlight and squinted at it once again. Twelve fifteen. The church clock struck once, confirming the quarter hour. Tokar wondered once again where this small town was, quarter past twelve, probably two or three hours from Verkhneudinsk and breakfast.

Tokar looked at himself in the small mirror that he had hung on the wall. He was getting old, too old for this kind of trip. He shuffled back to his bed and lay back down on the now cold mattress.

Fifteen minutes later the church bell struck twice, the locomotive's whistle peeped briefly, the soothing mechanical rhythms of the locomotive restarted and the train began to roll towards Vladivostok. Tokar slipped back into a deep sleep.

CHAPTER TWENTY-EIGHT

At breakfast the next morning, just as the train pulled away from Verkhneudinsk station, the door between the bullion wagon and the dining carriage was pushed open with a bang. The travellers stopped talking and looked at the man who had just appeared in the doorway.

The tall, handsome newcomer was wearing a charcoal grey greatcoat and a low fur *shapka* decorated with the badge of the Imperial double-headed eagle. The crimson shoulder cord that ran diagonally across his chest to the pistol which was holstered on his wide black leather belt indicated that he was an officer of the Imperial Russian Special Gendarmerie. The policeman simply announced:

'Inspector Lesnoy is dead.'

The whole carriage stared at the speaker in shock. The man, Detective Sergei Pravdin, scanned the carriage as he pulled off his leather gloves and removed his fur hat. No screams of terror, no wide-eyed panic, no impassioned denials of involvement, no fingers pointed, no denunciations of fellow travellers. Just a stoic, calm, acceptance of a sad fact. The mouth of the attractive young brunette seated in front of him opened briefly and shut. The young man next to her frowned in disbelief, half rose from his seat and then sat down again. Pravdin made a mental note of their reactions. It was as if he had

192

announced that a number of silver birch trees could be seen from the left hand side of the train.

'Ladies and gentlemen, I should introduce myself. I am Detective Sergei Pravdin of the Verkhneudinsk office of the Tsar's Special Gendarmerie. You are all now officially designated with the status "witness" and also "suspect" in the murder of Inspector Vladimir Lesnoy.'

Ekaterina, Pavel, Tatiana, Sofia and Alexander all sat looking more or less like carp in a glass tank. Only Dominic had a faint smile playing on his lips. When he saw that Pravdin was looking directly at him, he glanced out of the window at the sparse forest, bathed in a hazy, early morning, sunlight.

'Moreover, from this moment the bullion carriage is now a crime scene,' Pravdin continued. 'Nobody is to pass through this door without my express permission. We have approximately six days before we reach Vladivostok. Upon our arrival at our destination it is my intention to pass the murderer into the custody of the Vladivostok Gendarmerie.

'Each one of you will be interrogated. Because the murder was committed on a train, the investigation will be conducted under the Railway Investigation Acts passed by the Duma. Unfortunately, none of you will have access to a lawyer. You all have the right to remain silent, but your silence can and will be used against you in the Tsar's Criminal Courts.

'Finally, the murder of Inspector Lesnoy might well be connected to the large amount of Imperial gold bullion being transported to Vladivostok. Please, ladies and gentlemen, be careful, be observant, report any unusual or odd behaviour to me as a matter of urgency. We are all at risk.'

At that moment, the spell of silence that had descended upon the carriage was broken. As one, each traveller turned to the person sitting next to them and started trying to make sense of what had just been communicated.

'Order, order!' shouted Pravdin. 'Silence!'

Sofia stood up and said, firmly, almost defiantly, 'Detective, I have something to report.'

'Not now Miss,' Pravdin said.

'Please, I must insist. This is important, very important.'

'Miss, please sit down. We can talk later.'

'I want to…' Sofia's voice trailed off to an embarrassed silence.

Pavel raised his hand, somewhat apologetically.

'Yes?' Pravdin asked. His impatience was clear in his tone of voice.

'Are you interrogating everybody on the train? There are hundreds of passengers in second and third-class. Isn't it more likely that one of them is the culprit?'

Pravdin noticed the Pavel's gaunt, hunted look and his wife's odd, nervous habit of plucking at his jacket. A closer inspection revealed that one arm of Pavel's jacket was covered in a light dusting of tiny white feathery filaments. Pravdin replied brusquely, 'The first-class *spalny vagon*, dining car and security carriage are sealed off from the rest of the train. There is no access through from the other carriages. The guard is under strict instructions to keep careful watch each time the train stops to ensure that nobody enters this section without their ticket and identification papers being checked. I have already ascertained from the guard who was on duty last night that absolutely nobody entered from outside.'

Pavel nodded. 'I see, Detective Pravdin, thank you for the explanation.'

'Ladies and Gentlemen,' Pravdin continued, 'I am going to conduct a detailed search of the murder scene. I politely request that you all return to your private accommodation. You will be called one-by-one to account, in detail, for your movements last night, your relationship with the Inspector, may his soul rest in peace, and your background.'

He turned his bright blue gaze towards Sofia.

'Actually, Miss, perhaps you can help me.'

'Yes, of course. That is why…'

Pravdin interrupted her.

'I need a list of everyone who is travelling in this part of the train. Can you arrange that?'

Sofia nodded.

'Once you have written the list, please bring it to me. I will be in Inspector Lesnoy's cabin.'

Sofia nodded. She felt dumbstruck by the detective's piercing eyes and the combined sense of threat and security that he projected. She was both repulsed and attracted to his masculine energy, hypnotised by his power, control and authority. So very different from Lesnoy. This man was not one to be played with.

'Sir,' she said.

'Yes, Miss?'

'Sofia Maslova'

'Yes, Miss Maslova, what is your question?'

'Can I talk to you in private?'

'Miss Maslova. I have given you my instructions. Write a list of all the first class passengers and railway staff that have access to this part of the train and bring it to me. Do not deviate or distract yourself from that task.'

'Yes sir. It is just…'

'Ladies and Gentlemen,' Pravdin boomed, 'I now require you to return to your accommodation.'

Sofia looked at Tatiana. She looked like a ghost: heavy black circles under her eyes; an expressionless face that somehow communicated hate.

'Are you feeling unwell, mademoiselle?' Sofia asked, instinctively falling back into the habit of a servant.

Tatiana shook her head, lips firmly clamped together, and stood up. She looked as though she would burst into tears at the slightest trigger. Alexander looked worried, smiled sadly at Sofia and gently guided Tatiana away from the table.

'Sacha, Sacha,' Sofia hissed, 'Can you give me some paper?' Alexander handed over his notebook and a pen to Sofia. 'Here, you can turn it over and take notes from the back, but please don't lose it - all my poems are in there.

'Thank you.'

'Good luck,' he whispered, giving her an encouraging smile, that frankly, did nothing to make her feel better.

CHAPTER TWENTY-NINE

Left alone in the dining car, Sofia took Alexander's notebook and the pen. She wrote 'Passengers - *Spalny Vagon*', at the top of the page in black ink and underlined it twice.

The first name on her list was Mr Dominic Hare; she paused, the pen hovering over the white paper, and added Dmitry Zayats in parentheses with a question mark and then, after a hyphen, British. She considered placing the word Spy next to the word British, but changed her mind. That was just a rumour, gossip, with no real proof. She had better stick to facts.

Second on her list was Captain Pavel Ozertsov. After his name she wrote Cavalry Officer.

Third was Ekaterina Ozertsova - Wife of Captain Ozertsov.

This was followed by Alexander Zhuravlev - Writer, Poet.

Next she added Tatiana Shuyskaya. What should she put after that? Countess? Aristocrat? Sofia thought about Tatiana's mood that morning. How best to describe it? Sulky, sullen, spoiled baby? Sofia smiled to herself, considered it for a moment and then added 'Sleeping Compartment 2'. She went back to the top of her list and added the appropriate compartment number to each name.

197

Finally she added her own name, Sofia Maslova. How should she describe herself? Housekeeper? Maid? Ex-maid? Diamond smuggler? Killer? She simply added 'Sleeping Compartment 2', put the lid back onto the pen and left it at that.

It was only after she had counted down the list of passengers that she remembered Andrey Tokar. She picked up the pen once again and wrote Andrey Tokar - Imperial Bank official - Own sleeping compartment in the bullion wagon.

Who else? she wondered.

At the bottom of the page she added Staff: Cook, Waiter, Head Steward, Washer-up/Cleaner. She didn't really know any of their names. One of the Stewards was called Kirill, but he had left the train days ago at Mysovaya. The staff seemed to come and go as the train moved across the country. She wrote 'name and location unknown' by each job title.

She blew gently on the ink to dry it, shut the book and stood up.

CHAPTER THIRTY

Detective Pravdin braced himself before entering Lesnoy's cabin, but a sharp intake of breath as he took in the scene indicated that it was even more ugly than he had remembered.

The body lay sprawled on the narrow bed, its dark eyes still open and staring at the ceiling. The thin lips were slightly parted and a slug trail of drool trickled from one corner of the mouth across the cheek, almost reaching the left ear. In the temple above the ear, a neat puncture with a trickle of congealed blood disappearing into the dark hair formed an inverted exclamation mark.

The small table at the end of the bed had two glass tumblers on it. One lay empty on its side while the other still had a finger of clear liquid in it. Pravdin picked up the latter and sniffed at it. Vodka. He put it down and picked up the other glass. He wiped his index finger around the inside, rubbed his finger and thumb together and detected a trace of oily liquid. He lifted his fingers to his nose - more vodka.

Pravdin knelt down gingerly beside the body and looked into the dead policeman's bloodshot eyes. 'God rest your soul, Inspector,' he whispered before he gently closed the cold eyelids, creating an illusion of peace in the corpse. No signs of rigor mortis, he noted mentally. He noticed a few tiny feathers embedded in the drool, but not in the blood. A pillow lay on Lesnoy's chest and, on close examination, Pravdin found a cleanly-cut slit in the cambric cover, about half an inch long. Fine filaments of goose down filling were escaping from this cut.

Pravdin lifted the pillow, examined its underside and ascertained that the slit also appeared there, this time with a blood stain. He placed the pillow at the foot of the bed. A circular blood stain, the mirror image of the one he had found on the underside of the pillow, about three centimetres in diameter, and congealed with more feathers, formed a bull's-eye in the centre of Lesnoy's white shirt. Pravdin carefully undid the shirt buttons and located the corresponding wound in the middle of the chest. The dark hairs surrounding the wound were matted with dark red, almost black, blood, still sticky, but not a huge quantity.

The detective bent his head towards his colleague's mouth, which was partly open. He inhaled through his nose and caught the subtle but unmistakeable scent of alcohol. More vodka, most likely, from the empty glass. He looked around the compartment but couldn't see the bottle. However, he had noticed, as the train rattled its way along, the sound of something rolling around beneath the bed. Sure enough, on lying flat on his stomach to peer into the narrow space, he could see the gleam of glass.

Pravdin tried to reach into the dark recess, but his arm wouldn't quite fit. He stood up, removed his long coat and placed it on the hook on the back of the door. He lay down on the floor once more and tried again. This time he was just about able to insert the full length of his muscular arm and, after scrabbling his fingers around for a while, managed to grasp hold of what felt like a bottleneck. Awkwardly, he rolled away to withdraw his arm. He looked at what he was holding - an almost full bottle of vodka, undamaged, with the seal broken but the cork stopper still in place. He looked closely at the bottle but it seemed unmarked. He estimated that one large shot, or possibly two less generous ones, had been taken from the bottle. This corresponded with what he had noticed in the glasses.

Pravdin heaved himself off the floor and knelt by the bed to continue examining the corpse. This time he began his observations at the feet. Lesnoy was still wearing his boots, trousers and shirt. His jacket, however, had been carelessly discarded on the floor. Pravdin redid the buttons on the shirt and examined the head again. Close to the rivulet of blood, but almost invisible on Lesnoy's swarthy skin and partially hidden in his dark hair, he observed the deep purple stain of a hefty bruise.

Pravdin picked the Inspector's jacket off the floor, shook it and caught sight of a small object falling. He laid the jacket on top of the pillow at Lesnoy's feet and bent to pick up a pearl earring, with a clip-on clasp. He shook the jacket again, brushed it down, examined the lining, but there was nothing else. He prostrated himself again to look under the bed, once again without results. He returned to Lesnoy's jacket, searching in the pockets, and found a box of matches. Lying down with a sigh once more, he lit a match and held it just under the bed. Was it enough to pick up the lustrous gleam of a pearl in the gloom?

There was no sign of a matching earring, but in the flickering light of the match Pravdin noticed a cardboard folder. Just before the flame burnt his fingers, he blew out the match, pulled out the folder and stood up, stretching himself. He sat on the edge of the bunk, next to Lesnoy's booted feet and opened the folder.

Pravdin looked at the bundle of papers inside. On top, an envelope addressed 'To Tatiana and Sofia' had already been opened. He drew out two sheets of writing paper and glanced at them - two separate letters, embossed with an ornate coat of arms and both signed by Count Shuysky. He read the letters, folded them and placed them back in the envelope. Interesting, but what were these letters doing in Lesnoy's possession? He frowned. Sofia was the name of the young woman who had agreed to take notes for him. Was she also the Sofia to whom one of the letters was addressed? Or was that just a coincidence?

He placed the envelope at the back of the file and turned his attention to the rest of the contents. The next item was a leaflet:

Fourth Thursday Meeting
of Progressives and Intellectuals
International Working Women's Day,
6.00pm,
Moscow West Workers' Meeting Hall.
Speakers:
Viktor Skobelev, Valeriya Amosova, Alexander Zhuravlev

Beneath the announcement, the third of three grainy photographs, a young man with dark hair and a serious expression, had been circled in pen. Pravdin looked closely at the face. It looked somewhat like the man who had been sitting at the table with Sofia and who had given her the notebook.

The next two pieces of paper were internal memos from the Moscow division of the Special Corps of Gendarmes. The first was addressed to 'All Departments' from the International Surveillance department:

British agent, Dominic Hare, believed to have arrived in Moscow. Motives unclear - do not challenge - advise immediately if you gain intelligence on this man.

The second memo was addressed to Lesnoy personally:

My dear Vladimir, Grigory tells me you are going to be travelling on the Trans-Siberian railway on the night of 23rd February. Sorry to be a bore, but could you make your presence known to Andrey Tokar, the bank official who is escorting the latest 'cargo'. He is on our watch list and it would be as well to let him know he's being observed. It would save me sending another officer - and with the troubles in Petrograd we need all the manpower we can muster to keep control in Moscow. Kind regards, Kirill.

Under the memos, a letter stamped COPY, not in an envelope:

January 1917
Letter from Grigory Zyuzin, Moscow Chief-of-Police, to Ilya Brilyov, Verkhneudinsk Chief-of-Police.
Esteemed Brigadier Brilyov,
We have recently had a breakthrough in our ten year long investigation of the serial killer popularly known as 'the Potato Sack Killer'. We have reason to believe that he is now living and working in the Verkhneudinsk area and I am sure you will join us in wishing to apprehend him before he carries out yet another heinous crime, this time in your jurisdiction. To this end, I would be grateful if you could be so good as to afford all possible assistance to the senior detective, Inspector Vladimir Lesnoy, who has been leading investigations into this case. He will be arriving in Verkhneudinsk by train in the next few weeks, further details of his travel arrangements to follow. We would request that he is met at Verkhneudinsk by one of your officers of equal rank and accommodated with a desk and lodgings, ideally close to the Office of Gendarmes.
Yours faithfully,
Brigadier Grigory Zyuzin
Chief-of-Police
Moscow

The contents of this letter were no surprise to Pravdin. He set it aside and flicked through the rest of the papers - a thick pile, all relating to the murders: A page headed Index started with March 1907, Spassk, vagrant. Pravdin scanned down the page: April 1912, St Petersburg, ballerina; August 1914, Oryol Oblast, father, mother and three children, the list of murders covered almost half the page. The final item was December 1916, Verkhneudinsk, school girl. Pravdin sighed at the list of inhumanity and closed the folder. At that moment came a tentative tap on the door.

'Just a moment,' he called.

CHAPTER THIRTY-ONE

Sofia took the notebook and opened the door to the carriage carrying the gold. She peered through the bars of the cage, and was relieved that there was no sign of Andrey Tokar. She reached the door to Lesnoy's compartment and tapped at the door.

'Just a moment,' Pravdin's voice called.

As the door opened she caught a glimpse of Lesnoy's compartment, the sunlight making it look a lot less sinister than it had last night.

'Your list, Inspector,' she said, holding out the notebook towards him, 'I have written it on the back page.'

'Ah, thank you Miss Maslova.' He took the notebook and came out of the cabin, shutting the door firmly behind him. 'Let's go and sit down in the dining car where we can look at this properly.'

Sitting at one of the dining tables, opposite each other, Pravdin gazed levelly at Sofia. For the first time he had the chance to inspect her face. Her cloud-grey, rather too wide apart eyes, blonde hair and slim figure made her quite striking. There was something slightly 'other-worldly' about her looks. Beautiful, yes, but not conventionally pretty, he thought. He wondered if she might have the potential to kill. His experience was that men were random

205

murdering bastards, but women, even attractive young women, certainly had the potential to kill, especially if they felt threatened or humiliated in some way.

She briefly met his piercing blue-eyed stare, but looked away immediately. Yes, an attractive girl but excessively nervous, he thought, noting her unwillingness to look at him and the way she twisted a loose lock of hair round her finger.

Pravdin opened the book at the first page.

'The list is at the back,' Sofia repeated.

'Yes, you told me already. I was just curious about why.' He read aloud:

Oh, Russian mother, your sons have gone,
Your sons have gone, your sons have gone.
They have gone to fight each every one,
Each every one, each every one.
The river of blood runs in the red gutter,
The flag drips the bitter crimson of every son's life,
Of every son's life, of every son's life.

'Did you write that, Miss Maslova?'

Sofia blushed, 'No, no Inspector. I think that must be Alexander's work. This is his notebook; he kindly said I could make notes in the back.'

'"...*the bitter crimson of every son's life*..." Quite an imagination your friend Alexander has.'

'Yes, he is very poetic. A romantic with a *Russkaya dusha* and a sense of social justice.'

'A "Russian Soul", eh? You mean he is a revolutionary?'

'We live in a time of change, Inspector. Who knows what tomorrow will bring?'

Pravdin smiled slightly at Sofia's deflection of his question. 'Indeed, Miss Maslova. An age of change, what a charming way to describe chaos and anarchy.' Pravdin turned the notebook over and opened the back cover.

Sofia thought she could hear her own heart pounding in the silence as Pravdin looked through the list, running his index finger under each name in turn and occasionally pausing or tapping his finger at some detail. Eventually he reached the end of the list.

'What does this mean - "unknown"?'

'I don't know their names, Inspector. The problem is that these people change every few days. The staff who served us last night were replaced by a different crew at Verkhneudinsk.'

'I see. I will have to telegraph from the next station and ask my colleagues to interview the railway employees who disembarked there last night. Did you notice any of the waiters or stewards behaving in a suspicious manner? Do you know of any motive any member of staff might have had to murder a police inspector?'

'Well...'

'Well what?'

Sofia took a deep breath and finally forced herself to return Pravdin's steady gaze.

'Well... do you remember I said I wanted to tell you something?'

'Ah yes, something to do with the murder?'

'Yes, you see it was... well I didn't mean... but I did...'

Pravdin said nothing; his face remained impassive as he looked into Sofia's wide-set grey eyes which were now glistening with emotion.

'*I* killed Inspector Lesnoy!' There - she had said it! The pent-up relief of confession overcame her and she buried her face in her hands.

Pravdin remained silent and Sofia, who had half-expected him to secure a pair of handcuffs around her wrists instantly, eventually raised her head to look at him again. Was she imagining it, or was there just the hint of a wry smile on his face.

'*You* killed him? How?'

'I hit him very hard on the side of his head. With a

207

bottle of vodka.'

'Vodka?'

'Yes, and he collapsed.'

'I see. And may I ask *why* you attacked my colleague, Miss Maslova?'

'Yes, I can explain, of course. I want to explain. I need to tell you exactly…' Sofia's words were spilling from her lips faster and faster and Pravdin sensed her mounting panic. He made a 'slow down' gesture with his hands. 'Stay calm, Miss Maslova and speak slowly. I need to take notes.' He took the pen from where she had left it on the table, unscrewed the cap and turned over the page in the notebook.

'I suggest that you start at the beginning.'

Sofia looked embarrassed. The story she had to tell was not going to make her look good.

'At dinner last night…'

'That's not the beginning.'

Sofia looked puzzled. 'Where should I start?'

'Please start at the very beginning. I need to know about you, who you are, your background, why you are travelling on this train and so forth.'

'I am Sofia Ivanovna Maslova. I live and work, or rather I lived and worked, at the Shuysky Palace in Moscow. I was the housekeeper there and also personal maid to Countess Tatiana Shuyskaya.'

'Her maid?' Pravdin interrupted. He sounded a little surprised.

'Yes. Countess Tatiana was my mistress.'

'The girl with the dark hair?' asked the detective; his eyes seemed to drill deep into Sofia's soul, 'And how long have you been in service?'

'Well, I suppose you could say almost twenty-three years.'

'Twenty-three? You hardly look old enough.'

'I was born into the service of the Shuyskys. My foster parents worked at the Shuyskys' dacha. I owe everything to the Shuysky family.'

'You do know that Tsar Alexander II banned serfdom fifty-five years ago, don't you?'

Sofia nodded sadly.

'Yes, inspector, I know that's why he is called The Liberator. But banning an institution, proclaiming laws against it, does not change the culture. That takes longer, much longer. I speak like a slave or, as you suggest, a serf because, in truth, that is what I am.'

'Miss Maslova, as you said yourself, the world is changing. There is no need for you to be haunted by the spectre of slavery.'

'Easy for you to say. A man, a policeman, with the authority to send this person to jail or that one to a *katorga*.'

Pravdin sighed. 'Please continue with your story.'

'My confession.'

'Your confession, then. Please continue.'

'Just eight days ago the palace was attacked by a gang of militant Bolsheviks. Countess Tatiana and I escaped, just in time.'

'How did you manage that?'

'We had already made a contingency plan. We passed through a hidden door in the garden wall and were met by a troika that took us to Yaroslavsky Station. We were lucky, I think, to escape with our lives.' She looked directly, almost defiantly, he thought, at Pravdin.

'Very melodramatic, Miss Maslova. What happened next?'

'We boarded the train and it left Moscow at 11.15 that night. The following day we met our fellow *spalny vagon* passengers in the dining car. We dined with different people every evening. Inspector Lesnoy seemed to take a special interest in me and Tatiana.'

'A special interest?'

'Yes, he knew a lot about the family. Actually it turned out that we had played with him as children. His father was the Shuysky's family doctor. His father was there the day I was born.'

'An extraordinary coincidence. And what form did this "special interest" take?'

Sofia blushed and looked away again, staring out of the window at the snow-covered landscape.

Nearly a minute passed. Pravdin said nothing.

'I'm sorry…'

'No, no, it's quite all right. Please take your time, Miss Maslova, we have plenty of it!' Pravdin smiled encouragingly, gently.

'He seemed… well I suppose he seemed to… to like me,' she shook her head in embarrassment. 'It sounds conceited, but…'

'No, not at all, Miss Maslova. You are merely stating what you observed, which is exactly what I need you to do. You are, if I may be so bold, an attractive and intelligent young woman. It would be quite natural for any man to find you interesting and to enjoy spending time in your company.'

Sofia finally allowed herself to smile back, briefly. She felt relieved that he was taking her so seriously. Quite different from Lesnoy's lewd and unsubtle flirtatiousness.

Pravdin continued, 'So you spent some time in the Inspector's company over those first days on the train. Was anything different on that final evening, the evening he died?'

'The evening I killed him, you mean,' Sofia looked defiant again.

'The evening you believe you may have killed him, yes.'

'That morning, just before breakfast, I discovered a note had been pushed under the door to our compartment.'

'A note from Lesnoy?'

'Yes, it said: "I know more about you than you know about yourself. We must speak privately. Tonight, come to my cabin, after dinner. VL"'

'Those were the exact words?'

'Yes. I read it over and over, so many times that I know it by heart. I still have the note if you want to see it. I hid it in my luggage.'

'And what were your thoughts when you read it?'

'I was angry.'

'Angry?'

'Yes, angry at his presumption, but also intrigued.'

Pravdin nodded. 'Yes, I can understand both those emotions. Anything else?'

'Maybe embarrassed.'

'Why embarrassed?

'At his low opinion of me. His expectation that I would go alone to his cabin. I am not that sort of girl.'

'But you decided to comply with his request?'

'I don't remember "deciding" exactly. I felt I had no choice. Nobody wants someone else to know a secret about them when they don't know it themselves.'

'Of course not. So you went after dinner? Didn't the Countess try to stop you?'

'I made an excuse about returning Lesnoy's jacket which he had lent me.'

'And you went alone, late at night, to the sleeping compartment of a man who, by your own admission, was attracted to you?'

'Inspector, please believe me - I would never normally go alone to the private quarters of a gentleman. I am not proud of my unladylike behaviour. But I felt curious.'

'Miss Maslova, I am not a member of the moral police. There is no law in Russia that forbids a woman to be alone with a gentleman in his quarters. It might not be appropriate, but if you are confessing to being alone with Lesnoy, I can tell you now that you won't have to serve a single day in prison. However, if you are confessing to his murder... well murder is quite a different matter.'

A silence descended between them.

Sofia looked out of the window and sighed.

211

'It wasn't murder. I did kill him, but it wasn't murder.'

'What was it, then? An accident?'

'Yes, an accident - self-defence.'

'But he asked you there to tell you something. What was it he wanted to tell you?'

'I don't know. I... he... it all happened before he told me.'

'Go from where you arrived at his compartment.'

'He opened the door and said, "Ah! I knew you wouldn't be able to resist my invitation." I replied, "I have come to return your jacket; please say what you want to say quickly so I can return to my mistress. She is waiting for me."'

'And then?'

'He laughed in a very unpleasant way and said, "Your mistress? I have something to show you - but you have to come in."'

'So you went in?'

'Yes, reluctantly. He shut the door and picked up a folder from his bed.'

'Did he show you the contents of the folder?'

'No. He waved it in front of me and said, "I have good news, my dear Sofia," then someone knocked on the door. It was Mr Zayats. He had brought the bottle of vodka which he had promised to Lesnoy.'

'Mr Zayats?' Pravdin suspended his note-taking and turned back to the passenger list. 'Dominic Hare?'

'Yes. He asked Lesnoy for money. Lesnoy put the folder back on the bed and went to get his wallet.'

'Did Mr Zayats see you?'

'I don't think so. Lesnoy only opened the door a crack and I was behind it. He put his finger to his lips to tell me to keep silent.'

'Then Mr Zayats went away?'

'Yes. Inspector Lesnoy opened the vodka and poured two glasses, gave one to me and said, "Perfect timing! Now we can celebrate! *Na zdorovie*!" Then he drank his in one go. I put my glass down and said "Just say what you have to say so I can go."'

Pravdin, rapidly taking notes, heard a change in Sofia's voice. He laid the pen down and looked at her, concerned.

'Do you want to stop, Miss Maslova?'

Sofia shook her head and took a deep breath. 'No, I want to get this over with. Lesnoy said "Perhaps you'd prefer to celebrate in a different way," then he attacked me.'

'Attacked you? Did he hurt you?'

'Well, not exactly, not immediately. He grabbed my shoulders and…'

'Wait a moment, I need to understand exactly how this "accident" as you call it, happened. Please would you stand up, Miss Maslova.'

Slowly, reluctantly, Sofia rose from her seat and Pravdin did likewise.

'Let us say that this empty glass is the bottle and the small table here is the table at the bottom of the bed. These chairs are more or less where the bed is located. Now you stand in position so I can see where you were in relation to the bottle.'

Sofia thought for a moment, then stepped into place.

'Now, imagine that I am Lesnoy. Where should I stand? In front of you? Facing you?' Sofia nodded. 'A little further back?' Sofia shook her head. 'A little nearer?' She nodded again, unable to speak as Pravdin stepped close enough for her to touch him.

'Then you say he grabbed your shoulders. Will you permit… I'm sorry, I don't wish to distress you, but will you allow me?'

Sofia nodded again, unable to look him in the face as his strong fingers firmly, but gently held her shoulders.

'And then? You hit him because he touched you?' Pravdin laughed, 'I am not convinced that this level of physical contact constitutes an attack, Miss Maslova. Or did he go further?'

213

Sofia bit her lip and nodded.

Pravdin's expression became more serious. 'I realise that this is distressing for you, but I wish to help you, so it's important for me to understand exactly what happened.'

'He pulled me towards him.'

'Like this?' Pravdin's left cheek was now just an inch or two from her own. She noticed his shirt collar was just beginning to fray, how neatly his left ear was shaped and the pleasant aroma of wood smoke and cinnamon scented cologne.

'Yes,' she whispered, 'He tried to… he tried to kiss me.'

Pravdin turned his head infinitesimally towards hers and for a split second Sofia thought he was going to kiss her neck. A tidal wave of desire flooded through her and she gasped out loud. At the same moment the detective stepped back with an embarrassed look on his face.

'I'm so sorry, Miss Maslova, I didn't mean to startle you.'

Sofia was astonished to find herself smiling at him. A ridiculous feeling of happiness came over her.

'No, no, Detective Pravdin. It's quite all right. I understand that you need to reconstruct the crime. It's for my own good, isn't it? To establish that I acted in self-defence. Please, let me show you.'

She stepped back into position. Pravdin continued to stand, looking slightly embarrassed. Sofia reached out, took his hands and placed them on her shoulders. 'When he tried to kiss me, I slapped him.' Sofia made as if to slap Pravdin, stopping just short of his cheek. The detective flinched, almost imperceptibly, but Sofia noticed the twitch in his eyelid. 'Then he grabbed me by the throat and bit my ear.'

Pravdin touched her left earlobe. 'I can't see any teeth marks.'

'No. I was wearing earrings - clip-on pearls. He hurt his teeth on the metal clasp and got angry. He spat out the earring and started squeezing my throat, tighter and tighter until I couldn't breathe.'

Pravdin placed his fingertips lightly on either side of Sofia's neck. 'I don't wish to hurt you, Miss Maslova, so I won't squeeze, but is this how you were standing?'

'Yes, he squeezed and squeezed. I thought I was going to die. Then I remembered the vodka bottle. I reached out, like this,' she stretched her fingertips towards the glass and picked it up.

'With your left hand?' Pravdin gazed directly into her eyes and Sofia looked steadily back at him.

'Yes, but I transferred it into my right hand, to get a stronger swing. Like this.' She passed the glass behind her back and swapped it to her right hand.

'Then you hit him?' 'Yes.'

Sofia moved the glass in slow motion towards the side of Pravdin's head and tapped it lightly on his temple.

'That's not very violent, Miss Maslova,' Pravdin smiled.

'I don't want to kill another policeman, Detective Pravdin. Then I really would be in trouble! No, I picked up the bottle by the neck and swung it at the side of his head. I hit him hard. He let go of my throat and fell back onto his bed.'

'And you felt for a pulse? Checked his breathing? Confirmed that his pupils would not constrict with bright light?'

'No, I ran away. He looked dead. I thought he *was* dead.'

'And you didn't even stop to pick up this?' Pravdin reached into his jacket pocket and pulled out the pearl earring.

'No - may I…?' She reached out for the earring but Pravdin shook his head and moved it out of her reach.

'I have to keep this, as evidence,' he said, firmly.

'I see.'

There was a moment's silence while they each tried to assess what the other was thinking.

215

Sofia spoke first. 'Evidence of… of self-defence?'

'Perhaps. It's a pity that nobody witnessed your fight with Lesnoy. If your story about a violent struggle could be corroborated, your defence would be a lot stronger. Unfortunately, as it stands, it is your word against that of a corpse.'

Sofia looked crestfallen. Then a thought occurred to her. 'Perhaps Mr Tokar heard what happened.'

'Mr Tokar?'

'The bank official.'

'Why might he have heard you?'

'Well, he sleeps right next to Lesnoy's compartment.'

'Next door?' Pravdin seemed surprised. 'Was he definitely there last night?'

'Yes he is always there. He is locked into the cage and sleeps in the area behind the curtain.'

'Locked in?'

'Yes, one key stays in Moscow, the other is in Vladivostok. There is no way in or out. It is the perfect system to protect the gold.'

'Well, we ought to visit this Mr Tokar, but we have done enough for today. You go back to your compartment. Please inform the other passengers that dinner will be served as normal at the usual time, but no discussion about the case will be allowed. Tomorrow morning we will interview Mr Tokar. Let's see what he has to say about your fight with Inspector Lesnoy.'

CHAPTER THIRTY-TWO

Sofia passed down the corridor and knocked at each compartment door, relaying Detective Pravdin's instructions. Finally she knocked on the door of her own compartment and, not hearing any objection, opened the door. Tatiana was sitting on the bed and Alexander was standing by the window, leaning against the wall.

'We need to talk…' the young Countess began.

'Tatiana, I am really not in the mood.'

'Well I am, and you need to hear what Alexander has to say.'

Sofia turned to Alexander, who looked worried.

'Well, Sacha, tell her.'

'Tell me what?'

'Tell her Sacha, tell her about the night of my birthday ball. You *destroyed* my life, Sofia. My dear father, my beautiful home, my status, everything. You *sooka*, how did I trust you? We gave you everything. My dear father, may he rest in peace, he treated you like a daughter. You are nothing without the Shuyskys. And this is… how… how could you…' Tatiana broke down in tears and Alexander moved to comfort her.

'May he rest in peace?' Sofia asked in shock. 'What do you mean?'

Alexander turned to her. 'Viktor, your friend from the

217

Women's Day meeting, killed the Count. I was there.'

Sofia stared at him, in disbelief.

'My God, I prayed that it would not happen. How sad.'

'How sad?' Tatiana said calmly, wiping away her tears.

Sofia could already tell this was going to end badly.

'*How sad*?! Bitch, killer, *sooka*! *You* led that bloodthirsty mob of criminal socialists to the palace. You idiot, *dura*. You have destroyed everything. Hiding your evil plan behind your fake concern, looking down at our generosity, our care, my friendship. My father loved you. He loved you Sofia. And this is how you repay him. You go to some Bolshevik meeting and help a gang of drunken ruffians invade my precious home. Attack my precious father. Kill him. Kill him, do you hear? Burn the palace down. Two hundred years of history turned to smoke and cinders in minutes. Your friend Viktor did it, but you might as well have fired the shameful shot into Papa's poor generous heart yourself. I can never forgive you, you troll!'

Sofia stared blankly at her former mistress and erstwhile friend. The Count was dead. Tatiana was right: Sofia had caused the trouble, she should have known Viktor was up to no good. She had been a fool. A stupid *dura*. Sofia looked at the floor in shame. Tears welled up in her eyes. The first fat drop slipped through her eyelashes and rolled down her cheek. Many more followed; they ran down her face and dripped off her chin. She looked back at Tatiana and whispered '*Prosti*, I am sorry.' She wiped the drips away from her face with her hand, turned and left the compartment.

'*Sooka*!' screamed Tatiana as Sofia pulled the door shut.

CHAPTER THIRTY-THREE

The following morning, after breakfast, Pravdin and Sofia went to interview Andrey Tokar in the bullion carriage.

'Mr Tokar? Are you there?' The detective gripped the thick wrought iron bars and looked at the pine wood boxes all branded with the double-headed eagle of the State Bank of the Russian Empire.

'Is that the gold?' he asked Sofia.

'Yes, I believe it is.'

'My God, that must be worth a fortune.'

He shouted again, 'Tokar, Tokar, I am Detective Sergei Pravdin of the Verkhneudinsk Gendarmerie. Please show yourself immediately.'

A grumbling and grunting indicated that the bank official was alive and, by the sound of it, getting dressed. Pravdin looked at Sofia.

'Is everything alright Miss Maslova? You look tired.'

'I did not sleep well, I must look a mess.'

Pravdin smiled as he remembered the reenactment they had done the previous day. 'I should apologise for yesterday. I am sorry if I behaved in a way that disturbed you. I hope that you did not suffer from nightmares last night.'

'No, no, Detective, it was nothing to do with that,' Sofia stammered. She felt her customary blush creep up

219

her neck as she recalled how his hands had gripped her shoulders and the way he had stepped towards her during their reconstruction of her self-defence. They smiled sheepishly at one another.

'It was very helpful, to understand what happened.'

Sofia heard herself say, for no real reason, 'Thank you Detective.'

Pravdin banged on the iron bars. 'Mr Tokar, Imperial Gendarmerie here. Show yourself immediately.' He winked at Sofia who wished he would stop looking at her.

Finally, after some more grunting and huffing, Andrey Tokar appeared from behind the curtain which screened off his sleeping area.

'A fine bedroom you have,' said Pravdin, nodding at the boxes of gold. It looks as though you still have a lot of unpacking to do.'

Sofia smiled; she realised that she liked this detective. She wondered if he was married and found herself feeling schoolgirl happy that there wasn't a ring on his finger.

'May we come in?' Pravdin asked.

'Into my prison?' said Tokar, tucking his shirt into his trousers. 'No, nobody comes in and I can't get out.' He smiled ruefully, 'I am almost certainly the richest "prisoner" in the world, but nevertheless, I am a prisoner, and at the moment I'd give anything to escape from this damned money cage.'

'May I present Miss Maslova to you,' Pravdin said, sweeping his hand towards Sofia and accidentally on purpose brushing her hand with his.

'Yes, yes, I have had the pleasure of meeting the beautiful Miss Maslova. After three days of silence I was starting to go mad. I asked the steward to tell the first class passengers that I would welcome some company. Miss Maslova and I have discussed all sorts of topics - music, art and the revolution - at some length. Crime fiction too, Detective. Sherlock Holmes in particular.'

'Don't forget your castle in Spain,' Sofia interrupted.

Pravdin raised his eyebrows enquiringly. 'We played a game where we imagined what we would do if we actually owned the gold in these boxes. Mr Tokar said that he'd buy a castle in Spain with a prize-winning herd of fighting bulls.'

'You remembered my ambition? Let me see if I can return the compliment. Miss Maslova said that she wanted to go to America, live in an luxury apartment in New York, and also in a villa with a private swimming pool in Los Angeles. And drive a Buick. Correct?'

Pravdin cleared his throat. 'Well, I'm sorry to interrupt these enjoyable fantasies, but perhaps we could return to the less hospitable Siberian climate. As I mentioned, Mr Tokar, I am Detective Sergei Pravdin of the Verkhneudinsk office of the Gendarmerie. I am here on police business. Did you know that my colleague Inspector Lesnoy was murdered on Wednesday night, in the very next compartment to yours?'

'Yes, I heard that awful news. Do you know who did it?'

'Not yet Mr Tokar, but rest assured that I am carrying out the fullest possible investigation. Now, I have asked Miss Maslova to act as my secretary, my note taker. I have some questions for you. You understand that everything you say will be recorded in evidence. And what you say can be used in a court of law?'

'Of course Detective, ask me anything. I didn't know your colleague, Lesnoy, very well, but he seemed a decent enough man.'

'Clearly, Mr Tokar, your particular circumstances mean that you are not a suspect in my investigation. You see, being locked into a cage has some advantages after all.'

Tokar gave a sad smile. 'What can I tell you, Detective?'

'You are an employee of the Imperial State Bank?'

'Yes, the State Bank of the Russian Empire. I am head of one section of transport security, specialising in railway transport. It is a good job, a responsible job. Yet one that

221

necessitates my travelling in quite primitive conditions, as you can see, for some weeks every year. However the armoured trains and the detachment of Czech guards keep me, and the gold, safe and sound.'

'Is it standard operational practice for a detective from Moscow to accompany you on these trips?'

'No, no, he wasn't associated. I mean, Inspector Lesnoy wasn't anything to do with the logistical operation that I am managing. He told me that he was on his way to arrest a multiple killer, one whom he had tracked for several years across Mother Russia. Of course it was quite satisfactory to have another officer of state to accompany the bullion transport, but he had no official role in the operation.'

'So why was he allocated the sleeping compartment next to yours?'

'Well, as I said, having a officer of the Gendarmerie sleeping next door is an asset. The station master at Yaroslavsky station asked me if I would mind Inspector Lesnoy sleeping in the bullion transport carriage; I said that I found that arrangement quite satisfactory. You see Detective Pravdin, the biggest dangers of these long trips aren't Cossack brigands or Bolshevik bandits but boredom and loneliness. Suicidal thoughts are never far away. The incessant snow and forest, the milky sun, the awful food... Vodka keeps the demons at arm's length, but she can be a *sooka*. One of my colleagues killed himself last November. Since then the first class passengers have been allowed, encouraged even, to visit the bullion wagon and to engage the security controllers in conversation.'

'Mr Tokar,' said Sofia, 'I think that I speak for all my fellow passengers when I say how much we have enjoyed making your acquaintance. Being locked in a cage with all this wealth must be so boring. What happened to your colleague is very distressing. I can't imagine what it would be like to be isolated from other humans for weeks at a time.'

Sergei nodded in sympathetic agreement with Sofia. 'Tell me a little about yourself, Mr Tokar. What is your background, where do you come from?'

'My father worked at the Royal Mint in St Petersburg; *his* father was a silversmith in Moscow. Precious metals run in my blood. I attended technical school in Moscow before joining my father at the Mint. I was lucky. I got promoted from the smelting floor to the Imperial Bullion Depository. Transferred to Moscow. What else can I tell you, Detective?'

'How often have you made this trip?'

'Many, many times. This is my third trip from Moscow to Vladivostok since this time last year. I escort the bullion out and hand it over to the American consul general, or sometimes, as on this occasion, to the Captain of an English Royal Navy battlecruiser, at the quayside in Vladivostok. Our foreign friends sign the chitty to confirm that they have taken charge of the gold and they arrange for it to be loaded onto the appropriate ship. From Vladivostok it goes to San Francisco in the United States or to England. In return they supply the military material needed to fight a modern war against the Germans. Guns, ammunition, uniforms, boots, trucks, petrol, even tanks. Without the gold and the support it buys we would be finished. Even the mercenaries of the Czech Regiment who guard this train need bread and guns. The sad reality is that either the Germans or the Bolsheviks would have taken over the Russian Empire many months ago without our vast reserves of gold.'

'Was anything out of place, has anything unusual happened this trip?'

'Apart from having an officer of the Moscow Gendarmerie living next to my cage, nothing. The food has been slightly better than previous trips, and we ran out of vodka, but apart from that everything has been quite normal.'

'The vodka ran out? Tell me about that.'

223

Sofia interrupted, 'On Wednesday the last bottle of vodka was served.'

'Not the last. As a senior officer of state I was offered the last bottle of Zorokovich. I can claim such necessities on expenses so despite the outrageous price charged by the steward I bought it.'

'When was this?'

'Wednesday after lunch. I am ashamed to tell you that I drank alone that afternoon and into the night. It was my wedding anniversary. I felt rather melancholic and lonely, so like all good Russians I fell into the warm embrace of mistress vodka.'

'You are married?'

'Yes to the love of my life, Anna. I miss her very much when I am away for so long.'

'So you were drunk on the night of Inspector Lesnoy's murder?'

Tokar nodded sadly. 'I was at best semi-conscious. The vodka gave me the "dreaded rotor", you know, when the ceiling slowly twists this way and that. Eventually I slept. I had the strangest dream that night. The Zorokovich must have been tainted with ergot. I dreamed about a baby pig at a circus.'

Sofia laughed 'That sounds entertaining. What happened?'

Pravdin brought the focus back to the investigation. 'While I am fascinated by your amusing porcine dreams, I prefer to take the investigation one step at a time, please. Mr Tokar, tell me what happened after dinner. You dined on your own that evening?'

'Yes, well, as I said, I was melancholic. I didn't want to mix with the others. I had the fish and then the reindeer *shashlyk*. I finished the bottle of vodka and went to bed.'

'So Tokar, am I correct to understand that by this time you were blind drunk?'

'I was, but I do remember some comings and goings.'

'Comings and goings? Elaborate please.'

'The first thing I remember was a woman talking to Lesnoy. Then Mr Zayats, the Englishman, knocked on the door and I clearly remember the sound of a bottle being opened. What else? A fight, yes. I think I heard a woman shouting 'No, no, stop it, get off me. Or maybe that was the pig squealing in my dream. Oh yes, I do remember. I smelled a perfume - *L'Heure Bleue.*'

'You have smells in your dreams? Is that possible?' Sergei looked at Sofia and smiled his blush-inducing grin. 'How can you be so sure it was *L'Heure Bleue*? I presume that is the name of a perfume?'

'Yes, it's French - by Guerlain. Last November, I went to a conference of National Mints from all over the world which gathered at the *Monnaie de Paris*. While I was there I bought a small bottle of *L'Heure Bleue* for my wife. I have the scent imprinted deep in my brain.'

'Ekaterina - Mrs Ozertsova - uses *L'Heure Bleue*,' said Sofia. 'Why would she be visiting the Inspector so late at night?'

The banker and the detective smiled knowingly at each other. 'Well at least he didn't die of loneliness!' Tokar quipped.

'No, his cabin seems to have been quite the *Nevsky Prospekt*. So the last thing you remember, before the dream, was the perfume?'

'I seem to remember that a door opened and shut. Just a click and a squeak. But that was after the perfume, I am sure of it.'

'Thank you Mr Tokar. You have been most helpful. I assume that if I need to talk to you again you would not object?'

'Not at all Detective. I am locked up here. I crave human contact, so of course I remain at your service.'

'Detective Pravdin, we didn't hear Mr Tokar's dream,' Sofia said.

'Mademoiselle Maslova, in the ten years I have served in the Tsar's Gendarmerie I have never solved a crime with the help of a dream interpreter, a ouija board, a Baba Yaga's mushroom tea, nor one of those drumming Siberian Shamans.'

'Well I'd be interested in hearing it,' said Sofia.

Pravdin shook his head in exasperation but smiled indulgently. 'Oh, very well, then - go on, Mr Tokar, you have a captive audience in Miss Maslova.'

Tokar looked delighted to have the opportunity to recount his dream. 'I was in a park like the Hermitage Gardens in Moscow. We, that is Mr Zhuravlev, Captain Ozertsov and myself, chased and caught a baby pig which, for some reason was dressed as a clown. It was wearing a ruffle around its neck and a conical white hat with black pom-poms on its head. We decided to take it back to the circus. A huge circus tent had appeared in the park. Once we arrived we all seemed to have become circus clowns. The ringmaster, who looked very like Countess Shuyskaya, cracked a whip and told us to load the baby clown-pig into a big circus cannon, you know, like the one they use to fire young women into a net. My goodness the pig was squealing as she was put into a cannon, she really wasn't happy. A tall half-naked muscle man, with the face of my boss, rang a countdown on a huge brass gong. Ten, nine, the crowd was going wild with excitement, eight, seven, screaming and shouting, six, as the gong sounded the pig was shouting to the muscle man, "Who the hell are you?" We just laughed and then, after a dramatic pause, the cannon fired and the piglet flew through the air, with little butterfly wings flapping like crazy. Then the dream stopped. I woke up. I don't know what happened to the pig or the clowns or the circus.'

'That's amazing,' Sofia said, 'Was Tatiana really the ring-master? How strange. You know I can just imagine her in that role. My aunty in Novinki used to interpret dreams...'

'Sofia, we must go now,' Pravdin interrupted, gently. 'Mr Tokar, thank you once again for your help.'

As they walked out of the carriage Sofia turned to the detective. 'Should I add the dream to the notes?'

Pravdin laughed. 'If you want to waste your time, paper and ink, then please - go ahead.'

CHAPTER THIRTY-FOUR

Sofia and Detective Pravdin left the caged banker and returned to the dining car. The steward was clearing away the tables; obviously everyone else had already eaten lunch.

Sofia felt safe with Pravdin. He touched her shoulder and indicated where they should sit. She smiled to herself; if nothing else, his attention and apparent respect for her as his assistant in the investigation so far had helped distract her from her bad tempered falling out with Tatiana. She found herself disappointed with Alexander. He should have explained more clearly what happened at the Meeting Hall.

Sofia frowned as she did a roll call in her head. 'What are you thinking?' Pravdin asked, smiling at her distracted expression.

'I was just adding up,' she said. 'By my calculation, at least three or maybe four people visited Inspector Lesnoy's compartment on the night he died.'

Pravdin nodded, looking closely at Sofia's face. 'Let's see. Three definites: you, the Englishman and a mysterious woman wearing expensive French perfume and possibly a fourth suspect, who pulled the door shut with a click. The only women who had access were you, Mrs Ozertsova and the Countess. The perfume is circumstantial but seems to point to Mrs Ozertsova.'

Sofia nodded. 'When I returned to my compartment after my fight with Lesnoy, I was quite upset as you can imagine. I must have fallen asleep quite soon after I got into bed. I didn't hear anything else during the night.'

'Well, I intend to interview everyone on the list. At the moment they are all still suspects and all potential witnesses. Once I have heard everybody's story I hope to be able to work out the truth about the murder of my colleague. After we have had lunch will you fetch Mrs Ozertsova? I will begin with her. I would like to you continue keeping notes for me. This is already getting more complicated than I had imagined.'

'Of course, Detective Pravdin, shall we order something to eat?'

After lunch Sofia left Pravdin and went to find Ekaterina. The two women returned without delay, Ekaterina looking white-faced and twisting a lace-edged handkerchief nervously in her fingers. Pravdin was looking out of the dining car window as the bleak grey and white Siberian landscape crept past. He didn't turn around immediately to focus on Ekaterina, but kept his eyes flickering, trying to identify individual trees in the forest.

'Please sit, Mrs Ozertsova,' he said. 'There is no need to be nervous - I just want to ask you some simple questions.'

Ekaterina sat at the table with Sofia next to her. Pravdin turned from the window to give her a long, appraising stare before he spoke again. Ekaterina twisted her handkerchief more nervously than ever. Pravdin put his nose in the air and sniffed theatrically.

'What a delicious scent you are wearing - what is it called?'

Ekaterina glanced at Sofia with a puzzled look. 'It is Guerlain's *L'Heure Bleue*,' she murmured, disconcerted by the apparently irrelevant question.

'Delightful. The same distinctive fragrance that Mr Tokar noticed the night before last, wafting past his cage.'

'Mr Tokar?'

'The bank official guarding the gold, Mrs Ozertsova. You know him. Mr Tokar knows you. You had to pass him on your way to visit Inspector Lesnoy.'

'I didn't go there, I haven't seen anything,' Ekaterina said nervously, avoiding his gaze.

After a long and uncomfortable silence Pravdin said, 'I see.' It was clear that he knew Ekaterina was not being truthful. 'No matter, but of course your lack of candour makes me even more curious.'

Ekaterina looked anxiously at Sofia, who shrugged - she was starting to enjoy observing Pravdin's interrogation technique. She wanted to ask him why he had not pressed Ekaterina about her apparent lie about visiting Lesnoy.

'We'll come back to last night eventually, Mrs Ozertsova, but I want to take you back a few years.'

'A few years? What is the relevance, Detective Pravdin? I can't see...'

'No, of course you can't, but please don't worry about my methods. You know that there was a killing, a murder. These tragic events don't usually happen by chance. We are social animals; we do not live and die in a vacuum. For a murder to be committed there are various factors which have to be in place. It's one of the first lessons we learn during our initial police training - the "Three elements of a murder". Firstly, the murderer must have the opportunity to kill; secondly, he - or she - must have the means to carry out the evil deed. Last, but not least, there must be a motive. And the motive is not always immediately apparent. It might be theft or revenge, moral outrage or fear. Fear of the truth, for example, or fear of losing everything which one holds dear, one's home or husband.' Pravdin paused to give Ekaterina time to reflect. 'What do you think, Mrs Ozertsova? Are any of those motives understandable, or even excusable in your view?'

'No! of course not, Detective Pravdin. Killing is always wrong. I...'

Pravdin interrupted her. 'Tell me, Mrs Ozertsova. How

long have you known Inspector Lesnoy?'

'Well, let me see...' Ekaterina laid her handkerchief on the table and counted on trembling fingers. 'I think it was the second day on the train. Six days ago, maybe seven. The first evening after the train left Moscow - all the first class passengers were at dinner here and we introduced ourselves then. Isn't that right, Sofia?' She turned to Sofia expectantly to corroborate her story.

'And that is where you met him?'

'Yes.'

'Where you met him for the *first* time?'

'Yes. I... I think so.'

'You think so?'

'Yes.'

'But you don't know, you cannot be certain?'

Ekaterina said nothing more.

Sofia nodded encouragingly and sympathetically at Ekaterina, feeling rather sorry for her and somewhat disconcerted by Pravdin's insistent questioning. She broke the uncomfortable silence. 'Yes, Ekaterina, that was seven days ago. We all met for the first time at dinner on the first evening.'

Pravdin changed the subject. 'How long have you been married, Mrs Ozertsova?'

Ekaterina frowned. 'How is that relevant, Detective, I don't understand why...'

Pravdin interrupted her sharply. 'With respect, Madame, it is not for you to question me. It is for me to question you. I am the investigating authority here and you are a suspect in the murder of Inspector Lesnoy. If I decide that a question needs to be asked, it will be asked. If I decide that a question needs to be answered, it will be answered. Do I make myself clear?'

Ekaterina twisted her wedding ring around and around her finger. Then, sensing the Detective's eyes had travelled from her face to her hands, said, 'We have been married for three years.'

'I understand your husband is a military man, a cavalry officer. Was he called to the front?'

'Yes. He left shortly after we were married. He was wounded and taken prisoner on the first day of fighting. He was held in a German prison camp for over two years. He only returned a few weeks ago, in a prisoner exchange. We swapped wounded and sick German prisoners of war for Russian men, captured by the Germans. Pavel was traded at Tornea, in Sweden. His finger had been amputated, then he suffered from typhus and later the lack of fresh food gave him scurvy which reopened his wound. It became infected. They thought he would die. When he recovered he was allowed to come home, despite his being an officer.'

'As Tolstoy said, *"If there was no suffering, man would not know his limits."* Your husband has suffered more than most men. Does he know his limits? Does he have any limits?'

Once again Pravdin paused to let Ekaterina consider the meaning of his question. Before she could answer he asked, 'Why are you on this train, Mrs Ozertsova?'

'We wish to leave our past behind and begin a new life. My husband has family, his brother and sister-in-law, in America; we are on our way there.'

'Where was your home in Russia?'

'In Oryol, south west of Moscow.'

'Turgenev's birthplace. I know it quite well. In fact my colleague Inspector Lesnoy, may he rest in peace, was stationed there in 1914. And you never met him?'

'No, never. Well, I don't think so. I can't possibly remember everyone I have ever met. I suppose it is possible our paths crossed, but I certainly didn't recognise him.'

'Indeed. Well, let us move on to what happened two nights ago. What time did you go to bed?'

'I don't remember exactly. Just after ten I think. Mr Zhuravlev left first, from the other table. Then… then I left next, is that right, Sofia?'

'Yes. You came over to our table and said goodnight to Tatiana and me. You kindly lent Tatiana your shawl because she was cold.'

'Did you also say goodnight to Inspector Lesnoy?' Pravdin asked.

Ekaterina put her trembling fingers to her forehead and shook her head nervously. 'I don't know, I really don't know. I expect I said goodnight to everyone, just to everyone in general.'

'Yes, you said goodnight to all of us,' Sofia encouraged her. 'Don't you remember the Inspector made that stupid joke as you were leaving?'

'"Stupid joke"?' Pravdin asked, sharply.

Ekaterina laughed nervously. 'You mean when he called you Countess Sofia?'

Sofia rolled her eyes. 'Oh God! Don't remind me! He said "If you're cold, Countess Sofia, I'll keep you warm," and forced me to take his jacket.' She shuddered in recollection.

'Was that his only comment, Mrs Ozertsova?' Pravdin asked.

'Yes. I don't remember anything else.'

Sofia laughed. 'No - don't you remember, Ekaterina, he called you a strange name, "Kiki" wasn't it? "Goodnight Kiki," is what he said.'

'Why would he call you "Kiki"?'

Ekaterina shrugged. 'I have no idea. It didn't mean anything. He had just had too much to drink and didn't know what he was saying.'

'What *is* your given name?'

'Ekaterina.'

'Is "Kiki" a diminutive of Ekaterina?'

'I have never been called "Kiki". He was drunk. I thought nothing of it.'

Pravdin looked at Ekaterina for a while in silence.

'So after that, you left the dining car and returned to

your cabin. Did you remain there for the rest of the night?'

'I went to wash, then straight to bed. I was very tired. I haven't been sleeping well on the train and I needed an early night.'

'Did you hear your husband return to your room?'

Ekaterina hesitated. 'I don't think so. I must have been asleep when he came back.'

'So you have no idea what time he returned?'

'Not exactly.'

'And you don't know what time he left the compartment later on?'

'He did not leave the compartment; he was with me.'

Pravdin didn't answer, merely raised his eyebrows. 'And was he asleep when *you* left the cabin?'

'When *I* left?! What *do* you mean, Detective. I never left my bed - never! What are you insinuating?'

Sofia could hear the stress and confusion in Ekaterina's voice and noticed how her fingers were nervously twisting and untwisting the handkerchief.

Pravdin looked kindly at Ekaterina and spoke gently. 'Calm yourself, Mrs Ozertsova. I'm not insinuating anything. It's just that someone thought that you might have visited Inspector Lesnoy during the night.'

Ekaterina glared at Pravdin with a stony, expressionless face.

'Who told you that? Did someone see something? They can't have done - it's just not true! It is impossible. What did they see?'

'Well, I admit, nobody actually saw you. It was just an impression, a "sense", shall we say, that you might have been there. But of course, if you tell me you weren't, I shall take your word for it.'

Ekaterina seemed to relax slightly.

Sergei took the notebook from Sofia, flicked through the pages, then returned it to her.

'Let's move on, then. You slept all night and nothing. Correct?'

'Correct.' Ekaterina was breathing normally again and her flushed face was returning to its usual porcelain perfection.

'So if - and please note that I say "if" - your husband had left the cabin later, you wouldn't have been aware of it?'

'No… yes… I don't know… I can't believe…' she tailed off, miserable again, tears brimming.

'This brave man who has no limits, could he kill another man?'

'My husband *is* a brave man, an honourable man.'

'Is he not a proud man, Mrs Ozertsova? He fought for his country and suffered a great deal these past years. He deserves respect and expects loyalty from those who love him - the same loyalty he showed to his Tsar and to Mother Russia. If he had reason to suspect for one moment that his loyalty had been compromised, betrayed, who knows what he might feel. What he might be compelled to do.'

There was silence. Sofia had stopped writing and put down her pen. Pravdin waited patiently while Ekaterina struggled once again to compose herself. At last she was able to speak.

'My husband fought for his country, yes. He suffered, it's true, but he is not a violent man. All he wants is a new life, away from all the troubles here, away from his past - our past.'

'You don't believe he would kill out of revenge, then, Mrs Ozertsova? But what about for love?' Pravdin spoke softly, with emotion, 'If Captain Ozertsov loves you deeply, madam, and I have no reason to doubt that, do you not think he would do anything for you? Anything to protect you from danger?'

'Like what?' Ekaterina's voice was almost a whisper.

'I have no more questions. You may return to your compartment. Good day Mrs Ozertsova.'

After Ekaterina had left, Sofia turned to Sergei. 'Why

were you so hard on her?'

'Hard on her? She knows something. She is a clever woman, a survivor. We have more to learn from her. Did you know that Inspector Lesnoy kept notes about everything - and everybody?'

Sofia blushed.

CHAPTER THIRTY-FIVE

Sofia woke early the next morning. It was barely light and she felt exhausted from her previous day's work. She pulled the eiderdown quilt up over her face, determined to get some more sleep before she had to start again, but it soon became clear that this was impossible. Her mind was too crowded with thoughts - about the killing of Lesnoy, about what she had done, about the statements that Tokar and Ekaterina had given - and thoughts about Pravdin.

It was only forty-eight hours or so since that extraordinary moment when Pravdin had made his shocking announcement. Sofia tried to remember exactly what her first impression had been. Although the announcement had been shocking, she hadn't been surprised. No, she hadn't intended to kill Lesnoy but, when Pravdin announced that Lesnoy was dead, she had assumed that it was her fault.

What had she felt, realising this? Guilt? Not exactly, she knew that what she had done had been done in self-defence, with no forethought or planning. She hadn't taken any weapon with her - the bottle of vodka had simply been the object closest to hand.

Horror? Well, violent death always has an element of horror, but there had also been an element of relief that Lesnoy had ceased to exist. No, the overwhelming feeling had been one of detached acceptance. It had happened; it was a fact.

Since then, though, Sofia had been through a whole range of emotions. When they had interviewed Tokar, there had been a sense of a great weight lifting from her. So she hadn't been the only one to have visited Lesnoy and, thinking back, perhaps she hadn't really hit him that hard, just enough to stun him and allow herself to escape. At the time it certainly hadn't occurred to her that he might be dead - only the next morning when the announcement was made. Then there had been feelings of excitement and curiosity: both Tokar's and Ekaterina's evidence had revealed other possibilities, other clues as to what might have happened.

Sofia got up, washed and dressed, being careful not to wake Tatiana, and wondered whether it was still too early to go to the dining car and see if breakfast was being served. It was much too early to start the next round of interviews, but perhaps Pravdin would be there and they could review the evidence so far. She blushed and smiled to herself. What was she feeling now? She couldn't put a name to it, but it was a good feeling, she liked it.

In fact, Pravdin didn't appear at breakfast until most of the others had finished. Sofia had been there well over an hour and was on her third cup of tea with a spoonful of jam. She tried hard not to show how happy she was to see him, nor how disappointed she was that he barely acknowledged her while he ate. She reminded herself that very soon everyone else would be returning to their cabins and that she would be remaining there with him, just the two of them.

Gradually the dining car emptied and they were left, at separate tables, Pravdin still drinking his tea and looking thoughtfully out of the window. At last he turned to her with a warm smile which made her insides turn to molten butter.

'Miss Maslova, good morning. Apologies for my late

arrival; I was awake until the small hours this morning, reviewing the case notes and trying to make sense of the evidence. I'm very impressed with the standard of your notes, by the way. You seem to have not only transcribed all the witness statements exactly as they have been presented to us, but also to have added some very pertinent ideas and interpretations. That's why I couldn't get to sleep, you see, I kept thinking about your observations.'

For a split second, Sofia hoped he had been going to say, 'I kept thinking about you...' She smiled back at Pravdin who picked up the notebook from the seat beside him and beckoned her over.

'Shall we get back to work, Miss Maslova?' Pravdin drained his cup as Sofia came to sit opposite him. 'Who is next on our list?'

'Alexander Zhuravlev, though I really cannot imagine that he murdered the Inspector.'

'Why do you say that?'

'He is a gentle soul. A poet. A romantic. I just cannot imagine him murdering anyone. In fact a couple of nights ago, at dinner, we discussed the use of violence by the Bolsheviks. He was absolutely against it. He said that violence never solved anything.'

'Interesting. What else can you tell me about Mr Zhuravlev?'

'Well, he and Tatiana...'

There was a pause; Pravdin raised his eyebrows in anticipation.

'He and Tatiana?'

'Well, you know...'

'Know what?'

'You know, they are... how can I explain...'

'Try.'

'Well, they are becoming very close; they are sweethearts I suppose one would say.'

Pravdin tried to look stern, but Sofia could see he was

suppressing a smile. 'All right, all right, enough of your romantic nonsense, this isn't "War and Peace"!' He waved a hand at her dismissively and spoke gruffly. 'Go and fetch Mr Zhuravlev. I want to talk to him.'

Sofia stood up and glared at him. Pravdin looked at her cross face.

'I am sorry, Miss Maslova, I mean *please* would you be so kind as to go and fetch Mr Zhuravlev.'

Sofia inclined her head slightly in gracious acknowledgement of his more polite request, and left.

'Sit down Mr Zhuravlev,' said Pravdin. 'This is just an initial and very informal discussion. You are not a suspect, merely a potential witness.'

'I am very pleased to hear that, Detective Pravdin. How exactly can I help you?'

'Help me by starting at the beginning. Continue through the middle and finish at the end.'

'Very well, I last saw Inspector Lesnoy at dinner on Wednesday night... '

Pravdin held up one hand to halt Alexander mid-flow.

'Just a moment, Mr Zhuravlev, please start at the beginning.'

'The beginning?'

'Yes, please.'

'I first saw Inspector Lesnoy at... '

'No, no - at the very beginning.'

'Well, I boarded the train at Yaroslavsky Station. When was that? Nine, ten days ago? My God, it is difficult to remember. All the trees and snow are quite hypnotic... '

Pravdin shook his head.

'I'm sorry, Mr Zhuravlev, I obviously haven't made myself quite clear. I prefer you to start at the *very* beginning. *Your* beginning. Who are you? Where do you come from? What are you doing on this train?'

'Oh, I see. Let me introduce myself. I am Alexander Borisovich Zhuravlev. Born on the eleventh of December

1885, aged thirty-one. I was born in Moscow, but educated in Petrograd where I worked at the office of Naval Intelligence, writing reports about the war against the Japanese. I was made redundant during the cuts after the war. When my father died I moved back to Moscow. I live a modest life - not married, no children, no responsibilities. I am a writer, a poet to be precise. Unpublished as yet, but I have plans.'

Pravdin interrupted 'A poet?'

'Yes.'

'Unpublished?'

'Yes, it is a difficult time.'

The Detective cleared his throat, smiled and started speaking in a sonorous voice:

> *Workers,*
> *Which of you will grieve*
> *For this broken young soldier?*
> *Does he not seem too insignificant for our concern?*
> *Yet in my heart I never will deny him.*
> *Sad, like a rain shower in February,*
> *He suffered death*
> *In a storm of lead and steel*
> *Because he chose to stand.*
> *To stand for you.*

Alexander blushed.

'Yes, Inspector. It was printed as a pamphlet, but not exactly published, I mean, not sold in a bookshop. But yes, that is one of mine.'

Sofia couldn't help but smile.

'"One of yours"? Please, Mr Zhuravlev, no need to be modest. You are a leading poet of these interesting times. An intellectual. You give heart and soul to the cruel, bloody Bolshevik cause. You are very well-known, certainly among the Okhrana officers I know. Oh yes, some of my friends in the secret police have spent days, weeks thinking about how to capture you; some, no doubt are, at this very moment, thinking about how to torture you. Every office of the Tsar's Gendarmerie has a rather nice photo-etching of your handsome face. With a beard, but it is most certainly you.'

The colour drained from Alexander's face.

The Detective continued: 'Listen, Tovarishch Poet, Comrade Sacha, I'm not here to arrest a scribbler, no matter how red he is. Nor am I totally unsympathetic to your revolution. For me it is simply a matter of timing. Is 1917 really the most convenient moment for radical changes? Personally, I am not convinced.'

'Inspector, I assure you that I would never betray Mother Russia. I further assure you that I am not responsible for the death of Inspector Lesnoy.'

'An excellent sentiment, certainly, but the question of your innocence or guilt is for me to decide once my investigation is complete. Please continue with your witness statement. Where were we?'

Pravdin looked at Sofia. 'Can you remind Mr Zhuravlev of his last words?'

Sofia ran her finger along the handwritten line, '"Not married, no children, no responsibilities. I am a writer, a poet to be precise. Unpublished as yet, but I have plans."'

'So, Comrade Alexander, you "have plans"? Please elaborate. Why are you going to Vladivostok?'

'Well, I had to leave Moscow in a hurry. I got tangled up in a rather unpleasant series of events. You see, Detective, I am fiercely opposed to violence. I believe that a revolution with its roots in blood and guts and splintered bone, will carry that birthright through into the future. A bloody, cruel revolution will give birth to a bloody, cruel society.'

'I see, please continue. Tell me about the "unpleasant series of events".'

Alexander hesitated and Pravdin noticed him glance anxiously at Sofia. When he spoke, it was with a sense of reluctance. 'I suppose I should start at the meeting to celebrate International Women's Day at the hall on Pokrovka Street.' Again, he glanced meaningfully at Sofia, but she seemed unwilling to catch his eye. 'The meeting, how can I explain… the meeting got rowdy. Inflammatory statements were read. Provocative evidence was presented. I am sure you know the kind of thing.'

'No, comrade poet, I do not know "the kind of thing". Please explain.'

Alexander didn't know what to do. He stuttered and stammered while turning a bright shade of red.

Eventually Sofia interrupted. 'Inspector, I believe that Mr Zhuravlev is trying to protect me.'

Pravdin's piercing blue eyes turned towards Sofia. 'Please elaborate, Miss Maslova.'

Sofia pushed a blonde tendril of hair back behind her ear and looked steadily back at Pravdin.

'That evening, the twenty-third of February, I was there.'

'Where?'

'At the meeting. The International Day of the Working Woman celebration. I was tricked, manipulated into going along, but, nevertheless I admit that I was there.'

'You accompanied Mr Zhuravlev to the meeting?'

'No, I was taken there by someone else, someone whom I thought of as a friend; however, this "friend" betrayed me.'

'So you met Mr Zhuravlev there?'

'No, well, yes, I…'

Pravdin waited patiently while Sofia bit her lip and began to look flustered. He turned to Alexander. 'Perhaps you can be clearer on this matter, Mr Zhuravlev. Did you see Miss Maslova at this meeting?'

Alexander looked out of the window at the endless birch woods flashing by. 'Yes Inspector, I saw her there. I helped her to escape. The agitators used Sofia as a provocation to attack the Shuysky Palace.'

'And you helped them to sack and rob the palace?'

'Oh no! Certainly not. Quite the reverse. I did my best to stop them, but I am no Horatius.'

Pravdin smiled sympathetically and quoted Macaulay:

And how can man die better
Than facing fearful odds,
For the ashes of his fathers,
And the temples of his Gods?

Alexander cast his eyes down. 'I was knocked out. By the time I came to and reached the palace, the mob had set it alight. I found the Count, but he was badly injured. With his last breath he made me promise to follow his daughter to the station, to protect her. It was the least I could do.'

'His daughter?'

'Countess Tatiana.'

Sofia was looking at Alexander, tears running down her cheeks. Pravdin patted her hand gently.

'Why the tears, Miss Maslova?'

Sofia couldn't speak. She just shook her head in misery.

Pravdin turned back to Alexander. 'This is all quite messy isn't it? Revolutionary mobs, a dead Count, a dead policeman, and you, Comrade Poet. You seem to be at the centre of this storm. Why don't you tell me what happened the night of the murder?'

'Inspector, may I speak frankly? It's true, I am a revolutionary, but I am no Bolshevik. I believe in peaceful change. I could not murder in cold blood.'

'What if it came down to a choice between you and Lesnoy? Wouldn't it be different if you had to save your own skin? Weren't you worried that he had recognised you from those photographs posted in every gendarme station? The threat of imprisonment or hard labour somewhere in this god-forsaken wilderness,' Pravdin gestured towards the bleak scenery beyond the window, 'Wouldn't that be enough to drive you to an act of violent desperation?'

'I admit I was nervous of Lesnoy at first. He tried to wind me up, to mock me, but I soon recognised him for what he really was - a drunkard, a bully, a coward. Once I got to know him, I stopped feeling frightened. I don't believe he could be bothered with me either, quite honestly. He thought I was small fry, a nobody. There were others he seemed to be more interested in and in return they seemed more bothered by his interest.'

'For example?'

'For example, Mr Zayats, or Mr Hare as he is otherwise known. He isn't who he seems. He is an agent, working for the British government. And he has some interesting baggage with him: three different passports in his attaché case, along with an automatic pistol: a Colt, I think, with a silencer.'

Pravdin indicated to Sofia to make a note of this information, then regarded Alexander's face closely.

'What else do you know about Mr Hare?'

'He has poison, or rather, he had poison; and a bottle of unpalatable, low-grade vodka.'

'Gun, poison, vodka - quite an arsenal of murder. Do you think he killed Inspector Lesnoy?'

'I don't know, Detective. The Englishman is difficult to read. Lesnoy tried to get him rattled, but it was impossible to tell whether or not he had succeeded. These British agents are completely ruthless. They think nothing of eliminating someone who is becoming an inconvenience. I suspect that Hare has more to hide than his real nationality. You know, Inspector, I'm almost certain he has other, dirtier secrets.'

'Well that's all very interesting, but let me tell you what I *do* know. *You* had access to the pistol, you also had access to the poison and the vodka. You knew that Lesnoy recognised you as the "Red Catullus". You knew that you were in danger. How long, do you think, would a sensitive literary soul survive in a *katorga* in Siberia? I very much doubt if paper and pencils are issued to inmates.'

CHAPTER THIRTY-SIX

Everyone else was already seated for luncheon when Dominic Hare arrived in the dining compartment, but there was a strange hush. Ekaterina and Pavel appeared to be ignoring each other; Tatiana looked as though she had been crying and Alexander, always pale, appeared even more ashen-complexioned than usual. The tension in the atmosphere was palpable.

It was Detective Pravdin who broke the silence.

'Aha! Mr Zayats at last. We were all worried that you had disappeared. Jumped off the train, perhaps?'

Dominic gave Pravdin a cold stare. 'That would be an exceptionally stupid thing to do, Detective. Even assuming one didn't break every bone in one's body, one would soon either die of cold or be eaten by wolves. I can assure you that I have no reason to wish to leave the relative comfort and safety of the train. Now, what's on the menu today?'

He rubbed his hands together and sat down next to Sofia and opposite Pravdin.

'Well, I can recommend the venison stew - I had it yesterday,' said Pravdin.

'Excellent! Sounds delicious.' He turned to the waiter who had appeared beside him. 'The venison, please, and a bottle of water.'

'Water!' Pravdin sounded incredulous. 'I thought you were a hardened vodka drinker, Mr Zayats. I've been told that you even travel with your own supply.'

'I do like to keep my own reserves, that's true. But I drink it only sparingly.'

'Indeed, well, you can tell me about that later. I would like to interview you after lunch, Mr Zayats, if you don't mind.'

'Of course - I shall be pleased to be of any assistance I can.'

The food was served and consumed in silence. Detective Pravdin was the only one who spoke at all, commenting on the view from the train window which was relentlessly, endlessly bleak. *Verst* after *verst* of snow-covered landscape with barely a sign of human life. They really were in the middle of nowhere.

After tea, the rest of the passengers returned to their private compartments, leaving Dominic, Pravdin and Sofia sitting at their table.

'Do you wish to interview me in private, Detective Pravdin?' Dominic asked, glancing sideways at Sofia.

'Miss Maslova will stay. She is assisting me with the investigation.'

'I see. So, what can I tell you? I am at your complete disposal - ask me anything you like.' Dominic leaned back in his seat and opened his hands in a gesture of frankness and cooperation.

'Thank you, Mr Zayats, you are certainly an exemplary Russian citizen and I thoroughly appreciate your help in investigating this outrageous crime. An officer of the Tsar's Special Gendarmerie - murdered! A true patriot like yourself must be horrified by such an appalling act of brutality.'

Dominic merely nodded slightly.

'So, tell me about yourself, Mr Zayats; who are you and what are you doing on this train? Before you answer, I should warn you that I am well aware of your true identity.

247

You are not a Russian at all, are you? And your name is not Dmitry Zayats, is it?'

Sofia stopped writing notes and looked up, curious to know what he would say. She glanced nervously at Dominic, then at Pravdin, then back to Dominic again.

'I think you must be aware, Detective, that if you wish me to give a full and frank account, then we need to observe strict confidentiality. Miss Maslova is a charming young lady and I am sure she is proving to be a very useful assistant, but I'm afraid I must insist that she leaves before I say anything.'

Pravdin hesitated momentarily, staring at Dominic, then nodded. 'Very well then, Mr Zayats. Miss Maslova, may I ask you to return to your compartment during this interview. I will take notes myself.'

Once alone, the two men stared appraisingly at each other. Eventually, Pravdin broke the silence. 'So, let me ask you again – who are you, where are you from and what are you doing here?'

'You indicated you were already aware of my identity. But if you want confirmation, I will gladly give it to you. My real name is Dominic Hare. I am a British citizen and I am here as an agent of the British government.' Dominic reached into his jacket pocket and produced a passport which he passed to Pravdin. His Majesty, King George, is anxious to do everything he can to help his cousin, your Tsar Nicholas, and my purpose in being on the train is to safeguard the valuable cargo being transported in the next carriage. My assignment is to ensure it reaches its destination.'

'Which is where?'

'Well, Vladivostok, initially, but from there it will be loaded onto a British warship for the next leg of its journey to London. The gold is being used to purchase weapons for the fight against those bloody revolutionaries. You see, Detective, you and I are on the same side in the war against the Bolsheviks.'

'Indeed, that is most reassuring, Mr Hare. I am most grateful for your protection against those "bloody revolutionaries" as you so accurately describe them. But surely none of them is aboard the train. Not in this exclusive first-class section at least?' Pravdin raised his eyebrows questioningly.

'Oh, I'm sorry, I thought you had interviewed my cabin mate. I assumed that you had questioned Mr Zhuravlev about his background and political sympathies?'

Pravdin snorted scornfully. 'That lily-livered young pup? He likes to think of himself as a revolutionary, but he's not the sort to cause the Tsar any concern. He can wield his pen as elegantly as any dueller with a sword, but his pretty words are hardly a serious threat.'

'Maybe not, but his horror of violence may only extend as far as actual bloodshed. I have come across young men like him before in my career. They may not wish to plunge a weapon into a fellow human's heart, but they are still capable of killing. If they can find a method of murder which is "clean" and leaves them detached from guts and gore, they are surprisingly capable of using it when it suits their need for self-preservation.'

'How interesting, Mr Hare. I assume you are talking about a method like poisoning, for example.'

'Exactly.'

'And you really believe that Mr Zhuravlev has a convenient supply of some sort of lethal poison in his possession, ready to eliminate any passing policeman who seems to be on his tail?'

'Oh, come now, Detective. Don't tell me that our gentle poet didn't assist you with your investigation by informing you of the contents of my attaché case? It's just the normal standard issue – pistol, poison and passports. What every British agent needs for his jaunts abroad.'

'Yes, Mr Hare. You are quite right. You will be happy to hear that he was touchingly reluctant to incriminate you. I am well aware that both you – and he, as you so accurately pointed out – had the means to murder the Inspector.'

'I am happy to admit that I had the means, but that is all - I had no motive. As I said, Inspector Lesnoy and I were on the same side - both of us had the interests of the Tsar at heart and wished to ensure that the gold was safely delivered to its intended destination.'

'It's true that you don't have an obvious motive, but I'm not entirely convinced by your protestations of loyalty. You have admitted to having the means. I think you also had the opportunity. I have witnesses who can place you at the scene of the crime at the approximate time of death. What can you tell me about that?'

'Well what have you been told exactly?'

'Mr Zayats - Mr Hare - I respectfully beg to remind you that *I* am the one asking the questions. Please give me a full account of your evening, from the dinner onwards.'

'Fine. I was sitting with Captain and Mrs Ozertsov at dinner. It was a pleasant evening, although everyone seemed a little on edge. The Inspector was becoming upset about the lack of vodka and I think the tension began to rub off on everyone else.'

'So you got involved, I have heard. Tried to smooth the situation over?'

'Yes, I had a bottle of vodka with me. Alexander and I had already tried it, but it was revolting - quite undrinkable to my palate. Lesnoy, however, seemed to be at the point where he would drink anything, just to get the alcohol coursing through his veins. I said I would fetch my bottle after dinner and bring it to him in his compartment.'

'Very well, but just stay with the dinner for a moment. What did you eat and what did your table companions eat?'

'I had the Baikal cod, I think. Ekaterina had the same, though she didn't eat much of it.'

'Was that normal for her?'

'She's typical of her class - attractive, well-groomed, well-dressed and likes to watch her figure. In that respect no different from the other young ladies in our carriage. None of them ever ate very heartily. I think this evening was exceptional, though. Ekaterina had just a couple of mouthfuls before pushing it to one side of her plate. It was quite tasty, so I don't believe it was purely dislike of the dish. She looked nervous and preoccupied from the beginning of the meal and I suppose her state of anxiety resulted in loss of appetite.'

'Interesting. Any idea why that might have been? Was something or someone in particular making her nervous? Did you, for example, sense any tension between her and Captain Ozertsov?'

'Not really. They struck me as a couple who were still very much in love. I understand they had been separated for several years soon after their marriage - Captain Ozertsov was a prisoner-of-war. They seemed close - the way they sat, for example, and he was always very attentive and concerned for her well-being and comfort. It was just the same that evening.'

'So why, then, do you think she might have been anxious that night?'

'I don't know; I didn't feel I knew them well enough to ask such an intrusive question.'

'Obviously, but Mr Hare, you are a trained British agent, surely an expert in the art of observation and analysis. I am simply asking you to speculate on the reasons for Mrs Ozertsova's state of mind on that evening.'

'Really? You, Detective Pravdin, are a trained officer of the Tsar's gendarmerie, an expert in cold hard facts. I am astonished that speculation has any place in a serious investigation of this kind.'

'On the contrary. The facts are vital, of course, and I want all the facts laid before me. But the psychology behind the facts is equally important and that element requires interpretation and, yes, a certain amount of speculation. Your expert insights and my local knowledge combine to create the ideal combination to solve this case.'

'Ah! Pravdin, I clearly observe your use of flattery to persuade me. My psychological skills are developed enough to realise that, at least. All right, I'm willing to humour you, Detective and play along with your game.'

'Excellent. So let's continue from the end of the meal, when everyone began to leave the dining car. What do you remember about the sequence of events?

'Alexander left first. I thought that seemed a little odd because he and Tatiana seemed to be enjoying each other's company so much. If that had been me, I'd have wanted to stay with the young lady as late into the night as possible. I was talking to the Ozertsovs, though, so I didn't hear him say why he was going so early.'

'Who was next?'

'Ekaterina said she was very tired and asked me and her husband to excuse her.'

'Did the Captain not offer to accompany her?'

'No. That did strike me as a little odd - he was normally so attentive. On the other hand, she gave the distinct impression that she wanted to be alone. And he hadn't finished his meal.'

'Did she say goodnight to the diners at the other table?'

'Yes, she said she was tired and excused herself. She stood up and bent to kiss her husband on the top of his head - a very tender gesture I thought at the time. He took her hand in his and kissed it and they smiled at each other. As she passed the other table she bade them goodnight.'

'Could you hear exactly what was said?'

'Yes. Tatiana was cold and Ekaterina offered her the shawl she was wearing.'

'And the men?'

'Alexander had already left. I didn't hear her say goodnight to the Inspector specifically, but he certainly said goodnight to her.'

'Do you remember his exact words, Mr Hare?'

'Yes. He said "Goodnight, Kiki".'

'Did you think that was strange at the time, for him to address her in that way?'

'Yes, extremely peculiar and his tone of voice was distinctly impertinent – bordering on downright rude in fact.'

'How did Mrs Ozertsova react?'

'I couldn't see her face - she had already turned her back to leave the compartment.'

'How about Captain Ozertsov? You were sitting opposite him, so I presume you observed his reaction?'

'Yes, he had returned to eating his meal once his wife had begun to take her leave, but he looked up sharply when Lesnoy spoke and I noticed him grip his wine glass very tightly.'

'Indeed? Was he also eating the cod?'

'No, he had the steak that evening. It looked good - just the right amount of blood.'

'Did he say anything?'

'To the Inspector? No. But he began talking rather loudly and rather fast about a beautiful horse he'd once had, Belaya Iskra I think he called it. He had taken the horse with him to East Prussia to fight in the war with the Fourteenth Cavalry Division, but it was killed in combat on the very first day of fighting, in the same skirmish in which the Captain lost his finger and was taken prisoner.'

'Was there a particular reason why he introduced the topic of his horse at that specific moment, do you think?'

Dominic shrugged. 'He had mentioned the horse before, how beautiful it was - a grey, he said; and how loyal and faithful.'

'Just like a wife, eh?' Pravdin smiled.

'Just like a wife should be, yes.'

'Like your wife?'

'I have no wife, never have had, Detective. From my observations of my fellow men, wives are not always as loyal or faithful as they should be. Horses, yes; dogs, even more so.'

253

Pravdin laughed, 'Ah yes, you Englishmen and your dogs, it's a well-known love match! Personally I prefer women, even the unfaithful ones. An element of uncertainty in a relationship adds to its piquancy in my view.'

'Certainly Miss Maslova is an attractive alternative to a horse. Attractive and, even better, intelligent. I imagine she is proving to be a valuable assistant in your investigation, Detective.'

'She is indeed. A pity she isn't here to take notes on this occasion - her insights into her fellow passengers are proving to be most useful. Female intuition I suppose. However, let us return to the evening in question.' Pravdin consulted his notes. 'After Mrs Ozertsova left and after your conversation about the horse, what then?'

'Miss Maslova and Miss Shuyskaya, or rather Countess Shuyskaya, left soon after Mrs Ozertsova.'

'So then three of you - you, Captain Ozertsov and Inspector Lesnoy remained in the dining car.'

'Yes. Captain Ozertsov and I continued our conversation, about the horse, about the war, about the world...'

Sergei interrupted, 'And Lesnoy sat by himself at the other table?'

'Well not exactly. As soon as the young ladies left he became more restless than usual. He turned round in his seat to face our table and began haranguing me about the vodka. "Stop talking and go and get the bloody vodka, Zayats." I tried to ignore him, but in the end decided to get the wretched stuff, just to shut him up.'

'So you returned to your cabin for the vodka. Was Mr Zhuravlev there?'

'Yes, he was asleep, or appeared to be at least. I got the bottle out of my case and took it back to the dining car.'

'Immediately?'

'No, actually, not straight away. I decided to let him stew a bit, lay down on my bed and read my book for half

254

an hour or so. Then I went back to the dining car. There was nobody there, so of course I assumed Lesnoy was in his own cabin. I went through into the armoured carriage, past the gold cage.'

'Did Mr Tokar witness you?'

'I didn't see him. I assume he was already asleep behind his curtain.'

'So, then…' Pravdin gestured for Dominic to continue.

'I heard voices coming from Lesnoy's cabin. I knocked on the door and they fell silent. Lesnoy came to the door and I gave him the bottle.'

'Did he invite you in? For a drink?'

Dominic laughed. 'No, I thought that he would probably try to avoid paying, so I put my foot against the door to stop him shutting it on me and reminded him that he had promised me two roubles for it.'

'And he gave you the money?'

'Yes, reluctantly. He growled, "stay there," and went over to his bed where he had the money in his jacket pocket.'

'So it's clear he didn't want you entering the room. Why do you think that was?'

'Well, it might just have been that he wanted to drink himself into oblivion without my help. Having paid for the vodka I doubt he was very keen to share it. I'd have refused him anyway - as I said, it wasn't very pleasant.'

Pravdin looked thoughtful. 'Did he notice that the bottle wasn't full?'

'I don't think he would have noticed. Alexander and I had only had a small sip each. The bottle still appeared to be unused.'

'So you didn't need to top it up with anything to make it appear full?'

Pravdin picked up a fractional hesitation before Dominic replied. 'No, I didn't top it up.'

'Any other reason why he wouldn't have invited you in?'

M P Peacock

'We were hardly the best of friends, Detective. And, as I said, I suspected there might already be someone else in there.'

'Any idea who?'

'Miss Maslova, perhaps. She and Lesnoy seemed to know each other quite well. I can't imagine it was Countess Tatiana - she was more interested in the poet; and Mrs Ozertsova surely wouldn't have compromised herself by visiting his cabin alone.'

'You're convinced it was a woman, then?'

'That was the impression I got from the voices I heard. I suppose it might have been Captain Ozertsov. They were the last two left in the dining car. Perhaps Lesnoy had invited him back to join him for a drink, but...' Dominic shrugged and broke off.

'But you don't think that's likely?'

'Not really. I don't think there was any love lost between those two. The Captain would have wanted to get back to his own cabin, to see how his wife was.'

'So after Lesnoy paid for the vodka, you went back through the dining car to your own cabin.'

'Yes.'

'You didn't see or hear anyone else on the way?'

'No. Oh, actually yes, the steward was in the dining car, clearing the tables.'

'Did you speak to him?'

'I probably said goodnight. I don't think he replied. He seemed annoyed, in fact, muttering to himself and looking beneath the tables as if he'd dropped something.'

'Or was missing something, perhaps? An item of cutlery?'

'Cutlery?' Dominic frowned, perplexed as to the Detective's train of thought. Then his expression cleared and turned to one of intense interest. He leaned forward and tapped his forefinger excitedly on Pravdin's notes.

'"*Gde nozh, gde nozh?*" - that's what he was muttering! Doesn't that mean "where's the knife?"'

256

Pravdin nodded and picked up his pen again. 'Yes, Mr Hare. Your knowledge of Russian is really very good. It does indeed mean, "Where is the knife?"'

CHAPTER THIRTY-SEVEN

Pavel poured the last few drops of coffee from the pot into his cup and swigged it down, pulling a face at its chilly bitterness. He smiled at his wife and said, 'I only drink this stuff because in America they don't have good tea; I need to get used to it.' She smiled at him, but he could see the stress in her eyes and the tension in her neck and shoulders. Most of the other passengers had already finished breakfast and returned to their cabins. Only Sofia and Detective Pravdin remained, reading from a notebook and making quiet comments. Even as Pavel rose from his seat, murmuring, 'Come, my dear,' and offering his hand to Ekaterina, he knew perfectly well that he was next on the list of suspects to be interviewed. He was unlikely to get very far.

In fact, Pravdin allowed Pavel to reach the door that led from the dining car to the *spalny vagon*, and turn the cold brass handle. It was only as Pavel stood back to allow Ekaterina to pass in front of him that he heard the Detective's clipped, commanding tones:

'Captain Ozertsov - a moment of your time, if you please.'

Pavel spoke softly to his wife. 'You go back to our cabin; I won't be too long.' Having seen her pass safely over the somewhat rickety connecting platform, he shut

258

the door and walked back towards the table where Pravdin looked at him with his intelligent, penetrating gaze.

'Please sit, Captain. As you know, I have spoken to your wife and fellow passengers about the murder. Now it is your turn to answer some questions.'

'Very well,' Pavel nodded agreement and tried to look unconcerned, 'I will tell you what I know, but I doubt if it will be very useful; I cannot imagine how I can help your investigation. You know, I can honestly say that I had never met Vladimir Lesnoy before we found ourselves on this damned train - what, nine or ten days ago? What possible motive could I have for his murder?' He glanced at Sofia. 'Unless, of course, it was to protect the national strategic supply of grain vodka, eh Miss Maslova? I suppose that might be enough to drive even a sane Russian to commit a murder.' Pavel suddenly forced a somewhat false laugh and Pravdin and Sofia gazed at him, wondering when he was going to stop his nervous jabbering.

Pravdin remained stony-faced. 'You never came across Inspector Lesnoy during the war?'

'No, never.'

'In which regiment did you serve?'

'The Fourteenth Cavalry Division; and to be totally clear, I never came across him before the war either. Did he even fight? He had the air of an avoider if you ask me; a sly, not very pleasant man.' Pavel's tone was scornful.

'Well, you are correct, he did not join the army, but we, the officer corps of the Gendarmerie, have all done our bit. In fact, Lesnoy was stationed for a time in your hometown, Oryol. Are you sure you never met him when you were home on leave?

'I had no leave. I was wounded early on and taken prisoner. I was only exchanged quite recently. I went directly from Haparanda to Petrograd then briefly to Oryol and then home to my wife. It honestly feels as though I have been living on trains for the last month. Once I was home it took me all of ten minutes to persuade her that we should leave Russia and start a new life in America. I have a brother in California who will help us.'

'But the war continues and Mother Russia needs her warriors during these difficult times. Are you not being a cowardly avoider yourself, Ozertsov? Deserting your country in her hour of greatest need?'

Pavel held up his disfigured left hand, the ring finger just an ugly purple stump and the middle finger badly crooked and scarred. 'I am no longer wanted by dear Mother Russia. Her army has cast me off like a spent matchstick, kicked into the gutter. I have a pittance of a pension and nothing more. There is nothing left for me here.'

Sofia had stopped writing notes and gazed sadly at the former soldier, his thin face overlain with an unkempt bitterness, giving him a tragic, slightly wild look.

Pravdin stroked his chin thoughtfully and looked long and hard at Pavel.

'Very well, let's accept that you hadn't previously met Inspector Lesnoy and had no prior motive for killing him. I still need you to take me through everything that happened on the evening of the night he was killed. I want to know what your movements were and what you observed of everyone else's movements.'

'When I went to bed - my wife was already...'

'No, no, Captain Ozertsov, we need to start before that - much earlier in the evening, when you were all seated here for dinner. Tell me, for example, what you ordered from the menu.'

'I - I really can't remember. We have been on this so-called express train for ten days and I have had every possible item from the menu several times. What could it possibly matter, what I had on that particular evening?' Pavel sounded irritated and somewhat flustered. 'Can't we just get on with this damned interrogation? I want to return to my cabin and make sure my Ekaterina is all right. Since this awful business, she gets quite anxious if she is left on her own.'

'Please indulge me, Captain,' Pravdin smiled charmingly. 'It is in the little details, the seemingly irrelevant minutiae, that we often detect the most important indications. A murderer will often take enormous care to conceal the most obvious clues to his crime, but it is much harder for him - or her - to think of all the small hints and marks he may have left. For example...' Pravdin broke off to borrow Sofia's notes and riffled through them, 'One of your travelling companions... ah, yes here it is, mentioned that you had ordered steak and that you were the only person to choose that particular dish on that particular evening.'

'Y - yes, I think that is probably correct. Now I think about it I did eat the steak that evening. It was probably horse, not beef, but I still don't see...'

Pravdin flicked through the notes again. 'Well, someone else overheard the steward complaining later that evening that one of the steak knives was missing. The knife you had used.'

Pavel shrugged. 'What can I tell you? It was there on my plate when I left the dining car.'

'But you were the last to leave, were you not? So there are no witnesses to that. Why did you wait at the table until everyone else had left? I am surprised you didn't return to the cabin with your wife.'

'Ekaterina was very tired that night; she left early and I hadn't finished eating. Also, Mr Zayats and I were in the middle of an interesting conversation.'

'A very experienced detective in Petrograd once told me that if a suspect gives more than one explanation of his actions in a statement then it is safe to assume that nothing he says should be believed.'

Pravdin stared coldly at Pavel for what seemed to Sofia an eternity. Pavel avoided Pravdin's stare and focused instead on massaging his damaged fingers.

Eventually Pravdin continued 'Very well. So, as you've

just brought it up yourself, let's go back a little earlier in the evening, to the moment when your wife decided she was tired and left the table. Did you say anything to her?'

'I expect I said "Goodnight my dear, I'll be along shortly" or something to that effect.'

'And did anyone else wish her goodnight?'

'I really don't remember.'

'So Coco left and…'

'*Kiki*…' corrected Pavel without thinking, suddenly stopping short and blushing to the roots of his dark hair, 'I mean, *Ekaterina* left and…'

Pravdin interrupted. 'It is curious that you call her Kiki. How interesting. Your wife denied she had ever been known by that diminutive.'

Pavel spoke through gritted teeth. 'It's just a silly pet name we used to use when we first met, when we were younger. She hates me using it - anyone using it now.'

'That is strange. Does she not like to be reminded of those idyllic days of young love, Captain Ozertsov?' Pravdin glanced at Sofia with a wry smile on his face, 'I thought all women enjoyed hearing tender terms of endearment. What made her decide that she hated that name? Have you any idea?'

Pavel stared at Pravdin, wondering just how much he already knew. 'I don't know,' he said, feeling more and more threatened, 'She thought it was ridiculous, childish, unsophisticated. We both grew up a lot during the war, unfortunately we had to do our growing up apart.'

'Did you also grow apart? Did Mrs Ozertsova feel lonely while you were interned? She could hardly be blamed if she…'

Pavel leapt to his feet, knocking the table and toppling the empty tea glasses. The clatter made Sofia jump and jogged her hand as she wrote, creating a jagged scratch of ink on the page.

'I don't know what you are insinuating, Pravdin, but you can stop right there. My wife and I love each other, we are faithful to each other and we are going to have a new life together, a fresh start. It's exactly your kind of dirty-minded tittle-tattle that we wish to get away from.'

'Sit down, Captain; sit down and calm down,' Pravdin ordered. 'I am not insinuating anything against your wife. If you yourself are convinced that she has been a model of fidelity and rectitude, then I am sure you must be right. I am simply doing my job, trying to solve a brutal murder. Someone on this train - more precisely a first class passenger - is responsible. It is my unpleasant duty to question each and every person who had the means and the opportunity to commit the crime, to ascertain whether any of them had a possible motive to do so. I have no choice but to question you and your wife as suspects. Please, Captain, sit down and answer my questions.'

Pavel sat down but remained silent and Pravdin remained silent too. Pavel's anxious, heavy breathing slowly calmed and Sofia laid down her pen and looked first at one man, then the other.

Eventually, Pravdin turned to her. 'Miss Maslova, just remind me what you told me yesterday morning, when we were interviewing Mrs Ozertsova'.

Sofia frowned. 'I can't really remember; I'm sure it wasn't important'. Pavel looked completely wretched, she thought, and she didn't want to make the situation worse for him.

Pravdin tutted, impatiently. 'Come now, Miss Maslova, you know perfectly well what I mean. You were talking about Inspector Lesnoy. You said that when Mrs Ozertsova left the dining car to go to bed, he said something to her.'

'Just 'goodnight' I think'. Sofia could feel Pavel's eyes boring into her and was careful to avoid catching his eye.

Pravdin persisted. 'Not, "Goodnight Mrs Ozertsova"? Or "Goodnight Ekaterina"? Or some other name? Kiki for example?'

Sofia nodded once but said nothing. Pravdin looked at

her and wondered if she could be trusted.

'Captain, once your wife had gone to bed you were left at the same table as Mr Zayats. Inspector Lesnoy was alone at the other table. Why didn't you ask him to join you?'

'Lesnoy had drunk too much, as usual, and he was spoiling for a fight. I think it was because the last bottle of vodka had been finished. Mr Zayats had promised to give him - or sell him - a bottle from his own personal supply and Lesnoy was waiting for Zayats to finish his conversation with me and go and fetch it. In fact he was quite rude and obnoxious, continually interrupting our conversation to try to make Zayats hurry up.'

'So eventually Mr Zayats went to get the vodka?'

'Yes and as soon as he left, Lesnoy also got up from his table.'

'Did he say anything to you?'

Pavel hesitated. 'No. Well, he said he was going to use the bathroom and that if Zayats came back with the vodka he should deliver it to his cabin.'

'And did Mr Zayats return?'

'Not while I was still there. As soon as Lesnoy had gone the steward came in to clear the tables and I didn't wait around. I went straight back to my cabin. I didn't see Zayats on my way back, so I don't know what time he took the vodka to Lesnoy, or even whether he did so at all.'

'Was your wife already asleep when you entered your cabin?'

'I assumed so; I could hear her breathing steadily. She didn't say anything. I didn't turn the light on; I changed into my nightclothes in the dark and climbed into my bed.'

'You definitely changed straight away?

Pavel frowned. 'Yes, why?'

Pravdin leaned over to look through the notes again. 'I noticed when I arrived the following morning that there were some tiny feathery filaments stuck to your jacket.'

'Feathers?!' Pavel laughed incredulously. 'Do you think I was plucking a goose, Detective? I think more likely you are chasing a wild one!'

Pravdin gave a world-weary smile. 'Yes, a very good joke, my friend, but the feathers are not so funny. They looked like the duck down one finds in the soft pillows of *spalny vagon*. Tiny, soft feathery filaments which might float out into the air if the pillow were cut open.'

'Was there such a pillow in the Inspector's cabin? A pillow which had been cut?'

'I'm sorry, Captain, but the scene-of-crime details are confidential at present. Until I have heard everyone's witness statements and had time to analyse them and draw a satisfactory conclusion, I am not at liberty to divulge any such information.'

'But, Detective Pravdin, how was Lesnoy actually killed? Surely we all need to know. After all it might have some bearing on the information you are given.'

'As I said, Captain… I expect everyone to give me all the information I ask for, fully and frankly. It is up to me, not up to any of you, to decide whether the information is relevant to the case or not. Any attempt to hide anything or to mislead me is illegal and punishable by law. Let us return to your account of the evening. You changed and got into bed. Did you fall asleep immediately?'

'Not quite immediately, but not long after.'

'And your wife? Did she remain asleep as far as you are aware? Did she leave the cabin at any time?'

'No! Definitely not!'

'But if you fell asleep "not long after" how can you be sure she did not wake once you were asleep and leave the cabin while you were dreaming of your new life in California?'

'Why on earth would she?'

'Who knows? You might not know as much about your wife as you think you do. As I have explained, over and over again, I have to explore every possibility, however unlikely you think it might be. How about you, Captain? Did you remain asleep all night, or did you have occasion to leave your cabin again?'

'No, I just slept.'

'You weren't tempted to join Mr Zayats and the Inspector in their late night vodka drinking session?'

'Not at all. Mr Zayats had confided in me that it was the worst alcohol he had ever had the misfortune to sample. Almost undrinkable. He thought it would be funny to sell it to the Inspector. Lesnoy was almost permanently plastered so he probably wouldn't have noticed what it tasted like. Zayats himself wasn't planning to stay and socialise, just get his roubles and leave the Inspector to drink himself into oblivion.'

'Did Mr Zayats mention adding anything to the vodka to make it more palatable?'

'He didn't say so. Do you think he did? Was there any vodka left in the bottle in Lesnoy's cabin - no, don't tell me, you can't divulge such information! Ridiculous!' Pavel shook his head in frustration. Once again Sofia though how strangely the Captain was acting.

'You are a fast learner, Captain. Just to return to your wife, for a moment. I do have some evidence that she left your compartment while you were asleep.'

'Evidence?! What evidence? And don't tell me that you can't divulge it. I have the right to defend myself and my wife if somebody else is spreading scurrilous lies about us.'

Pravdin asked Sofia for the notes again and looked through them for some time before finding what he was looking for. 'A fragrance - identified as *L'Heure Bleue* by Guerlain - was identified just outside the Inspector's cabin very late on that evening, after everyone else had retired to their cabins for the night. Your wife uses that scent doesn't she?'

Pavel was silent and Pravdin repeated his question. 'Doesn't she, Captain?'

'Yes, but...' Ozertsov put his elbows on the table and

sunk his face into his hands, rendering the words, 'Oh dear God!' almost inaudible.

Sofia felt her heart go out to him. Poor Captain Ozertsov, she thought, then suddenly, something lit up in her brain. She gently touched the back of Pavel's hand, making him lift his head and look directly at her.

'Don't you remember, Captain? Just before your wife went to bed, Tatiana said she was cold and Ekaterina kindly said she could use her shawl. She put it round Tatiana's shoulders as she left the room and told her to keep it for the night. I remember Tatiana saying, "It's a lovely shawl and what a delicious scent".'

A look of relief came over Pavel's face. 'Yes, that's right,' he murmured.

'How interesting,' said Pravdin turning to look at Sofia. 'Perhaps it is time to call in your friend and ask her some questions. Go and let her know that she will be required after lunch, Sofia.'

Now it was Sofia's turn to look crestfallen.

CHAPTER THIRTY-EIGHT

Sofia entered the restaurant carriage and saw Tatiana sitting at the far end of the car with Alexander. Sofia decided that, after three days of almost complete silence, she must break the thick layer of ice that had formed between them. Sofia walked down the aisle to Tatiana's table and addressed Alexander.

'Sacha, I need to talk to Tatiana in private. Would you mind taking your lunch with someone else today?'

Alexander looked up at Sofia, surprised at her request. He turned to Tatiana and said, 'I think that is a very good idea.' He looked around at the other tables and continued, 'I'll go and sit with the Englishman.' He smiled at Tatiana, patted her hand reassuringly and left the table.

Sofia sat down opposite Tatiana, who maintained a mask of emotionless disinterest in Sofia's arrival.

'Tatiana. I am truly sorry about my involvement with the death of your father. Nothing I can say or do will help, but this has been a horrible experience for all of us. I am as upset as you are.'

Tatiana simply said. 'I know.'

'We cannot go on like this, This silence is too awful. We will be in Vladivostok in less than a week and then we'll need to decide what to do about going to America.'

'Yes. I'm not sure what our plans are.'

'Our plans?'

'What Alexander and I are going to do.'

An uncomfortable silence settled between them. Sofia changed the subject. 'Detective Pravdin wants to interview you after lunch.'

'I have nothing to say to him.'

'Well he is an officer of the Special Gendarmerie; you don't have any choice but to answer his questions.' Sofia hesitated. 'He can have you arrested if you refuse.'

Sofia reached out to touch Tatiana's hand but Tatiana moved it away before they touched. Sofia sighed, regretting the distance that had grown between them. She wished that they could exchange the confidences and secrets as they had done in Moscow. Sofia missed the happy, silly, carefree Tatiana. She wanted to hear her friend joyfully babbling about how Alexander was the man she loved. Sofia would have liked to confide her growing attraction to Pravdin. In spite of the bad feelings between them, deep inside Sofia still felt a deep affection for her friend and former mistress. Sofia didn't want her to be anxious or upset by Pravdin's questions and she could have kicked herself for having drawn attention to the perfumed shawl. Please, Sofia thought, why can't we be friends again? Please don't blame me for all the bad things which have happened; please don't blame me for ruining your life.

A waiter brought Tatiana a plate with a small pie and some pickled vegetables. Tatiana shoved her food around her plate miserably and avoided making eye contact with Sofia. Eventually she spoke. 'What am I going to say to Detective Pravdin? I don't know anything. Why would I want to kill Inspector Lesnoy? I had no reason.'

Sofia tried to sound reassuring. 'It's just routine, Tatiana. Pravdin is talking to everyone. It doesn't mean he suspects you - why would he? He just needs to find out whether you heard or saw anything.'

Once everyone else had returned to their

compartments after lunch, the two girls remained in the dining car and Pravdin came to join them at their table.

'Right. Time to get out your notebook again, Miss Sofia. I have some important questions to ask Countess Shuyskaya.'

Tatiana raised her chin defiantly and looked at Pravdin with a slightly haughty expression. Sofia knew her so well that she could see beyond this superficial defence mechanism to the frightened young girl underneath.

'What do you want to know, Detective?' Tatiana said. 'That night I went back to my room and fell asleep straight away. The next thing I knew, it was morning and you arrived to tell us that the Inspector was dead.'

'Well, let's go back a little further, shall we? I need to know a little more about you - your background, what are you doing on this train. Kindly begin by telling me a bit about your life and how you come to be here.'

Sofia was relieved at how gently Pravdin was speaking to Tatiana. She noticed that Tatiana's hands had begun to shake. She looked back at her friend, gazing into her eyes searchingly. Yes, she thought, you do still need me when things get tough. She reached out towards Tatiana's hands and this time Tatiana welcomed her gesture; tentatively, the girls smiled at each other for the first time in three days.

'I am the only daughter of Count Nikolai Lvovich Shuysky,' Tatiana began, 'I have two elder brothers who are fighting the German invaders. My mother died when I was a baby. I grew up in our palace in Moscow and spent summers in the family dacha. Sofia was my…' she paused and gently squeezed Sofia's hand, 'Sofia was my friend as far back as I can remember. She is my best friend.'

'Thank you, Countess, that is helpful.'

'There is one particular detail about my childhood which I think you should know. I don't want you to find out later that I have been hiding anything from you.'

Pravdin raised his eyebrows and nodded with interest.

'At the dacha, when I was a child, Sofia and I used to spend the summers together with my brothers. Occasionally a friend of my brother Konstantin would come to stay with us. He was the son of Dr Lesnoy, our family doctor. The boy was Vladimir Lesnoy.'

'Ah, yes, I think Miss Maslova mentioned that you had a prior connection with Inspector Lesnoy. Do you have any particular memories of him?'

'Only that he used to tease us and annoy us. Just as my brothers used to. When we were little girls, Sofia and I thought boys were nothing but an irritation.'

Pravdin smiled. 'I don't imagine that you or Miss Sofia killed Inspector Lesnoy because he pulled your pigtails when you were young, but his propensity to irritate is something that I have heard of from others too. Please continue with your story.'

'I don't think I saw Vladimir after 1904 whenI was about ten years old. Then when I was thirteen I went to school in Paris for five years. Since I got back, Sofia and I have been living with my father in Moscow, but life has become more and more difficult. As you know, Detective, the Socialist Revolutionaries hate people like me and my family.'

Tatiana stopped speaking, seemingly unable to continue. Sofia could feel her squeezing her hands tightly and sensed that she was struggling to continue. Pravdin opened his mouth to speak but Sofia gave him a sharp, warning glance and he said nothing. Tatiana took a deep breath and began again.

'About ten days ago a mob came to our home in Moscow to kill us. My father had been prepared for that awful moment and had made a plan for my...' Tatiana glanced at Sofia, '...our, escape. I didn't want to leave him, but he insisted that Sofia and I had to leave Moscow. We managed to get to Yaroslavsky Station and bought tickets on the first available train to Vladivostok. It was so frightening, so awful, I tried to be brave but...'

The memories of that night were too much. Tatiana broke down in tears, gripping Sofia's hand. 'Oh, Sofia, Papa is dead and the palace has been burned to the ground. I don't know what to do - why are we here and where are we going? What's the point? I wish I had stayed with Papa and died in the fire with him!'

Sofia stroked Tatiana's hand and tried to soothe her. 'It is tragic, horrible, but your life is still worth living. Think of Alexander and how much he cares for you. Don't you want to be alive so you and he can be together?'

Tatiana said nothing but continued to sob and Pravdin sat in silence to allow her some time to recover her composure. At last her tears slowed and she sat up and turned to him again, her eyes red and her face pale.

'What else do you want to know, Detective? Ask me anything you want.'

'If you're sure you are able to continue, Countess...' he said, gently.

'Yes, I am.'

'Well, tell me about the first few days on the train, before the Inspector's death. What did you observe about your fellow passengers?'

'Captain Ozertsov and his wife are very pleasant, but they often seem very tense. I suppose that is not surprising - they are in a similar situation to us, escaping from danger, trying to look forward to a new life, but it isn't easy.'

'Did they seem tense with each other or with their fellow passengers?'

'They certainly seemed uneasy when Inspector Lesnoy spoke to them. I can't imagine why - they don't seem the sort of people who would have ever been in trouble with the police and I would have thought they would feel reassured by having an official from the gendarmerie on the train.'

'Did you ever overhear any conversation between them and the Inspector?'

'Not very much. The Inspector seemed to know the

town where they came from - Oryol. I think they talked a little about life there.'

'What about Lesnoy's dealings with the other passengers. Did you notice any other tensions?'

'He asked Mr Zayats a lot of questions.'

'Did Mr Zayats answer willingly?'

'No,' Tatiana laughed for the first time that afternoon, 'Mr Zayats seemed to be very expert at not answering questions. I think he is probably hiding something - a mystery man. His accent is not Russian, is it - I think we all realised that, but I have no idea where he is from or what he is doing here. Alexander thinks…'

She broke off mid-sentence and bit her lower lip nervously as though she was worried she had said too much.

'What does Mr Zhuravlev think?'

'Oh, he's not being serious. He's a poet, you know, he has a vivid imagination.'

'And what imaginary role did Mr Zhuravlev cast Mr Zayats in?'

'You already know that - Alexander told me what he had told you.'

'True, quite true. Does Mr Zhuravlev - Alexander - tell you everything, Countess? I have the impression - and I hope you will not think it impertinent for me to say so - that the two of you have become quite close. Do you have plans for a life together once you reach Vladivostok?'

Tatiana blushed. 'We have only known each other a very short time, Detective, and amidst so much stress and confusion. First our escape from Moscow,' her lip trembled, 'and then the sad death of Inspector Lesnoy. There is too much uncertainty for us to talk about our lives, our plans for the future. I feel as though I am surviving from moment to moment.'

'Those doubts must make living for the day even more important. To have met Mr Zhuravlev with his passionate *Russkaya dusha* and his optimistic belief in the inherent

273

goodness of humanity, that must be a great comfort to you.'

Tatiana looked thoughtfully at Pravdin. 'Yes, that is so. I hadn't thought about it in that way, Detective, but what you say is true.'

'Shall we move on to the night in question, Countess? Please tell me what happened from the moment you sat down to dinner on the night the Inspector was killed.'

Tatiana sat up straight, smoothed her dress and composed herself.

'Sofia, Alexander, Inspector Lesnoy and myself were seated at this table, where we are now. Mr Zayats, Captain and Mrs Ozertsov at the next table. Alexander and I were talking about poetry; the Inspector was trying to flirt with Sofia, wasn't he, Sofia?'

She turned to her friend for confirmation. Sofia shrugged. 'I suppose so. I don't think he knew what he was doing or saying, he was so drunk.'

'Is that right, Countess?'

'He drank a lot of vodka. But it had run out that evening, so actually he hadn't been able to drink as much as usual. He was irritable at the start of the meal, but Sofia tried hard to charm him into forgetting.'

'He was still thinking about nothing but his vodka, though,' Sofia broke in. 'He kept calling across to Mr Zayats on the other table - "Don't forget that bottle you promised me, Dmitry!"'

'Do you remember who left the dining car first, Countess?'

'Alexander left first. I was quite surprised. We were in the middle of a conversation about *Over the Barriers.*'

'The poem by Boris Pasternak?'

'Yes, indeed!' Tatiana exchanged a look with Sofia as if to say, who would have guessed that this Detective from the back-of-beyond might have read Pasternak? Sofia smiled back as she thought how different Pravdin was to Inspector Lesnoy.

'I think Sofia and I left next - we were so tired and, honestly, we'd had enough of the Inspector's loud voice and alcoholic nonsense. No, actually, someone else left before us - Ekaterina. She didn't look very well, did she, Sofia?'

'No, she looked quite pale and drawn.'

'Did she say anything before she left?' Pravdin asked.

'Not that I remember. I think Sofia and I said "goodnight" to her and she just smiled.'

'Anything else?'

'Yes, Inspector Lesnoy said "goodnight Kiki" to her. I remember thinking how rude of him to talk to a lady like that, so over-familiar. He sounded as though he were mocking her. She looked shocked and angry - so would I have been if he'd spoken to me like that.'

'How did Captain Ozertsov react?'

'I couldn't see him.'

'Let me just take you back a little before that, Countess. Didn't Mrs Ozertsova say anything else to you? Or maybe give you something?'

'Did she?' Tatiana frowned in concentration and shook her head. 'Do you remember anything, Sofia?'

Sofia's heart sank. Of course she had known that Pravdin would bring this up eventually.

'I think perhaps Detective Pravdin wants to know about the shawl which Ekaterina lent you. I... perhaps somebody mentioned it in their witness statement.'

'Oh, yes, of course, I had quite forgotten. After Alexander left I felt a little chilly and as I said goodnight, Mrs Ozertsova noticed me shiver. She asked if I would like to borrow her paisley shawl - it was very kind of her.'

'So you accepted the shawl and put it round your shoulders?'

'Yes, that's right. She put it around me, in fact.'

'And did you say anything?'

'I said something like, "You're so kind - it's a lovely shawl and what a delicious scent; I shall wear it all night."'

'And did you?'

'We went back to our cabin and...' Tatiana's voice once again started to crack into a sob.

'It's all right, Countess, I don't wish to upset you. Just try to complete your account of the evening - we are nearly finished. Just a few more details. Did you and Miss Maslova leave the dining car together?'

Tatiana took a deep breath and tried to control her emotions.

'Yes, we left together, not long after Ekaterina.'

'And you both went straight to bed?' Pravdin glanced at Sofia, who avoided his look.

Tatiana glanced at Sofia and hesitated momentarily.

'No, not exactly. We entered the cabin and I saw an letter on the floor which must have been pushed under the door. It had my name on it, so I picked it up.'

'Did you recognise the handwriting?'

'Yes. Well I wasn't absolutely sure, but I thought it was from Alexander. I recognised it from seeing the poems he had written in his notebook.'

'Did you show Miss Maslova?'

'No. I wasn't sure what would be written inside. I thought it would be better to open it in private, when I was on my own. I hid it under the shawl and put the shawl and the letter on my bed while I got undressed.'

'Did Miss Maslova notice?'

'I don't know. Did you, Sofia? I'm sorry, I just wasn't sure what Alexander would have written.'

'I saw you pick an envelope off the floor. I didn't really think about it. To tell the truth I was a little distracted at that moment.'

'Were you? I remember you said something about a jacket and you left the cabin.'

Pravdin broke into the conversation. 'Miss Maslova went to return Lesnoy's jacket. Didn't that strike you as being strange, Countess?'

'No, I just thought it was fortunate. It gave me the

chance to open the letter and glance at its contents at least.'

'And that is what you did?'

'Yes - yes, I did and it was awful. I wished I'd never read the words.' Once again, Tatiana broke down in tears, and Sofia held her hand. 'It was from Alexander, but it was not the love letter or poem I'd expected. The words jumped out at me: "revolutionary mob... palace... fire... Count Shuysky... dead..." It only took a second for me to absorb the terrible news he had been too frightened to tell me face to face.'

Again, Pravdin allowed Tatiana time to calm herself before continuing to question her, as gently as he could.

'Had Miss Maslova returned by then? Did she find you crying after reading the letter?'

Tatiana frowned. 'No, she didn't return as quickly as I had expected. I changed into my nightdress, wrapped the letter in the shawl again and put them both under my pillow. Then I turned out the light, lay down in bed and cried.'

'Did you hear Miss Maslova return?'

'I don't think...' Tatiana looked nervously at Sofia.

'It's all right, Tatiana, Detective Pravdin already knows my story - I have been completely frank with him. You didn't hear me return, because when I did get back you were sleeping peacefully. Did you cry yourself to sleep?'

'Countess Shuyskaya. There is just one more fact I need to check and then you are free to go. Did you at any point leave your cabin, return through the dining car, and go from there into the carriage where the gold is stored, to visit Inspector Lesnoy in his cabin?'

Tatiana looked incredulous.

'No! Absolutely not!'

'So you didn't visit Lesnoy at all that night, wearing your borrowed shawl with its scent of *L'Heure Bleue*?'

'No, Detective! I swear on the memory of my beloved father, I did not.'

CHAPTER THIRTY-NINE

Pravdin sighed. Sofia looked at him and said, 'You can't seriously believe that Tatiana killed Inspector Lesnoy. It doesn't make any sense.'

Pravdin rubbed his temples in an attempt to reduce the tension he was feeling. 'What makes you think that?'

'Well, she doesn't seem to fit any of your "Three elements of a murder" theory. Firstly, Tatiana had no access to a weapon or means to kill, secondly she has no motive and thirdly she didn't have the opportunity to commit the crime.'

'That's not strictly true. I agree with your analysis, it seems most unlikely, but we cannot rule your friend out, if you think carefully about it. The perfume locates her at the time and place of the murder. The weapon? Even an innocently soft pillow can kill. Motive? This is less clear, but I presume that Lesnoy's father attended Tatiana's birth. Might he have had too much to drink, given his son's proclivities? Might Tatiana have taken revenge for the death of her mother at the shaky hands of an inebriated family doctor? Who knows what secrets hide behind that pretty face?'

Sofia sighed; tired, she rubbed her eyes, tilted her chin up, rested her head on the back of her chair, and shut her eyes.

'I give up, I give up, I… give… up…' she whispered as if to lull herself to sleep.

The train's hypnotic rhythm gently rocked her to sleep. For a brief moment she found herself transported back to the dacha, alternately rising and falling on the swing that had been knotted to a high branch of the big willow tree in the garden; the dappled sunlight flickering and dancing across her eyelids. Memories of calm and peace.

'You should go to sleep' Pravdin whispered.

She pretended to be asleep. 'Shhh… I am asleep.'

'Sofia, you should go to bed.'

A small smile crept across her lips.

'Assistant Detective Maslova, I order you to go to bed.'

Her fingers slowly crept her across the table and she waved her little finger at Pravdin's big, paw-like hand. He wanted to hook his little finger, which was as thick as her thumb, around hers and engage her in a gentle finger fight. He knew exactly where such a tangle of fingers would lead. He struggled to remain professionally detached. He wanted to lift her hand to his mouth and kiss it. He wanted to hold her face in his hands and kiss her lips. But he could not risk the integrity of the investigation.

'Go to bed, Assistant Maslova.' He spoke gently to her. 'Sofia - that's an order.'

Sofia finally opened her eyes slightly, noting his use of her given name. 'Am I a bad person… Sergei?' she asked.

'No, why do you say that?'

'I've enjoyed these days investigating with you. Who would have thought that death and blood, a cruel, violent murder of a man I knew, would have made me feel… feel so…'

'Alive?' Pravdin said, finishing her sentence.

'Yes, alive; does that make me a bad person?'

Pravdin grinned.

'It is quite natural, I think. Being so close to death, being so intimately connected with a murder, it is exciting. Why do you think I love my work? Not for my salary!'

Sofia thought about her melancholy. 'But now we have finished the interviews, what will we do? We have talked to everyone on the list. Will you even need me?'

'We need to think. Put our thoughts in order. We cannot do that while we are exhausted. And yes, my dear Assistant Detective, I will need you. You help me think; you are the one who "soothes my savage breast"'.

Sofia looked at how their close their fingers were. She was disappointed and, at the same time, impressed that he hadn't touched her hand. The truth was that she felt calm in his presence. She didn't want to stop talking to him. Maybe she had become addicted to solving the bloody puzzle of Lesnoy's murder with him.

Like a puppy that refuses to drop a bone she went back to the investigation. 'What do you make of Captain and Mrs Ozertsov? I find him a little strange, but she is really lovely, a good person.'

'Yes, he is an odd fellow. I know these privileged cavalry officer types. They are difficult to read, to understand. I expect that being locked up in a camp in Germany for several years, with a couple of thousand unwashed, typhus-ridden, starving serfs, changes your perspective on the big themes of life. Love, freedom, loyalty. I detect a ruthlessness running through both of their characters. I would not call either of them "lovely".'

Sofia looked sad. 'But Sergei, we are all focused on surviving at the moment. The Ozertsovs gave up everything: their house, their land, most of their belongings - everything except one another. I think their love is strong. I pray that they make it safely to California.'

Pravdin looked at her. 'You make survival sound quite romantic. Has it occurred to you that a survivor will do almost anything to carry on living? I think that if Captain and Mrs Ozertsov felt threatened, they would be quite capable of killing. The Captain spoke like a man who has killed before.'

Sofia fell silent, thinking about the different

possibilities. 'And Alexander? I can't see him actually murdering anyone.'

'Alexander Zhuravlev - our revolutionary poet,' Pravdin laughed. 'My dear, sweet Sofia, you should know that these quiet, romantic types are the worst of the worst. Their dainty words depend on having a vision of the dark side. Their passion and emotions can drive them to all sorts of excessive, irrational, behaviour. Tatiana's young admirer is not the innocent intellectual he wants to project. Honestly, he'd turn from an angst-ridden cissy into a psychotic, bloodthirsty killer in an instant if he suspected someone he loved was in danger.'

'Someone he loved? Like Tatiana, you mean?'

'Exactly.'

'Was she in danger?'

Pravdin did not respond.

The rhythm of the train was broken for a moment as they clattered across some points and then over a bridge.

'I think it must have been Dmitry,' Sofia said, changing the subject. 'He is a trained killer. Have you heard his stories about Africa? The way he talks about the Boers, he must have killed lots of them in the Orange Free State. He pretends to be a charming Anglo-Russian gentleman, he wants you to believe that he is everyone's favourite uncle, but I don't trust him one bit.'

'I'm not convinced he was involved,' Pravdin said. 'Zayats gets his orders from the Foreign Office in London. Their agenda doesn't include killing an unimportant Inspector. Do you believe that he would put his mission at risk by getting tangled up in a pointless murder?'

'But he does have poison and the bottle of cheap vodka which he could have used to kill Lesnoy. We know he was at Lesnoy's door.'

'Very true, but what is his motive? Two out of three doesn't persuade me of his guilt.'

Sofia's tired eyes shut involuntarily.

'Miss Maslova, Sofia...' Pravdin hesitated, 'Dearest

Sofia, you look exhausted. Please, go to bed. Leave me the notes; I'm going to order a cup of tea and review the whole case.'

'You know who killed Lesnoy, don't you?' She sat up abruptly, alert to something in his tone.

'Better to say "I have a strong feeling". But feelings often confuse the truth. What I do know is that there are six suspects and someone is guilty of murder.'

'Six?' Sofia said, frowning, 'So you haven't even ruled me out?'

Pravdin laughed and stood up. He offered her his hand and gently pulled her up from her chair. He pulled her towards him and paused. Sofia closed her eyes and parted her lips slightly, ready to receive the kiss she had been thinking about for the last three days and nights.

'Detective Pravdin,' interrupted the steward, 'Mr Tokar wishes to see you.'

Sofia felt the sparks that were jumping between them fade and die, just as the glowing embers from the engine were snatched from the locomotive's funnel by the icy wind and blown out in an instant.

'Do you want me to take notes?' she asked.

'No, Sofia, you go to bed.'

Sofia turned and walked through the dining carriage towards the door to the *spalny vagon*. As she left, she heard Pravdin order a cup of tea. When she reached the door she turned and looked at the handsome policeman looking intently at the notebook open on the table.

'Good night, Sergei,' she called, softly.

He was too focused on the notes to hear her.

CHAPTER FORTY

Pravdin scanned the pages of the notebook. He was searching for notes that Sofia had made at the start of the investigation.

After a few minutes he stood up and went through the door into the bullion wagon.

'Tokar?' he called, 'Where are you hiding?'

Andrey Tokar, unshaven and looking rather crumpled, pulled back the curtain and greeted the blue-eyed policeman.

'Ah, Inspector Pravdin, you got my message, good. Listen, I think that Lesnoy was alive.'

Pravdin smiled. 'There is no doubt that he *was* alive. You and the other passengers saw him walking and talking right up to… to what? Midnight of the night he was murdered.'

'No Inspector I was thinking that maybe I heard him alive the next morning.'

'Why do you think that?'

'Dream analysis.'

'Dream analysis? Come on Tokar - next you'll be asking me to believe that the tea leaves at the bottom of your cup reveal the face of the killer.'

'Listen to me, Detective; remember the dream I had about the piglet?'

'Yes, the flying pig and the clowns.'

'This afternoon I was taking my after-lunch siesta. I had exactly the same dream.'

'The pig, the circus clowns, the cannon?'

'Yes, with the clowns, but not the cannon, but the squealing pig woke me up, and guess what. The squealing was real, but it was not made by a baby pig.'

'So what kind of baby was it?' Pravdin was tired and found it difficult to feign interest in the bank official's strange story.

'The squealing was the train. Braking before a station. We stopped at a station at about 4.15 this afternoon - didn't we?'

'Yes, some small town, I can't remember where.'

'That's when I woke up.'

'So, now you are telling me that the squealing pig in your dream was actually the sound of the train coming to a stop?'

'Yes. Exactly. The night Lesnoy was killed, we stopped at another small town at midnight, a couple of hours before Verkhneudinsk. I remember looking out of the window when I woke up, just after the dream. Do you recall that in my dream there was a muscle man sounding a giant gong? That must have been a church bell ringing. Five times'

'I thought you said it was midnight?'

'Yes, midnight Moscow time, but that was five o'clock local time.'

'Listen, Tokar, I am tired; I am not convinced of your dream analysis. I want to go to sleep but I still have to review the interview notes. I suggest you get some sleep.'

'Hang on, you don't understand. I think my dream was influenced by reality. I believe that the piglet was actually Lesnoy. When the pig shouted, "Who the hell are you?" that must have been Lesnoy.'

'You think so?' Pravdin frowned as he tried to make sense of Tokar's bizarre story.

'Tell me, Pravdin, how was Inspector Lesnoy actually killed? Was he shot? I think the cannon I heard in my dream was a gun shot. Please tell me - this nightmare is destroying my nerves.'

Pravdin sighed, 'Look Tokar, I have five or six suspects, five quite credible motives and four possible methods. I am sorry to disappoint you, but a gun is not on the shortlist of murder weapons. I have a lot of cold hard evidence to review and tomorrow I am hoping to be able to reveal who murdered my colleague, as well as how and why. Nevertheless, I will certainly take your flying pigs into account. However, in my limited experience the interpretation of dreams is better left to experts like that Austrian Freud or our own Nikolai Ossipov, not simple police detectives like me and certainly not Bullion Transport Officers like you. Good night, Tokar.'

'Please Detective, I know it is a lot to take in. I have written it down for you. Think about it. You will see that it all makes sense.'

Pravdin took the note that Tokar had poked through the bars of the cage, glanced at it and put it into the notebook. 'I'm going now, but I promise that I will read this and if I have any questions about dream analysis, I will come and see you later.'

CHAPTER FORTY-ONE

The steward rapped at the doors of the first class passengers. He repeated, 'Breakfast will be served in twenty minutes, ladies and gentlemen, breakfast in twenty minutes,' as he passed down the corridor.

The tall figure of Detective Sergei Pravdin stood at the far end of the dining carriage, blocking the door to the bullion wagon. He nodded a greeting to each of the passengers as they arrived for breakfast. He smiled to himself as he recognised the guilty looks that each one gave him as they glanced in his direction and muttered 'Good morning Detective.'

Once everyone was settled and tea had been served he cleared his throat.

The muted conversation in the carriage fell away and soon the carriage was silent, except for the distant pulse of the engine and the sound of plates being readied from the kitchen. He noted that Dominic was sitting with his back towards him, while all the other passengers had chosen to sit in seats facing him.

'Ladies and gentleman,' he started, 'I would like to begin by thanking you all for your cooperation over the past four days. I know it has not been an easy or pleasant time for you. However, my investigation is now complete.'

There was silence. Sofia looked intently at him and

squeezed Tatiana's hand. After a long pause, Alexander spoke.

'Do you mean, Detective Pravdin, that you have solved the case? That you know who murdered Inspector Lesnoy?'

'Yes, Mr Zhuravlev, I mean exactly that.'

Everyone looked at him expectantly. Dominic Hare twisted around in his seat to look at Pravdin and said 'Well Detective, if one of us is the murderer, shouldn't you get a move on and arrest him - or her - immediately?'

'It isn't quite that simple, Mr Zayats. Please, I ask you all to indulge me a little longer and allow me to narrate the "story" - the very interesting story - of the brutal and needless killing of Inspector Lesnoy. Please feel free to continue with your breakfast while I begin.'

Everyone glanced at each other nervously, unsure about what was coming next. Nobody seemed inclined to eat the boiled eggs and slices of cold sausage which had been served. Pravdin began his story.

'On the night of Wednesday the first of March, all of you dined in here as usual. Captain and Mrs Ozertsov and Mr Zayats, you sat together at that table. Countess Shuyskaya, Miss Maslova, Mr Zhuravlev and Inspector Lesnoy sat together at this one.' Pravdin paused and looked directly at Alexander.

'Mr Zhuravlev, you were the first to leave the dining car. You returned to your cabin to write a letter to the Countess; however, from the witness statements I have evidence that you also took the opportunity to pry into Mr Zayats's possessions. Were you looking for the vial of poison which you knew was in his attaché case, or for his gun?'

Alexander blushed furiously and began to stutter, 'I wasn't prying, I was looking for my own gun, which I had reason to believe Mr Zayats had taken.'

'So, you admit you wanted a gun?'

'Yes, but not to kill Lesnoy.'

'I'm not so sure. Lesnoy had made it clear that he knew you weren't merely a Romantic poet. Far from it, you are one of the leading members of a group of revolutionaries who are hell-bent on violence and overthrow of the Russian state. In fact the reason you were on the train was to escape arrest after playing a leading role in a murderous attack on the Shuysky palace. You fled the scene of your crime and jumped on board the train, only to find that you were cooped up with a member of the Special Gendarmerie who recognised your pretty face from the posters on his office wall.'

Alexander leapt to his feet. 'That's completely untrue! Tatiana knows I wasn't involved in the Shuysky palace attack. Far from it - I tried my utmost to stop it and, when I couldn't, I swore to make amends by carrying out the Count's last wishes. That's why I got on the train - to protect his daughter.'

'That doesn't account for why you suddenly felt the need to carry your gun on that particular night. How do you explain that?'

'I… I don't know,' Alexander sat back down. 'I was feeling threatened, anxious about being arrested. Lesnoy was volatile - friendly one minute, aggressive the next. Every time the train stopped at a major town I expected him to arrest me and put me into the custody of the local police. I knew he was getting off at Verkhneudinsk and I thought my number was up.'

'So you wanted your gun handy to resist arrest? To shoot Lesnoy and his colleagues in the line of duty? That in itself is a capital offence, Zhuravlev.'

'But I didn't do anything - Lesnoy was dead before we got to Verkhneudinsk.'

'So you must have been relieved when you heard of his death?'

There was a long pause while Pravdin and Alexander held each other's gaze.

'Well, Mr Zhuravlev?'

'Yes, I was relieved if you want the truth. Relieved that someone else had got me off the hook. But I didn't do it - I swear it.'

'But you had a motive and the means…'

Alexander interrupted. 'No, I couldn't find my gun in Zayats's case.'

'You found the vial of poison, though. Weren't you tempted to use that to poison Lesnoy?'

Alexander shook his head in exasperation. 'I didn't even contemplate it. How would I have administered it? I had a quick look for my gun and, when I couldn't find it, I went to bed.'

Pravdin nodded. 'Very well. Luckily for you, nobody has testified to seeing you anywhere near Lesnoy's cabin that night. Reluctantly, you are no longer a suspect, Mr Zhuravlev, but when we arrive in Vladivostok you will be questioned about your role in the attack on the Shuysky Palace and the murder of Count Shuysky. Any attempt to resist arrest will make your punishment a lot more severe.'

Alexander looked at Tatiana and shook his head, half relieved, half despairing. Pravdin turned his attention to Sofia.

'Miss Maslova. Investigating Officers of the Special Gendarmerie are trained to regard any civilian who gets involved in a criminal investigation with particular suspicion.'

Sofia blushed with mortification. How dare Pravdin humiliate her like that! She opened her mouth to protest but Pravdin held up a warning hand.

'We have to be on our guard for anyone trying to gain access to confidential case details or attempting to misdirect the investigation. However, you have proved to be an exemplary assistant and a real asset to the investigation. I thank you.'

He smiled warmly at her and Sofia smiled back.

'Moreover,' he continued, 'You were the only suspect to come clean about your actions voluntarily. You confessed to hitting my colleague on the head with a vodka bottle, but having heard the evidence, and reconstructed your struggle...' Here Pravdin paused and looked at Sofia while she blushed again, this time with pride, 'I have officially noted your actions as self-defence and, while you probably knocked Lesnoy unconscious, it is almost impossible to batter a man to death with a glass bottle, unless it is a champagne bottle, made of thicker, stronger glass. Normal bottles break before the skull of the victim. Being stabbed to death with a broken bottle is all too common in Russia. But being bludgeoned to death with a champagne bottle is limited to the upper classes. So, I am certain you did not kill Inspector Lesnoy. Please consider yourself completely exonerated in this case.' He inclined his head somewhat formally at Sofia and she mirrored his gesture solemnly. Pravdin looked around the room and his eyes rested on Dominic.

'Mr Zayats, or do you prefer to be called by your real name, Mr Dominic Hare?' Dominic shrugged and murmured, 'I have no preference, Detective.' Sofia noticed him looking at his pocket watch. It seemed strange - did he have an appointment to keep elsewhere, she wondered?

'Very well, Mr Hare, loyal servant of King George of England, perhaps you could be good enough to look at me while I am talking to you.' Dominic shrugged and turned in his seat to face Pravdin. 'When I first began my investigation, you were the prime suspect. The reason was simple - of all the possible perpetrators here in the first class carriage, you are the only one with the appropriate psychological profile and professional experience.'

'That is not strictly correct, Detective,' Dominic answered calmly, 'Captain Ozertsov is a trained soldier. I'll wager he has killed a great deal more men than I have.'

Pravdin shrugged. 'I take your point, Mr Hare, but there is a difference between the anonymous deaths which a soldier is responsible for in the chaos of war and the cold, clinical assassinations which a spy is trained to do. Is that a fair assessment?'

It was Dominic's turn to shrug. 'Possibly. Please do continue your interesting story, I am very keen to learn what I am supposed to have done and why.'

'Let's start with the "why", then. On the face of it, your motive might have been the fear of discovery of your true identity. You made a valiant attempt to pass yourself off as a Russian but realised that Lesnoy had established that you were an English agent. However, I don't believe you were seriously bothered by his discovery; you enjoyed playing your little game of cat-and-mouse, or should I say hare-and-tortoise. But in truth the whole charade was nothing more nor less than a red herring.'

Dominic snorted. 'Perhaps I should retrain as a zoo-keeper, Pravdin. Come on, you're wasting time. You know perfectly well I didn't kill Lesnoy, so why don't you move on to your next suspect.' He glanced at his watch again.

'Don't be in such a hurry, Mr Hare. Let me tell you what I know of your movements on the night of the murder. You left Lesnoy and the Captain in the dining car to go and fetch the vodka which you had promised to Lesnoy. You found Mr Zhuravlev asleep and you topped up the vodka with a deadly dose of the poison which is part of your espionage kit. Then you took the vodka to Lesnoy's cabin with the intention of poisoning him.'

Dominic remained impassive, so Pravdin continued. 'You were worried that Lesnoy had got wind of your real scheme when he overheard you sending a telegram at Yaroslavsky station.'

There was a lengthy pause. Only Pravdin noted the almost imperceptible flicker in Dominic's eyelid which confirmed he had uncovered the truth. 'However, when you handed over the lethal vodka you thought you heard someone else in the cabin.'

'Yes,' interrupted Dominic, 'And you've just told us that it was Miss Maslova, who used the bottle to knock Lesnoy unconscious, so he didn't drink it anyway. Come on, Pravdin, I'm off the hook - admit it.'

'In fact, Lesnoy did drink a small amount. He offered some to Miss Maslova, too, but luckily she didn't drink any. Off the hook for murder, yes, I do admit it. But you can still be tried for attempted murder and I will be investigating your other plot too, so don't imagine you're going to get off lightly, Mr Hare.'

Dominic turned away again as if he really didn't care. The Ozertsovs exchanged anxious glances and Pavel took his wife's hand in his own. As they had anticipated, Pravdin turned his attention to Ekaterina.

'Mrs Ozertsova, I realise that this has been a very upsetting time for you. However, I do not feel that you have been entirely honest with me. You categorically denied ever having encountered Vladimir Lesnoy before you met him on this train. But if that is the case, why did you seem to detest him so vehemently from the moment you saw him?'

Ekaterina gritted her teeth. 'He was a drunkard, a rude, boorish drunkard. He was not a gentleman. I'm sure everybody else will agree.' She looked around for approval at her fellow passengers and there were murmurings of assent.

'Yes, so I have heard. Well, perhaps I understand, then. You are of a sensitive disposition and Lesnoy's drunken crassness offended you. Particularly on that final, fateful evening when he went just too far.' Pravdin noticed Pavel grasp his wife's hand more tightly. He continued, 'Several of your fellow passengers noticed your reaction when Lesnoy said "Goodnight" to you. But let's not dwell on that for the moment. You returned to your cabin and, according to your husband, you were still there when he came in a little later. However, I do not believe you were asleep.'

'That is true, Detective, I was awake when Pavel came in, but I went to sleep soon after.'

'Well, that may be so, but before you went to sleep you

left your cabin for a short time. I don't know whether the Captain had fallen asleep himself or whether you went with his blessing, but I am sure that you returned to the dining car and from there passed into the armoured carriage and into Lesnoy's cabin. Mr Tokar smelled your scent, *L'Heure Bleue* - it reminded him of his wife.' Pravdin stopped talking and looked steadily at Ekaterina, waiting for a reaction.

Ekaterina sat in silence, making no attempt to deny the accusation. Eventually Pravdin said, 'Shall I go on?' Ekaterina shrugged, but Pavel broke in angrily.

'No, Pravdin, you have said enough. My wife is not a murderer, so let's just stop this charade right now.'

'In that case you won't mind if I turn my attention to your own role in this crime, Captain. And I will do so in just a moment, but for the sake of completeness, let me finish what I have started. Mrs Ozertsova went to Lesnoy, perhaps not with the intention of killing him. She may simply have wanted to talk to him, or possibly to buy his silence with a bribe. However, when she entered his cabin he was unconscious on his bed, knocked out by Miss Maslova. In a moment of madness Mrs Ozertsova saw an opportunity to silence Lesnoy for good. Battered and drunk, he was in no state to put up a struggle; what could be simpler than to remove the pillow from beneath his head and hold it over his face, pressing it down until he finally stopped breathing and moved serenely from unconsciousness into death. So clean, so quiet, hardly a murder at all, eh Mrs Ozertsova?'

'I didn't plan to kill him, I just wanted him to go away, to leave us alone…' Ekaterina finally broke down and sobbed into her husband's shoulder.

'Hush my darling, it's all right - you didn't kill him. I know you didn't.'

'That is an interesting comment, Captain,' Pravdin said. 'You are quite correct that your wife's attempted suffocation of Lesnoy failed. You know that, don't you?'

'Yes, I do know,' Pavel murmured.

'When your wife returned, *you* were pretending to sleep. You waited until you were sure that she was sleeping and then you went to visit the inspector yourself, taking with you the steak knife which you had "borrowed" from the dining car.'

Ekaterina looked up and stared at Pavel. 'No, no!' she gasped.

Pavel looked ahead, stony-faced. 'I did it for the honour of my family name.'

Pravdin nodded, an almost sympathetic look on his face. 'Yes, I do believe you are an honourable man, Captain, but there is nothing honourable about murder, particularly when your victim is quite unable to defend himself.'

Pavel stood, his military background very visible in his bearing, and gazed steadily at Pravdin. 'You are correct, of course, I have committed an unforgivable sin.' He laid his hand tenderly on Ekaterina's shoulder and spoke softly to her. 'Please forgive me, my darling, I couldn't bear to see you hurt.' Then, louder, with just the hint of a crack in his voice, 'What happens now, Pravdin? Do you put me in chains?' he held out his hands in front of him in a pantomimed invitation to be handcuffed.

Pravdin smiled at the Captain and gestured for Pavel to sit again. 'I expect the real murderer has just breathed a sigh of relief. They must have thought they had got away with it. You, Captain, and quite possibly your wife, may be charged with attempted murder, but you should thank your wife for saving you from the *katorga* camp. The pillow she placed over Lesnoy's head and chest acted as a protective buffer and while your vicious stab through the pillow drew some blood, you caused little more than a superficial wound. No, in spite of all your best efforts, none of these attempts made on my colleague's life was actually the cause of death - none of them was the mortal blow.'

Sofia looked puzzled. 'I don't understand what you mean, Detective, what was "the mortal blow?"'

'I use the term loosely - what I mean is that, clearly, there were several strikes on Lesnoy's life that night. Firstly, Mr Hare's attempt to poison him; secondly, your defensive blow with the bottle, Sofia; thirdly, Mrs Ozertsova's suffocation; and fourthly, the Captain's stabbing. I must say I am tempted to arrest the lot of you, and charge you with "joint endeavour in the commission a murder". However, you each acted independently and each of you is, in my view, guilty to a differing degree. If cowardice, stupidity, incompetence, paranoia and inhumanity were illegal, Mother Russia would be a better place. However these are not currently crimes and I cannot in good faith arrest any of you for the murder of Inspector Lesnoy.'

The first class passengers seemed dumbstruck. Nobody spoke, nobody moved. Eventually Sofia said, tentatively, 'But you said there was a mortal blow, a fifth "strike". If it wasn't any of us, then who…?' Her voice tailed off. As she spoke, the rest of the passengers were looking around at each other in turn, trying to work out which of them had not been ruled out. As Sofia's question hung in the air, everyone's gaze had come to rest on the same person. Sofia gasped and at the same instant all colour drained from the beautiful face of Countess Tatiana Shuyskaya.

CHAPTER FORTY-TWO

Detective Pravdin laughed. 'My dear Countess, I apologise. I had no intention that your fellow first class passengers should jump to such a wildly improbable and ill-informed conclusion. It is ironic that everybody else, each with their own degree of culpability, should now believe that Lesnoy was murdered by the one person who definitely had no opportunity, no means and, most importantly, no motive.'

Abruptly Dominic stood up. 'You bloody fool, Pravdin, why are you practising these idiotic deceptions on us? You have now ruled all of us out, so why are you wasting time with these irrelevant stories. Just tell us who did it - who murdered Inspector Lesnoy?'

'Andrey Tokar,' Pravdin announced.

There was a split second's silence before everyone started talking at once. Eventually Dominic spoke up. 'Don't be bloody ridiculous, man; Tokar is locked into a steel cage. How could he possibly have killed Lesnoy?'

'Ladies and gentlemen, listen to me please. Mr Tokar has confessed to the murder. He told me last night. I need to take a formal statement of his confession. Sofia, would you please take notes. Mr Zhuravlev, I'd like you to be a witness. Countess Shuyskaya too, if you please.'

Still shocked at the news, Alexander, followed by Tatiana and Sofia, filed past Pravdin and stepped over the coupling between the carriages. The noise of freeze-dried wind, the clattering wheels and the distant thump of the steam locomotive was louder here and the fierce wind made it much colder. Through the gaps in the iron footplates Sofia watched the snow that lay between the tracks rush by. She paused for a moment wondering how she had found herself tangled up in such a strange and sorry mess. 'It wasn't meant to be this way.' she said to herself sadly, 'Come on Sofia, you can do it.' Just then a high-pitched scream pierced the cold and Pravdin pushed past her and into the bullion wagon.

Sofia pulled herself forward and stepped into the secure carriage. Tatiana was alternately screaming and gasping; her mouth was wide open, her eyes looked as though they might pop out of her skull at any moment, her fingers were stretched wide apart in agony. Initially Sofia could not understand what had triggered such an extreme reaction. Tatiana's slim body, supported by Alexander, was slowly collapsing with shock, revulsion and the vomit reflex. Sofia turned to look through the bars of the cage.

Death is never picturesque. Certainly, some deaths are more horrific than others. Tokar's death was neither distinguished nor heroic. There was nothing noble about the grey-pink and red mixture of brains and blood that had been splattered over the carriage ceiling and walls. Nothing artistic about the large puddle of brown-red blood that was congealing into a clotted mess on the floor. There was nothing wise or kind about Tokar's pale waxy face lying on the floor, eyes wide open, his shattered mouth blasted with black specks of burnt cordite.

As Sofia's shock slowly faded it was replaced by the sound of Tatiana's sobbing and retching. Sofia was surprised to find herself considering forensically the process that had led to Tokar's death. Brain splatter, blood puddle, cordite burns… must be a bullet, no bullet without a gun, where was the gun? And there it was: the method, a service revolver, lay on the floor near Tokar's right hand.

What's next in Sergei Pravdin's investigative process? Motive and opportunity. Tokar was, by his own admission, feeling melancholic. Motive: melancholia. Opportunity? Sofia looked at the blood; several hours of congealing, she thought. Alone in the cage for hour upon hour, Tokar had ample opportunity to carry out his last, desperate act. If you asked someone to sketch the scene of a suicide, the scene in the cage is what they would draw. She turned to Pravdin who was standing, gripping the cage bars, staring at the body.

'Sergei, look, there is a piece of paper; Tokar has left a note.'

'Can you reach it?' he asked. Sofia knelt down and put her arm through the bars and tried to stretch her arm by waving it to the left and to the right. But her arm was not long enough.

Alexander, still holding Tatiana in his arms said, 'Mr Hare has a walking stick. Maybe we can use it to reach the letter. I'll go and get it.'

Alexander gently steered the sobbing Tatiana back into the dining carriage, and guided her into a chair. 'Mr Tokar is dead,' he announced.

'Why am I not surprised?' said Dominic.

'Mr Hare, Detective Pravdin needs to reach a letter written by Tokar. May he borrow your walking stick, please?'.

'I'll get it immediately.'

Alexander returned to the bullion wagon with the eagle-headed cane, passed it through the bars and dragged the piece of paper across the floor; as he did this a key slid out from the paper. Once the paper was close enough to the edge, Pravdin reached into the cage and picked it up.

'What does it say?' Sofia asked, softly.

'It confirms my suspicions. You two come with me. I'll read this to everyone next door.'

Once all the passengers were seated Pravdin began to read:

I, Andrey Tokar of Gogolevsky Boulevard, Moscow, do humbly beg forgiveness from my darling wife, Anna, my beautiful children, my parents and from God for the wrong I have done. Since last April, 1916, I have been involved in a fraud to steal gold bullion from the Russian Imperial Bank. To this date I have stolen almost 15,000 roubles worth of gold and silver.

Once Inspector Vladimir Lesnoy had discovered my crime, I had no choice but to shoot him dead. I confessed my action to Detective Pravdin but I am not a strong man. I cannot face life in a katorga or execution for financial treason against the crown. Now my hands are stained with blood, I realise that my time is up. I cannot go on.

Please, forgive me,
Signed
Andrey Tokar

The dining car remained silent. Pravdin placed the suicide note on the table in front of Sofia who unfolded it and slid it over the table to Tatiana who had the notebook open in front of her.

Dominic raised his hand. 'Detective, my understanding was that Mr Tokar was locked into the security cage in Moscow and the only other key was in Vladivostok. How could he have killed Lesnoy?'.

Pravdin replied, 'That was my understanding also. Two keys, one in Moscow and one awaiting his arrival in Vladivostok. However, when we found Tokar a few minutes ago, we observed a key on the floor by his body. So it seems he did have the ability to come and go from his cage, after all.'

A quiet discussion among the passengers followed.

While Pravdin was speaking Tatiana had flicked through the notebook to the first blank page. A jagged edge of torn paper marked the place where a page had been torn out. She slid Tokar's suicide note over the notebook, rotated it and aligned it with the torn edge. She tapped Alexander's hand and pointed at the perfect match. Sofia and Alexander looked closely at what Tatiana had done. Alexander carefully placed a brass key onto the page and made a slight twisting action with his right wrist, as if opening a lock. Sofia and Tatiana looked at him expectantly. Then, slowly, he whook his head and wagged his index finger to indicate that it didn't work.

Tatiana whispered, 'The key doesn't work?'

Alexander whispered back, 'It doesn't even fit into the lock. How did Tokar get that piece of paper from the notebook?'.

'Ladies and Gentlemen,' Pravdin announced, 'I now confirm that the investigation into Inspector Lesnoy's murder is over. You are all free to go about your business as normal. Once again, The State Gendarmerie of his Highness Tsar Nicholas Romanov thanks you for your cooperation. Let us please put this sad episode behind us and enjoy our breakfast.'

Sofia noticed the corner of a piece of loose paper in the notebook. She pulled it out and saw the embossed letterhead of the State Bank of the Russian Empire. She looked at the handwritten note.

Squealing - train brakes
Gong - Church bell
Five O'Clock (midnight Moscow)- Babushkin (three hours before
Verkhneudinsk)
'Who the hell are you?' - Lesnoy?
Circus cannon - gun shot'
Piglet - Lesnoy???
Was Lesnoy shot?
Murderer - ???
Detective Pravdin, I urge you to consider my evidence. Please do not disregard it.
Sincerely Tokar

Sofia carefully folded the note to show only the signature and placed it on top of the suicide note.

The three friends looked at the mismatched scrawls

and then at each other.

The sound of a revolver being cocked made them jump.

Pravdin was pointing his pistol directly at Tatiana's face. She raised her hands.

'Sergei! What, in the name of God, have you done?' Distraught, Sofia could barely articulate her words.

Pravdin said, 'Alexander Zhuravlev, can you please put your hands up, very slowly, and tell everyone what you have discovered.'

Alexander did as he was told.

'The key we found by the body doesn't work; it doesn't even fit in the lock,' Alexander answered.

'Which is significant why?'

'Tokar could not have killed Lesnoy.'

'And you Countess Shuyskaya, please tell the good people of First Class what you have found.'

'Th... that...' Tatiana stammered, 'That Mr Tokar's suicide note was written on paper torn from your notebook. And I believe that only you and Sofia had access to it for the last days.'

'Brilliant, quite brilliant. Who would have thought that two such *duras*, two soft-headed dimwits, would solve the mysterious death of Andrey Tokar.'

Sofia raised her hands like her two friends. 'And you, Detective Sergei Pravdin, you murdered Mr Tokar and also Inspector Lesnoy.'

Pravdin laughed. 'How did you work that out, pretty one?'

'Mr Tokar's dream. The piglet's squealing was the sound of the train braking to a stop at a town called Babushkin. The gong at the circus was the sound of a real church bell ringing, the pig saying "Who the hell are you?" that was Lesnoy, alive if not well at five o'clock in the morning. The cannon, I think that was a gunshot, fired by you, into Lesnoy's temple.'

'Why do you think I fired the shot?' Pravdin lowered

his pistol.

'Lesnoy knew all the first-class passengers - he had been travelling with us for a week. He wouldn't say "who the hell are you?" to any of us. It must have been someone unknown to him, someone who had got on the train at the station before Verkhneudinsk, someone with a gun.'

Pravdin looked at Sofia without emotion.

Sofia continued 'It seems that, despite all our best efforts to kill him, Lesnoy was still alive at five o'clock the next morning when you, Detective Pravdin, joined the train and shot him. You must have done it. You are the only stranger among us.'

Pravdin nodded. 'What impressive skills of deduction you have developed, Miss Maslova.'

'And when poor Mr Tokar related his dream and its interpretation, he unwittingly signed his own death warrant.'

'Yes, unfortunately Tokar had to be liquidated.'

'Don't be so modest, Pravdin,' said Dominic from behind him, 'You are more than a crooked provincial policeman. You are the Potato Sack Killer: the man Lesnoy was investigating, the man Lesnoy was coming to arrest. How many people have you slaughtered? Fifteen? Twenty? More?'

CHAPTER FORTY-THREE

Sofia was never completely sure whether she remembered the truth of what had happened next, or some imaginary, dreamlike version of subsequent events. Her memory of the moment that Pravdin fired his pistol was fixed in her memory in minute detail. She remembered his arm swinging up and his finger starting to tighten on the trigger. She remembered realising that he was going to shoot Tatiana.

She remembered standing so as to block Pravdin's bullets from hitting her friend. She remembered the flash of the gun, immediately in front of her, the jet of smoke and sparks. But not the noise. She remembered the feeling of being punched by the first bullet as it struck her in the ribs. She remembered being forced backwards against the table by the thump of the second bullet as it hit her chest and the third bullet as it smacked into her shoulder.

She knew that it was physically impossible but later she would describe, quite clearly, watching the first spinning bullet as it punched a hole in the velvet of her jacket, split three layers of horsehair canvas and passed through the cotton padding. She could not have actually seen it but she clearly recalled how the heavy lead bullet left her jacket and went through the silk of her dress and then into her bodice. The bodice she had made all those weeks ago.

Later she had found the second and the third bullets. They were split open like grotesque metal flowers, bright and shiny on the inside, dull and dented on the outside. Squashed and bent by the diamonds hidden in her bodice and caught on the rebound by the layers of fabric that surrounded them.

The energy from the bullets knocked her backwards. As she twisted and fell she saw Dominic Hare pull his own gun from under his perfectly tailored tweed jacket. She heard him shout, 'Get down!'

She found herself on all fours, winded, unable to breathe, staring with blinking-eyed astonishment at the grubby, rucked up rug that lay on the carriage floor. She found herself shocked that Pravdin had actually fired his gun, astonished at his inhumanity and surprised to be alive. She finally took a deep breath. She had survived.

Just as she inhaled she felt the carriage floor tremble and then shudder as the train suddenly braked. She heard Dominic stumble and fall over; his Colt automatic hit the floor and skidded, spinning past her left hand and under the table where it bounced against Alexander's boot. She did not actually see it, but later, when she told the story, she was able to imagine how Alexander's hand reached down under the table and picked up Dominic's gun. Still on her hands and knees, Sofia's head was safely out of the way when Alexander fired three bullets in quick succession into Pravdin's chest. Three holes, in the form of an neat, equilateral triangle around his heart, like the three-pronged bite of a giant bed bug.

Pravdin dropped, dead. First onto his knees and then flat onto the floor.

The train's emergency stop slid the dead policeman's body between Sofia's arms where she looked at his handsome profile. 'Oh Sergei,' she thought, 'what an ugly, cruel mess you have made.'

Sofia felt strong hands grip her arms as Pavel and Alexander picked her up from the floor. She stood, swaying on her feet for a moment, still looking at Pravdin's body and the pool of blood that was spreading out from under it.

Dominic knelt down by the body and felt for a pulse. He untangled the gun from the dead policeman's fingers and stood up. He looked around.

'Is everyone all right?' His question was answered by silence inside the restaurant carriage and the sound of shooting outside. The Englishman gently pushed Sofia's shoulders so he could pass by her, and picked up his automatic from the table where Alexander had placed it.

'Now listen. With the help of some colleagues, I have stopped the train. Shortly there will be a small explosion and we will start to transfer the gold from the armoured wagon to a truck. I need you all to go to back to your sleeping compartments and stay there.'

Alexander took Tatiana by the hand and led her up the carriage, followed by Pavel who looked stoic and Ekaterina who was shaken and tearful.

Sofia looked at Dominic. 'Mr Hare, If you are driving to Vladivostok would you please take me with you, I've had enough of this train.'

Dominic took her hand and said, 'Of course, Miss Maslova, the more the merrier. Incidentally, one question before you go: how was it that Pravdin's bullets failed to kill you?'

Sofia looked down at her punctured jacket. She gently wiggled her index finger into the bullet hole over her left breast and said, 'I've got a kilo of cut diamonds hidden in my bodice. I think they saved my life.'

Dominic laughed and shook his head incredulously. 'Sofia, you are an amazing young woman. I have to organise some logistical matters, but I give you my word that I will come and find you when we are ready to depart.'

CHAPTER FORTY-FOUR

As the truck rattled its way along the rough-surfaced roads of Primorskaya Oblast, Alexander opened the folder which Dominic had entrusted to his safe-keeping and flicked through the thick pile of papers. He was startled to see his own slightly-smudged but immediately recognisable face jump out at him from the flimsy pamphlet advertising the Fourth Thursday International Working Women's Day meeting. That bloody meeting, he thought, counting the days back on his fingers. Two weeks, yet it seemed like a lifetime. That meeting in Moscow had been the start of this whole horrendous episode. He looked at Tatiana, dozing next to him, her head resting so naturally on his shoulder and decided that perhaps the past fourteen days had not been an unmitigated disaster.

He continued to work his way through the papers. The torn corner of a cream coloured envelope caught his eye. As he fished it out his heart jumped; was it the letter? He pulled it free and held it in his hands like a precious holy relic, addressed in black ink to Tatiana Shuyskaya and Sofia Maslova below the Shuysky coat of arms. My God, he thought - finally, the letter which the Count had entrusted to his care, the letter which had led to him jumping onto the train. He gave Tatiana a gentle nudge, but she continued to sleep. Sofia, however, sitting on his other side, was wide awake.

'What's that?' she asked. With some trepidation, Alexander handed the envelope to her.

'It's been opened,' she said.

'Count Shuysky gave it to me to pass on to you and Tatiana, but I dropped it as I got onto the train. Lesnoy obviously found and opened it.'

Sofia drew out two pieces of fine-quality writing paper from the envelope. She unfolded the one which bore her name and read it in silence. She handed the other letter, bearing Tatiana's name, to Alexander. 'I think you should wake her, Sacha.'

The next time the truck stopped, Alexander left the two sisters together, embracing, crying and laughing at the long list of coincidences from their past lives that now made sense. He took another letter from the folder, this time a carbon copy of an official typewritten letter; he wanted to show it to Pavel.

January 1917
Esteemed Brigadier Brilyov,

We have recently had a breakthrough in our ten year long investigation of the serial killer popularly known as 'the Potato Sack Killer'. We have reason to believe that he is now living and working in the Verkhneudinsk area and I am sure you will join us in wishing to apprehend him before he carries out yet another heinous crime, this time in your jurisdiction. To this end, I would be grateful if you could be so good as to afford all possible assistance to the senior detective, Inspector Vladimir Lesnoy, who has been leading investigations into this case. He will be arriving in Verkhneudinsk by train in the next few weeks, further details of his travel arrangements to follow. We would request that he is met at Verkhneudinsk by one of your officers of equal rank and accommodated with a desk and lodgings, ideally close to the Office of Gendarmes.

Yours faithfully,
Brigadier Grigory Zyuzin
Chief-of-Police, Moscow

'Interesting,' said Pavel, 'So, Zayats - Hare - was right.'

On the back of the letter, in hand-written scrawl, were some notes ending with 'Sergei Pravdin' followed by a question mark.

'Is that Lesnoy's handwriting?' Pavel asked.

'It seems to match other letters in the folder. At first I assumed it meant that Sergei Pravdin was the officer coming to meet Lesnoy at Verkhneudinsk, but now I think that Pravdin was the main suspect, the killer.'

Pavel re-read the letter, pushed it back into the folder and pulled out a second sheet of paper. 'I think you're right, Alexander. *Bozhe moy*! Look at this list of crimes - a dozen, or more... March 1907, Spassk, vagrant... April 1912, St Petersburg, ballerina... I remember that one, she was a beautiful dancer - Ekaterina and I had seen her in Swan Lake at the Mariinsky. And this one, here, August 1914, Oryol Oblast, father, mother and three children... My God! that was no more than a few kilometres from where we lived, just after I'd left Ekaterina there on her own. If only I'd known how close that bastard had been...'

CHAPTER FORTY-FIVE

The truck jerked and bounced across the granite sett avenue that separated the cargo ships docked against the quay side and the railway. When they finally reached the square in front of Vladivostok Station the driver braked sharply. Tatiana and Sofia were jolted awake by the sudden stop. The metal hoops covered in canvas offered little protection from the cold wind blowing from across the bay, despite being wrapped in their furs, they leaned against Alexander for warmth..

Tatiana rubbed her eyes, yawned and blinked several times.

'Where are we?'

Alexander stood up, muttered, '*Dobroye utro Kapitan Ozertsov*', stretched his legs, cautiously pulled back the corner of canvas flap that hung over the back of the truck and peered out. Pavel, his arms still wrapped around his sleeping wife, was seated opposite Sofia and Tatiana. He smiled at his travelling companions and wished them a good morning, '*Dobroye utro damy*,' and gently kissed Ekaterina on the forehead to wake her.

Dominic banged on the side of the truck and shouted, 'Wake up, wake up, Vladivostok Station, all change, all change - next stop, San Francisco.' He appeared at the back of the truck, pulled the canvas door wide open and helped Alexander and the others down from the truck. Dominic grinned broadly at Sofia and clapped his mittens together to prevent the cold getting into his fingers. She gave him a tired smile in return. Tatiana and Alexander looked at each other, dazed from the bumpy, uncomfortable trip, and smiled weakly.

Dominic and the driver clambered up into the back of the truck and counted the crates, pulled six away from the others and shook hands.

'Right, I'm going to find the next boat to America and to book our tickets. Six berths, yes? We're all going to the United States aren't we?'

'Of course!' Sofia exclaimed. She looked at Tatiana and Alexander, who were silent. 'Tatiana! Come on! It's what our dear father wanted - a new life for both of us, somewhere safe. Alexander - tell her! Tell her you're coming too - we can all be together.'

Alexander took Tatiana's hands in his and gazed at her, seriously. 'I cannot leave. But... darling, you should go. Russia is in chaos. It is no place for you.'

'Five berths then?' Dominic was stamping his feet and clapping his gloved hands impatiently to stave off the cold. 'Come on, Alexander,' Dominic said, 'You should come. There's this place - Hollywood - where they make films. They need writers. Say the word and I'll go and buy tickets. One way to San Francisco! The land of opportunity, you'll love it there.'

Alexander smiled. 'I cannot speak English, let alone write in the noble language of Milton and Shakespeare. Thank you Dominic, but my head tells me to stay in Russia and my heart... my heart belongs to another.' The friends remained silent. Eventually Tatiana spoke. 'I'm not going to California either. I want to be with my Alexander. Going to America wasn't ever part of his plan.' She turned to Sofia. 'Remember, he was only on the train to look after us at Papa's dying request.'

'So four berths to California?' Dominic was itching to

get himself and his golden fortune safely stowed onto the first steamship and as far away from Siberia as possible. 'Sofia, come with me to sort out the travel arrangements while the young lovebirds decide what their plans are. Come on'.

Sofia hesitated and turned to Tatiana, taking her hand in hers. 'You know I love you, sister, but I'm going to America, whatever you decide. I want you to come with me - you too, Alexander - but if you decide not to… well, I understand.'

She hurried after Dominic and they walked towards the shipping offices with Pavel and Ekaterina, leaving the surly, bearded driver leaning against the back of the truck, smoking a pipe.

Tatiana and Alexander looked desperately at each other, neither wanting to speak first. Eventually, Tatiana broke the silence. 'Darling, your life is in Russia, in Moscow. I understand your dilemma. You want to go back and help the cause, not abandon your comrades, your beliefs. You need to be part of the new Russia. I love my sister, but I want to be with you now.'

Tears came into Alexander's eyes. 'I can't ask this of you…' Tatiana pulled her hands from out of her fur muff and gently took his face in her bare fingers, wiped his tears away and made him look her in the eyes.

'Yes, Alexander you can ask. I'm telling you - you must go back to continue your endeavour. If you don't, then the cruel, vengeful ones, the people who murdered my father and poor old Roberts, will take control of our motherland. That will be a tragedy. Alexander, if you want me, I'll be at your side. Don't worry - not as Countess Shuyskaya, just plain Tatiana.'

'Not plain Tatiana - beautiful Tatiana. My beautiful Tatiana, Tatiana Nikolaevna Zhuravleva.'

Alexander took her face in his cold hands and kissed her passionately on the lips. Tatiana felt as though she were melting into him. Eventually he stopped and held her at arm's length, trying to read in her eyes what she was thinking. 'Sacha… I am cold,' she murmured and he pulled her close to him again.

The driver clearing his throat brought them back down to earth. 'Your friends are returning,' he laughed and pointed with the stem of his pipe. Alexander looked anxiously at Tatiana again.

'You're sure?'

'I am sure.'

The SS George W Fenwick wasn't sailing for another two days. Dominic oversaw the loading of fifty-five crates of gold into the secure hold, leaving six in the truck for the driver to take back to his gang of bandits in Spassk Primorskiy. Dominic was forced to keep a low profile once HMS Suffolk docked and Royal Navy officers started to question the port authorities about the ambushed train and the shipment of gold that had gone missing.

The six exhausted travellers booked into the Versailles Hotel to await the sailing.

'Are you sure you don't want any of the diamonds?' Sofia asked Tatiana.

'No, you take them to America. I'll keep the emerald necklace and earrings; I can sell them when I get back to Moscow. Alexander and I will have something to live on.'

'If you ever need help, you must let me know.'

'Of course, we must never lose touch.'

The two bodices now lay on the bed, Sofia's distinguished only by the three small tears in the cotton fabric.

There was a knock at the door.

'One moment…' Tatiana wrapped herself in a hotel bathrobe as Sofia opened the door. It was Dominic and Alexander looking like excited schoolboys.

'Mr Hare is a magician!' Alexander exclaimed, unable to disguise his glee.

Dominic smiled modestly. 'Just a bit of common-or-garden bribery, I'm afraid. The Archbishop at the Cathedral of the Intercession of the Holy Virgin was only too delighted to receive a bar of gold - to help with his charity work, of course - in return for performing a modest marriage ceremony tomorrow at eleven thirty…'

Tatiana squealed with delight and flung her arms round Alexander.

'That's enough of that!' Dominic scolded. You and Sofia have a wedding to prepare. I'm taking my young friend off for his one last evening of freedom. Come on, Mr Zhuravlev, there are a lot of taverns in Vladivostok and we've only got one night to visit them all.'

THE END

ACKNOWLEDGMENTS

Thanks to all our Russian friends for their help and encouragement, particularly Svetlana Kuznetsova, Victoria Kreissmann and Ilsa Pichler, whose attention to detail and knowledge of Russian names were invaluable. Russian naming conventions are very complex and any mistakes are ours and ours alone. While all the characters in Murder on the Strike of Five are totally fictitious, Tatiana Racila, Julia Sazonova, Orsi Vincze and Andrei Tokar all provided inspiration. Andrew Critchley, Philip White and Lawrence Youlten all gave hugely valuable feedback and corrected our many mistakes. The Kino in Rye provided coffee and WiFi: what more could a writer need?

M P Peacock

Coming soon from M P Peacock

SPIRIT OF DEATH
Summer 1910. Jean Palmer's first job takes her to a house party in a castle on a beautiful Scottish island. When the first of Jean's new acquaintances dies it seems like a misfortune; when the second death happens Jean starts to investigate.

AS LONG AS YOU BOTH SHALL LIVE
Spring 1911. Jean Palmer has been invited to Italy for the wedding of an old school friend. At the reception in a romantic villa outside Florence, family members start dropping like flies and Jean's observational skills are in demand once again.

CPSIA information can be obtained at www.ICGtesting.com
Printed in the USA
LVOW07s1659280916

506567LV00004B/678/P